BOUND BY WATER

THE GENESIS SERIES

STELLA BRIE

COPYRIGHT

Cover Design: The Author Buddy (Perrin)
Editing: Kaye Kemp Book Polishing

PLAYLIST

"Nothing Is As It Seems" - Hidden Citizens

"Buried" - UNSECRET (feat. Katie Herzig)

"Down So Low" - Royal Deluxe

"Cry Me A River" - Tommee Profitt, Nicole Serrano

"Brother" - Sam Tinnesz

"Need A Friend" - The Broken View

"Not Going Down" - Kevin McAllister

"Forever & Always" - Written By Wolves (feat. Becks)

"For This You Were Born" - UNSECRET (feat. Fleurie)

"Thunder, baby" - Allegra Jordyn

"Truth Comes Out" - Willyecho

"Sand" - Dove Cameron

"Can You Die From A Broken Heart" - Nate Smith, Avril Lavigne

Playlists for all my books can be found on
Spotify @Stella Brie Author or YouTube @authorstellabrie

AUTHOR'S NOTE

This book is a Why Choose romance, which means the heroine does not have to choose between male interests.

Please take care of yourself and read at your own discretion. Recommended for 18+ due to mature content including violence, death of family and enemies, gore, and other sensitive subjects.

For the fourth time this semester, I'm going to be late. I look at my phone. Seven minutes to make it across campus. Mrs. Pembrooke, my boss and the university's head librarian, hates when students are late. It's one of her strictest rules, and since it's one of the few graduate-level work-study programs that allows me to promote my tutoring side gig, I can't afford to piss her off.

Freshly brewed dark roast fills the air, and I practically whimper when I pass by the little coffee shop. That is obviously not happening today.

I blow dirty blond hair out of my eyes, shift my heavy backpack, and pick up the pace, darting in and out of the students milling around the quad. Of course, it's almost noon, and the area is packed with those having lunch or visiting with friends. I stare at them with a wistful smile. I'm a little envious of the extra time they have to enjoy this warm fall day, but instead of dwelling on it, I promise myself I'll relax after I graduate.

I finally reach the other side of the quad and glance at my watch. Three minutes. Time to run. Unfortunately, the sidewalk is also crammed with students, so I take to the grass.

Stretching my long legs, I sprint alongside them, snippets of conversation and laughter barely penetrating the sound of my harsh breathing. At five feet ten inches, I eat up the distance quickly. Sweat trickles down my temple. Sixty feet. I'm almost there. I glance at my watch. Twelve o'clock. A minute late would earn me a frown, but not an outright lecture. I smile.

Suddenly, a tiny brown blur comes flying across my path, followed by a guy, tan arms outstretched, blue jersey shining in the bright sun. I blink in confusion. Unable to avoid each other, we collide in an explosion of pain.

Oomph. Air bursts from him the second his body hits mine, and he grunts. Slamming into the ground, my backpack slides off my shoulder, and then, it's just him and me skidding along the grass, rocks and dirt flying everywhere.

We finally come to a stop, but the world around me keeps spinning so I just lie there, focusing on the sky above, watching tree limbs laden with orange leaves sway back and forth. The heavy smell of sweat, dirt, and grass surrounds me.

The heavy body pinning me to the ground shifts, pressing his muscular frame into me, and I wince. I shift my gaze from the tree to him and stare until my sight sharpens. Square jaw. Firm lips compressed tightly together. High, cut cheekbones. Dark brown eyes snapping with irritation. I frown. Why is he pissed? He hit me.

Laughter and clapping fills the air, and I look past him to the faces above. Guys and girls snicker as they stare down at the two of us. Lovely. An audience to witness this glorious event. I groan.

At the sound, the guy lifts his body off me and jumps up.

"Shit, man, that was epic," a laughing blond guy wearing another blue jersey says, slapping his friend on the back. "You okay? Coach would kill me if I hurt his star player."

Epic. I mentally roll my eyes.

"Shut up," a deep voice above me orders. The laughter stops. "Sorry. We were playing catch, and I didn't see you crossing the grounds. Let me help you up."

Happy for the distraction, my eyes turn back toward him.

He extends his hand to me.

Wincing, I sit up, spit out the dirt coating my tongue, then survey the damage. My shirt is torn, with one shoulder hanging by a thread. I pull it off, grateful for the tank top I threw on underneath. Rolling my arms and shoulders, I decide nothing's broken. The palm of my right hand stings like fire, and I lift it up to examine the damage, finding a huge scrape, with grass and blood embedded in the shredded skin.

I look up and find Mr. Irritated is not only the university's wide receiver, but he's also Mr. Popular himself. Trent Hightower. Son of a senator. Politically connected, rich, and because he was lucky enough to also inherit his Italian mother's genes, extremely good-looking. Light brown complexion, thick dark hair, and a tall body honed from sports.

"Thanks," I say, raising my hand to take his.

Instead of taking it, he's staring intently at the mark on my shoulder. "Did I do that to you?"

Even after all these years, the mark with its deep red color and unusual shape continues to draw everyone's attention. It's why I always cover it. I automatically raise a hand to pull up my sleeve but forgot I took off my shirt. I sigh, wondering if I can find a hole to crawl into.

"No, it's an old scar," I reassure him.

"What's this? Another woman felled by the great Trent Hightower?" an amused feminine voice pipes up. Blond hair perfectly curled and bouncing with every step, the cheerleader strides up and pops a hand on her hip.

Everyone laughs like it's the funniest thing they've ever heard.

Blushing, I let him pull me up. Once standing, I murmur my thanks. My gaze slides from his handsome face to his broad shoulders and long legs. At almost 5'10" myself, most guys are my height or shorter. It's nice to stand next to someone over six feet.

He says nothing, only stares down at me with an unreadable expression on his handsome face.

Nervously, I glance at my watch. Five past noon. I'm so late. *Damn it.* I bend over, grab my backpack, shove my shirt in it, then hurry toward the stairs, leaving him standing there. Only once do I look back, but he's already turned away.

Built in 1754, the library is the epitome of the Georgian period with its symmetrical architecture, multi-paned windows, and stately entrance. Constructed of red brick, like all the buildings on campus, it should blend in, but its sheer size and grandeur is impressive.

The interior boasts the same feeling of prestige as the exterior with hand-carved oak bookshelves that stand floor-to-ceiling on all four levels and a dome that allows in light from above.

As my eyes adjust to the darkness inside, I find Mrs. Pembrooke waiting for me at the circular desk in the center of the room.

Her eyes widen when she sees my disheveled look. "What on earth happened to you?"

"A run in with a football player," I reply with a wince, setting my backpack under the desk. I grab a tissue and carefully try to wipe the dirt from my scraped palm. "Sorry I'm late."

In response, she jerks open a drawer and pulls out the first aid kit. "Go to the bathroom and clean up. I'll man the desk until you return." With a frown, she turns to the girl hovering at the counter. "How can I help you?"

While the girl stammers out her reply, I take the kit and make my way to the bathroom.

Lexie, another graduate student, sidles up to me along the way. "Good thing you look so bad. She was livid you were late again."

"I'm sure. If she would just let me shift my hours by thirty minutes, I'd never be late," I grumble, pushing open the door to the restroom. "I didn't even get coffee today. My advisor held a mandatory meeting for all the DPT graduate students. It's not like I could skip it."

Lexie gives me a commiserating nod and walks away. "I hear you. I'd better get these books shelved before she hunts me down."

Thank goodness this is my last semester on campus. The DPT, or Doctorate of Physical Therapy, program is no joke with its mixture of classwork and clinical rotations. Between this job, the tutoring, and sheer number of class hours I'm taking in order to finish early, I'm stretched to the max. But I keep reminding myself how close I am to finishing. The only thing I have next semester is a clinical rotation. Then I'm done.

Weary, I turn on the cold water and thrust my hand under it. Gritting my teeth, I clean out the debris and smear some antibiotic ointment on it, then stick a couple of Band-Aids across the wound. Finished, I turn my attention to the rest of me. The gruesome vision in the mirror has me twisting my lips. Tired forest-green eyes surrounded by pale dirt-smudged skin is only the beginning of the hot mess. My long, dirty blond hair is plastered to my sweaty face and full of dirt and grass. Without a brush, I finger comb through it, pick out the remaining green blades, and clean the dirtiest strands. Once done, I wash my face and arms. That's the best I can do for now.

Turning around, I glance over my shoulder and into the mirror behind me to see if there's anything on my backside. My tank top was pretty much covered by my other shirt, so it looks good, but my jeans are streaked with dark green and brown stains. Wrinkling my nose, I decide to wrap my torn shirt around my waist when I get back to the desk.

Picking up the kit, I return to find Lexie standing at the circular desk with a flower in one hand and a note in the other. She thrusts them at me.

"You didn't tell me you ran into Trent Hightower," she squeals. "Literally."

I look down at the recently picked pink rose and note. "I'm guessing this is from him?" When she nods, I open the folded paper.

Sorry I hit you! I hope you're not hurt too bad. Coffee sometime? 615-999-5555.

"That was sweet of him," I murmur, unsure how to respond. He's a senior in college, but still three years behind me. I fold the note and slip it into the backpack at my feet. "Do we have a vase?"

Lexie blinks. "Is that it? The best-looking guy on campus asks you out, and all you can do is ask for a vase?" She rolls her eyes and grabs a paper cup. "Put it in here." When I drop it in, she grabs a water bottle and pours some water in it. "Well?"

"It's not a date. He's just trying to apologize for running into me," I tell her. "It's fine. It was an accident. No need to ask me out for coffee."

She gives a sad shake of her head. "I don't get you. Trent

Hightower doesn't have to ask girls to go anywhere. They practically beg him. If it was me, I would jump on that so fast."

Ignoring her, I reach down and pull my ragged shirt out of my backpack, then flip it inside out and tie it around my waist. That will have to do until I get home. Mrs. Pembrooke swings by the desk, nods her approval, then gives Lexie a pointed stare.

Lexie sighs and grabs the stack of books waiting to be shelved off the counter. After she leaves, Mrs. Pembrooke walks off.

Sitting down, I stuff the first aid kit back in the drawer and start checking in the books on the return cart. Getting coffee with Trent will only make things worse. I just want to forget the embarrassing incident, and I'm sure he does too.

Several students come up to the desk, asking for various books, and after answering their questions, I continue the rest of the monotonous tasks until the students working the evening shift come in, then I grab my stuff. At the last second, I pick up the paper cup with the rose in it. Inhaling its sweet fragrance, I smile. The rose is beautiful, and it's not as if someone gives me flowers every day. I try to think of the last time I received some and realize it was my sixteenth birthday. The day of the crash. My smile dims, and I head out.

It doesn't take me long to get from campus to my little studio apartment above the garage. I walk up the steps and into the small, tidy interior. After dropping the backpack on a hook by the door, I set the cup with the flower in it on my coffee table and plop down on the couch. Thirty minutes of rest. That's all I need, then I can get up and throw something together for tonight.

What a crazy day. I shift and wince at my sore muscles. I'll definitely need a hot shower before bed. Although, it wasn't all bad. Trent's brown eyes flash in my mind, but I shove the image away and focus on the news I got this morning.

My DPT advisor gave his graduate students their final semester assignments for clinical rotations, and I'm so excited. I'll be working at the children's hospital, focusing on neurological rehabilitation, which is exactly what I want to do when I graduate. It's the whole reason I decided to become a physical therapist. To help kids get the help they need to live functional lives. Like my physical therapist, Kyle, did for me.

My cell rings, startling me, and Lionel's smiling face pops up on the screen. I glance at the clock and realize it's almost seven. My thirty minutes stretched into an hour.

Tired, my voice is rough when I answer. "Hi. Let me change clothes and grab the salad. Five minutes."

He chuckles and hangs up.

Lionel Vickers owns the apartment I live in, but he's more than just my landlord. He's also my surrogate father. A member of my dad's Army unit and one of his closest friends, he often came to our house for dinner. After the accident that killed my parents, I had nowhere to go and no other family. An underage orphan, the state wanted to put me in foster care, but Lionel stepped in and petitioned the court. As a colonel in the Army and long-time family friend, he presented a strong, stable environment, so they granted him guardianship.

We became closer the two years we lived together, and it didn't end when I went away to university for my bachelor's degree. He knew I needed to escape the memories but called and visited often.

When I returned home to complete my graduate program,

he surprised me with this apartment. Detached from the house, it affords me privacy while giving me the perfect excuse to stay close to him. Plus, he doesn't charge me rent. Having a free place to stay means I only have to worry about making enough to cover my books and other daily expenses. I get to practice being an adult without all the responsibility.

He gets peace of mind knowing I'm safe.

Muscles locked with stiffness, it takes me a second to stand and get my body moving. Lionel and I have dinner together on Mondays and Thursdays to catch up with each other. Although it's mainly for him to keep tabs on me, since his days consist of either working or golfing with his Army buddies. I smile at the thought and hurry to get changed and over to his house.

Salad in hand, I knock on the back door. When he hollers for me to enter, I step inside, and the aroma of fresh garlic and rich tomato sauce surrounds me, making me inhale in appreciation. Savoring the scent, I set my bowl down on the small breakfast table and turn to find him stirring a big pot at the stove.

Lionel Vickers is a big, barrel-chested man with a booming voice and hearty laugh. He's handsome and charismatic. As a kid, all the ladies at our family barbeques used to flirt with him, but he never even looked in their direction. And not once while I lived with him did he ever go out.

In his fifties now with a head full of grey hair, he's still fit and trim, but he never dates. I asked him why once, and he told me that his wife was the love of his life, and when she passed, she took his heart, and their son, with her. He would wait and meet them on the other side. It was the most romantic thing I'd ever heard.

He never talks about them. They died in a devastating house fire when I was around five, I think. I vaguely remember them visiting our house a few times. His wife was blond with a broad, easygoing smile. Their dark-haired little boy had been a couple of years older than me and bursting with energy. My mom used to tell me I followed him around like a puppy.

Now it's just Lionel and me, from six down to two. A sad pair, but we're all that's left between his family and mine, and we're thankful we have each other.

"Hmm. Smells good. You pulled out the big guns. Home-made sauce. I guess you didn't play golf today?" I ask, walking over to the fridge to get the pitcher of tea. I pour us two glasses and set them on the table.

Lionel loves to cook, but he insists on making everything from scratch. He pauses mid-stir to answer. "Nope. Brad's back gave out, so he had to cancel. How was your day?"

I frown. "His back goes out a lot. I thought I gave you some rehab exercises to give to him?" The exercises should have strengthened his back and stopped this constant relapse cycle.

Lionel slides a glance at me and rolls his dark green eyes, which oddly enough are similar to my dad's and mine. "I think he does them for a while, then stops when he feels better." He shrugs and takes one last taste of the sauce. "It's done. Grab a plate."

I pick up a plate and fill it with noodles, sauce, and bread, then take a seat at the table. He follows behind me, and for the first few minutes, we're both busy digging into the delicious meal.

"I swear, your sauce gets better and better. What did you do different this time?"

He chuckles. "I added a little bit of brown sugar." He eyes me closely. "You sounded like you were sleeping earlier. Any time you don't feel like coming over, just let me know. Dinner will be in the fridge when you're ready."

I smile at him. "Thank you, but I'm good. Once this semester is over, things will get easier." I've said the same thing a million times this year.

"If you'd let me give you money, you wouldn't need to work at all," he grumbles, a hint of irritation in his voice.

An old argument and not one worth pursuing. Pausing for a second, I wait until he's looking at me. "I got my final assignment for clinicals today... pediatric neurological rehabilitation!"

His frown turns into a huge grin, and he picks up his glass. "Congratulations. You've been looking forward to working with children for so long, and I know you'll be good at it. After all, you've been in their shoes and understand their frustration and pain." With a flick of his wrist, he clinks his glass against mine, then takes a sip.

I take my own drink, then set my glass down. "And since it's my last rotation, maybe they'll hire me after I'm done." I chew my bottom lip as I think about the possibility of staying here.

Lionel studies me closely for a second. "I know this is home, but I don't think you should limit yourself. With your grades, you can go anywhere. Why not apply to the best facilities and see what happens?"

I never told him how miserable I was when I went away to college. Parents, gone. My only lifeline, hundreds of miles away. It was hard to function, much less have a social life. Unlike the other kids my age, I couldn't pretend to be carefree and interested in the same frivolous things. That part of me died with my parents. For four years, all I did was study and work to save for graduate school.

After next semester, I'll face the same decision again. Stay or go. Every time I think about leaving, my stomach clenches in knots. I know I'm supposed to go and make a bigger mark on the world, but why? I can be content here.

"Maybe."

He presses his lips together but says nothing. It's not the first time we've had this conversation, and I'm sure it won't be the last. He knows I'm scared. I know he only wants the best for me. Right now, we're at a stalemate.

Desperate to change the subject, I tell him about getting hit by the football player. "After all that, I ended up being five minutes late for work. Ten, if you count the additional minutes I used to clean and bandage my hand." I hold up my palm for him to see the Band-Aids covering the scrapes.

Aware of my boss's strict policies, he winces. "I'm sure Mrs. Pembrooke was thrilled." His eyes scan the rest of me. "Any other injuries? What about your head?"

"All good," I assure him. "The guy felt so bad he brought me a rose and an apology."

An amusing glint appears in his eyes. "Really. Did he ask you out?"

Warmth flushes my cheeks. "For coffee, but he's younger than me, a senior, and very popular, so I know he's just being nice." I pick up the garlic bread, break off a piece, and shove it in my mouth.

"Too bad," he remarks with a sad shake of his head. "When are you going to realize there's more to life than studying?"

"After I graduate," I tell him firmly, as if it's been my plan all along.

Before the accident, I flirted with tons of guys at school, but something inside me changed afterward. Recovery and rehab took a long time. By the time I went back to high school, I felt out of sync with my life.

During my first year of college, I tried to be normal, but it was hard when I felt so awkward, as if I'd skipped a rite of passage in my teen years. I went on a few dates my freshman year of college, lost my virginity, but for the most part, they were disastrous, so I gave up.

My life is finally stable and on track. But if I'm honest, part of me is scared I'll do something stupid. It's not as if I have a lot of experience in dating or experimenting. When everyone else was fooling around, I was grieving. At the ripe old age of twenty-four, I'm not technically a virgin, but it's damn close.

I fiddle with my fork as I think about it. Maybe I should at least date. Next semester, though. I'm too busy right now. Trent's intense chocolate brown eyes flash in my mind again, but I brush the image away. Not him. Someone... less handsome. Quieter. Easier.

Lexie plops a pile of books on the counter and flashes me a huge smile. She's practically vibrating, she's so excited. Leaning over the counter, she whispers, "Guess who's here? In the library?"

I try to think of the name of the guy she's currently crushing on. "Hayes? Or Harley? Sorry, I can't remember."

Her lips twist into a wry smile. "It's Hayden, but no. Even better. Trent Hightower!"

Above her bent head, I see his tall, fit body weaving through the students. "He's coming up behind you."

She whips around, and I cringe. We're so obvious.

"Trent," she practically purrs. "Can we help you find something?"

He glances at the two guys with him and waves a hand to the right. "I'll meet you at the table with Kelcey and her friends."

My gaze follows and lands on a table full of pretty girls sitting nearby. Gorgeous and bubbly, and guessing by their uniforms, cheerleaders.

Once his buddies walk off, he turns back to us. "My

professor told me I could find a tutor here for my biomechanics class?" He looks at Lexie, then swivels his glance to me.

Lexie pouts. "Unfortunately, I'm a marketing major. Willa's your girl."

He slowly nods and flashes me a half smile. "Do you have a second?" When I dip my chin in answer, his gaze returns to Lexie, and he waits, saying nothing.

Enviously, I watch him silently command her. Is that something bred into the wealthy? Or are some people just born with the innate ability to get people to do what they want with little protest? I wish I could cultivate that level of confidence.

She sighs, then winks at me. "I'll go put these books away." She brushes against Trent as she pushes past him, her arms full again.

I wince. "Sorry about that. Lexie's a fan."

Eyes narrowed; he stares at me for a minute. What he's looking for, I'm not sure, but just as an uneasy feeling crawls up my spine, he steps forward and flashes a big, white smile. "That's nice, but I'm only interested in you."

Those words, coming out of his perfectly shaped lips, make the heat rise from my chest to my face.

He needs a tutor, I remind myself, trying to will the embarrassing blush away.

Placing his forearms on the counter, he leans in closer and presses his hands together like he's praying. "Kinesiology is my major, and I need to make sure I pass this class. Please tell me you have an opening?"

He pouts a little, turning his puppy dog eyes on me, and I can't help but laugh. Still feeling self-conscious, I reach for my phone and pull up my schedule. "Stop. You're killing me. I'm sure I have an opening." Trying to be fast when your fingers can barely function is impossible. *Focus.* Finally, my clumsy taps and swipes are successful.

When I glance up, his dark eyes are drilling into me as if he's trying to peer inside my soul. Uneasy again, I still for a second, but he blinks, and the intensity eases.

"What day works for you?"

Trent thinks about it for a second. "Probably Tuesdays. I have practice and games the rest of the week."

I secretly wince. Tuesdays are my worst days because I have three classes and work, plus I'm tutoring two others on that night. "Mondays would work better for me, but if you can't meet on Mondays, I'll work you in on Tuesdays. It will be late, though. I already have two other sessions that night. Can you meet at eight p.m.?"

He breathes out a sigh of relief. "Tuesdays at eight would be great. How much?"

"Thirty dollars a session, and I need a month upfront, which comes to one hundred and twenty dollars. Cash," I tell him. The money I earn from tutoring isn't much, but I use it to cover my daily expenses.

With a nod, he agrees. "Deal. Should we meet here?"

"Yes. Bring your weekly assignments. We'll do those together, then walk through the lectures for the following week," I reply. "Don't be late, and don't bring anyone with you."

He flashes a broad smile. "I'll be here at eight. Thanks, I appreciate it."

I raise my hand to seal the deal, and his large, warm hand engulfs mine. "See you Tuesday."

He walks off. Moments later, he's leaning over a vivacious blond, laughing at something she's saying. I wonder if that's Kelcey? They look close. His friends look from him to me, but it's obvious he doesn't want them to know anything, so I turn away.

TRENT IS FIVE MINUTES EARLY ON TUESDAY. I'M JUST finishing up with Maggie, another student, who I'm tutoring in biology. I signal for him to wait, and he slides into a nearby chair.

Eyes wide, Maggie looks from him to me and giggles. "What's he doing here? You're tutoring him, aren't you? Wait until I tell my roommate. She's been trying to run into him all semester." Her red lips curve in anticipation.

I silently groan. Trying to make my tone as dismissive as possible, I answer her. "He's just looking for a book for his biomechanics class. I told him I'd help him find it." I tap on the paper in front of me. "Great job on your quiz. Next week, bring your notes for the mid-term, and I'll help you study."

She nods, but I can tell all her attention is on Trent. "Okay." Tugging on her skirt, she stands and makes her way over to where he's lounging, then leans down to whisper in his ear.

I see something, maybe anger, spark in his eyes, but he quickly slaps on his mask and flashes her the same broad smile he shows to everyone. She writes something on his notebook, then winks at him and walks away.

After she's gone, he comes over and sits down next to me. "Hi."

I grimace. "Sorry about Maggie. Come on." Standing, I grab all my stuff and shove it into my worn backpack. "I told her you were here for a book. She'll get suspicious if we keep sitting here." When I dart a glance at him, he's studying me closely. "What?"

"I'm trying to figure out your angle."

I roll my eyes. "Look. I was under the impression that you

didn't want people to know I was tutoring you, but it doesn't matter to me one way or another. So, what do you want to do? Stay or go?"

"Where?" he cautiously replies.

I think about the tables scattered throughout the library. Most of them are out in the open. Except one. "We have a small conference room on the second floor. It's private."

With a strange expression on his face, he nods and gathers his books. "Lead the way."

I head up the back stairs to the room in the corner. Taking a ring of keys out of my pocket, I unlock it and open it wide. "See. Table. Chairs. Just a room, not a den of iniquity."

He slowly sits and places his stuff down on the table in front of him.

Following, I pull all my supplies out of my backpack and sit. "Did you bring the cash and your assignments?"

When he says nothing, I raise an eyebrow. "Look, it's been a very long day. I just want to finish and go home."

He pulls the money out of his pocket and hands it to me. Then he sifts through the papers on the table and pulls out a single sheet.

Counting it quickly, I stash the hundred and twenty dollars in my backpack and grab the paper. "Ok. Let's get started. We'll start with the five main components—motion, force, momentum, levers, and balance—then we'll move into the planes and axes of the body. Sound good?"

Some of the tension eases from his shoulders, and he clears his throat. "Sorry. This is going to sound conceited, but... girls are always trying to trick me into being alone with them. I kind of thought... that you..." He stops talking and shrugs one of his broad shoulders.

It's my turn to study him. He's definitely uncomfortable. I

get up and walk over to the door. "I'll leave the door open, okay?"

The last thing I want him to think is that I'm chasing after him. Yes, he's incredibly good-looking. But he's too young and, oddly enough, out of my league. I'm an ordinary person living a pretty boring life. He's a sports star from a wealthy and powerful family.

He chuckles. "You can close the door. I realize you're not interested in me."

I wave a hand. "It's fine. It's actually cooler in here with it open." I turn my focus back to the work. For the next thirty minutes, I outline everything I think he'll need to learn in the class while I work to get an understanding of his current level of knowledge.

"Honestly, I don't think you need much help. You've got a good grasp of the basics, and with just a few sessions, you'll easily understand the more advanced topics," I inform him, flipping my wrist over to glance at the time. "Next session, we'll jump into the axes and planes, then use the third session to dive into the various joints. For the fourth session, I'll give you an old copy of a final, and we'll see if there are any knowledge gaps."

A relieved smile flashes across his face. "Thanks, that sounds great."

"Okay. Time is up," I say gently, wanting to get home.

With a quick swipe, he grabs his stuff. "Right. I'll see you next week."

Yawning, I make a few notes on the session, then pack up my things. It's been a long day. My pajamas and comfy bed are calling my name. I swing my backpack onto my shoulders and make my way downstairs, passing giggling students along the way. Open all night, the library is a safe place for students to meet and study. I pass by a couple staring soulfully into each other's eyes. Or flirt.

Cool night air caresses my skin, and I sigh. I've spent the past seven hours in the library, working and tutoring. It feels good to leave.

Rustling has me turning toward the nearby bushes. The area around them is dark. Branches sway back and forth, but I can't see anyone. I dismiss it as the wind but freeze a second later when I hear a twig snap. My breath stalls. An animal? Peering into the dense foliage, I realize it's too dark to see anything. Holding my breath, I wait, but there are no other noises. Goosebumps appear on my arms. All my senses are tingling, telling me someone is there. I continue to wait.

A couple of students walk out of the library and pause beside me. Taking advantage, I snatch open my purse and grab my keys. Safety in numbers. With them next to me, I hurry down the steps, then swivel toward the parking lot.

Having arrived early today, I was able to grab the parking space closest to the library, so it doesn't take long to get to my car and jump inside. I immediately lock the door. When I look around, I don't see anyone. Feeling foolish, I take a few deep breaths to calm my racing heart. Probably a cat or raccoon or something.

By the end of the week, I'm practically jumping out of my skin. Ever since I walked out of the library that night, I've had the sensation of being watched. It's stupid. And paranoid. But every time I try to use logic to reassure myself it's nothing my gut kicks back. The feeling is so strong, I constantly have to stop myself from reaching up to rub the back of my neck.

"Willa!" the barista shouts from behind the counter.

With a jolt, I grab my mocha and dash out the door, even though I have plenty of time to get to the library for my shift. Head down, I hurry through the quad, making sure to stick to the crowds, feeling safer surrounded by people.

A heavy hand drops down on my right shoulder, and I let out a little scream. Hot coffee spills out of the top of the lid and slides down my hand, but I only clench the paper cup tighter as I turn to see who grabbed me.

A bright blue jersey meets my gaze, and I flick my eyes up. Trent's smiling down at me.

He laughs. "Didn't mean to startle you. I've been calling your name since you left the coffee shop."

I ease my grip and transfer the cup to my other hand.

Shaking off the spilled coffee, I press my slightly burned hand against the back of my jeans. "Trent! Oh. Um. Sorry, I didn't hear you. Thinking about mid-terms. What's up?"

He pauses for a second but then flashes that signature smile. "My dad is going to be out of town on Monday. I know your Tuesdays are pretty booked, so I thought we could switch days next week."

Surprised he remembered; I think about it for a second. "That would be wonderful, but I only work an hour on Monday. My shift ends around one p.m."

He nods and pulls out his phone. "That works for me. I'll grab us some lunch."

"Umm, don't worry about bringing lunch. I'm used to eating later," I protest.

"Well, I try to stick to a strict eating schedule for football, so I'll bring food, and if you want some, it will be there," he replies with a shrug, then holds up his phone. "I would have called you about switching, but I didn't have your number. Do you mind giving it to me?"

"555-493-7714," I tell him.

Usually, I give my number to the students I'm tutoring when I set up the schedule. I can't believe I forgot. My phone buzzes, and I pull it out of my pocket to see a text from Trent.

A shout from his friends has him turning away. "Thanks, Willa. See you Monday."

I tuck my phone away and give him a half-hearted wave. As I leave, I see the blond cheerleader from the library staring at me with a frown on her face. Her gaze darts to Trent, then back to me. When Trent leans down and says something to her, she jerks around to face the rest of their group.

I take a sip of my coffee and continue on to the library. The sensation of being watched has dissipated. Maybe it was Trent

I felt earlier. Or maybe my stressful workload is causing me to lose my mind. I laugh, but there's a hollow ring to it.

On Monday, I walk out of my apartment to go to class and find a manila envelope under my windshield wiper. I frown. Lionel usually leaves notes on my apartment door, but maybe it's mail or something. I grab it and jump in my car. After setting my backpack in the passenger seat, I open the flap and peer inside. It's full of little squares. Confused, I pull one out and gasp.

It's one of those tiny instant pictures. Almost like an old polaroid but smaller. In this one, I'm talking to Trent in the quad, his blue jersey shining in the sun. This was taken on Friday.

I reach in and grab another. Fingers clenching the corners, I take in all the details. Pink scrubs. I'm walking out of the rehab center. Clinicals are held on Thursdays.

With dread, I dump out the rest of the pictures into my lap. I pick one up, then another and another and another: me going to class, walking up the steps to my apartment, working in the library, and driving my car. My school, my home, my work, my car. All of the pictures seem to be from last week. One in particular catches my eye. I'm on the steps of the library, and it's night. This picture of me is framed with branches. I knew it. There was somebody in the bush on Tuesday night.

Hands shaking, I stare at Lionel's back door, wishing he was home, but I know he had an early tee off this morning. And he always turns off his phone when he's golfing. If I leave the pics without an explanation, he'll freak out. Kind of like I'm doing right now. I turn on the car and sit there, my mind racing, trying to figure out what to do. Should I go to the police?

A couple of tears slide down my face. More from nerves than anything. With shaking hands, I rub my face. I don't know what to do. Go to class like normal? Wait for Lionel to get home? After thinking for a minute, I stuff the photos back into the envelope and toss it in on the passenger seat.

My phone pings. It's an alert for a test I have in my second class today. Groaning at the reminder, I drop my head back on the seat. I can't miss it. There are no make ups. And I sure as hell haven't worked this hard to let my grades slip now.

Not knowing what else to do, I put the car in gear and head to class. At least at school, I'll be surrounded by people. Safe. Or safer than being home alone.

I don't understand. Who would want to stalk me? I lost touch with all my high school friends, what few I had, when I graduated. Besides Lexie and the students I tutor, I don't speak to anyone at the university. I don't date. Or even flirt. So, why me? I try to recall everyone I've come in contact with the last week. I don't remember speaking to any strangers.

After acing the test in my second period class, I slowly walk to the library for my shift, my eyes flicking from one person to another, trying to catch someone watching me. Most don't even glance in my direction. For the few who do, their gazes slide away almost instantly, as if they're dismissing me. Tense, I keep walking.

The library steps come into view, and my eyes automatically slide to the bushes on the left. Unable to stop myself, I walk over to them and lean in, peering through the branches to the steps beyond. Not quite the same angle. I move to another bush and do the same thing. This is the one. I step back and look around the bush. For what, I'm not sure. I look down. There's a faint impression of a shoe.

Whoever took the picture probably had to step into the bush to get a clear shot. Squatting down, I take a picture of it, then stand and study the image. The curved lines and perforations in the dirt make me think it's a tennis shoe or sneaker. It looks big. I place my foot beside the one in the dirt. I wear a women's size nine, which is pretty big. The shoe imprint dwarfs mine. Maybe a guy?

I back up another few feet, but too many people have walked the path near the bush, and I can't tell which ones belong to my stalker. I snort. I don't even know if this imprint belongs to him. Disappointed, I walk away and climb the stairs. Once I'm sitting at the circular desk, I pull the pic back up to study it.

Why would someone stalk me, of all people? It just doesn't make sense. There are a lot of prettier and younger girls at this school. And why would they tell me? Sending me those pictures is almost like shouting it from the rooftops.

The smell of chicken makes me look up. Trent is standing there with a bag of food in one hand and his backpack in the other. "I hope you like chicken. The Roasted Shop smelled so good when I walked by earlier. I had to get it for our lunch."

When I only stare at him blankly, he sets the bag on the counter. "Are you okay? You look... upset."

Embarrassed, I nod. "Yes, sorry. No. Chicken sounds good. I'm fine. It's just been a rough day. Why don't you go upstairs, and I'll meet you there in a minute. I have to wait until my replacement comes in."

"If you're sure," he says hesitantly. With one last look at me, he grabs the food and makes his way to the staircase in the corner.

Tall with powerful-looking legs, I can't help but watch him take the steps two at a time until he's at the door of the conference room. He turns the knob to enter, but nothing happens.

Shit. The keys.

He turns, and I hold up the keys. Thankfully, my replacement appears at that exact moment, and after filling her in on the tasks for the day, I quickly grab my backpack and head up.

"Sorry, I forgot it was locked," I tell him, shoving the key into the lock.

Once open, he strides past me, and the smell of roasted chicken intermingles with scents of cedar and citrus that I've come to associate with Trent. "I hope you're hungry. Even I can't eat all of this." He flashes me one of his infamous grins. The same one they always show on the big screen at the games that makes all the girls giggle.

It's potent, and my lips stretch into an answering smile.

Trent sets the bag on the table, then digs out the containers of food. "I got us chicken, of course. Green beans. Mac and cheese." He holds up the last Styrofoam box. "And the best chocolate cake on campus."

I help him open each box. "This looks amazing. I missed breakfast, and now I'm starving. Thank you." I pat his arm, and he gives me a wolfish grin.

"Most girls would be throwing their arms around me while declaring they couldn't possibly eat all this. You pat my arm," he says with a grin.

I give him a stern look. "I'm tutoring you, not dating you. Speaking of..."

He holds up a finger. "Food first. Then you can whip my brain into shape." His lips twitch, and he gives me a wicked grin. "The chocolate cake will be our reward." His eyes move from the dessert to my lips, then he winks.

For the first few minutes, we eat in silence, but Trent suddenly tosses his fork down. "Are you sure you're okay? I know it's none of my business. We don't know each other that well. It's just. Well... you looked scared earlier. Were you? Scared?"

I swallow the bite stuck in the back of my throat and stare at him. Words fill me, hovering on the tip of my tongue, desperate to get out. I want to share this burden with someone. I want this sick feeling in the pit of my stomach to go away. I want somebody to protect me. But I say nothing. Trent is a stranger.

Forcing a smile, I shake my head. "Something spooked me earlier. But I'm fine. Really. I appreciate you asking."

He says nothing for a long minute. "If you say so." Picking up his fork, he finishes his meal, but I can see the wheels turning in his head. "Here's my homework for the week."

With the change in conversation, the session shifts back to tutoring. For the next hour, we walk through the homework he aced and review the topics coming up next, but it's obvious things are strained between us.

"Come on. I'll walk you to your car," he states firmly, gathering his books.

Relieved to have some degree of safety, I don't even think of refusing but lead the way. Once I'm in my car, I wave my thanks and speed off. It's nice to have someone my age, or at least close to my age, worrying about me, especially a good-looking guy like Trent. It makes me feel normal.

I pull into the driveway and reach for my backpack and the envelope. When I don't see it, I jump out and hurry over to the other side of the car. Maybe it fell down into the door well. I throw open the door, but I don't see anything. The dome light isn't that powerful, so I turn on my phone's flashlight. Nothing. It's empty, and it's not on the floorboard either, which means someone broke into my car and stole it.

Lionel's furious. Face red, he paces back and forth, asking me to repeatedly describe everything from the clasp on the envelope to the photos inside. There was nothing special about the generic envelope, but he makes me find an image of one online and send it to him. He frowns when he hears the images were from some type of instant camera.

"Were the images clear?" He abruptly asks.

I sift through the images in my mind. "Most of them. A couple were sort of... grainy? The one at the clinic and me driving my car. Why?"

"Every detail is important," he says, his tone calm but commanding. "Clear pictures means they've been close to you. Instant cameras don't take the best pictures from a distance. I'd like to narrow down the camera. Can you find an example of the images online?"

Bringing up my browser, we start looking at various models until we can pin it down to two possibilities. Both have a maximum range of five to seven feet for a clear photo.

The lines around his mouth tighten as I tell him. "I know you're not dating. Have you spoken to anyone new in the last couple of weeks?"

"I picked up a new tutoring client," I reply. "The football player. We barely know each other and have had very little interaction outside of the library." I cross my arms tightly across my chest. "He walked me to my car earlier tonight because I looked scared."

Lionel pauses. "The same one who ran over you the other day?"

I groan. "Yes, but you can't think he's got anything to do with this. The guy doesn't have to stalk anyone. He's popular and good-looking; girls chase him."

"So?" Lionel remarks, lifting one eyebrow. "Someone starts stalking you shortly after you meet?" He snorts. "I don't like it. He remains at the top of the list." He reaches into a cabinet in the dining hutch and pulls out a small tackle box. "I'm going to dust your car for fingerprints."

Flabbergasted, I stare after him. "Do you even know how? And where did you get the supplies?"

Bewildered, I follow him to my car, but he doesn't answer. Too focused on the task at hand to pay attention to me, he methodically dusts around the windshield, the passenger doors, and driver's side. It takes forever, but I don't interrupt him. Instead, I impatiently shuffle back and forth until he's done.

He closes the tackle box and waves the samples at me. "I'm going to have a friend run these prints. You never know."

Once back inside, he slides the box back into the cabinet and turns toward me. "I'm going to set up surveillance around your apartment. For now, follow your normal routine. Anything out of the ordinary could spook your stalker, and I want to catch this bastard. Don't worry. I'll be close by in case you need anything."

I throw up my hands. "Shouldn't we go to the police?"

He thinks about it for a brief second, then shakes his head. "With the pictures gone, there's no evidence. Nobody has threatened you, and you don't even have a face or name to offer them. At best, they'll create a report, but they're more likely to dismiss you as a paranoid girl."

Frustrated, I realize he's right. Why didn't I put those pictures in my backpack?

Lionel comes over and pulls me into his arms. "I've got you, kiddo. I promised your father a long time ago that I would take care of you, and that was before you became mine. I'm not about to let some idiot take you from me."

With a shudder, I throw my arms tightly around him and breathe in the familiar smell of his aftershave. "Thank you. You're the best." Drawing back, I look into his dark green eyes, sparking with fierce determination. "Can I sleep here tonight?"

"I'd feel better if you did," he replies with a look of relief on his face. "I'll get your apartment wired with cameras and motion sensors tomorrow. I want to know when anyone steps foot near it."

Relieved, I ask him to go with me to get a few things from my apartment. When we enter, it's silent. Nothing's been touched, but I can't help but shiver at the thought.

THE NEXT DAY, I FOLLOW MY USUAL ROUTINE. CLASS, then the library. As I'm sitting there checking in books, I can feel someone watching me. I look up and scan the room. Trent's sitting a few tables away, watching me. For a brief second, I can't help but wonder if he's the one following me. As I return his stare, Kelcey slides into the chair beside him, capturing his attention.

Feeling stupid, I look away and continue stamping the pile in front of me with the return date. Lost to my thoughts, a polite cough startles me, and I jerk my head up to find Kelcey standing there.

She hands me a piece of paper. "Can you help me find Morgenstern's textbook on visual nursing?"

"Sure," I reply, taking the paper from her. When I open it, the book's title isn't on the sheet. Instead, it's a note. *They're watching you.* My gut twists when I read the words. 'They' implies more than one. *Who's they?* I open my mouth to ask her who she's talking about, but she interrupts me.

"That's okay," she says loudly. "I'll grab a copy from the bookstore. Thanks for your help."

Pivoting on her heel, she walks over to where Trent is waiting for her to join him. She links her arm in his and tugs him toward the door. He glances from her to me, then leans down and says something to her. She rolls her eyes and shakes her head.

Surely, she didn't mean Trent and his buddies. We barely know each other. Still, I can't dismiss it. Is this some sort of stupid hazing or bullying? I haven't told him or anyone else about the pictures. So, how does Kelcey know they're watching?

I fold the paper and put it in my backpack. Once my replacements come in, I move to the table where I usually tutor and wait for the first student to arrive. About mid-way through our session, I get a text from Maggie canceling her appointment. After quickly rescheduling for later this week, I finish up with the current session and make my notes.

Thankful for an early night, I grab my things and make my way outside. The moment my foot hits the stairs, my eyes are drawn to the bush. There's no rustling, and the night is silent. I don't feel like someone is watching, but fear makes me run to my car. Nobody follows me.

My relief fades the minute I sit in the driver's seat and see the photograph tucked into the instrument panel. It's an image of me taking a picture of the ground behind the bush. Unlike the others, this one has a circle in red ink, and dread fills me.

I was here.

There's an arrow at the bottom of the image. I flip it over and see a second picture almost identical to the first, but this one is grainier. The view is shifted slightly to the left. Someone is standing at the corner of the library, phone raised and pointed toward me.

But I'm not the only one.

My head jerks up. I immediately lock my door and scan the area around the car. Fear and rage bubble up inside me. Unable to see anyone, I can't help but hold up my middle finger. Flashing it from one side to the other, I scream *Fuck You!* even knowing my stalker can't hear me.

I drop my gaze back down to the image in my hand. There's something odd about it. I grab my phone and shine a light on the image. It takes me a minute to realize what it is. The nails. They look long. Too long. I blink several times and move the phone closer, then back. The tips are definitely pink and white. The image is too grainy to tell much, but those are nails. It's a girl.

My mind nearly explodes with the information. The shoe print in the bush was definitely big, telling me my stalker was a guy, but this has to be a girl. Kelcey was right. *They're watching.* But who? Some of her friends? Is this some kind of stupid hazing thing? Find an unsuspecting student and terrorize them?

All I want is to finish school and get a real job. Help others.

Is that too much to ask? There's so little in this world for me to hold on to. Lionel and my dream of helping others. That's it. If my stalkers think they can take those from me, *they* can fuck off. I'll fight tooth and nail to keep my little world intact. I lost everything once, but I'll be damn if I let it happen again.

Furious, I ignore my trembling hands and start the car, then floor it out of the parking lot. When I get home, Lionel's putting the finishing touches on the new security system. Jaw locked; I hand him the photograph and the paper Kelcey handed to me.

"It appears there are more than one." I sigh. "They're most likely students." I explain Kelcey's involvement and point out the second image. "Those look like nails to me."

A deep line appears between Lionel's brows as he stares down at the words on the back of the photo. For a long minute, he says nothing. "I don't like the fact that there are two independent parties stalking you." He taps the first image. "This person clearly doesn't like the fact that someone else is watching."

He nods his head as if he's in agreement with whatever he's thinking. "This is the one that worries me. What is their agenda?" Snapping a pic of the two images, he turns toward me. "An admirer? Maybe. If so, he's gone out of his way to follow your every move."

He's silent for a few minutes. Brow furrowed; he taps his fingers on the table next to the image. "My gut is churning, but before I try to find this asshole, I want to check into something. Make sure there's no chatter about you."

Confused, I stare at him, trying to figure out what he's saying. "Chatter? About me? What are you talking about? Isn't this enough to go to the police?"

He pockets the photo and thrusts his fingers through his grey hair. "There are a few things in your dad's past. In my past. Enemies. I doubt this is related, but I have to know for sure." His worried gaze darts to me. "I know this is confusing, but it's better to be safe than sorry. Once I know for sure, I'll be able to figure out our next steps."

My head rears back. "My father?" Even though it's been years, I immediately see his smiling face and humor-filled forest green eyes the exact same color as my own. He was always joking and teasing my mom and me. Everyone loved him. "What enemies?"

Lionel immediately reaches for my hands. "I can't tell you." He holds up his hand when I open my mouth. "Please don't ask. All these years, I've kept you safe, and I'm not about to stop now."

All these years. The words ring in my brain.

One thing had always bugged me about the night of the accident, but the police had quickly dismissed it. "Dad was upset that night. He and my mom were talking in the front seat, but I couldn't hear what they were saying. All I remember is his hands, clenching the steering wheel, us speeding up, bright lights." Panic rises in me. Breathing fast, I try to push past the lights to see more. "He yelled. Something slammed into us."

The car started flipping over and over. Somehow, my seatbelt came loose, and I was thrown out the window. I must have passed out. When I woke, I was lying in a large pond. Our car was farther down the hill. In flames. Then, I blacked out. I remember nothing until the hospital.

Tears roll down my face as I recall the worst night of my life. Their screams. The certainty of the flames. My body broken. My mind filled with horror. The past wraps its tight grip around me until all I can do is stare helplessly at Lionel as the abyss in my mind threatens to drag me under.

Lionel grabs my arms and shakes me. "Stop. I've got you. You're safe, and I promise I won't let anything happen to you."

I stare up at him. If my dad had enemies... "Did someone

deliberately hit us?" Holding my breath, I wait for him to tell me I'm wrong.

He sighs heavily. "The police ruled it an accident, but it wasn't. Your father was trying to get to me, but he waited too long. They got to him first."

Reeling, I pull away and stumble back from him and the truth he just blurted out. "Who got to him?" Betrayal punches me in the gut. "All this time, you hid this from me. Why? I deserve to know what happened."

His green eyes harden. "No, you don't." He returns bluntly. "Knowing could have gotten you killed. The best way to protect you was to show them that you weren't a threat. If I hadn't... I don't know what they would have done."

Frustrated at his lack of answers, I throw up my hands. "Who would I be a threat to? I was a sixteen-year-old girl." When he says nothing, I grab his arm. "Why can't you tell me?"

"Because if it's not the past, I don't want to open that door. Right now, you have a life. A future. More than anything, I know your parents would want me to do everything in my power to make sure you have the opportunity to live it. If I tell you anything, the future you envision will be gone," he reveals, to my astonishment.

He grabs my phone and punches in a number. "If I don't return by Sunday, call this number. I'm going to list it under Help. Tell the person who answers that the Colonel gave this number to you. Then tell them, Raven has found you. Repeat."

Bewildered, I spit out his instructions. Raven? The black bird that croaks in the trees? Panic sets in. "You're leaving?"

He nods. "I have to. Whatever the person on the phone tells you to do, you do it. I trust them. Completely." He fiddles with my phone for a few minutes. "I'm installing the security app on your phone. An alert will pop up if someone triggers the sensors. If someone is here, don't come home. Stay at the library or find an all-night diner until they leave." Bending close, he shows me where to find the app and how to use it.

"Follow your normal routine," he orders me. When I start to protest, he cuts me off. "I don't want you to trigger them into acting. Right now, they're just watching. Let them." He hands me my phone. "Can you do this for me? Please."

Helpless, I stare into his worried green eyes. "I'll try." With a cry, I throw my arms around him, hugging him tightly as I breathe in the scent of his old-fashioned aftershave and use it to calm myself. "Please be careful."

He squeezes me hard. "I love you, Willa."

"I love you too, Lionel," I whisper, my throat choking with the words. He means so much to me. A father who loved and protected me after mine was gone. "Please come home."

ON EDGE AND BARELY ABLE TO CONCENTRATE, WEDNESDAY is a disaster. When someone slams into me in the hallway after class, I scream. The guy's face turns red as he holds up his hands. I stammer an apology and practically run to my next class. I'm so exhausted by the end of the day, I crawl into bed early. But I can't sleep. Every time I hear a noise outside, I grab my phone and pull up the camera, hoping it's Lionel, praying it's not one of my stalkers. The only time my fear abates is when I push myself to remember the night of the accident, but it's an endless loop. The same sequence plays over and over without change.

I drag myself out of bed Thursday and make my way to the rehab center for clinicals. Thankfully, it's busy, and my mind is able to take a break from this nightmare and concentrate on my patients. But when I step out the door, I feel someone's eyes on me. I know they're there.

Nauseous, I fight the urge to run and casually stroll to my car, then get in. My hands shake as I turn the key. Tempted to keep driving until I'm out of the city, I force myself to return to my apartment. The second I walk in the door, I run for the toilet and throw up the little bit of food I managed to eat for lunch. Unable to face the apartment, I shut and lock the bathroom door, then curl up on the cold tile. It seeps into my skin and bones, numbing me, and for the first time in days, I feel safe. Unable to bring myself to leave my little refuge, I stay in the small bathroom the rest of the night, dozing on and off.

Friday arrives, and I sweep the hair back from my worn face. I need this week to be over. I'm so tired of trying to be strong. The sleep I got last night helped, but I feel fragile, like I could break at any moment. Scraping my hair into a bun, I drag myself out of the apartment to the university.

Once my only class is over, I contemplate going to the grocery store like usual, but I can't face the crowded aisles. My stomach rumbles loudly, telling me to eat something, and I decide to treat myself to a sandwich at the little bistro near campus.

Normally, I would walk, but the car feels safer, so I get in and drive over. It's not quite lunchtime and, thankfully, the place is relatively empty. I order a Tuscan Chicken Wrap combo with a drink and a bag of chips. Taking a seat by the window so I can watch the parking lot, I slowly pick at the meal. It tastes like sawdust, but I make myself eat it.

Lionel hasn't called. I'm trying not to worry, but it's hard. Ever since Tuesday, I've managed to avoid thinking about our discussion. The accident that changed my life that wasn't an accident. Some faceless enemy deliberately... murdering my parents.

Lionel and my dad were in the same Army unit. It's where they met and became fast friends, but is that also where they made enemies? My dad left the service and started working in insurance, but Lionel stayed in.

Why all the lies and secrecy? Who would think I was a threat? Who is Raven? Nothing makes sense.

"Mind if I join you?" Trent's deep voice startles me, and I jump.

With dread, I turn my gaze from the parking lot to him and reluctantly agree. "Sure." Coincidence? Suspicious, I study him, noting the dark circles under his eyes.

He sets his food down and slides into the booth across from me. "I was going to call you. My dad is returning to Washington early. If you want to move our tutoring session to Monday again, that works for me."

Will Lionel make it back by Sunday? I flash a wobbly smile, trying to make it seem like everything is fine. If he's following me, I don't want him to know I suspect him. "Sure, Monday sounds good." I pause for a second to find something normal to ask. "Why kinesiology?"

He swallows his food and shrugs. "I'm not good enough to get drafted. Kinesiology allows me to stay in sports and work with athletes." His lips twist in a wry smile. "And no, I'm not interested in politics like my dad." This last statement is tacked on in a slightly bitter tone.

Sounds like a sensitive subject. "Well, it's a great field. Your hands-on knowledge of sports and the way athletes move will be invaluable to your clients." I take a bite of my wrap.

"What about you? Why did you decide to go into physical therapy?"

I swallow and take a sip of my drink. "When I was in high school, I was in a serious car accident." I shudder and pause for a second to think about the word I've said a thousand times before but no longer believe. Accident. Everything I've known and done during the last nine years is based on a lie. I glance up at Trent and force myself to continue. "It took months of rehab for me to be able to walk again. My physical therapist, Kyle, was a miracle worker. I want to help others like he helped me." That part is true, at least.

His gaze moves from my face to my shoulder. "Is the scar on your shoulder from the accident?"

I lift a hand and rub a thumb across my sweater where it resides underneath. "Yes." I stop. The mark was there when I woke up in the hospital. Doctors couldn't tell me what caused it. They chalked it up to possibly hitting a tree.

His jaw clenches. "Was anyone else hurt?"

I frown. "In the accident?"

He scrunches up the napkin in his hand and leans forward.

Even though I rarely talk about it, the intensity of his expression is unnerving.

"My parents. They died," I murmur, not wanting anyone else to hear me.

"Your real parents?" he asks with an intense look.

"Of course, my real parents," I confirm, confused by his question. It's not as if I was adopted.

Releasing a long, slow exhale, he looks away for a second. "I understand. My mom died, too. It's tough to talk about, isn't it?" When his gaze returns to me, his eyes are blazing, full of anger and loss. The expression in their depths is riveting.

Is that what I'll look like? Angry? Lost? Is it because he needs answers? His mother committed suicide. It was all over the news. Beautiful model married to senator with an adorable son. She had everything. Yet, she purposely overdosed on painkillers. Why did she kill herself? The speculation had been rampant.

I can't imagine going through all that in the public eye. "I'm sorry. Losing a parent, or in my case both... it's an emptiness you carry the rest of your life," I whisper quietly. "The only thing I can do is remember them and the good times we had. Live my life the best way I can."

If anything, my words seem to make him angrier.

My stomach churns. Unable to finish my wrap, I roll up the paper around it to save it for dinner. Just in time, too. The bistro starts filling with students hungry for lunch.

Uneasy, my eyes dart from one to the other. "I've got to go. See you Monday. Just text me a time." Scrambling out of the booth, I grab my leftovers and walk away, leaving him to stare after me.

Lionel's text appears the next morning. Unable to sleep, I'm already up and drinking coffee when I see the notification pop up on my phone.

LIONEL: Returning Monday. Confirm.

After confirming receipt, I drop the phone on the couch beside me and let out a huge sigh of relief. He's alive and coming home in two and a half days.

Sunday and Monday. The rest of today. I can do this. Tempted to stay in my safe apartment, I quickly realize I'll go stir crazy if I don't get out. Normal routine, right? I force myself to get dressed. The fridge is empty, and that was the last of the coffee.

At the grocery store, I slowly walk up and down the aisles to kill time. Surrounded by bright packaging and smiling faces, the smothering feeling of being watched recedes a bit. It's just me and my sugary childhood cereal. I choke out a quiet laugh. Maybe I'm losing my mind.

After buying more groceries than usual, it takes me a few minutes to fit them all in the trunk of my little hatchback.

While I'm standing there, a huge black truck with tinted windows slowly rolls past me. I glance at it but can't see inside. Something about it makes me nervous, and I shove the last bag in and slam the hatch shut.

On the road, my eyes flick between the view in front of me and the rearview mirror as I leave the store until I'm sure nobody is following me, then I turn to go home. When I get there, I try to grab everything in the first load but can't quite carry it all. Rushing up the stairs, I dump the first load on the kitchen counters and hurry down to get the rest. I grab the few remaining bags and shut the door. As I walk back up the stairs, I see the same truck go by the house.

Completely spooked, I hole up in my apartment for the rest of the weekend with the app open and all the lights on.

LIONEL IS COMING HOME, AND I WANT TO BE ABLE TO TELL him I followed my routine even though it's the last thing I want to do today. So, here I am, waiting for Trent to show up for his tutoring session. He strolls into the conference room a few minutes late and plops down into the chair beside me. The lines around his eyes are tight with anger. He stares at me for a full minute without saying a word.

"Is everything okay?" I tentatively ask as he continues to sit there.

He snorts. "That depends." Full lips twist into a half sneer.

Someone is in a mood. "Let's postpone." I offer the words, although I have no intention of ever rescheduling.

He immediately shakes his head. "No. This is our last session. My father doesn't want me seeing you again." Shocked but relieved, I raise an eyebrow at his statement, and he elaborates. "*A Hightower doesn't need a tutor. You're either smart enough to figure it out or you're a failure.*" Bitterness seeps into his tone.

Appalled at the callousness of his father's words, I lean forward and clasp his forearm. "I'm sorry." The muscles bunch under my hand, and I jerk it away. "Well, let's cram two sessions into one, okay?" Relief eases the tight muscles in my shoulders. This gives me a clear out. Not wanting him to see, I look down at my papers and shuffle them around.

He reaches out and grabs my hand in his. "Sorry. I didn't mean to take our family drama out on you, and I actually don't have time to stay. Can we reschedule? Meet me tonight? At Murray's?"

Murray's is an all-night diner close to campus. The students love it because they serve breakfast all day, and it's a good spot to eat cheap and study. Since it's Monday, there will likely be some open tables.

But Lionel's supposed to return tonight. "I can't. Can you meet tomorrow?"

He vehemently shakes his head. "He comes home tomorrow. It must be tonight. Please." He flashes his best puppy dog eyes at me.

I stare at him, unsure of what to do. Maybe he's involved in all this, and maybe he's not. I don't know. It's just one more session. In a public place. Somehow, I find myself nodding. "I can meet at five p.m. for one hour. That's it."

He smiles broadly. "I'll see you there at five." Then he's gone.

The moment he leaves, I start having second thoughts, but I promise myself I'll cancel if Lionel gets home before five.

Four forty-five, and Lionel isn't here. I'm not even sure he'll see my text, but I send one anyway, telling him where I'm going. Hopefully, he'll text me the second he's home. This week has been crazy, and I need answers.

As I pull into a parking spot at Murray's, I swivel my head around, but I don't see anyone nearby, and not once have I seen the black truck today. It might have been just a coincidence, but until I know who's after me, I prefer to be safe than sorry. Public places and my apartment. That's it.

Striding into the diner, I spot Trent in the corner booth, typing furiously on his phone. Waiting until he finishes, I drop my backpack on the seat and flag down a server to order a Diet Coke before removing my coat.

"Thanks, Amy," he says when she brings it back to me.

Startled, I turn toward him. "Sorry, I didn't want to interrupt you, and I was dying of thirst." Gulping down half the glass, I set it back on the table and take a seat across from him.

His phone buzzes, and he swipes it up. "Sorry, I have to get this. Football stuff."

This goes on and on for the next fifteen minutes until I find myself itching to throw the damn phone out the window. Even when he's not fiddling with the phone, he's tapping his fingers on the table or looking out the window. Clearly, he's distracted.

Enough. "Look, I've got to go. We don't have to go over this stuff in person. You can text me if you have any questions. Free of charge," I tell him with a strained chuckle. This was a completely bad idea, and I'm pissed I gave in to his sad plea.

He holds up a finger and types another text.

With a shake of my head, I grab my backpack, put on my coat, and place a five on the table for the server. "Sorry." I slide out of the booth, and he flashes me a look I can't decipher, but for some reason, the sight of it makes my stomach cramp.

I wave at the server and point to the table where I left the money. With a sour taste in my mouth, I head out to my car, trying to erase the last few minutes from my mind. It's not until I'm reaching for my door that I see the black truck, parked two spots down from my car. There's nobody in it, but I immediately turn to go back into the diner. Unfortunately, it's already too late. A huge, burly guy steps in front of me.

"Where do you think you're going? We've been waiting for you," he tells me, beefy hands reaching for my shoulders.

I open my mouth, but another hand comes from behind and covers it, cutting off the scream before it even gets started. Panicking now, I kick out at the guy in front of me, and swing my backpack toward his face, but for a big guy, he moves fast and easily rips it from my hands.

I pick my feet up and slam them against my car, pushing back, hoping to catch the guy behind me off guard, but he only takes a half step back. *Damn, he must be big, too.* I can't see him, but the arm wrapped around my shoulder is bulging with muscles. He picks me up like I'm weightless.

Wild with fear, I jerk my legs up and down, kick back at his knees, and basically, throw all my strength at him, but nothing loosens his granite grip.

The guy in front of me folds his massive arms across his chest and laughs. "I was expecting a bit more from you. Are you sure that's all you've got?"

Terror rips through me. I start thrashing again, and the guy behind me heaves a large sigh.

"Tommy, stop fucking around. It's broad daylight. Grab her legs," a guttural voice orders from behind me.

Tommy scowls at his friend but moves toward me. "Hold your fucking horses. Just trying to enjoy the moment. Besides, Trent's going to take care of the cameras."

The words reverberate in my head. Trent's going to take

care of the cameras. Are they *kidnapping* me? What the fuck? Is this a game? Football hazing?

Some of the fear leaves me, and anger takes over. When the guy bends over to grab my legs, I bring my knee up and slam it into his big fat ugly mug.

Blood gushes from his nose, and he curses and yells.

The guy behind me chuckles.

"Mother fucker. You fucking bitch. I think you broke my nose!" Tommy screams at me while holding his hands to his face and pinching his nose. "I think it's time you took a nap." He waves a bloody hand at the guy behind me.

"Nighty night," the other guy whispers in my ear.

A prick to my neck, and the whole world goes dark.

A THROBBING HEADACHE WAKES ME FROM MY SLEEP. Hurting, I try to massage the pain away, but my arm is stuck. *Why can't I move my arm?* Confused, I roll my head to the side and look down at my body. The burgundy sleeves of my sweater have been pushed up to my elbows, and my wrists have been tied to the arms of the chair. I tug on them, but they refuse to budge.

I lift my head, but the weight is too much, so I let it fall back against the wood behind me. Blinking several times, I try to focus on my surroundings, but everything is spinning in a lazy circle.

What is wrong with me?

Keeping my head still, details slowly become clearer. In front of me, sunlight streams through a dirty window set high in a wall of equally dingy brown slats. A single door is encased on the same wall, which isn't very big... maybe five or six feet long.

I roll my head from one side to the other. The world spins again, and I close my eyes to make it stop. Seconds or minutes later, I'm not sure, I open them again and blink continuously until that side of the room comes into focus. A dirty sink with a two-door cabinet above it. There are dishes and a McDonald's bag on the tiny counter beside it.

Where am I?

Alarm buzzes at the edge of my brain, but it's cold, and I'm so tired, I can't think. My heavy eyes drift shut.

Crickets. A croaking frog. The sounds pierce my sleep, and I peel my eyes open. Moonlight streams through the window from earlier, flooding the small space. It's nighttime, and I'm still in this... shack, for lack of a better word. Time has little meaning, but the sun was up the last time I opened my eyes. The cold night air makes me shiver. I wonder how many hours have passed.

How did I get here? The last thing I remember was going to the diner to meet Trent. He was... distracted. On his phone. I left. He stayed. Two guys stopped me. Memories sweep through my mind, and I gasp. Those bastards kidnapped me.

My mouth is wooly like cotton. I swipe my swollen tongue across my dry lips, but it feels like sandpaper scraping across the delicate surface. I'm so damn thirsty. A tear rolls down my face, and I open my dry lips. It slides into the corner of my mouth, but the drop of moisture barely registers.

I wonder if Lionel's home and searching for me. A half-sob escapes at the thought, but I squeeze my eyes closed until it subsides. Crying isn't going to help. I'm already severely dehydrated, and I need to get out of here. The fog lifts a little. *Think, Willa.* I straighten and look down at the ropes tying my wrists to the chair.

Thick, tan, rough. They look immovable. I jerk on my wrists, trying to see if the ropes are loose enough for me to pull my hands through, but they're too tight, and the rough rope scrapes the raw skin underneath, so I stop. Whoever tied these did a fantastic job.

Frustrated, I look around for something sharp to cut them off. My eyes land on the window, but it's too high. There are a few items in the sink, but the dim light makes it difficult to see what they are.

I try to stand, but something tight pulls at my ankles. Bending over, I peer down at my legs. Also tied. Picking up my feet, I try to move my ankles away from the chair legs, but they don't budge.

Think, damn it.

Tapered chair legs. An idea pops into my head. Could I slide the ropes off the chair if I stand? Scooting to the edge of the seat, I carefully place my weight on my feet and stand up as far as I can. Hunched over, I jerk my arms and the chair up and down. The skinny chair legs move the tiniest bit. Elated, I do it again. And again. Sweat drips down my face to the floor below, but I don't stop. Time slides by until finally the chair legs slip free, giving me enough room to maneuver. I use one foot then the other to shove the loosened ropes off my legs, then do a little dance to get the blood moving in my feet again.

With a swipe of my shoulder, I wipe the stinging sweat from my eyes so I can see better and figure out what to do next. Lionel taught me to solve problems one step at a time. Feet are free, but I can barely walk with the rest of me tied tightly to the chair. Still hunched over, I shuffle over to the sink to peer inside.

My eyes immediately focus on the faucet, and my tongue glides across my cracked lips. Freedom first, water second, I promise myself, turning my gaze to the bottom of the sink. A bowl. Spoon. My eyes light up when they see the last item. A glass. That would work. Now, how do I get it, and more importantly, break off a piece large enough to use?

Back aching fiercely, I decide to sit while I figure this one out. Could I shimmy myself up onto the counter and grab it with my teeth? Maybe, but the grime coating its surface makes me grimace, and I'd have to smash the glass with it in my mouth.

My only other option is to take off my shoes and socks and use my feet to grab it. I think about it for a second. It could work. To test it out, I lift my feet up and over the sink. This is the answer. I swing them back to the floor.

Kicking off my shoes, I use my toes to shimmy off my socks. Barefoot, I slide down in the chair until my butt is touching the edge and lift my legs up and over the lip of the sink again. I move them side to side, but I can't reach the glass. Maybe I need a few more inches. I lift my butt off the chair into a bridge. Pain shoots across my back, begging me to stop, but I refuse. My toes graze the top of the glass. With a grunt, I shove my hips up another painful inch and stretch farther. It works. Carefully wrapping both feet around the top of the glass, I grab it. Pausing for a second to make sure it's secure, I then lift my feet and swing them in front of me.

Now comes the hard part. I place the side of the glass against the sharp metal edge of the Formica counter and take a deep breath. Closing my eyes, I tap the glass against it, harder and harder, until it breaks. Sharp pain streaks across my arch and inhale sharply. A quick glance at my feet reveals a small, jagged piece of glass in my foot. I shake my head. I'll worry about that later. The top of the shattered glass is one large piece with sharp edges. Perfect. I smile.

I wipe my face with my shoulder again. Now comes the hard part. Tongue between my lips, I slowly lower my feet until my fingers can grasp the big piece. Once I'm sure I have it, I drop my feet to the floor. Cramps in my hamstrings make me grit my teeth, but after a few seconds, the muscles loosen, and I can shuffle closer to the pool of moonlight.

Thankfully, they only tied my wrists to the chair, not my hands.

Hunching over my right arm, I twist my wrist as far as I can and start sawing at the closest piece of rope. Tiny pieces of glass rain down on my wrist, grinding into the tender skin, but I don't stop. I can't. I need to get out of here before someone comes back.

Hours go by. Every minute is excruciating. My back burns from holding its hunched position. My fingers are numb from gripping the glass, which sweat has made slippery, but I don't dare let go, not even to dry my hand. I'm so close. There are only a few miniscule strands of rope left to cut. I lift my shoulder and wipe my blurry eyes with my sleeve. Just a little more.

Sun begins to stream through the window. Daylight. Fear fills me.

Another piece gone. Sawing takes so much time. Desperate, I slip the final two strands under the tip of the sharp glass and pull upward as hard as I can. Blood seeps from my palm, mixing with the sweat, but the bits of rope are no match for my determination and, finally, snap under the pressure.

Not willing to lose the glass, I toss it in my lap and yank against the strands. Loose now, the remnants release their hold. I slide my arm out and immediately move to untying the knots holding my other arm to the chair.

Adrenaline and fear rise as the sun moves higher in the sky. I yank my arm out and stand. The world spins around me, but I manage to lift my foot to the chair and remove the shard of glass stuck in it. Thankfully, the cut doesn't look too deep. Despite the blood, I slip into my shoes and socks, stumble to the door, and drag it open.

Trees. Everywhere. As far as I can see. In disbelief, I step into the clearing and turn in a circle. Nothing. It's only me and the brown shack in the middle of the fucking woods. I walk around the side of the little wooden structure and spot the first sign of hope. Two long ruts carved into a path. A driveway that looks like it goes on forever, but it must lead to a road.

Roads mean cars and people. Right? For a brief second, I think about going back to get a drink of water from the faucet, but fear and the passage of time prevent me from returning. Biting my lip, I move to the edge of the driveway, nearest to the trees, and put one foot in front of the other. Glad I'm wearing my tennis shoes.

An hour goes by and no road. I cross my arms to ward off the chill in the air. It will be much colder once the sun sets. An edge of despair creeps up on me. There seems to be no end in sight. Humming a cheery song, I trudge on, unwilling to give up, hoping my body doesn't give out. I remind myself that a person can go days without food. Water is my main issue. A body begins to shut down without that vital substance. It was stupid to let fear stop me from getting a drink.

Silently berating myself, the new sound doesn't register at first. It's not until I notice a flash of black in the distance that I see the truck and hear the slight roar of its massive engine. It's coming this way. Terror fills me. My heart slams in my chest. Turning, I run into the woods and crouch behind a tree. Dirt spews up, choking me, as it flies by, but it doesn't stop.

I slide around the tree to peek at it. It's them. When they're out of sight, I push my trembling legs to move quickly. Half shuffling, half jogging, I fix my gaze forward while keeping my ears peeled for the sound of them returning. A sob escapes.

My head swivels to the forest on my left, but there is nothing to guide me, and I'm too afraid to move away from my only clear point of direction. The driveway. Rumbling fills the air, making the choice for me. They're coming back this way.

I turn to the left. The engine drops to a low throttle. I look over my shoulder and see it crawling along, looking for me. I slow, moving from tree to tree, trying to stay hidden. The engine cuts off. I hear a shout. Without thinking, I shove away from the protection at my back and push myself to move.

Seconds later, a hard body slams into me, taking me to the ground, and I scream. We slide along the floor of the forest. Trent's expensive cologne wraps around me, and I'm taken back to the day we met. Déjà vu. Except this time, our collision wasn't an accident.

Instead of getting off me, he sits up and pins me to the hard, dirty ground. Flashing a victorious smile, he shouts, "Got you!" Then laughs. "Sorry for leaving you so long. Had to make sure dear old dad went back to DC first."

It makes me want to puke. Glaring up at him, I swallow the knot of fear in my throat and spit in his handsome face. "What the hell are you doing? I don't care if this is a stupid football prank or whatever. It's gone too far. Take me home."

I know it's not a prank, but I'm hoping he thinks I'm too dumb to realize it.

A long, tanned finger smooths the hair out of my eyes and tucks it behind my ear. "Good try, but you forget, I know how smart you are." Pounding feet brings his head around, and he eyes the guy behind him. "About time. Get some rope from the truck."

Throat tight with emotion, I burst into tears at the thought of being tied up again. "Why are you doing this to me? I've never done anything to you. I need to go home. My uncle will be looking for me." Even though Lionel wasn't my uncle, it had always been easier to describe him that way. He's so much more though.

He shakes his head. "I left a note in your apartment telling him you were too scared to stick around and would text him in a few days."

"He won't believe you," I tell him, conviction ringing in my voice. Lionel would never believe it.

He lifts a broad shoulder. "It doesn't matter. He won't find you." His voice is pleasantly mild, but his eyes burn with a fierceness I've only seen once—when he spoke about his mother.

"Why?" I whisper. "Just tell me why you're doing this to me. I deserve to know."

"Because your kind killed my mother," he snarls, fury riding hard on his face.

Is he crazy? "My kind?" What the hell is he talking about?

He cocks back his fist, and I flinch as it comes toward me, but instead of hitting me, it slams into the dirt beside my head. "Don't lie to me. What is your power? We've been watching you, but I haven't been able to figure it out. Tell me."

My brow wrinkles. Power? I shake my head vigorously. Has he lost his mind? "Listen. I don't have any power. I promise. If I did, I'd have used it to escape. Instead, I had to break a glass and saw my way out of those damn ropes. Think about it." That's it. Find the logic. Convince him.

A mirthless laugh fills the air. "You do. Maybe you don't know it yet, but you do. I knew it the first moment I saw that mark on your shoulder. Then I looked up your parents in my dad's files. Your father had the power to control air," he informs me, his voice ringing with smug superiority and a hell of a lot of anger. "We know this genetic anomaly is hereditary, passed through the blood. We used to think only Rh-negative people had powers, but we're discovering they have the ability to pass it on to their children."

My mind reels with the information he just dumped on me, but one thought keeps reverberating... he's truly crazy. Lost his mind. I hear the sound of footsteps coming closer. Does he believe this crap he's spouting, or is he just following orders?

I shake my head. "You're wrong." Tears trickle down my face. "If I had power, I would have used it hours ago to get free. Are you telling me I could have snapped my fingers and poof! The ropes would have magically disappeared?" The laugh that comes out is tinged with hysteria, but I don't care.

His brows crash together. "It's not magic. You have psychic powers."

I snort. "Oooh, psychic. Why didn't you say so? Let me close my eyes and see if I can use my mind to make you disappear." I shut my eyes and wish with all my heart that I'll open them and find out this is all a nightmare. I open them. "Damn. You're still here."

He gets off me, and a familiar-looking beefy arm jerks me to my feet.

I smirk at the white bandage on his face. "How's the nose, Tommy? Looks broken to me."

In retaliation, he slaps the back of my head.

Instant pain. Tears swim in my eyes, but I blink them away. *Fuck him.*

They tie the rope around my hands and feet and carry me to the truck. They're holding me so tightly, I can't even wiggle.

"Where are you taking me?" I force out, terror clogging my throat. *Oh God!*

"For a swim," Trent replies sarcastically. He reaches into his back pocket and pulls out a blindfold and ties it across my eyes. Blackness descends.

"How did your mother die?" The words tumble out of my

mouth. I need to know why this is happening. "Please. I thought she committed suicide."

They lift me, then the cool uneven metal beneath my tied hands tells me I'm in the back of the truck. Someone jumps in beside me. An arm wraps around my shoulders and hauls me backward. The scent of cedar and citrus tells me it's Trent.

He clears his throat. "She stopped to help a woman sitting on the side of the road who was crying and rocking a baby in her arms. My mother thought there was something wrong with the baby, so she made her driver stop. The bodyguard got out and approached the woman. She incinerated him."

Appalled, I inhale sharply. "What do you mean, she incinerated him? She set him on fire?"

His low tone fills with hatred. "The woman was a pyrokinetic. My mother and her driver tried to get away, but the vehicle burst into flames with them in it. Then, she turned her powers on herself and the baby. Her inability to control her power cost them their lives."

I shake my head vigorously, unable to believe what he just told me but also because I want him to believe me. "I'm so sorry that happened to you, but I told you. I don't have any powers. I swear. On my life." I start crying. "Please let me go. Please."

Cruel fingers reach out and grip my chin, turning my head in his direction. "When my father told me what happened, I made a promise to myself and my mother. I would do everything in my power to rid the world of each and every one of you. Nobody should suffer like she did or live without their mother like me."

I reach out and grab his shirt in my fist, desperate to get his attention. "I don't care what your reports say. I've never had powers. Don't you think I would have used it to save my mother and father? Instead, they were trapped in the car, and I had to watch them burn, hear their screams, while I lay useless in a pool of water." My voice is raw, and I feel him freeze. "I would have given anything to save them. To have them here with me today." I hiccup as the terror of the memory clogs my throat.

His hand grabs mine, and for a long minute, he holds it. "I'm glad you know how I feel."

Hope flares inside me.

He places my hand on my leg and pats it a few times. "It won't save you, but maybe we'll go a little easier on you."

His words are a death knell reverberating in my head. Nothing I say will change his mind. Hope dies. The truck stops. My adrenaline shoots higher, but so does my despair. Tied up, blind, and trapped in the middle of the woods. My chances of escape were slim earlier but are now zero.

The bed dips as Trent jumps out of the truck. Large hands slide around my ankles, and yank me out of the truck, letting me fall onto the hard-packed dirt.

Pain radiates from my tailbone to my head, and I rock side to side in agony, but there's little time to contemplate it before I'm dragged a few more yards.

"Rough her up. I want to remove the ropes before we toss her over the side," Trent orders.

A dark chuckle is all I hear before the shit-kicking boot drives into my stomach and side. Pain explodes, but no matter which way I roll, I can't escape it. I bring my arms up to protect my head and carefully work the blindfold down until I can see.

Smelling of sweat and anticipation, he bends down and laughs. Another kick slams into my side, and I swear I hear a faint crack. Excruciating pain follows.

Tommy is my sole attacker. Guess his friend couldn't make it today. With a glee-filled diabolical smile, he jerks me up from the ground, cocks his meaty fist back, and smashes it into my face.

Howling from the impact of his fist, I drop to my knees and

bring my hands up to catch the blood pouring from my broken nose. I know I should run, but where? Through the pain and tears, I flick a glance through my lashes and find trees almost everywhere. A dark pit lies in front of me, slightly beyond this clearing. There's a muffled roar to my right, but the ringing in my ears makes it impossible to determine what it is.

Is this my final resting spot? I stare at the brown, hard-packed dirt under my knees. Could be worse, I guess.

Someone steps closer, and I cower, afraid of what's coming next. The blood slows to a trickle, and the area around my nose goes numb.

Unfortunately, that asshole, Tommy, isn't done. He clocks me on the side of the head, hard enough to send my body crashing to the ground. I bring my hands back up to protect my head, accepting his fresh rain of blows without fighting back. Bones snap. Ribs crack. He continues his assault. His harsh breaths fill the air after each hit.

Time slips. Fog creeps into my brain. The bright sun dims, and twilight appears. The crisp air reminds me that it's fall. It even smells like it, with the air full of the musty, earthy scent of dried leaves and pine. My mind drifts. Maybe it's time to see my mother and father. To be together again. I bring up our final day and my favorite memory.

The crash happened the night of my sixteenth birthday. Too old for a party, I asked for the cute designer purse I'd been coveting for a while. Instead, my parents surprised me by taking me out of school for an entire day of shopping in New York City. We laughed, tried on clothes, and of course, they gave me the purse. It was an utterly perfect day, filled with sunshine and laughter. Strolling around the city with them, I *felt* older, more sophisticated, which was only emphasized by the fancy dinner we had that night. It was the most magical of birthdays. I smile.

Strong arms lift me up and hold me tightly.

The warmth feels so good against my cold body, but I resist the urge to curl into it. I peel open a swollen eye to peer at my captor. Anger, burning deep inside, erupts when I see Trent's handsome face.

"I..." I can barely speak through the pain, but his satisfaction at my faltering forces me to continue. "I hope you... see my face... close your eyes. Rot in... hell, Trent Hightower."

A sad smile slips across his face. "I'm already there, Willa Taylor." With those final words, he walks across the clearing toward the dark pit.

My sluggish heart picks up speed while frustrated tears leak from the corner of my eyes. I'm not ready to die. A scream builds in my throat, along with a desperate plea, but I can't get it out before he tosses me off the cliff.

Terror rips through me, and the scream tears from my throat as I fall through the darkness. My broken body flails wildly, but the wind does nothing to break my fall. Seconds tick by at an excruciating slow pace, as if my mind wants to savor every breath of life left in my body. Roaring assaults my ears, and a cool mist coats my face and arms, bringing temporary relief to the pain. *Is that a waterfall?* I see the rush of water for a brief second before my body plunges into the cold pool at the bottom.

Water wraps around me, almost like a cradle, as I sink to the soft ground several feet below the surface. All sounds cease in this underwater bubble. Ever since the accident, water has terrified me. Unwilling to risk triggering myself, a shower was my max. I wait for the familiar panic to start, but all I feel is a sort of resignation. This is...was...my worst nightmare. Not anymore. My head drops to my chest. Maybe my mind understands there are worse deaths to endure. Or maybe it's time to accept that water was always going to be my end.

Between one thought and the next, I open my mouth, fully expecting it to pour in and fill my throat and lungs, thereby ending my pitiful existence, but in an unexpected and dizzying rush, the water builds under my body and shoves me to the surface.

Air fills my lungs as I automatically gasp for life. Again and again, I inhale. Busy trying to live, I don't hear the shouts above until a rope splashes into the water next to me. Startled, I glance up and see Tommy shouting at Trent, who's rapidly rappelling down the rocks.

Panicking, I swivel my head around and search for the nearest bank. Body broken, I sob when I raise my arms, but somehow, with the water's current propelling me, I manage to push through the pain and swim over to the bank. Using my elbows, I drag myself up onto the rocky shore, but the second I'm out of the water, the little strength I have gives out, and I collapse onto my back. Rocks dig into my body as I stare at the stars above, knowing Trent's coming to finish me off.

Tommy's voice cuts off. A large splash alerts me of Trent's arrival. Seconds later, he stands over me, dark brown eyes filled with determination.

Trent shakes his head. "Maybe it's better this way. I'll be able to see the life leave your eyes and know, without a shadow of doubt, that I saved this world from another monster."

He drops to his knees beside me and reaches out with his finger to sweep the hair from my eyes. "Your eyes are beautiful." Large hands reach out and wrap around my throat. "Such hatred in them. Good. I want you to hate me the same way I hate you."

He starts squeezing, and I reach up and claw at his hands, trying to pry them off. My fingernails dig into his soft flesh but make little headway. Strong and muscular from years of catching the ball, his hands are steel bands locked around my throat. Unmovable. Tears slip from the corners of my eyes, gliding silently into my hairline. For a second, despair causes me to let go. My hands fall to the ground beside me while I stare helplessly up at him.

Satisfaction flares in the dark depths of his brown eyes.

My vision dims, and the air stalls in my lungs. Sounds almost cease to exist. Everything is muted. All my focus is on Trent. Panic tries to take hold and drag me under, but my debilitating fear fades when I see him smile.

How dare he smile at my death?! Bastard!

My blood burns with the need to wipe that fucking smirk off his face. I bring my hands up, fists clenched, and pound them into his chest. *Fuck this. Fuck him. I deserve to live, dammit.* Broken and exhausted, the end is close, and yet I've never felt more determined than I do in this moment. Something shifts inside me. A spark. Familiar but forgotten. The same feeling I felt the night my parents died.

Cool liquid encases my shoes and ankles, then slides up to my thighs. Creeping like a shadow, silent and steady, it waits for my command. My last breath of air is almost gone. This is it. My one chance. Lifting my hands from his chest, I instinctively lock my fingers in a circle, mimicking the monster sitting on top of me, and in response, the water rises behind him and wraps around his throat.

His eyes widen, and that fucking smile disappears. Hunching over, he tries to finish me off, squeezing with everything he's got. The edges of my vision blacken to a pinprick, but I manage to jerk my hands backward. At my command, the rope of water around his neck responds and pulls him back. His hands loosen, and I manage to gulp in some air.

With a sneer on his face, he taunts me. "You don't have what it takes to kill me."

Apparently, the water isn't squeezing him to death, only holding him back.

"I'm coming, Trent!" Tommy shouts from the cliff above us.

I watch as Tommy begins to rappel down.

"Wait!" Trent yells at him.

But it's too late. Seeing my tormentor moving toward me, I panic and slam my hands together. The water around Trent's neck instantly closes, crushing his windpipe and breaking his neck. Firm lips open wide in surprise, but there is nothing he can do, and his body folds to the ground, eyes staring sightlessly in my direction. Dead.

I killed him. Oh god. Oh god. Oh god.

With a roar, Tommy's shit kicking boots hit the rocky ground, and I watch him rush toward me, his muscular body eating up the distance.

Shaken from Trent's death, I scramble backward, one hand raised in defense, but no matter how hard I try, I can't get my battered body to move faster than a shuffling crawl.

Unfortunately, Tommy's quicker than he looks, and his rage at seeing Trent's lifeless body makes him move even quicker.

Terrified, I scream for him to stop, but he doesn't. The water responds. Rushing to meet him, it forms a column around his body, trapping him inside and stopping him in his tracks. Face twisted with rage, he pounds at the wall of water surrounding him, cursing me loudly. His words promising more pain and my death when he gets free.

Still on the ground, I push to my knees and stare at the wall of liquid locked around the one who broke me. My trembling hands clench into fists at the thought of the beating he gave me, and in an unconscious move, I raise them high, and with a hoarse yell of fury, I slam them down on my thighs. In a bizarre mixture of horror and relief, I watch the water shoot up and hover above Tommy for a brief second before it rushes over him, drowning him in the deluge. His angry shouts cut off, and although he fights the inevitable, he, too, drops like a stone to the ground.

Head pounding fiercely, I fall to my side. My body is done. I lay my cheek on the cold rocks beneath me. Unable to stop myself, I flick a glance from Tommy to Trent. *At least I took them with me.* They won't be able to murder any more of *my kind,* whatever that means. I watch the water recede, but it's restless. It ebbs and flows, as if it's waiting for me to call it.

The soothing movement lulls me into a meditative state.

How could I have not known this was in me? Did I use it the night of the accident or was the pond I landed in pure coincidence?

Pain makes me shudder. Even breathing hurts. It doesn't matter now. Too broken to move more than an inch, I feel death crawling toward me, his cold breath on the back of my bruised neck. Saddened, I let my tears fall as I mourn the life that's no longer mine.

BRIGHT LIGHT SHINES BEHIND MY CLOSED LIDS, BUT IT'S the sound of roaring water and the liquid covering me that makes me frown. Confused, I lift gritty lashes and stare at the sun shining down on me. *Where am I?* My hand reaches up to brush the hair back from my face and finds stiff, wet strands. The water slips away from my body. I lift my head and see Trent and Tommy staring at me. Dead where they lie. Memories flood my brain, and I sit up.

My pain is gone. What should have taken weeks to heal has been reduced to hours. I lift my hand to poke and prod at my ribs and head, but I find no soreness or broken bones. Zero.

Nada. Zilch. It's a freaking miracle. My gaze shifts to the water covering my legs. Or maybe it's something else.

My hand trembles as I reach down and run my hand across its liquid surface. Cool. Wet. It responds to my slightest touch, following every move I make.

"Thank you. For everything." I can't help but talk to it. Thank it. For a second, it lingers, then slowly recedes into the pool below the waterfall.

Unwilling to dwell on this—whatever this is—I cautiously get to my knees, and when that doesn't hurt, I stand. My legs are shaky and weak but easily support my healed body. I shift my gaze from the water to Trent.

For a long moment, I stare at him. In the bright light of day, his words and actions are even more astonishing. He truly believed I had power. Because his father had a file on mine. Because my dad had the power to control air. In fact, he bet my life on it. Too bad for him and Tommy... he was right.

What do I do now? I wipe away the tears falling down my cheeks. Crying won't help. I need to get out of here and find Lionel. He'll know what to do. I look around and find nothing but the same forest from last night, looking thicker and denser down here.

I need to go back up. My eyes scale the steep rocks in front of me, intently searching the face for any sign of a path. I encounter nothing but tiny crevices in the sheer rock and the rope they used last night. Apparently, that's my only option.

Sighing heavily, I trudge toward Tommy, my feet shuffling through the rocky bank, and stop. My lips curl as I stare down at him. His beefy fists are curled into his side, knuckles raw and bruised. A stark reminder of what he did to me last night. The urge to kick him over and over races through me. and I raise my foot, letting it hover over him for the longest time, but then I use it to shove him onto his back.

Reaching down, I pat his front right pocket and find what I need. My nose wrinkles in disgust, but it's my best shot of getting out of here quickly. I slip my fingers into his wet jeans and dig until I find the keys to that loud and obnoxious truck of his. Pulling them out, I carefully tuck them into my pocket and step over his prone body.

On the ground behind him, a buzzing sound comes from the black cased phone on the ground. I stare at it, wondering who is calling, when a thought hits me. I bite my lip, contemplating what to do, and realize I don't have a choice. Snatching it up, I hurry back to Trent and pat him down until I find his phone too. Slipping each of them into my back pockets, I race to the rope.

Time to get the hell out of here.

What took them minutes to descend takes me an hour to climb. Heaving myself to the top of the cliff, I lie there on my stomach, breathing rapidly while I stare down at the two bodies below. Tommy looks bloated in the mid-day sun, but Trent's handsome as ever... Well, except for the red mark around his neck. For a second, I see the broad, blinding smile he used to throw around carelessly.

Dread coils in my stomach, and my breath catches. I didn't check his pulse. Is it possible he's still alive? Worried, I stare at him for several minutes. Is he smiling? I squint in the bright sun. Nothing. There's not a single movement or twitch. He's not smiling. I take a deep breath in and hold it, then breathe out. Obviously, my extreme guilt is trying to convince me I didn't kill two people last night.

Unsure, I can't help but stare at Trent as I nervously stand and quickly pull up the rope. Stupid, but I don't trust anyone right now. Not even myself. Once it's on top of the jagged cliff, I heave it onto my shoulder and stalk over to throw it in the back of the truck.

Hopping into the driver's side, I pull out their phones and

toss them into the passenger seat, knowing I'll have to ditch them. Whoever keeps calling Tommy might decide to use the location app, and I can't take the chance they'll find him here.

The engine roars to life, and the truck rumbles underneath me. Thankfully, I'm tall enough to reach the pedals and comfortably drive this massive beast. Turning around on the driveway, I floor it. Rocks and dirt spray up under the truck and behind me. I desperately hope these ruts lead to a main road.

Fifteen minutes later, I pop out of the trees and come to a stop in front of a paved two-lane road. At least it's not dirt. My eyes dart from right to left. There are no signs to tell me where I'm at, and there's no traffic going by either. Leaving the truck running, I hop out and walk into the middle of the road, hoping to spot something farther down to help me decide.

I get to the center line, look down the road to the left, then swing around and look to the right. It's road and trees as far as I can see, which means I'll have to guess. With a sigh, I turn back to the truck, and that's when I see the faintest impression right in front of the tires. It would have been impossible for me to see from inside the cab, but standing here, I get a clear view of the dusty tracks heading right out of the driveway.

Jumping back into the truck, I turn right and press hard on the gas pedal, hoping I'm not wrong and this is the way back to town. The road continues on and on, forest on both sides, for another twenty minutes until I hit an intersection. Stopping at the light, I see a sign for the interstate and hit the blinker. Traffic clears, and I make the turn. As I do, I see a brown sign to help visitors find the entrance for the Shanty Lake State Resort Park, and I know exactly where I'm at—only twenty minutes from home.

Breathing a deep sigh of relief, I get on the southbound interstate and head toward safety. Along the way, I use the sleeve of my shirt to wipe the phones as best as I can and throw them out the window at two different intervals, hoping it throws off their location for at least a while. Trent's a senator's son, though, so I doubt it will work for long.

Finally, I spot the brown house Lionel purchased long ago, and it's as if a dam breaks inside me. Tears stream down my face. I didn't think I'd ever see it again. Or him. Loud sobs fill the cab as I hunch over the steering wheel, unable to do anything but cry.

The truck door swings open, and a gun appears in my peripheral vision. "Hands up."

I raise my shaking hands.

"Get out of the truck nice and slow. That's it."

My voice cracks as I say his name, "Lionel."

He swears up a storm, and the gun disappears. Strong hands clasp my shoulders as he hauls me the rest of the way out of the truck and into his arms. The scent of his old-fashioned vanilla shaving cream is the most comforting cloak.

"Damn it, Willa. Where the hell have you been? I've been worried sick about you."

Lionel rocks back and forth, his hand cradling my head. "Some fool left a note. As if I'd believe it." He snorts, but I can hear the worry in his voice.

"I killed them," I whisper, not wanting to say the words out loud, but knowing he needs to understand the seriousness of the situation. I pull back and stare at his deeply lined face, tears and snot running down mine. "With water." The sheer disbelief in my voice is still there, even after the proof of the night.

He briefly closes his eyes. "I hoped your powers would never surface. Your parents did, too."

"So, it's true?" I ask, blindsided by his answer. That means other things could be true too. "Trent said... his father had files on my parents. On my dad. Said he could control air." My lips stumble over the words, floundering under the weight of everything.

Lionel's green eyes sharpen. "Trent who?"

Askance, I stare at him. "Trent. The football player I've been tutoring. The one I ran into that day on the lawn."

He stiffens. "You never told me his name. What's his last name, Willa?" From the way he's holding his head, I'm getting the feeling he knows something I don't.

"Trent Hightower," I murmur with a frown. "His father is Senator..."

"Thomas Hightower," Lionel finishes for me. "Fuck. If you're not on his radar now, you will be. The second he finds out his son is dead; he'll use his extremely considerable power to find out who killed him." He reaches out and grips my elbow. "Is this his truck?"

I shake my head. "Tommy's truck." When he raises an eyebrow, I elaborate further. "His friend and fellow football player. Big guy with a vicious right hook." My fingers ghost along the right side of my face.

Lionel's fingers grip my chin as he turns my head to the left. "I don't see anything."

"The water healed me," I tell him, still unable to believe it. "Killed them and healed me."

Eyes wide, Lionel's head dips in a sharp nod. "Tell me everything that happened."

In a shaky voice, I haltingly explain about them kidnapping and beating me. When I get to what I thought was the end of my life, my voice is barely audible. "Trent hated me. His only thought was to rid the world of my kind. Up until then, all I felt was fear and anger at my impending death. But when I got to the very end, my anger twisted into hate, and it... triggered something inside me. The water rose up and answered my call." I finish the story with how I got out of there and what I did coming home.

"And it healed you while you were sleeping," he repeats, shaking his head, his tone full of disbelief. "That's a new one, but we'll deal with it later. Let me make some calls. Ditch this truck. Get a plan together." He points to my apartment. "Right now, I want you to stop thinking about last night and go upstairs. Shower. Pack. Whatever you can fit in one carryon and your backpack. That's it. Leave everything else behind. Got it?"

Numb, I stare at him, wondering why we aren't calling the police, but how do we explain the whole 'ability to control water' thing.

He turns me around and barks, "Go!"

My feet automatically move toward my apartment. Once inside, more tears roll down my face as I realize the impact of what all this means. The life I'd so carefully planned, the career, staying here... it's all gone. I still can't believe it. Two days ago, I was living a normal life. Or so I thought. Trent already had me on his radar at that point.

My mind races to recall everything he said last night, but all I get are bits and pieces. Fear must have blocked some of it out. I grab clean clothes and turn on the shower. Stepping in, I flinch when the beads hit my skin, but curiosity has me raising my palm up to catch a few drops. I stare down at the transparent liquid shimmering in my hand. I have so many questions. Why me? Trent said my father's power was air. Why did I not get his power? How does it choose?

The roar of the truck startles me, and I quickly dump the water and wash up. Minutes later, I'm standing in my bedroom, trying to figure out what to wear. Lionel didn't say where we're going. My shoulder throbs, and I lightly run a finger over it. There are no cuts or anything. Stepping closer to the mirror, I pull at the skin and squint. The mark on my shoulder looks darker with more defined edges, but there doesn't appear to be any damage. Maybe I banged it on the cliff or pulled a muscle during my escape.

Shaking it off, I walk over to the closet and pull out a tank top, a long-sleeved shirt, and a sweatshirt, then layer them with my most comfortable and worn pair of jeans. Finally, I thrust my feet into some socks and tennis shoes. Since it's cool outside, I grab a coat. Finally, I pull down my suitcase and backpack and stuff them full with my favorite clothes, shoes, and toiletries. My whole life in two bags. Will this be my life going forward—on the run with only these items?

Opening the front door, I take a moment to stare around the small apartment that has meant so much to me for the last couple of years and bite my lip. I loved this little place. Where will I end up now? The thought pangs me with a sense of déjà vu. I wondered the same after the accident seven years ago, but Lionel jumped in and took care of me. I know he'll do the same now.

With a heavy sigh, I close the door on the past and trudge down the stairs toward Lionel's house. I wonder where he took the truck.

It's not until I'm reaching for his back door that it hits me. The mark on my shoulder. When we collided that day, Trent couldn't stop staring at it. Then, last night, he said the mark made him look into his dad's files. I step into Lionel's house and find him running around the house.

"Where did the truck go?"

He waves a hand. "A friend picked it up. Took it to a junkyard."

A small blue square comes toward me, and I automatically reach up and catch it. It's my passport.

"Are we leaving the country?" I ask with a sinking feeling in my stomach.

He waves a hand. "I don't know yet. Once Brad gets back to me, I'll have a better idea." Stalking over to the cabinet, he yanks out a drawer and sticks his hand inside the hole. A second later, the hutch swings open, revealing guns, boxes of ammo, and stacks of money.

"Brad, your golfing buddy? Why would he have a plan?" I quietly ask him, the magnitude of what he's been hiding becoming more apparent with every action he takes. "Who are you?" Lionel doesn't answer. I point toward the bag he's filling. "Guns. Money. I told you I killed two people, and you don't bat an eyelash. What the hell is going on, Lionel?"

Hands on his hips, he stops, takes a deep breath, then turns to face me. "We don't have time for me to explain everything right now. Senator Hightower is more than just a senator. He leads a team of soldiers and scientists whose main job is to capture and study people with psychic abilities. If we don't get out of here, you'll become his next experiment."

I shake my head. "How do you know all this? At least tell me that part."

His eyes study me intently for a few seconds, then he slowly raises his finger and points to the cloth napkin lying on the table in front of me. A small flame appears. Fire. He reaches over and casually picks up the burning cloth and drops it in the sink, then holds up his hand. There's not a burn on it.

"You control fire," my shaky voice is barely a whisper, telling him how freaked out I am.

He thrusts a hand through his grey hair. "My ability is fire, but I'm not powerful enough to do much more than flames. The military knows, but because mine is a low-level psychic ability, Hightower has never been interested in me."

He reaches out and grabs a framed photo on the hutch.

"My son, though..." His voice breaks when he says those words. "He could command fire. Masses of flames, explosions, you name it. His abilities started showing when he was a year old. We tried to teach him how to control it, but he was too young to understand. The day they died... the fire got away from him."

Horror at the thought of the pain he must have felt, knowing what happened, and the overwhelming guilt weighing him down because his son had gotten his abilities. "I'm so, so sorry, Lionel." What a terrible burden to bear—for him and his son, Greer.

"Did my parents know about all this?"

He nods and thrusts the photo into his backpack.

"Why didn't I inherit my father's ability?"

He lifts a shoulder. "I don't know. Nor do I know why your power waited until today to show up." His eyes are distant for a second. "Abilities are evolving so fast, and we don't have a good way to predict the changes. That's the reason Hightower was given command of the task force. To find the origin of our powers and to determine if we're a danger to society. Unfortunately, his wife died at the hands of someone with psychic power. Since then, he's used extreme methods to capture the most powerful individuals. The powers above him know little of what he's doing, nor do they ask. Basically, they condone his handling of the situation." Bitterness coats his voice.

He strides over and grabs my shoulders. "I failed my son, but I won't fail you. I promise, Willa. I'll do everything in my power to get you to safety."

"I know," I assure him, patting him on the back. "Don't worry. I'll do whatever you tell me to do."

Tension eases from his shoulders and he heaves a sigh, his relief almost palpable. "You need a new identity, but we don't have time to do this right. For now, I'll have Brad use Greer's information with your photo." His tone is gruff as he sifts through papers in the hutch. A second later, he holds out a paper, and I take it from him.

"Greer's birth certificate," I say, reading the document. He was only a couple of years older than me. "Am I disguising myself as a boy?"

"Greer was actually my mother's name, too," he says with a small smile. "It can go both ways." He pulls out his phone and positions me next to the white wall in the hall. "No smile." Once he snaps the photo, he sends a copy of it and the birth certificate to Brad.

I take a deep breath. "Greer." I repeat the name a few times. It will take time to get used to it. "I'm honored." Tears well up, but I refuse to think of this as a permanent change. It's temporary until I get somewhere safe.

While Lionel stuffs weapons and other necessary items into a large duffel bag, I grab food and drinks for us. We don't know whether we'll be traveling by car or plane, but it gives me something to do and keeps my mind from replaying the details of last night over and over.

An hour later, we back out of the driveway in my little hatchback. Once we meet up with Brad, he and another friend will continue on in my car, ditching it a few hours away from the city to throw off Hightower's men. I bite my lip, hating the thought of putting someone else in danger, but Lionel chuckles and informs me that they're ex-Army Rangers and extremely capable of taking care of themselves.

Brad's older, like Lionel, but he's not what I imagined, with his shaved head, tattoos, and military demeanor. As he listens to Lionel, his eyes never leave the area around us. His friend is pretty quiet, too, his voice barely above a murmur when he asks for my keys. I bite my lip, looking around the abandoned gas station off an exit in the middle of nowhere.

"Give Mace your coat and phone," Brad orders me.

I glance at Lionel and see him nod, so I hand my phone and coat to the other guy. Cold sweeps around me, making me shiver, but it's eclipsed by the oversized dark hoodie tossed into my arms. When I look at Brad, he motions for me to put it on.

"Mace is about your size. With a wig and some modifications, the cameras will think he's you," Brad's voice is clipped as he explains the reason for the switch. "We'll try to buy you a day or two. Make the most of it." This time, he's looking at Lionel.

While I put on the hoodie, Lionel and Brad talk quietly about the plan. Their low murmurs are almost impossible to hear, but I catch the words train, major, and Raven. Headlights shine as a vehicle takes the exit, and we all tense. Lionel moves me to the rear of the car and pulls out his handgun. Brad slips into the shadows of the building. When it passes by without slowing, I breathe a sigh of relief, but none of the men do.

"What?" I ask, bewildered by the expressions on their faces.

"Keys," Lionel barks without answering me. Brad tosses him a set of keys, and hands him a small black backpack. "Go pack has cash, IDs, couple of burners, and a few other necessities. I've tagged it with a tracker. Train station is two clicks to the east. Watch your six. I'll let Phoenix know you're on the move and hand off your coordinates. Good luck."

Phoenix? Is that a person? I wonder but don't interrupt.

The two clasp hands, and Lionel gives him a quick salute. "I owe you."

Brad snorts. "Hell, I owe you at least a couple of life debts. See you on the other side." He walks over and slips into my car, which has been running with the lights off for several minutes.

Lionel motions for me to join him. "We've got a little over a mile to walk. Let's get moving before the car comes back."

My eyes dart around the dark parking lot. "Why would it return?"

He shines his flashlight onto a small dirt path on the side of the highway, and I walk toward it.

Lionel's voice is gruff as he answers, "It might not, but we don't believe in coincidences. Too many close calls." An engine revs in the distance. "Pick up the pace."

I start jogging, and as I get to the bridge, Lionel pulls me under it. A car passes by, then a few minutes later, another follows.

"Slide your backpack onto your shoulders and carry this one for me. I'll take my duffle and your suitcase," he informs me in a hard voice as he hands me the pack Brad gave him. "Let's go. Double time."

Having grown up with Lionel, I recognize his order to pick up the pace and start running. Thankfully, we're both in good shape, so it doesn't take us long. Eight minutes later, we're slowing to a walk on the outskirts of a train station parking lot.

"It's a commuter stop," he informs me. "We're going to change directions once we hit the main line." His eyes dart around the surprisingly busy terminal.

With gritty eyes, I glance up at the board. Six o'clock. These must be people getting home from work. When Lionel motions for me to follow him, I tighten my grip on the backpack in my hands and board the train he indicates. Once we're on, he dives into the pack in my hands and pulls out two tickets.

Destination is... Philadelphia, but I doubt we'll go that far. I want to ask Lionel, but the seats around us are filling with people, and I'm too scared someone will hear me, so I just lean my head on the window and stare out at the station.

Minutes later, the train rolls out of the station, and it isn't long before I see the outskirts of Philly. We get off at a stop in the suburbs. Lionel buys two tickets to Chicago, but on the way to board, he steps to the side, points to the restroom, and hands me a bag. "Put it on. Throw the hoodie in the trash. I'm going to switch too. If you come out before me, don't move from this spot."

Nervously biting my lip, I nod and take the bag from him. The restroom is full, so I dart into one of the stalls. Reaching into the plastic sack, I pull out a red jacket and a ball cap. After putting it on and using the restroom, I throw the hoodie into the bag and emerge from the stall to an empty room. Tossing the bag into the trash, I wash my hands and pull my hair into a low bun to hide it better, then put the cap back on. Lionel's waiting when I come out. Instead of the green jacket he had on earlier, he's wearing a navy windbreaker and a knit cap.

He throws an arm around me and leans down to whisper, "Head to the parking lot."

Confused, I glance at the train to Chicago but instead of boarding, I turn toward the exit. Someone in a dark hoodie bumps into me, and I let out a little scream, but when I hear a low voice apologize, I shake it off and flash an embarrassed smile in their direction.

Lionel digs into his pocket and pulls out the set of keys Brad tossed him. "Lot C. We're looking for a blue Nissan Rogue." When we get to the parking lot, we head to the section. Once there, he repeatedly clicks on the fob until one of the nearby vehicles answers back with a chirp.

Piling our luggage into the trunk, he points to the passenger side, and I slide in and wait for him. The dome light shines briefly on his face as he gets into the driver's side and starts it. Deep lines bracket his mouth and eyes. He looks tired.

"Do you want me to drive?" I offer, although I don't know where we're going.

He pats my hand. "It's not far. Once we're in D.C., we'll grab the 11:30 train to Atlanta. Why don't you catch some sleep? It's going to be a long night."

I shake my head. Sleep is the last thing on my mind. "Can't. There's too much I need to know." He glances at me but nods. "How do you know Brad?"

I don't know why that's my first question, but it helps to start with something... simpler than the subject of psychic powers. I'm having a hard time wrapping my mind around that part.

His shoulders relax a bit. "Army. Your father knew him, too. We served together on a few missions. After your father got out, Brad and I stayed in."

"And the other guy? Mace," I ask, thinking about the fact that Brad knew my father. I wish I'd known earlier.

"He served with us on the last few missions," Lionel says with a shrug. "Good guy."

"Do they have powers, too?" I ask, almost afraid of hearing the answer.

"Yes," Lionel says with a lift of his chin. "I can't tell you what they are, though. We tend to keep our abilities to ourselves, and they're not here for me to ask permission."

Fair enough. "Did you and my father get your powers in the military?"

"No," he quietly answers, then continues. "Thirty-five to forty years ago, random people started exhibiting powers. Most of them were low level. Telepathy. Clairvoyance. Precognition. The government ran a few tests, then dismissed them. But when the powers became more complex, they started to investigate further. It took them a while, but the government discovered the common factor was RH-negative blood. Some think our abilities were triggered by gamma rays from a meteorite that swept by earth, others theorize it was a natural evolution of the human race." He shrugs. "Sometimes I wonder if it's something we haven't thought of yet. There are a lot of theories and few answers."

Trent had mentioned something about RH-negative blood. "I'm O+," I remind him, confused.

He wipes a hand down his face. "I know. The first generation was purely Rh-negative. Once the second generation, our children, started exhibiting powers, we realized it was evolving. The second generation could either be Rh-negative or a carrier of the Rh factor. Because of your father, you're a carrier."

The numbers are mind-boggling. "If all of them have power and their children are inheriting it too, you're talking about a quarter of the human race."

He shrugs. "At a minimum." His hands tighten on the steering wheel. "A third generation is being born," he reminds me. "World leaders took immediate action when they realized how much of the population was impacted. In the United States, Congress created two groups. One to study us, led by Senator Thomas Hightower, and the other to support our rights, led by Senator Jack Harrison. Sort of a check and balance system."

He continues. "We call Hightower's military group Raven, because they're the harbinger of death for our kind. Hightower is supposed to use his position to find answers, not kill us, but after his wife died, he went off the deep end. Normal humans getting eclipsed by those with powers is his biggest fear, so he's made it a mission to hunt us down, especially the individuals with rare, almost unstoppable powers."

Taking a deep breath, he finishes. "When you first told me about being stalked, I thought they'd somehow found out I changed your records."

"What do you mean, you changed my records?"

"At your dad's request, I changed your birth certificate so they would think you were adopted," he admits with a sigh. "Honestly, I wasn't sure it would work, but Hightower never came after you. I didn't realize you'd run into his son."

"Trent knows I'm not adopted. Do you think he told his dad?" I ask, even though I'm scared to know the answer.

"I don't know. You've never used your power before last night, right?" he replies, asking for me to confirm.

"No," I answer. "But I have an idea of what might have first triggered Trent."

My fingers run lightly across my shoulder as I explain my theory. "The day I ran into him, my shirt came off, exposing my scar. He kept staring at it, but a lot of people do, so I didn't think much of it. I told him the truth; it was an old scar from the accident."

A line forms between Lionel's brows, and I shrug and

continue, "Trent said the mark made him wonder if I had powers. Apparently, his father keeps files on everyone who has powers, so he looked up my parents. Dad was in there."

"It would have said adopted parents, but maybe he figured out my ruse. I don't know anything about a mark. Neither I nor my son had one," he says, tapping his fingers on the steering wheel as he thinks about this new development. "We'll pass the information on to Phoenix."

"Who's Phoenix?" I ask.

"That's what we unofficially call the group led by Jack," he replies absentmindedly. He must still be thinking about the mark. "Over the last few years, I've worked with them to get people to safety. That's where I'm taking you. Phoenix will help you establish a new identity and help you figure out how to wield your powers. Until we get there, Brad created a couple of IDs for you with Greer's name on them. They're in the pack he gave us. Keep it close at all times."

I nod. "It sounds like you know him." When he raises an eyebrow, I clarify. "Jack."

"I do," he answers, then further explains. "We served together. And I worked with his son too. He's a major in the Army. They're men with integrity."

High praise coming from Lionel. "And they're in Atlanta?" I ask, watching the miles fly by. We're a little over an hour outside of D.C. I grab my backpack and pull out some bottles of water and snacks for us.

Lionel grabs a bottle and chugs half of it down. "That's where we'll meet them. Oliver, the son, runs Phoenix."

"If they're supported by the government, why do I need IDs with Greer's name on them?" I ask, confused by the whole thing.

"Tickets on public transportation require a government issued ID, and Greer's was the easiest option to pull together quickly," he replies. "But once you reach Phoenix, they'll likely help you establish a new, more foolproof ID and background to keep Raven from finding you."

"Will that mean I can return to school?" I ask softly, hoping that's the case. I know it's silly, but for years I've thought about nothing but helping others, especially kids.

I wait for him to answer, but he simply lifts a shoulder in response. For the rest of the drive, I can't help but think about everything. There are so many emotions bombarding me, thoughts bouncing all over the place, I can't sleep. Yes, I'm angry and scared, but a part of me feels blindsided by the truth that has been hidden from me for all these years.

My dad had the ability to control air. Even saying it to myself doesn't make it feel real. I never remember him doing anything out of the ordinary. He was my dorky dad who told jokes and loved us. I frown. He could have at least warned me. I was a teenager, not a child, and quite capable of understanding. Now, it's as if the past has ambushed me.

At the worst possible time, too. Twenty-three, ready to graduate, start my new life, and in a blink, everything blows up. My dreams gone. If I'd known it was a possibility, I could have done a better job of hiding or going to school far away from the Hightowers. If I hadn't been late for work and collided with Trent, I'd still be living a normal life, doing boring things like studying, not racing to hide from the government. If, if, if.

"We're close to the station," Lionel tells me in a tired, gravel-filled voice. "But we're not getting on the train. I don't like the idea of being trapped for fourteen hours. We need to be mobile. Stay here. I'll get us another car."

Before I can ask questions, he's gone. I sit in the quiet car, waiting for him to return, my eyes darting from one end of the parking lot to the other, scared someone will find me. Every time someone comes toward the car, I nervously duck down.

The door opens, and I jump, but it's only Lionel.

He eyes me for a second. "Leave your jacket here. Red is too noticeable." After I take it off, he gives me the navy blue one he's wearing. "After I leave, wait five minutes. There are cameras everywhere. Pull the collar up and your hat down low. Don't look up or around. There's a grey Nissan Altima three rows back and five cars to your right. Grab the backpacks and make your way to it. Crouch down beside the passenger door when you get there." He takes the red jacket and slips it on. It barely fits, but he doesn't seem to care. He grabs my suitcase and his duffle from the back and closes the door.

I watch him cross the parking lot and enter the station silently counting down the minutes. My heart races as I wait. Five minutes is an eternity. Finally, I hit the mark. Easing out of the car, I grab both packs and make my way back to the Altima.

It's more humid in D.C. than it was in Philly but still chilly. When I find the car, I follow his instructions and crouch down beside the passenger door, praying nobody comes along. I glance at the car beside me and find peeling grey paint. It's definitely seen some miles.

Laughter drifts in the night air but never comes any closer. I hug the packs to my chest, barely breathing, as I try to listen for footsteps. Minutes go by, and a bead of sweat rolls down my temple and falls to the ground.

A hand clamps around my mouth, and I let out a muffled scream.

"It's me," Lionel says harshly. "Once I start the car, get in and store the packs up front with you."

I nod, and he disappears. Seconds later, the car light comes on, and I hear my door unlock. The car starts, and I slide into the passenger seat.

He turns off the interior light but not before I see the wires sticking out from under the dash. "Are we stealing this car?"

My voice is high-pitched in disbelief. I've never even had a speeding ticket.

"Put on your seatbelt," he orders me. When I continue to stare at him, he heaves a sigh. "We're borrowing it. I'll make sure we leave it where it's easily found."

Appeased, I smile. Unlike the last vehicle, this one smells old and a bit musty, which makes my nose wrinkle in protest, but the floor is surprisingly immaculate when I place the two backpacks on it. Someone takes really good care of this car. I hate the idea of stealing, or borrowing, someone's only car.

"This sucks. What if it's their only mode of transportation?"

A line appears on his brow. "Better their car than your life." When I don't answer, he lifts a shoulder. "The newer models are harder to steal."

I raise an eyebrow at this piece of knowledge but also reach for the seatbelt. "Fine. But maybe you can find out who they are and send them some money." When I turn to buckle myself in, I see my suitcase and his duffle in the back seat.

His lips quirk up in a smile. "Deal." He puts the car in reverse and slowly drives out of the parking lot.

"How long is the drive?" I ask him, stretching out my legs.

"A little over nine hours," he says with a glance out the window. "Get some rest."

Exhausted from the last few days, I take off the jacket and stuff it under my head. Eyes closed; I can't help but think about everything he's told me and sadly wish I didn't know any of it. All I want to do is go back to being normal.

L ionel's harsh voice brings me out of a deep sleep. "Wake up, Willa. Slip the go pack on your back and put your jacket on over it." The engine whines as the car picks up speed.

Scared, I immediately sit up and do as he asked.

"What's happening?" My body sways right, then left, as he jerks the wheel from one lane to the other.

Lionel grimaces when he looks at me. "They found us."

Bright lights shine from behind along with the roar of an engine. Startled, I turn around, but I can't see anything. Whatever they're driving, it's big. "How?"

He lifts a shoulder. "I don't know. I knew our chances would be slim once they were on our trail." He glances at the car next to us. "Their technology is top-notch, government spyware. They can find anybody, anywhere. The plan was to buy us enough time to get to Phoenix." He slams his palm onto the steering wheel. "Damn it. I didn't expect them to find us this quickly. We're still five hours from Atlanta. Tighten your seatbelt."

We're flying down the interstate as fast as the old car will go, the guardrail a blur beside us, but it's obvious we can't outrun them.

"What are we going to do?" My voice trembles as I ask, although the real question I'm wondering is what they'll do when they catch us.

Lionel doesn't answer. His knuckles are white as he grips the steering wheel. At the last second, he takes an off ramp, cutting off a few cars on the right. Horns blare and tires screech as they hit the brakes to avoid hitting us. Not once does Lionel slow down. Nobody follows.

At the bottom of the exit is a gas station. Lionel jerks the wheel, and we fly into the little lot, coming to a stop at the pump on the farthest end. "Get out and stand near the trees. They'll be here soon."

I jump out, but I only take a few steps back.

Is he getting gas?

He inserts his credit card and goes through the motions. I hear the screech of tires. They're coming. I clench my fists, wondering what he's doing. He flicks the lever on, locks it in place, then drops the flowing pump on the island between the two lanes. Gas starts flowing across the pavement on both sides.

He runs over to my side of the car and jerks open the rear door. Grabbing his duffle, he drops it on the ground beside him, then rifles through it until he finds the guns and ammo. Laying each of them on the ground, he loads them, then takes position over the hood of the car.

I move in closer to him and watch a black SUV screech to a halt. "Original."

Lionel chuckles but the corners of his eyes never crinkle, which tells me how worried he is right now. "No matter what, stay down."

Five men wearing dark fatigues get out of the vehicle, but strangely, one stays in the vehicle. He doesn't move, but I can see glimpses of him when the overhead light shines down on his light brown hair.

Lionel shoots off a round, hitting the ground near the lead guy, making me jump. "That's far enough. Who are you, and what do you want?"

Undeterred, the guy takes another step closer.

Lionel curses quietly under his breath. "The next one goes in your leg. Don't test me, boy. Stand down." The hard cut of his military tone tells him he means business.

The guy stops and motions to his other companions to do the same. "We're here for her, and one way or another, she's coming with us. You pick. Alive or in a bag."

"She's not going anywhere," Lionel shouts back. He raises his hand to cover his mouth. "Brad put burner phones in the pack. Grab one. We need to let him know we're in trouble. It's a long shot, but maybe I can hold them off until he gets us some help."

I strip off the windbreaker and backpack, then dig into it. Pulling out one of the small black phones, I start to hand it to Lionel, but he shakes his head. "Dial 555-4906. Let me know when someone answers."

With shaking fingers, I dial the number. "Carl's Pizza Parlor."

I hold out the phone to Lionel, but he again shakes his head and whispers the following words. "Track the target. Falcon and little bird. Snafu. Out." He motions to me, and I quietly murmur the words into the phone.

"10-4. Sit tight."

"Now, hang up and turn it off," he tells me. "Put the pack and your jacket back on."

Confused, I wonder how they'll find us without a phone, but I do as he orders. What do I know? I've never been on the run.

The men in front of us cluster together, and I see them talking quietly.

Lionel tenses.

"This isn't going to end well for you," the lead guy calls out with a broad smirk on his face. He dips his head and one of the guys disappears into thin air.

"Fuck!" Lionel says, throwing his hand out. The gas flowing between us ignites and the flames race from one end of the gas station to the other, covering almost the entire surface and creating a nearly impenetrable wall between us and our enemies.

With the fire providing cover, he turns to me. "Your dad would never forgive me if I allowed those bastards to kill his only daughter. The second I fan the flames higher; I want you to take off into those trees. Don't stop. Don't look back."

I vehemently shake my head. "I'm not leaving you, Lionel. I've already lost one father. I'm not losing another because of this stupid psychic bullshit."

Suddenly, something hard is pressed against my temple. Out of the corner of my eyes, I see a man's hand. I'm guessing it's a gun.

"Drop it or she's dead," a calm voice orders Lionel.

Lionel freezes for a split second, his eyes assessing the man beside me. Then he slowly places his gun down on the pavement. He stares at the man the entire time, and as he rises, I see a small movement behind him.

Slightly behind his leg, Lionel circles his finger round and round in slow motion. I frown slightly, wondering if he's using his power or trying to signal to me, but I can't tell. Shuffling my feet, I try to move a little to the left to see it better, but the guy grabs my elbow and jerks me close.

"Kick it away," the man orders, his voice completely emotionless.

Lionel kicks his gun toward the trees.

"Why are you doing this?" I ask breathlessly, the smoke making it harder to breathe. "You have powers just like me. Why are you working for them?"

"You know nothing. Less than nothing. They're everywhere. No matter what you do, they'll track you down. You might as well come with me and save yourself a world of pain," he mockingly sneers, but there is a gravity of defeat in his low tone. "Start moving."

Instead of taking a step back, Lionel moves forward, startling the guy. "You're not taking her."

The guy presses the barrel of the gun into my temple, and I wince. "Either she comes with me, or I'll shoot her. Vince doesn't tolerate failure. Neither does Hightower."

Lionel takes another step forward.

Something tickles my hand, and I look down and see a small green weed or a vine, slithering up from the ground. It glides silently along the side of my body like a snake until it starts to encircle my wrist. I raise my hand to take a closer look and watch the small plant wind itself around my arm as it moves higher. Is the guy next to me doing this?

He starts coughing, and it galvanizes me into action. I immediately pull on the thin green rope, hoping to get it off. It loosens but instead of falling to the ground, it heads up my arm to my shoulder. I try to turn my head to look at it, but the gun barrel stops me. All I can do is stand there and stare at Lionel, praying he can do something.

Lionel's brows crash together at the sight of the vine on my shoulder. Turning back to the guy, he pulls up a string of fire from the ground. "Burning alive isn't pleasant. Let her go."

The plant wraps around my throat once, and I inhale sharply. Lionel's curses. Terrified, I raise my hand to jerk it away, but the vine moves even faster, avoiding me to latch onto the barrel of the gun. It jerks it away from my temple. The gun goes off with a roar, and I scream, then clap a hand over the pain in my ear. Quickly shoving away from the guy, I watch the vine disappear into the ground.

After I move, the guy's pants ignite, and with a yell, his attention immediately shifts to his legs, but the second he looks down, Lionel launches forward, tackling him to the ground. Horrified, I watch the flames crawl up their bodies as they roll around on the ground, each one trying to get the upper hand. Darting a glance around, I look for something to put out the fire, but an agonized yell makes me turn back to the two men.

My attacker is completely engulfed in flames. At the last second, he opens his mouth, as if to gasp for air, but the fire steals his last breath.

I force my eyes from him to Lionel, fearing the worst, but he waves a hand, and the fire moves away from his body. Hands trembling, I reach out to help him stand, my eyes scanning his body for burns, but there's not a single one on him. His clothes aren't even singed. It's as if the fire didn't touch him.

He tucks a piece of hair behind my ear. "That was close. Are you okay?"

"My ear's ringing, and things are kind of echoing, but I'm alive. How are you not burned?" I reply in a shaky voice.

He glances down at his outstretched hand, which is shaking violently. "Fire is a part of me. We need to go."

"What's wrong?" I ask, but then I see the fire dying behind him.

He tilts his head in the direction of the trees. "My power is almost depleted. When it goes, the fire will die. Our only option is to run. Brad will rally the closest troops, but I don't know when they'll get here. We need to buy him some time."

With a firm nod, I tighten the straps of the go pack on my back and look around for my other bag. At the same time, a loud crack pierces the night air and Lionel's body drops. One minute he's standing in front of me, and the next, he's on his knees, staring at his chest.

Kneeling down, I follow his gaze and see red blooming across his shirt. "No, no, no." I press my hands to the wound while I help him lie down. Blood seeps from the wound without stopping.

"Don't you dare die on me. Do you hear me, Lionel? Just hold on. Let me find something to stop the bleeding, then we'll get out of here."

He grabs my hand. "Stop. I'm not going anywhere, Willa. They must have hit my spine. I can't feel my legs." Pain tightens his face for a second, and his breathing becomes ragged. "But I can hold the fire while you escape."

Sobbing, I shake my head, refusing to leave him. "I won't leave you. I love you. You're my dad, too." I swipe at the tears on my face and cough as the smoke clogs my throat. "Please don't make me."

"Do it for me. For your parents. Live to fight another day. They'll be coming for you. Find Phoenix," he grits out, holding out his hand to fan the flames higher. "I can't hold it for much longer. This is your only chance. Don't make me watch them take you." He holds my gaze until I reluctantly nod. "I love you, Willa. Smart, beautiful, a heart of gold. I couldn't have asked for a better daughter. Make me and your dad proud."

Another shot rings out, hitting the side window of the car and shattering the glass. I duck, throwing my arms around my head, while I try to shield Lionel as best as I can. He swears fiercely, and I watch his hand shake uncontrollably. I know it's taking everything in him to maintain the fire, and the longer I wait, the harder it is for him. Tears streaming down my face, I realize I have to leave him here, alone on the ground, holding the barrier up between us and the bad guys.

Aware of the flames creeping closer, I bend down and brush his thick head of grey hair away from his face, then force myself to swallow the huge lump in my throat so I can tell him how much he means to me.

"I love you, Lionel. When I lost my parents, it felt like my world ended and I would be sad forever. But you... came along and helped me find joy again. You've been my best friend and a great dad." I kiss his cheek. "Thank you for everything."

Heat blasts me in the face, and with a sob, I stand, grab my other backpack, and start running. I see Lionel's gun and scoop it up. At the edge of the forest, I pause to take one last look at him, but he's covered in flames and a sob bursts out of my raw throat. How do I leave him like this?

Guns fire over and over, and I instinctively duck, but nothing comes close. That's when I see a guy running full speed in my direction. It's the one they left in the car. Tall and lean, he's shouting at me and pointing to the trees, but I don't know whether I can trust him. Scared, I raise the gun and pull the trigger. Nothing happens. Dumbfounded, I look down at it.

Without stopping, the guy reaches me and grabs my other hand, then jerks me into the cover of the forest.

"We're going to have to run," he shouts, trying to be heard above the shots still ringing out behind us. "They'll move fast. And once the teleporter tracks us, it's all over. We need to put several miles between us and them. Hurry!"

Trees and plants magically move to the side, creating a clear path for us. It's almost spooky the way they move, as if they were humans parting in a crowd. The second we pass, they close tightly, leaving no trace of us.

"It was you! With the vine," I say, unsure of whether to trust him. I decide not to tell him the guy with the gun is dead. "Thank you!"

He keeps running, his strong hand gripping mine, but manages to answer my unspoken question.

"They found me yesterday," he replies with a grim smile as he holds up his other wrist, which has a handcuff dangling from it. "Let's just say I wasn't happy about going with them."

I open my mouth to ask him a question, but there's a loud boom behind us and the night sky lights up like a fireball. Jerking to a stop, I stare at it, and suck in a harsh breath. Lionel. Would the explosion kill him? Or would it give him a chance to escape? Oh god, I shouldn't have left him.

"We can't go back," he tells me when he sees me turn in that direction. "You don't have to give up on him. You never know... he might make it... we're a pretty resilient bunch, but I'm sure the last thing he'd want is for you to return."

It takes everything in me not to go back, but I know he's right. I flash him a small grateful smile. "What's your name?"

The slight quirk of his lips tells me he's pleased I asked. "River. You?"

I stare into his unnaturally bright green eyes and wonder if that is their true color. "Greer. My name is Greer. Thank you for saving me back there." And for the second time tonight, I lose a piece of myself as I leave Willa behind, too.

River cocks his head and abruptly changes direction. He continues to firmly hold my hand, and I continue to follow him. For now. I don't know whether I can trust him, but I know I need his help. My ear is still ringing from that shot. I don't know how to operate the gun in my hand or the first thing about hiding from these people.

Plus, the longer we walk, the more erratic the path gets. Thankfully, brief glimpses of the interstate tells me we're sticking relatively close to it. Worst-case scenario, I could leave him and try to hitchhike, but it scares me to even think about it, which makes me snort. I'm practically useless. How do I even begin to navigate this new reality of mine?

River suddenly presses me up against the tree with a finger held to his lips. Tensing, I wait, wondering what he hears, but seconds later I hear it, too. A distinctive swooshing sound coming from above, blades cutting through the still night air to hold the metal bird in the sky. Helicopter. A beam of light hits the ground in front of us, and I shrink against the tree. It sweeps from one side to the other, coming closer and closer. I bite my lip, knowing it's going to reach us any second now. Barely breathing, heart pounding, I stand perfectly still, praying I'm wrong.

River's body is taut against mine as his eyes sweep the forest around us. Suddenly, he crouches down near the base of the tree and tugs on my hand. Unsure, but willing to do whatever he thinks, I squat next to him. He moves in closer, pressing me into the trunk, his body hovering over mine, until we're as small as possible. Once we're in position, hundreds of crisp fall leaves magically begin to cover us, forming a dome of protection.

For the second time in a few days, I'm in a forest, fearing for my life, but this time, I'm not alone. Even if I didn't feel him plastered against me, his spring-like scent fills the air around us, lightening my dark thoughts until I feel a sliver of hope. River's heated breath brushes across my neck, and I suck in a sharp breath at the sensation but remain still.

It's a good thing, too. The bright spotlight sweeps over the leaves, illuminating them for a brief second, then slides away.

Relieved, I start to stand, but River grabs my hand and gives it a squeeze, so I ease back down. Listening intently, I realize the helicopter hasn't left.

For what seems like an eternity, we listen to it lazily sweeping across the sky. Sometimes the light swings across us, but most of the time, the metal bird hovers above as if it's waiting for its prey to run.

A drop splashes on my hand, and I jump. Instead of brushing away the sweat, River dips his chin and rubs it on his shoulder. Confused, I look at his hands and realize they're still outstretched at his side, holding up the leaves. Yanking my sleeve over my hand, I carefully wipe the sweat from his face, especially his eyes. When I'm done, he briefly lays his forehead against mine as if to say thanks.

The night air is cold but in our little enclosed haven, we're generating enough warmth for the two of us to be comfortable. I lean back against the tree and wait for River to let me know when it's safe for us to leave. After a while, he eases down to his knees to wait them out.

Finally, the helicopter moves on, and with a muffled curse, River drops his hands, and the leaves cascade over us. Blinded by the crunchy leaves, I quickly shove them out of my face, then brush them away from my shirt. River hasn't moved. He's still hunched over in front of me with his fists planted on the ground.

Touching his shoulder, I softly ask, "Are you okay?"

He nods his head and tries to stand but immediately falls back to the ground. With a harsh laugh, he raises a finger. "I'm going to need a second."

I clear the leaves from my body and start on his. Plucking a few out of his hair, I silently give him time to recover while I get rid of the musty-smelling leaves. Once his hair and shoulders are free of debris, I sit and wait. The chilly night air sweeps across my skin, leaving goosebumps in its wake, but I ignore it.

With one hand on the tree for support, he finally stands. "Sorry. With all the power I've expelled tonight, it's taken a little bit out of me." He shares a look with me as if I should know what he means, so I nod and don't tell him I've barely even used my power. "We need to get moving before the guys on the ground catch up with us."

I frown. "You think they're still following?"

He lifts a shoulder. "If not the original crew, then another. They have a limitless supply of soldiers at their disposal." Taking my hand in his, he takes the lead. Although this time, our path isn't quite as clear as if he doesn't have enough to power to make the plants do his bidding.

A couple of hours later, the sun rises, and he tenses. "We need to figure out our location and determine the best place to lie low. They'll be able to track us better in daylight. Are you sure you need to go to Atlanta? It's too easy for them to find someone in the city. Too many damn cameras."

I haven't told him about the go bag on my back or the plan to find Phoenix, only the need to get to Atlanta. All he sees is the backpack full of clothes I'm carrying in my hands, although I'm sure he's noticed there's something under my jacket.

"I'm positive. Lionel thought it was the best place for me." I don't elaborate, but surprisingly, River simply shrugs his acceptance.

We decide to follow the interstate south and, thankfully, find a truck stop at the next exit. Semis fill the busy parking lot. But it's the smell of greasy diner food that makes me whimper while my stomach growls. It must be time for breakfast.

"I'm starving. How about you?"

"With the amount of power I've used tonight? I could eat a mountain of food," he says with a chuckle. "Tell me you have some money in that backpack of yours." His flashes pleading green eyes in my direction.

I laugh, but it echoes in the morning air, and a sob escapes. Surprised, I clamp a hand over my mouth, but I'm unable to stop the tears. Lionel's gone, and I'm standing in a parking lot talking about food and laughing with a guy I don't even know and probably shouldn't trust. Granted, River saved my life, but he's a complete stranger, nonetheless. For several minutes, hysteria causes me to swing between laughter and crying, until River sweeps me into his strong arms and presses my face against his hard chest.

"It's okay. Everything is all right. We're going to find a way to get you to safety. I promise," he assures me, his voice gruff with emotion. "Laugh. Cry. Just don't scream. A big burly guy is staring at me across the parking lot. I don't want him to think

I'm hurting you. And I sure as hell don't want to get into a fight with him. Dude is BIG."

With a sniff, I stop crying and swivel around to look. Sure enough, a large beefy guy with ginormous biceps is staring at us. I laugh. Not in a hysterical way either. Thankfully.

I stretch up and whisper in his ear, "Can't you use your superpowers?"

River glances around in an exaggerated way. "Shhh. We're not supposed to let humans know about us. Cardinal rule. So, no, smarty pants, I'd have to fight him the old-fashioned way. Fist to fist, and since his fist is the size of my face, I'd like to avoid that scenario. After all, I like my pretty face."

Tilting my head back, I stare up at him. It's the first time I've stopped and really looked at him. A few inches taller than my 5'10", he appears to be around my age, 23 or 24 years old, or maybe a year or two older. A strong jaw and high cheekbones have given his face strong defined features, but his bright green eyes and mischievous smile make him truly striking. Definitely hot, not pretty, and I'm pretty sure he's used his face many times to get his way.

Instead of a smile, I roll my eyes. "Let's go eat before your ego ruins my appetite." I tap the smudge of dirt at the end of his nose. "You should probably wash up, too."

This time, he laughs and slings an arm around me. "Wherever you go, I shall follow. Lead on, my lady who has the money."

He swings open the door to the diner and a blast of warm air rushes out to greet us, which I embrace wholeheartedly after walking for so long in the chilly air. The serviceable diner is packed with people eating breakfast, and the familiar sound of chatter, laughter, and utensils scraping plates eases the tension around my shoulders. My stomach growls. Mmm, everything smells more delicious and buttery than I expected.

Several individuals stop eating to stare at the two of us, but one glare from River turns their gazes away. I look from them to him, trying to see what they find so scary, but all I see is a charming smile and handsome face.

A wooden sign points right. Restrooms. I pivot toward them, but River grabs my elbow.

"We need to get in and out. They'll be looking for us," he tells me, bursting the little bubble of safety I'd found in the moment. He glances at the parking lot. "Don't talk to anybody. Five minutes. I'll meet you right here." His eyes are intense as he relays the message.

"Be quick. Got it," I tell him with a reassuring nod, knowing he has more experience with our enemy than I do. "Back soon."

With those words, I enter and beeline to the nearest stall, stripping off my jacket and the hidden go pack underneath and dumping them on the floor. I've had to pee forever. Once I finish, I grab my stuff and head to the sink. When I see myself, I shake my head. River didn't tell me leaves were sticking out of my hair, my collar was torn, or there was a line of blood from my ear to my shoulder. No wonder everyone was staring at us. I look rough. Chuckling, I reach up and pull out a couple more leaves and get hit with the strangest sense of déjà vu. The last time I stood in front of a mirror disheveled, picking dirt and leaves out of my hair, was the day I collided with Trent in front of the library.

I stare at my tear-stained face, trying to internally compare the two moments, and even though I try hard to point out the differences, they feel exactly the same. Last time, the harmless collision led to Trent trying to kill me. What if I'm making the same mistake all over again? Will I stand in front of another mirror in the future and regret meeting River? I sigh, completely unsure of what I should do.

Quickly cleaning my face and hands, I make myself more presentable, then I pull out a few bills from the go pack and place them in the front pocket of my dirty jeans. Putting on the go bag and my jacket, I then grab the larger backpack by the handle and carry it out. I'm sure River's realized I'm carrying something on my back, but I refuse to let him think it's more than a large purse.

When I open the door, he's leaning against the wall, waiting for me. His hair is wet and roughly combed back from his face, and the dirt is gone. He immediately steps forward and takes my hand in his.

"Someone cleans up nice. I wish we had time to sit and eat. Talk. Get to know each other. Unfortunately, we have to keep moving."

As I was also thinking about his good looks, I can't help the blush that spreads across my face. "I know, but I need food. We'll get something to go."

The thought of running without him is still lingering in the back of my mind. I hesitate for a second and stare up at him, knowing I should drop his hand and hitch a ride out of here. I open my mouth to let him know, but not a single word leaves my lips. I can't find the will to let go of my only security. Even if it turns out badly later, I'm willing to take the chance. Mind made up; I follow him to the counter.

We grab a couple of stools to wait for our food. His bare wrist makes me pause. "You got rid of your jewelry."

"Didn't want anyone to think I was the bad guy," he murmurs in response. His eyes find mine and he winks.

Several truckers sit down at the counter next to us to eat their breakfast while they swap the latest route and road updates. I lean over and quietly ask them where they're headed. Most are going north, but one guy, an older trucker with kind brown eyes, tells me he's headed south toward Birmingham, Alabama. I glance at River, and he gives a slight shake of his head, so I say nothing. My lips turn down at the thought of walking all day and night in the chilly weather.

With a sigh, I turn toward the parking lot to watch for any sign of the black SUV.

Minutes later, the trucker gets up to leave. He stops at my stool and looks us both up and down. "If you need a ride, I'm leaving in ten minutes. Should be enough time for you to get your food and join me." He leaves, heading to the parking lot on the right.

"We need to catch a ride," I tell River. When he shakes his head, I throw up my hands. "Why not?"

"Do you want to get him killed?" he whispers in my ear. "If they find us with him, they won't hesitate. Trust me. I've seen it happen."

The thought of being responsible for that man's death is sobering, but it doesn't deter me. "No, but I also don't want to die. It's only a matter of minutes until they catch up to us. We can't outrun them." Frustrated, I flag down the server. "Excuse me. Can you tell me where we're at?"

She studies us for a second. "South of Greensboro. Why?" Her eyes dart between me and River. "Are you lost?"

"What's the next big city?" I ask her, not wanting to tell her our destination.

Her eyes narrow. "Next big city is Charlotte. Why don't you just tell me where you're going? I've got customers waiting."

I take a deep breath. "How far is Atlanta?"

She thinks about it for a second. "Roughly four and a half hours, give or take, by car. Is that all?" When I nod, she huffs and speeds off, coffee pot in hand.

River groans. "You might as well put a neon sign out front."

My cheeks flood with embarrassment, but I defiantly shrug.

"I don't care. You can stay here. Or go your own way. I need to get to Atlanta."

The server comes out of the kitchen and hands us our food. "Well, what's it going to be?"

Gut clenching in knots, but completely prepared to leave without River, I hand him his breakfast sandwich. My fingers scrunch the bag tightly, waiting for him to answer.

He stares down at me with a strange look on his face. "Fuck it. Let's catch a ride in a big rig." I laugh and he shakes his head. "Haven't you ever heard of stranger danger?"

I glance down at the glass of water on the counter and motion to the server. "Can we get these two waters to go?" I don't know how to use my powers, but it couldn't hurt to have a little water with us.

Doug's big rig is silver, and he's standing by it when we come out. After laying down a few ground rules, basically telling us that if we give him trouble, he'll drop us on the side of the road, he helps us into the cab.

Married with grown kids, Doug's been on the road, driving semi-trucks for twenty years, and he's seen a lot. He seems like a pretty decent man, but I'm thankful River came with me. I would have been nervous without him.

I'm pretty sure Doug's wondering what our story is, since it's obvious we're not kids running away from home, but he doesn't pry into our personal lives.

River asks him a question about some sports game, and his face lights up. The two of them dive into the details of the game, and I watch the miles roll by. Having had little sleep the last two days, the warmth of the heater quickly lulls me to sleep.

Laughter wakes me some time later, but cocooned in River's arms, I let myself drift in and out for a while until the truck slows. Concerned, I force my gritty eyes open to see what's happening. Orange cones and a flashing light indicate a construction zone ahead. We inch along until we can merge with the rest of the traffic into one lane, then slowly pick up speed again.

I wonder how long I've been asleep. I yawn and look around. A clock on the dash tells me it's been about two hours. We have quite a way to go. Unwilling to move, I lay my head back against River's arm, savoring the comfortable nest he's created around me. Normally, I wouldn't be so at ease with a complete stranger, but there's something about him that makes me feel safe.

He bends down and peers into my eyes. "Hello, sleepy-head. We're north of Atlanta, with roughly two and a half hours to go. Sleep some more if you want."

With a big yawn, I glance away. "Sorry, I didn't mean to fall asleep on you."

He brushes a strand of hair from my cheek. "I liked it."

His words make me turn back to him, and I instantly get lost in his eyes. "What about you? Did you get some sleep?"

"I'm good," he replies. "Better than I've been in a long time." The brightness of his green eyes is startling up close.

I stare up at him. "Glad we took the ride, aren't you?" His arms feel good, but there's been so much that's happened the last few days, I can't quite feel the same level of happiness in this moment.

His eyes dim, and I'm sad that I ruined it, but he simply teases me. "Except for your snoring. But I'm glad we're not walking in the cold."

My mouth drops open. "I don't snore."

River looks over at Doug. "Doug, you heard her, didn't you?" His tone is full of laughter, so I can't tell if he's telling the truth or not.

Doug chuckles. "I learned a long time ago to keep my nose out of other people's business." He reaches over and takes a swig of his coffee. "Is there a particular spot in Atlanta where you want me to drop you?"

I open my mouth to answer, but River beats me to it. "If you can drop us off within the I-285 perimeter, somewhere close to Sandy Springs, we'll be able to make our way to the nearest Marta station."

Doug gives a quick nod. "Can do."

"It sounds like you've been to Atlanta?" I ask River, surprised he didn't mention it.

"A few times, visiting friends," he informs me with a tight smile. "You'll like them."

Them? I want to ask, but the directness of his stare silently urges me to wait until we're alone to ask questions. I dip my chin in agreement.

The rest of the drive is light and easygoing, with Doug telling us funny stories about his kids and grandkids, and before I know it, we're saying goodbye to our friendly truck driver at a gas station in Sandy Springs. After getting directions from the store clerk, we head out in the direction of the nearest Marta stop. Ten degrees warmer here in Georgia, the walk isn't nearly as bad now.

Once we get to the station, he makes me wait out of sight for a few minutes. When he returns, he's holding two ball caps, and I realize I lost mine last night at the gas station. He hands one to me and puts the other on his head.

"I thought you didn't have any money," I murmur, placing the hat on my head and pulling the brim down low.

"I don't." His voice is low. "We're only a few stops from the university. One of my friends likes to hang out there." His arm remains around my shoulders while we walk, but I notice his attention is on the people around us. Eyes swiveling from one side of the large open room to the other, he maneuvers us through the crowd to the counter, where I pay for our tickets, then onto the correct platform.

Once we're on the train, he motions for me to sit but chooses to stand like a shield between me and the rest of the world. As people get on and off at each of the stops, I watch River shift to let them pass, with none getting even close to me... My protector. It feels good.

Giggling has me turning to the seats on the right where a couple of college-age girls are eyeing River and whispering to each other. Hearing them, he turns briefly, causing them both to flash flirtatious smiles, but he simply turns away. Pouting, they look at me, and I smile back. I don't blame them. There's something about him that draws your attention. I know I can't stop looking.

Somewhere around the fourth or fifth stop, he motions for me to stand, and with his hand at my back, we exit the train at Midtown Station, where he ushers us onto a bright yellow trolley.

Once seated, he leans over to the girl next to him. "Do you mind if I borrow your phone? I left mine at home and need to text a friend that I'll be late." A soft feminine voice agrees, and he quickly takes her phone and sends off a quick text. "Thanks."

River turns toward me. "Jordan is a friend I met last year. Great guy. Similar to us. If he's still here, I'm sure he'll let us stay with him a night or two." The grin on his face tells me he's looking forward to seeing his friend again.

I fiddle with the zipper on my jacket. "Is he going to be okay with you bringing someone else with you?" He lifts a shoulder, and I bite my lip, wondering what we'll do if he doesn't like me. "We could go to a hotel. I've got enough money for a couple of nights."

His eyebrow rises, and he shakes his head. "Don't say that

out loud and don't tell anyone, especially not Jordan. He'd steal it in a heartbeat, and I wouldn't blame him. People like us..." He pauses. "We live close to the bone with few morals. Trust is rare. The only way to survive is to be on guard all the time."

"Should I trust you?" The question slips out before I can stop it, but I lift my chin and force myself to meet his bright green eyes.

The corners of his mouth turn down, but his eyes never leave mine. "No." Confused, I drop my gaze to my hands. "Our kind will do anything to avoid capture. Nobody wants to be an experiment. Always remember that."

He seems to have plenty of experience with Hightower and his group, but does he know Phoenix is out there offering protection against them? Maybe once I'm in contact, I can convince River to join me and give him some hope in this dim world of ours.

The driver announces the next stop, and River pulls me to my feet. "Let's go. He's usually in the chemistry building."

Once we get off and start walking, he links his fingers with mine. Sidewalks full of students walking from one building to the next make me envious and homesick for my old life. Not for things, but for Lionel and my dream of getting a doctorate. Everything happening to me feels surreal and a part of me keeps hoping it's just a really bad nightmare.

"Jordan is a Cryo and utterly fascinated with all things chemical," River says with a chuckle. He darts a glance at me and suddenly stops. "Are you okay? Did you see someone?" His head turns from one end of the campus to the other.

I place my hand on his arm to stop him. "Sorry. No. I'm being silly."

He tilts his head and studies me. "What is it?"

"It's stupid. Really. I miss my life, including school." When I hear the words out loud, I'm even more embarrassed by them.

After all, I'm alive. That should be enough. "Let's go." I tug on his hand to get him moving, but he doesn't budge.

"That's not stupid. In fact, I'm jealous," he admits in a low voice. "I had to leave and go on the run my freshmen year of high school. That's when my powers showed up. I was taking biology, and we were conducting an experiment with plants. Mine sort of took off like Jack's beanstalk. My mom has powers, so I instantly knew what it meant. I ran home, and we left that night." There's a slight tinge of red to his cheeks. "My mom home schooled me after that incident, but I always wanted to go to college."

I throw my arms around him, hugging him tightly. "I'm so sorry. For both of us and our lost dreams. Do you think anything will feel normal again?" I look up at him, hoping he has the answers, but he shakes his head.

"No," he replies with a twist of his mouth. "It sucks, but only because we can't enjoy our powers out in the open. We're special, but we can't let anybody know, so we run and hide and try to pretend we're just like everyone else when we're not, and we never will be again. It's not fair."

I ease back and study the bitter expression on his face. "I'm sorry." For a second, I hesitate but realize he should probably know in case they find us. "I've only used my power once." I bite my lip as I continue to tell him how clueless I am. "I don't even know what the official term is for my powers."

His whistle pierces the air. "Once?" He sees my slow nod and sighs. "What is your power?"

"Water," I reply hesitantly. "It responds to me, although I'm not exactly sure how yet."

"You have the power of hydrokinesis. We use the nickname hydro." He begins walking again, tugging me along with him. "It takes time. When I first came into my powers, they were sporadic and unpredictable. Unfortunately, we don't have time for you to gradually learn how to control yours. Maybe Jordan will have an idea on how we can fast track them."

Warmth travels from my hand to my chest. I've never wanted to hold someone's hand, but I like the fact that he's always reaching for mine. "What's a cryo?"

He leans in and murmurs, "A cryo controls cold and ice."

I blink. That's unnerving. "What are you called?"

His lips curve in a big smile and he taps his temple. "A phyto. Phytokinesis is the ability to manipulate plants with your mind, although my power extends to all of nature."

"Impressive powers, but the nickname lacks something," I tease him, quickly dodging his tickling fingers. "Are there a lot of powers?"

"More than we know," he replies as he stops at the corner of a huge grey building. "Let's go around to the front steps." He pulls me toward the entrance. As we get closer, his face lights up. "Jordan!"

I follow his gaze to a young man around our age, standing in the shadows of the building. Stocky, with light brown hair and intense brown eyes, the guy studies me for a second, his hand tapping restlessly on his thigh.

"Tell me that's not who I think it is," he orders River, a bite in his tone. "The sites are full of chatter about a girl Raven is hunting." He backs up. "There's a description of her floating around but no name or pictures. Tall. Dishwater blond. Green eyes. Our age. Is this her? Why did you bring her here? I don't want any part of this, man."

River drops my hand and holds up both of his. "I seem to recall helping you escape Raven yourself last year. You know me." Jordan starts to walk off. "Man, I need your help." The guy stops moving. "Just hear us out. We're only here for a night or two. That's it. Look, it's lunchtime. Why don't we grab some food, and if you still want us to leave, we will."

With a surly look in my direction, the guy shuffles forward. "Fine, but you're buying, and we're staying on campus. I know this place like the back of my hand, and if I see one sign of Raven, I'm out of here and you're on your own."

River grins like the guy agreed to be his best friend. "Totally understand, man. Is the BBQ joint still open?"

Somehow, River convinced Jordan to let us stay. It was remarkable to see but left an oddly unsettled feeling in the pit of my stomach. Every word he said was the truth but living and hearing it are two different things. Or maybe it was the slant River put on it. As if I'm a newborn baby bird that needs protecting until I learn a few survival skills. I mean, I actually don't know much about this world, but the *way* he said it guilts Jordan into helping us against his better judgement.

Still, I can't say I'm unhappy as I stare at the house in front of me. Jordan's place is a two-story white house with siding that needs a fresh coat of paint, a rough, cracked asphalt driveway, and some seriously overgrown landscaping. All of which sounds terrible, but for some reason, the worn house looks cozy.

Cold winter wind pierces my jacket. Shivering, I huddle into my windbreaker, and River bends over to rub his hands down my shoulders. He looks at Jordan. "Let's get inside. The temperature is dropping."

Jordan gestures toward a set of stairs on the left side of the house that leads up to the second story. "I live upstairs."

Inside, it's not much warmer, but at least it's shielded from the wind. Size wise, the apartment is similar to the studio I had at home, with one side of the room serving as the living area and the other side as the bedroom. Shabby green carpet runs the length of the room. Along one wall is a tired-looking brown and golden yellow floral couch that looks like it came out of the seventies with a scratched up wooden lattice-laced coffee table sitting in front of it. A large, outdated TV with the letters RCA sits on a small stand on the opposite wall.

In the bedroom area, a small blow up bed takes up most of the floor, with only a stack of books topped with a coaster and small lamp that seems to be serving as a nightstand beside it.

Jordan's eyes flick to me and he sneers, "Not fancy enough for you?"

"Reminds me of home," I inform him, and surprisingly, it does, maybe a bit more sparse than my garage apartment and the furnishings a bit more worn, but it's comfortable. "Where can I put this?" I hold up the container of leftover BBQ from earlier.

He leads me around the corner to a tiny hallway. Along one side is a small hanging closet with only a few clothes in it and on the other, a kitchenette with a small college refrigerator, a sink, and a single cabinet for dishes. Jordan motions to the fridge. "In there."

As I place the Styrofoam container in the fridge, I notice it's pretty bare. A couple of waters, a pack of ham, and a bottle of mustard. I place the BBQ on the top shelf and close the door. Standing, I look at Jordan. He's watching me closely, as if he can't decide whether I'm going to steal his food or make a disparaging remark.

"Thanks," I tell him. Wringing my hands, I walk back to the living room. "What now?" I direct my question toward River, who's standing in the middle of the room.

"I need to grab us a few things," he tells me. "Burner phone, little bit of food that we can take with us when we leave, and some fresh clothes." He pulls out the cash I gave him at the BBQ place. "Do you need anything?"

Uneasy with the thought of him leaving me here with Jordan, I open my larger backpack and dig through it to give myself a moment to think. All my toiletries are in there, along with a few clothes. "No, I'm good." I really, really want to take a shower, but if River's leaving, I'll wait until later.

Jordan plops down on the couch and picks up the remote. "Can you pick me up a loaf of bread?" Not once does he look at River.

"Sure," River answers with a shrug. "I'll be back shortly."

River pulls me to the door and leans down to whisper in my ear, "If I'm not back in an hour, take your things and leave. Don't wait for me."

Unnerved at the thought, I stare at him. "Why can't I go with you? If we see them, we can run together."

He forces a smile. "Jordan told us earlier that most of the chatter is about you. The longer you stay hidden, the better. I'll be back." Leaving no room for argument, he opens the door and heads down the stairs.

With a sigh, I close it behind him and walk back over to the couch. "Mind if I join you?" Without answering, Jordan slides over, and I curl up in the other corner. I'd love to take off this windbreaker, but I don't want Jordan to see the go bag. "What's your major?"

He gives a harsh laugh. "I wish." When he sees the frown on my face, he lifts a shoulder. "Hard to register for school when you're hiding from the government."

When I smile sadly, he shrugs. "Don't feel sorry for me. Auditing the classes means I get to learn everything I want for free. A top-notch education for zero dollars. The only thing sad about it is that I won't be able to get a real job afterward." His eyes travel around the small apartment. "And make enough money to afford something better."

"I miss school," I admit to him, feeling like we have some common ground. "I was only a semester away from earning my Doctorate in Physical Therapy. Maybe I'll be able to go back someday."

He snorts. "I doubt it, but you're still in the initial stages. Every day you'll wake up full of hope, and every night you'll go to sleep with less. Until one day, it's gone." He flashes a knowing smile when he sees my chin lift, but he changes the subject. "So, Greer, what's your power?"

River formally introduced us at lunch, but it's still startling to hear someone call me by my new name. I stare at him, unsure of whether I should tell him the truth. I guess he reads me well because he simply turns his attention back to the TV while he waits.

"Water," I admit to him. "Just water."

Both eyebrows shoot up as he stares at me in disbelief. "That's it? I don't get it. Water is an extremely basic power." His eyes narrow. "What's the real reason Raven is after you?"

If I told him I killed Senator Hightower's son, he'd immediately kick me out. "I don't know. One minute, I was a student, attending school and tutoring for money, and the next, I was being stalked. My guardian knew about... all this. We went on the run."

His face is blank. "Where's your guardian?"

I tell him what happened at the gas station, and he stiffens beside me. "That's where you met River? You didn't know him until a couple of nights ago?"

It sounds bad when he says it like that, but I didn't really have a choice. Or maybe I'm afraid to do this alone. I've come to realize how sheltered I was from the world.

"Nope. I left Lionel on the ground, fire raging around him, and between one second and the next, River was dragging me into the forest to hide." Guilt laces every word, but I can't help it. Logically, I know Lionel couldn't walk, but my heart still believes we could have found a way to escape together.

A line appears in the center of Jordan's forehead. "I see. River to the rescue. He does that, you know. Last year, I was running with a group. All of us had powers. One of the guys, Lance, had the ability to bilocate, and he was kind of the designated leader of our group. Great guy. Amazing power. He met River on the streets and slowly brought him into our pack."

He takes a long swig of his water. "For months, we all lived together in a large, abandoned warehouse. Protected each other. Pooled our resources. We were family. Until one day, it ended. Raven found us. I was headed back when River yanked me into a nearby alley. We watched them swarm the building and take everyone into custody. We stayed together for a couple of days, but I didn't feel safe anymore, so I left."

Leaning forward, he places his elbows on his knees and stares at the floor, his face twisted with memories. "River saved me, but sometimes, I feel so damn guilty about it that it pisses me off. Lance did so much for all of us, and I didn't even try to save him." He turns his brown eyes toward me. "That's why you can't stay more than a couple of nights. I refuse to go through that again."

Understanding dawns. He's grieving, too. "Don't worry, we'll be gone after we get some rest." When his shoulders relax, I decide to change the subject. "What's bilocate?"

His voice is full of awe as he answers. "Lance literally had the ability to be in two places at the same time. Both looked real. You couldn't tell which one was the original. An extremely rare psi. He's the only one I or anyone else has even heard of with that power. I confirmed on the boards."

"What boards?" I ask, confused by his answer.

"There are websites out there for people like us. On the dark web. Hidden from the rest of the world," he answers in a gruff tone. "It's how we stay up-to-date and share information, like Raven's location, so we can give each other a heads up."

"Would you share them with me? I think I'm going to need all the help I can get," I ask him, biting my lip. River was right. *I'm a baby bird with zero knowledge and no survival skills.* Worse, I don't even know how to use my powers to defend myself.

Jordan studies me for a second, but my worry must be showing on my face because he capitulates. "I can get you access, but don't be surprised if they don't speak to you. It takes them a long time to trust anyone new." He grabs his laptop and sets it on the coffee table in front of us.

River returns while Jordan is showing me the various boards and online forums. There's even a subreddit cleverly hidden in plain sight where they can ask each other basic questions like how to find a place to live without showing an income. The members use code words to convey information to each other and help each other out.

Overwhelmed, I know it's going to take me a while to catch on to everything, but it's reassuring to know others are out there. Hiding. Surviving.

River pulls out the loaf of bread along with a few other groceries. Jordan hops up to show him where to put them.

Taking advantage of River's return, I grab my backpack and head toward the bathroom. "Would you mind if I took a shower?"

Jordan waves his hand, his attention on the food River bought.

River's bright green eyes linger on me for a second, then he pulls out a box of dark brown hair color. "I got you this. You don't have to use it, but it might help."

I take it from him and stare down at it. "Thanks." Change my hair? I bite my lip. I should. It would help, but ever since Trent and his buddies kidnapped me, I've felt pieces of me being chipped away. I don't know if I can lose another right now.

Uneasy with the situation, and unsure about the amount of hot water in this small apartment, I strip down and take a quick shower. Dirt runs down the drain, mostly from my hair, but soon it's clean again. The whole time I'm in there, I mull over all the information I've picked up in the last few days and I... hate it. I don't want to know any of it, much less use it, but I might have to if Phoenix doesn't find me.

Tears slip down my cheeks and fall to the small pool below. I wish Lionel were here. He always had the best advice. The kind that always made me feel better. Safe. Loved. I tip my face to the water and wash away the sorrow. Later, I promise myself. When I'm safe.

After my shower, I pull on a fresh pair of jeans and layer on a clean tank and sweatshirt. I look around, but don't see a hair dryer, so I towel dry my hair the best I can until it's damp, then pick up the box of hair dye. Best on clean, dry hair. Relieved I don't have to change my appearance right now, I set it on the sink. Maybe later.

The small black backpack Brad called a go pack sits on the floor next to my larger one. I open it and stare at the burner phones, wishing I could remember the number Lionel made me call, but it's useless. Taking a chance, I grab one and hit send, but nothing happens. With a sigh, I return the phone and zip it closed.

I can't keep wearing my windbreaker in the apartment, but

I also don't want to let the bag out of my sight. Maybe I can stuff it in the larger bag for now. When we leave, I'll make sure to put it back on. Squatting down, I rearrange my clothes, putting the gun on the bottom, and placing the small go pack near the top with my purse. I want to be able to grab both quickly.

Jordan leaves early the next morning to get to a class he's auditing, but we stay behind to relax for a while. River wants to know what our next step is, but since I don't know what to say, I classically avoid the subject with the excuse that I need to dye my hair if we're leaving tomorrow like we promised Jordan.

Most of the girls in college dyed their hair, but I never did. I'm not sure if it's because I was clinging to the past and the girl I used to be, or if I really cared about such mundane things.

Before the accident, I was a bubbly sixteen-year-old with a bevy of friends I'd known since kindergarten. After the accident, I didn't know how to return to being that girl. My grief created a wall between myself and everyone else. I didn't blame my friends. None of them had gone through something devastating. They didn't know what to do or say, and eventually they stopped coming around.

Existing not living became my motto. Getting through school quickly so I could leave and do what I had determined was my purpose in life. Looking back, I wonder if I was in such a hurry to grow up just so I could have more control over my life. Boy, did that turn out well. Here I am, with no family, relying on strangers for food and shelter. Adrift again.

With a sigh, I follow the instructions on the box, and an hour later, I step out of the bathroom with a small smile on my face. I love it. My original blondish-brown color washed me out, but the dark brown makes my green eyes spark with life and my fair skin glow.

Clearing my throat, I stand in front of River and nervously wait for him to comment. "It's still wet, but I think it looks good."

He doesn't answer, only stares at me for a solid minute, and my toes scrunch together in my socks.

"Beautiful," he finally rasps, putting me out of my misery. "The brown makes your eyes stand out. Have you never tried this color?" He moves closer to me. Lifting his hand, he captures a wet strand and rubs it between his finger and thumb.

"I've never dyed my hair," I admit with a casual shrug. "I was too busy studying to worry about my appearance." That sounds a lot better than telling him about my parents and the accident and the permanent numbness that encompassed me for a long time.

He sweeps a hand toward the coffee table. "I made us a quick lunch. Once we eat, we can walk around the university and stretch our legs. Maybe we can also figure out where we're going next." His eyes dart to me as if to gauge my response.

Sitting on the sofa, I pick up a chip and eat it, trying to figure out how to tell him about Lionel's plans. "Lionel was in the Army, and because he had powers, he knew about the two organizations the government set up." I stop and try to explain how this whole thing started. "Up until a few days ago, I was at university, getting my degree. Someone—or maybe a couple of people, I'm not sure—started stalking me. Taking pictures and putting them in my car. Lionel was investigating to find out who did it. I was kidnapped and used my powers to... escape. When I came home and told him what happened, he instantly jumped into action, and we went on the run."

Trusting River to help me get to Phoenix and trusting him with the whole story are two entirely separate things. Right now, I don't know what Senator Hightower, or his organization, knows about my role in his son's death, but if I tell River, he might decide the risk is too great and leave.

"He was in the Army with Jack Harrison. Do you know him?" I say after taking a bite, which I'm barely able to swallow.

River's mouth compresses. "He's the Senator supposedly trying to get us some civil rights, but nobody has seen any progress. Why?"

Ouch. "Apparently, he runs a group called Phoenix that helps people like us. They provide safety and a new identity." My voice trails off because that's all I really know about the group. "That's why Lionel and I were headed to Atlanta."

River tenses. "How do you contact them?"

I take a deep breath and look into River's green eyes so I can see his reaction. "My bag has a tracker."

A shutter comes down over his expression, giving me no clue as to his thoughts. "I see. So, we're waiting for them to find us?" He casually picks up his sandwich and takes a bite, but his eyes never leave mine.

I bite the inside of my cheek. He told me not to trust him or anyone, but I sort of expected more of a reaction from him. "I guess. I'm not really sure. We were able to call for help at the gas station, but since then, I haven't seen anyone. I don't know what happened, and unfortunately, I can't remember the number."

"I see," he replies in a calm voice. "Eat your sandwich and

stop worrying. I'm not mad or upset. I told you not to trust anyone, including me, and I meant it." He looks down for a second. "I'm just not sure you've put your trust in the right people. I'm not the only one who feels that way either. You can ask Jordan about them, too. If Phoenix is actively helping those like us, I've never heard anyone talk about it."

A little hope crumples inside me, but I remind myself that Lionel was confident about his plan, and I completely trust... trusted... him. Pain rushes through me at having to use the past tense. It's like my parents' death all over again. Learning to use all the past tense ways to say they weren't alive.

It takes a lot of effort, but I force myself to finish the sand-wich. Being on the run, there's little certainty in the next meal, and after seeing the bare shelves in Jordan's small fridge, I refuse to waste a single bite.

I lift a hand and run it down my hair. Frizzy, but dry. I grab my large backpack and head into the bathroom to get ready. Thankfully, I packed a flat iron, so I smooth it out and pop in a couple of curls around my face, then brush my teeth and add a little make-up. When I finish, I stare at my reflection, partially wondering who the person in the mirror is because she doesn't look like the Willa I know. Maybe she's Greer?

Lionel's son, Greer, had dark brown hair similar to my current color, but even at a young age, he had a strong person-ality and a sense of fearlessness about him. Maybe using his name will give me some of those same traits. I hope so.

Conscious of the time, I grab the smaller backpack and slip it on, then with a wry smile, add the windbreaker. Feeling like a hunchback, I turn from side-to-side in the mirror. To my relief, Lionel's voluminous jacket hides the slight bump. A knock on the door makes me jump, and I open it to find River on the other side.

He scans me from head to toe with an appreciative glint in

his eye that makes me blush. "Great, you're ready. Let me brush my teeth, then we can go."

I slip my purse over my body and place the larger backpack on the floor by the couch. My fingers twitch slightly at the thought of leaving anything behind, but I force my hand away from the bag.

River returns and holds out his hand. "Grab your hat and let's go."

My nose scrunches up at the thought of wearing the baseball cap again, but it shields my face from the cameras, so I put it on. When I look up at River, he's smoothing down the back of his hat.

Without thinking, I reach up and finger a lock of his light brown hair. "Maybe you should go blond." I smirk, but with his bright green eyes, it's not a bad idea.

He leans down and whispers in my ear, "You've discovered my secret. I'm really a blond. Unfortunately, it's too noticeable."

His breath sends a shiver down my spine, and I nervously giggle. He's already too attractive. As a blond, girls would get whiplash turning their head to look at him. Snickering at the thought, I pivot and head out the door.

Jordan's apartment is only a couple of blocks from the university.

"Are you sure it will be safe?" I ask, stepping over the cracks in the sidewalk.

His hand brushes mine and immediately latches onto it. "At our age, universities are a great place to hide. We can easily pass for students. Wearing a hat or a hoodie is the norm. Everyone walks around with their head down, looking at their phone, so anybody watching through the cameras won't think it's unusual."

"How many years have you been on the run?" I ask; his

matter-of-fact tone makes me wonder. He said freshmen year, but I don't know how long it's been.

He glances down at me with the saddest look in his eyes. "Forever."

When I open my mouth to say how sorry I am, he suddenly points to the domed building up ahead. "That's the observatory. Want to see?"

Avoidance is something I completely understand. "Definitely."

He pulls me into the building. After passing through a small lobby, we enter a large open area with bookshelves full of books, tables and chairs scattered throughout, and a display case full of items. But the best part is the star carpet. Bemused, I can't help but stare down at the gold and silver star pattern.

We walk around the room, skimming the books, until we reach the display case. Inside are several instruments I assume have to do with astronomy, but the only ones I recognize are the compass, sextant, and telescope.

River spots a sign that says "Observatory" with an arrow. "Come on." He flashes a broad grin and tugs me down the hall. When we get to the large doors at the end, he quietly opens it but shuts it quickly when he hears someone lecturing. "Damn."

"Maybe next time," I say, but when River's smile dims, I realize there probably won't be a next time. "Let's get out of here." This time, it's me in the lead.

When we get outside, I squeeze his hand. "Thank you for taking me in there. I loved the stars on the carpet and the cool stuff in the case."

He says nothing for a minute, but then his back pocket buzzes. He pulls out a small black phone and looks at the screen. When he sees my raised eyebrow, he shrugs. "Picked up a burner at the store yesterday."

His fingers dance along the keyboard as he replies. "Jordan

wants us to meet him at the Preston Center." He looks around and then types a couple more sentences before taking off, me in tow.

"What's the Preston Center?" I ask him as we stride along.

"It's basically an activity center. There's bowling, ping-pong, an indoor track, a gym, and several other things that students can do," he explains with a grin. "Sorry about earlier. It kind of hit me that I might have to say goodbye to you soon."

I tug my hand from his and come to a complete stop in the middle of the sidewalk. "What are you saying? If I go with Phoenix, I won't see you again?" My voice trembles, and I know he can hear it, but I don't care. The thought of him not being there didn't even occur to me.

He draws in a deep breath and turns to face me. "I don't know anything about them, and quite honestly, I'm not keen to place my trust in another organization. Even if they say they're the good guys. Why do you need to go with them?"

"I know you don't trust anybody, but I trust Lionel's plan. He would never put me in harm's way. Not only did he know Jack, but he also ran missions with his son. Both of them are part of Phoenix. He trusted them, which means I do too," I state quietly but firmly.

He rubs a hand down his face. "What if they only want you?"

I hear the worry in his voice and fake a confident shrug. "I won't go without you." What if they said no? Would I really not go without River? No, I wouldn't, but it would be tough to turn down a safe place.

"I'm afraid that the longer I'm out here, the more likely Raven will catch me," I admit, biting my lip at the thought. I think about his earlier answer. "I don't want to run forever." His eyes fill with some unknown emotion as he stares down at me, listening intently. "Maybe you could stop running for a while and try it out?"

He pulls down the brim of my hat and taps the end. "I don't know. The thought of letting someone else worry about things for a while is tempting but also terrifying. Let me think about it."

"There's a lot of chatter today," Jordan says, scarfing down the burger we bought him. "I don't like it. I'm going to go home, grab some stuff, and disappear for a few days. Break up the routine."

River exhales a long breath. "I hear you. Do you mind if we stay at your place for a couple more days? We're waiting for Phoenix to contact us."

Startled to hear him casually mention it, my breath catches. I nervously turn toward Jordan to see his reaction.

He slowly sets the burger down. "Phoenix? You know Lance tried to find them but never had any luck. They're a myth, man." His eyes dart to me. "Did you put him up to this?"

I blow out the breath I've been holding. "They're not a myth. Lionel was in the Army with two of their leaders. That's who we were going to meet when Raven ambushed us at the gas station."

His expression hardens. "Well, where the hell have they been hiding? Every day, Raven hunts us down and nobody comes to our rescue. We simply disappear as if we never existed." There is a slight hoarseness to his reply that tells me how much this bothers him.

My lips curve down. "I don't have all the answers, but when I find out, I'm going to post them to the board. Maybe it's time more of us helped each other."

His derisive snort is not the least bit reassuring, but I don't care. If I hadn't had Lionel and River, I'm not sure I'd be sitting here eating a hamburger right now.

River leans across the table. "Thanks for helping us. I won't forget it. You have my number for the next couple of days. Once it stops working, you'll know we've left. Watch your back."

Jordan dips his chin and inhales the rest of his food, then stands. "Thanks for lunch." He clasps River's hand with his and gives him a slap on the back and a hug. "Put the key under the mat when you leave."

River watches him leave. "Told you. Phoenix isn't the hero." He points to the back. "I'm going to the restroom, then we can leave." He takes our tray of trash with him to dump on the way.

Good thing I finished my burger, or I'd find it hard to eat. Biting the inside of my cheek, I can't help but wonder if I'm making a huge mistake, but what else can I do? Go on the run with River? It's an option, but eventually, the money will run out. Then what?

River sits down beside me. "I'm sorry. Hope is a scarce commodity, and I don't want to destroy yours." He stares down at me with those bright green eyes of his, reminding me of his unnatural ability to command plants. "Let's go see a movie."

The words are so unexpected I don't reply at first.

"I mean it," he insists with a laugh. "The small theater on campus gives a discount for students, and you don't even have to show an ID. We'll grab a big bucket of popcorn and escape the real world for a couple of hours. What do you say?"

I'm tempted. The thought of returning to Jordan's small apartment and sitting there is not appealing at all. "Extra butter on the popcorn?"

"In the middle and on top," he confirms with a chuckle. "Let's go."

I slide out of the booth and follow him, relieved to have something normal to do for a while instead of worrying. It's not as if the world is going to fall apart in the next couple of hours.

When we get to the theater, there's only one movie scheduled in the next twenty minutes—an action-packed Jason Statham thriller—so we grab tickets and popcorn, then sit in the darkened room, snacking and swapping favorite movies until it starts. It almost feels like a real date... something I haven't done in forever.

The minute the lights go down, River laces his fingers through mine and leans in close. I turn my head to find him watching the screen, but when I continue to stare at him, he turns his head toward me. His eyes roam my face, lingering for a second on my lips before raising to meet my stare. Whatever he sees makes his green eyes darken with intent.

Butterflies dance in my stomach at the thought of kissing him, and I inch closer.

"I've wanted to kiss you since the first moment I saw you," he murmurs in a wistful tone. His lips hover above mine. "But I don't want you to think I'm trying to influence you."

"No," I tell him in complete agreement.

River gives a wry smile and starts to pull away.

Realizing how that sounded, I slide my hand around to the back of his neck to stop him. "I don't think you're trying to influence me." Staring into his eyes, I want him to see the desire swirling in me. "And I'm not kissing you because you saved me." It's important he knows that, too.

His chest rises as he takes a deep breath. "Is that a yes?"

"Yes," I tell him breathlessly.

His lips descend on mine, and the kiss is firm and delicious, and so freaking good, I'm astonished. The last time I kissed someone, I was an undergrad, and we were drunk at a party, so it kind of sucked. But even my best kiss couldn't compare to this one. It's the right blend of... everything. Unhurried but with depth, more than lust, less than love, the perfect blend of *I like you and you turn me on*.

His hand cups the back of my head, and he shifts until his other arm is around my back, pulling me into his body. Wanting to hold him tighter, I wrap my arms around him too.

The kiss intensifies, our hunger rising together, but a cough behind us quickly douses the flames, and we both jerk away, breathing rapidly. The heat on my cheeks tells me how flushed I am, but the darkness is a great cover.

He takes my hand in his. "That was one hell of a kiss." His voice is quiet but with a slight roughness to it that tells me he was definitely as affected by it as me.

I smile at the thought and turn my head toward the screen. "Yes, it was."

Best kiss of my life. I mean, I don't have a lot to compare to it to, but it's in a league of its own. He's been running for a long time, so I'm sure he's kissed a lot of girls. A tinge of jealousy hits me, but I shove it aside. Honestly, if that's the result, who cares?

From the moment I met him, I've felt safe and protected, but also completely comfortable with him to the point where I've constantly let him hold my hand. His charming ways make me laugh, but his depths make me want to know more. It's rare to find someone who makes me feel this way. I like him.

For the rest of the movie, we steal small glances at each other as if unsure of this attraction between us but unable to let the idea go. My mind is full of what-if scenarios that seem stupid in the light of everything, but I couldn't care less.

The movie ends, and the lights come on, but neither of us moves. Lost in our own world, we sit there, savoring this moment, actively resisting the return of reality. Unfortunately, the usher comes in and starts collecting trash, a signal for us to leave.

River tosses the empty popcorn bag into the trash. "Let's grab a pizza and take it back with us. We can always eat it later."

This time, it's me who slips my hand into his. "Sounds good, but no pineapple or other weird stuff like anchovies."

His mouth twitches. "I knew I liked you for a reason. How do you feel about a BBQ chicken pizza?"

"Love it," I tell him, letting him guide me across campus to get the pizza. Five minutes later, we're walking back to Jordan's, pizza in hand. "Did you like the movie?"

He laughs. "I couldn't tell you a single thing that happened in it. All I could think about was that kiss." His voice is full of disbelief, as if that's never happened to him.

"Best movie ever," I state with full confidence. It was too. It's my turn to laugh at the incredulous expression on his face. "The kiss too."

Satisfaction fills his face, along with an edge of heat. "I..." Two black SUVs shoot past us, and he immediately moves us into the doorway of a nearby convenience store as a third one flies by. "No, no, no."

"It's them, isn't it?" I ask, already knowing the answer. I'm not sure I'll ever look at a black SUV the same way again. "What do we do?"

He thinks about it for a second. "Let me text Jordan." He hands me the pizza and pulls out his phone. After sending it, we wait, but there isn't a response. "We can't stay on the street.

I know a back way to Jordan's that will allow us to check things out. If they're not there, we can grab our stuff and find a new place tonight."

He takes off with me following close behind. Fear chokes the breath in my lungs, making every breath a trial. River turns down a back alley and slips into a stranger's backyard. I glance at the windows to see if anybody is home, but they're dark. At the side of the house, he stops at the gate and peers through the wooden slats.

Curious, I join him and gasp. We're directly across from Jordan's apartment and the street is full of SUVs. The door to the little studio is open and men are going in and out with stuff, including the backpack filled with my clothes and toiletries. One of my shirts is hanging out, making it clear they've already gone through it.

Dismayed, I stare at it. They're taking the only stuff I own. Why do they even want it? It's obviously not full of anything dangerous. *Damn.* I take that back. Lionel's gun was in the bottom of the bag. Anger makes me grit my teeth. At least, I've got the go bag with me.

River motions for me to follow and silently leads us back to the alley. He leans down to whisper in my ear. "They'll spread out until they've canvassed this whole area. I know a place we can go tonight where they won't think to look."

Numb, I nod and let him lead me away.

For the next few blocks, he keeps a steady pace and until we get to the other side of the university, his only words directional. Finally, he stops.

"I haven't seen anyone following us, so I think we're good. Do you want anything to drink?" He motions to the convenience store on the corner. "The place we're going is pretty rough."

I nod and trudge into the store with him. The clerk behind the counter barely glances at us, which is a good sign, I guess.

"Water, please."

He grabs a couple bottles of water and a phone. "I'm going to try Jordan one more time. If he doesn't answer, I'll ditch this one." His explanation makes little sense to me, since I don't know what can or can't be traced, but I nod in agreement.

When we leave the store, River turns right and begins walking at a fast pace.

Uneasy, I look around. "Why are you hurrying? Do you see them?" I can't help the tremble in my voice.

He stops. "No, sorry. I didn't mean to scare you, but we need to hurry. It's dark, and this isn't the best part of town. Fifteen minutes, I promise." He takes off again.

True to his word, a short time later, we stop in front of an old warehouse. Built of grey cinder block, it's two stories tall and completely non-descript with its lack of signage. The white door is peeling paint and padlocked, but at this point, I don't care. I'm so exhausted, I'm ready to break into it myself.

River quickly picks the lock and opens the door. "Careful." He points to a large metal piece sticking out of a huge pile on the floor. "The warehouse is full of old car parts and some other stuff, but there's a path through the center to the offices in the back."

Light from the streetlamp outside shines into the second-story windows above us, illuminating part of the room, which is full of similar stacks of large metal parts and bins containing smaller pieces. It's not two stories, like I thought, but one story with very high ceilings.

I immediately sneeze three times. "It's also full of dust." Dust at least an inch thick covers everything in sight.

River's staring at the phone in his hand. "Damn it. He hasn't answered a single text."

With a frown, I grab River's sleeve. "Do you think Raven has Jordan?"

He lifts his head and gives me a confused look, but it's quickly replaced with a shake of his head. "I'm sure he's fine. The office used to have a couch in it. Let's see if it's still there."

The line between his eyebrows tells me something is bothering him, but I'm not sure what it is. "How did you know it was Raven?" If Phoenix was following the tracker, they might have noticed the long periods we spent at Jordan's apartment and made an educated guess we would return.

He glances at me over his shoulder. "The patch on their arm. It's their insignia."

The guys at the gas station had been in suits. Yesterday, they had been in blue uniforms, but I didn't notice an insignia or a patch. Of course, I'd been too busy staring at my bag.

When we get to the offices in the back, I'm surprised to see a spacious room. There's a pretty good-sized leather couch across from a large, grey metal desk and an old school leather office chair. Along the side wall is an ancient coffee maker and a few cabinets. River sets the pizza down on the counter under them.

He seems awfully familiar with this place, and it reminds me of something Jordan told me. "Is this where you, Jordan, Lance, and the rest of your group hid for a while?"

Surprise flashes across his face. "He told you?" When I nod, he sighs. "Yes. It gave us all a safe place to stay for a while. Better than the streets."

I frown. "But didn't Raven catch Lance and the others here? They know about this place!" Fear makes my voice rise. Why are we hiding where Raven can find us?

"It's the last place they'll look for us," he insists, taking my hand. "Look, it's only for one night. I don't know that many safe places here. We'll rest up and figure out where to go, okay?" He stares at me while he waits for an answer.

"I hope you're right," I concede with a sigh. "One night."

We have food, water, and shelter. That's infinitely better than being in handcuffs in the back of one of those SUVs, I remind myself. Wrinkling my nose, I grab a rag from a nearby table and wipe down the old leather sofa. It's going to be a long night.

Downtown Atlanta is too hot with Raven in the vicinity. River and I decide to head to the suburbs tomorrow. We found a motel or two that seems promising. River assures me they're the kind that take your money and don't ask any questions.

Tonight, we dine on cold pizza and water. What started out as a fantastically awesome day went to hell fast, but oddly enough, I'm sort of okay. Does that mean I'm getting used to this life?

I glance around the office. "How many of you lived here? And why isn't it freezing?"

"Seven of us." River leans back with a shrug. "Whoever owns the building must control the temperature remotely. The thermostat is set on sixty, and we could never find a way to change it."

"Tell me about them?"

He flexes his fingers as if he doesn't know what to do with them. "Lance was the best guy. He noticed me using my powers one day and invited me to lunch. When he found out I had no place to stay, he invited me back here." River grins at the memory.

I turn toward him, getting comfortable on the couch. "He sounds like a good guy."

"He was awesome. Always taking care of us. Finding cash jobs for the necessities. He was even working on a plan to get us an apartment," he says with a soft snort, looking around the office. "None of us really cared where we were, though. Having a semi-permanent place like this one was better than any place we'd stayed in a while. We were like family." His voice drops off, heavy with emotion.

"How did seven guys sleep in this tiny place?" I tease him, trying to help him through the guilt he must be feeling.

Jordan told me about how he and River watched them round up the rest of the guys and how guilty he still feels.

He motions to the right. "There's a bathroom and another office behind that wall, along with a back door for a quick escape, not that it did any good." This time, there's a bitterness to his tone.

I slip off my shoes and lay my head on his shoulder. "Tell me about the others."

"I can't," he murmurs, rubbing his palms on his thighs in agitation.

Underneath his usual spring scent, an underlying burnt wood smell like a bonfire fills the air, and it tells me more than his words. I get it. For a long time, I couldn't talk about my parents. When I did, it was only to Lionel... someone who knew and loved them, too.

"I understand. How about your parents? You said your mom has powers?"

He's silent for several minutes but then begins. "My dad left when we were kids. My mom is wonderful. Protected us for years. Always moving us before Raven could even get a sniff." His voice is warm and full of love. "She has telekinesis. The ability to move objects with her mind. She's not very powerful even for a first gen, but she only used it to make us laugh or swat us on the butt with a wooden spoon."

His smile fades. "Her biggest fear was that we would be born with a high level of power or a rare talent. She felt that once the government knew about everyone, it would be bad. She was right. Her generation was largely ignored. Then, our generation came along, and Raven started rounding up the most powerful of us."

The more I hear, the more scared I am of this whole thing. How do I live being scared all the time?

"We?" I ask softly.

His breath catches. "My sister and me."

"I've always wanted a sibling. What's she like? Do you ever see her or your mom?" I ask tentatively, almost afraid of his answer.

This time, his smile is brighter. "Lily is wonderful. Smart, beautiful, and at seventeen, growing up way too fast. Unfortunately, she's extremely powerful. Her talent is telekinesis but on a significantly higher level than anyone else with those powers." His mouth turns down. "If I get a chance to visit them, I take it, but it's rare."

"Does your sister look like you?" I ask, picturing a blond girl with green eyes. Scooting down into the leather couch, I tuck my cold hands into the crook of his arm and huddle closer.

"We used to look alike. Same blue eyes and blond hair," he replies with a small smile. Confused, I stare at him. "My powers grew exponentially, and when they did, my eyes turned green. It happens sometimes. Lily's are still blue. Brighter, though."

It's obvious he misses them. "I'm sorry. It sounds like you're a close-knit family." Although I try to hide the envy in my voice, I'm sure he can still hear it.

He squeezes my hand. "We are. There's nothing I wouldn't

do for them. Nothing." Laying his head on the back of the sofa, he wraps his arms around me and rubs up and down, generating some warmth. "Try to get some sleep. Tomorrow's going to be a long day."

"GREER, WAKE UP," RIVER TELLS ME, HIS VOICE URGENT. "We've got company."

I shoot up from where I'm sleeping, only to be met with River's arm across my chest and a very large gun in my face. The man in front of us is wearing dark camo fatigues. I search for an insignia, but I don't see anything on his arms. Some kind of dark knit material covers his face, leaving only his eyes and mouth visible.

"Name," the man in front of me barks, his gravelly voice sounding almost irritated.

I'm caught by his amber eyes. Ringed with burnt orange, they're so striking it takes me a minute to respond. "Greer... Vickers." It's tough to say Lionel's last name. "Who are you?" My voice is shaky, but it's hard not to be scared when a soldier is standing in front of you with a gun.

He ignores my question and looks at River. "You?"

"River Fulton," he states with a slight smirk.

He ignores River and taps the thing on his throat. "Greer confirmed." He pauses. "Affirmative. On our way out."

He eases back a step or two, but the gun never lowers. "Get up. We're leaving."

Not liking his attitude, I glare at him. "What's your name?"

He says nothing, only jerks his head toward the door.

Afraid we'd have to leave in a hurry, the only thing I took off last night were my shoes. I'm still wearing the bag and my windbreaker. Reaching down, I jam my foot into one sneaker, then the other. The minute they're on, River grabs my hand and pulls me up, leading us out of the office. GI Joe falls into step behind me.

The second we pass through the office door, more men in fatigues with their faces covered close in on us, guns aimed in our direction. Unnerved, I stumble and almost fall, but the man behind me reaches out and steadies me.

Glancing back, I reluctantly murmur my thanks, but of course, he doesn't answer. Another man falls in behind him. Swallowing hard, I grip River's hand tighter and carefully watch each step. Outside, the sun is shining, and the air is crisp. Two dark SUVs are idling in front of the door. Seconds later, we're completely surrounded by men.

The big guy behind me wraps a single arm around my body. "Now."

A tall, lean men standing beside the first SUV reaches out and touches River on the neck. "Sleep." Two men catch him as he instantly drops.

Unable to move, I open my mouth to scream, but a hand clamps across my lips. "Sleep" is the last word I hear.

SOMETHING TAPS MY FACE A COUPLE OF TIMES, AND I reach up to brush it away. An irritated sigh, followed by a gruff order to get up, wakes me immediately. I sit up with a glare and find myself in unfamiliar surroundings with a guy squatting in front of me. Correction, a man. Big, with broad shoulders and thick thighs, he squats easily as if he's used to it.

His jaw is chiseled like granite and based on the tic I see, clenched tightly in irritation. Scruff covers his strong cheekbones and slightly crooked nose. Even his dark brown hair is closely cropped and molded to his skull. Pouty lips are the only thing soft on this guy. The longer I stare at him, the more the line across his forehead deepens until he's scowling. If it wasn't for those strange amber eyes of his, I wouldn't know he was the same guy who came for us at the warehouse.

"Where am I?" I ask, flicking a glance around the grey room. There's a large window along one wall. Looks like an interrogation room. "Am I in jail?" I sit up a little straighter and realize my go bag and windbreaker are gone.

"I'll be the one asking questions," he curtly informs me. He stands and stalks over to the table in the center of the room. "Come over here and sit."

Uncertain whether I'm in jail or not, I rush over and sit down in the cold metal chair. Folding my arms, I watch him as he sits across from me.

He picks up a file and notepad. "Name?"

"Greer Vickers," I reply with a sigh.

"Address?"

A laugh escapes. "None."

His head pops up and his eyes narrow. "Previous address?"

"A friend's place," I answer quickly.

He leans forward. "What was your friend's address?"

I shrug. "I don't know." His eyes start to glow, and I realize I'm definitely not in jail. Whatever his power is, it's starting to show. I swallow hard. "I promise. I don't know his address. Can you tell me where I am?" *Can you tell me if you're Raven?* I want to scream but somehow hold back.

He ignores my question and looks back down at the file. "Parents?"

"Where's River?" I counter, lifting my chin.

"Down the hall," he replies to my surprise. "In a room

similar to this one. Answering questions." His jaw hardens further. "Parents?"

"Dead," I tell him. "All of them are dead. I'm the only one left. Happy now?" Angry tears fill my eyes, and it pisses me off. "Where am I?"

His hand rises to his ear, and he says nothing for a second. "Someone's here to see you." He stands up and opens the door.

Brad, with his shaved head and tattoos, is standing in the hallway, and I immediately burst into tears.

"Lionel's dead," I push the words out between sobs. "He decided to drive instead of taking the train. They caught up to us on the highway. We pulled into a gas station. They shot him." My words are barely coherent as I try to tell him what happened to his friend.

"Shh," Brad says, his voice gruff and thick with emotion. He awkwardly pats me on the back a few times. "Take a minute to breathe, then we'll talk. Everything's going to be okay. I promise."

He points to the metal chair on the opposite side of the table. "Slide me that chair and get her some water. This isn't a prison cell. Have some fucking compassion."

The other guy practically stomps out of the room, only to return a few minutes later with a cup of water. "Here."

I sniff. "Thank you." I take a few sips and several deep breaths. "Sorry. Seeing you reminded me of Lionel and that night. Everything hit me at once."

The corner of Brad's mouth turns down. "Lionel was one of my best friends. I didn't realize he fell at the gas station. We didn't find any bodies at the scene. Of course, there wasn't much left. The explosion took out most of it."

"That's weird. There should have been at least two bodies," I murmur. Did Raven take them? I explain everything that happened at the gas station up until I ran into the forest.

Brad leans forward and props his elbows on his knees. "The second you called and told us you were in trouble, we set out, but by the time we got to the station and searched the forest, the tracker was heading south. We didn't know if Raven had taken you or if you'd somehow escaped."

I stare down at my hands. "I didn't realize it would take you so long, and I was afraid to stay in the area." I pause and explain how River pulled me into the forest and hid us from Raven. "The next morning, we found food at a diner and a trucker willing to take us to Atlanta. Once we got here, River's friend, Jordan, let us stay with him."

Brad stroked his chin. "How did River get his collar off?"

Confused, I stare at him. Collar? Like a shirt? "I'm not sure what you're asking."

"When Raven captures one of us, they snap an electronic device around our neck," he explains with a blank expression on his face that tells me he's familiar with the devices and how they feel. "It blocks access to our powers. Was River wearing anything around his neck when you met him?"

"No, he had a handcuff on one of his wrists," I reply with a shake of my head. "When they first pulled up, he didn't move when everyone else got out. I didn't see him again until he was running toward me."

Brad exchanges a look with the big guy. "I see. We'll ask River about it." The other guy nods and leaves the room. Brad leans back in his chair. "We would have picked you up sooner, but we weren't sure who your new friends were, and we couldn't take the chance they were spies for Raven. So, we set up surveillance with the hope that we could get you alone. It wasn't until Raven found Jordan's apartment that we realized how close they were to finding you, too."

"Did you see Jordan?" I ask, biting my lip. "We saw Raven at his place, but didn't see him."

Brad's gaze is steady when he replies. "He left before Raven got there. Tell me something. Do you trust River?"

That's a relief. "I do," I answer with a wry smile. "He continuously tells me not to trust anybody, including him, but I do. I wouldn't have escaped without him, and since we've been in Atlanta, he's helped me hide from Raven."

Brad's brow furrows. "I see. What do you know about him?"

I give him the few pieces of information he's told me. "Not a lot. He's powerful, can manipulate plants, and has been on the run for a long time. He has a mom and sister, but I don't know where they're living." Brad gives me a long look. "I get it. It's not a lot of info. But I keep coming back to the fact that he didn't have to save me. He could have escaped on his own, with nobody being the wiser. Everyone at the gas station was focused on me and Lionel."

He runs a hand down his face. "Time will tell."

The other guy comes back but says nothing.

I clasp my hands tightly together. "Is this Phoenix?"

Brad nods. "This is their headquarters. There are several facilities around the country, but this is the main one." The guy behind him growls something, and Brad jerks his head toward him. "At ease, soldier. She didn't even know about this world until a week ago. Who's she going to tell?"

Wait. A week? Surely, it's been longer. I count the days in my head. Nope. "I hope the rest of it is nicer than this room." I can't help the snarky comment. Right now, I feel like I'm in jail. I don't know a lot about this world but kidnapping me leaves a sour taste in my mouth.

Brad hesitates. "It's utilitarian. The original facility was used as a top-secret government compound, and little has changed. Phoenix uses part of it as sort of a halfway house. Here you'll learn survival skills, how to harness your powers, how to tap into the Phoenix network, and other stuff to help you in the real world. Once you're ready, they send you back out with a new identity."

"So, it's temporary?" I ask with a relieved sigh.

"Affirmative," he says. "I know this is a lot. What can I do to help?"

Lost, I don't know how to answer him. "Once I see River, I'll feel a lot better. Neither him nor Jordan think Phoenix are the good guys, but because of Lionel, I'm willing to give this place a shot. I honestly don't have anything or anyone to lose. River has a mom and sister, though. I'm not sure if he'll want to stay." That thought is sobering.

"I understand," Brad says, standing up. He motions for me to stand, too. "Go with Quaid. He'll get you settled in, and if you want to talk, I'll be here for at least another day or two."

So, the big guy's name is Quaid. Kind of suits him. I give Brad a brief hug. "Thank you. If it wasn't for you and Lionel, Hightower and his men would have found me pretty quickly. I just wish Lionel had made it. I'd feel a lot more comfortable with him here." My parent's deaths left a huge hole in my heart, but Lionel's death shattered it. At least, this place will give me time to decide what to do next.

Quaid's face is one big scowl as he takes my elbow and guides me out the door. I'm tempted to jerk away, but I don't want him to label me a troublemaker. Still, it's tough. There's something about him that makes me want to smother him. Maybe it's the intense energy flowing off him, practically smacking me in the face with his testosterone.

Or maybe it's his complete disregard for someone else. I grit my teeth and hurry along. At this pace, I'm practically running.

"Can you slow down? Not all of us are the size of a mountain," I huff, trying to keep up.

He completely ignores me. Like not a word. What is it with him?

His long, muscular legs eat up the endless white hallways, one corridor after another, the monotony of them broken only by the occasional overhead fluorescent light. He finally stops at... surprise... a white door.

Sliding his badge across the mechanism, he opens it and gestures for me to enter. "This is your room. Someone will come by in a couple of hours and take you to the cafeteria for dinner." His voice is curt as he explains. "Feel free to take a shower. Fresh clothes are in the closet." His hand gestures to the two closed doors in the room. He eyes me for a minute, then abruptly turns and walks out, shutting the door behind him.

Arrgh. What is it with him? Of course, everything in here is also white. Floors, ceiling and walls, of course, but also the dresser, mattress, and the bedding folded on top. It's sterile and the polar opposite of my warm, cozy little garage apartment.

Narrowing my eyes, I walk over to the door and turn the handle. Locked. My blood boils, but there's nothing I can do about it.

Flinging open one of the other doors, I find a closet with grey sweatpants and sweatshirts hanging on the rack, and I grimace at the drab but functional garb. Guess it will do. I grab a set and throw it on the bed, then walk over to the dresser and pull out a sealed package with a basic pair of white underwear, a sports bra, and socks. Is this it?

Panic at the thought of living here with nothing to call my own has me plopping down on the new bed to breathe in and out a few times. This whole scene is wigging me out. If it wasn't for Brad, I'd be in full-on panic mode. Phoenix is nothing like I expected. I feel trapped and scared. Did I make the wrong decision? Maybe River was right, and Phoenix isn't the good guy.

But Lionel wouldn't have worked with them if they didn't have integrity. I clench my hands into fists and get a handle on my emotions. Neither my father nor Lionel raised a coward. Take a shower. Get some rest. Go to dinner.

Roughly three hours later, there's a knock on the door. Stealing myself to face Quaid's scowling countenance, I'm surprised to see a good-looking guy standing in the hall dressed similarly to me. Dark brown hair with equally dark eyes and a tanned complexion, he easily looks like he could be Trent's brother. When he flashes an eerily similar perfect white smile, I instinctively take a step back.

He holds up his hands. "It's okay. I'm Gabe, and I'm here to take you to dinner." His chuckle echoes in the empty hallway.

Uneasy, I motion for him to start walking and fall in slightly behind him. I don't want to be caught off guard.

"It takes a little while to get used to things around here, but it beats the street. There's food, a roof over your head, places to practice your power, and people just like you," he assures me. "It's safe here. And I'm sure you'll make friends in no time. Like me."

He reaches for the door and swings it open. A sea of grey sweats greets me. Creepy.

Gabe reaches out to grab my elbow, but I step away from his grasp. "I see my friend over there. Thanks for helping me find the cafeteria." I don't actually see anyone, but he reminds me too much of Trent. Not sure why. There's just something about him.

"Okay, find me when you're ready to leave, and I'll walk you back to your room," he says with a shrug and a slight frown.

Not a chance. Although, I have no idea how I'll find my

way back when everything looks the same. I'm a sight naviga-tor. Turn left by the Starbucks, and right by the McDonald's. That's how I navigate roads and life. White on white isn't helpful.

Arms circle me, and I inhale sharply, but the crisp notes of spring with an underlying scent of sweet honeysuckle ease my fear.

"River!" I turn in his arms and hug him tightly. "Are you okay? They didn't hurt you, did they?"

He raises a finger to his lips and pulls me into the corner. "They have cameras everywhere. I left my room earlier and went exploring, and they sent someone to escort me back." His green eyes are darting around the room behind me. "Who was that guy with you?"

"Gabe. My door was locked, so I had to wait for him to escort me to dinner," I tell him, then remember how he picked the lock on the warehouse. "Maybe I need to learn lock-picking while I'm here."

His lips twitch. "Couldn't hurt. I can't always be the one to rescue you."

I laugh, but I'm only half-joking. If they're offering the skills I need in this new life, I'm all in. Whatever they want to teach me.

"Brad's here," I tell him. When he gives me a confused look, I explain further. "Sorry. One of Lionel's best friends. He helped us escape." I go on to explain how Brad and Phoenix have been watching us. "Brad said Jordan left before Raven raided his place."

Instead of being happy, River frowns. "That's what they're telling you, but how do you know for sure? Until I see Jordan again, I won't hold my breath."

"Lionel trusted Brad, and that's good enough for me," I tell River. It's not that I don't understand how he feels, but I'm not sure his isolated approach will work for me. "I trust you, but I need more than just you in my life."

He flashes me a wry smile. "I told you not to trust me, either." He sweeps a lock of hair behind my ear. "More people means more risk."

"Not for me. People have a habit of dying and leaving me all alone," I state quietly. There's only so much I can take until there's nothing left of me to salvage.

He leans in and places a sweet kiss on my lips. "I understand. I do." He insists. "I'm starving. Let's grab some dinner. Then you're coming back to my room with me. I don't like being alone. Gives me too much time to think."

The thought of lying in a real bed with him makes my cheeks flush.

He leans down and whispers, "Sleep, nothing else. I swear."

Maybe I should be relieved he's a good guy, but I'm not.

CHAPTER 20

QUAID

After wrapping up my report from our surveillance, I head to Oliver's office to discuss our next steps. When I arrive, Oliver Harrison, my oldest friend and Phoenix's commanding officer, is standing with Brad, watching the monitors on the wall. The cameras show River and Greer walking around the cafeteria. I wonder how Oliver is going to handle the situation. We knew Greer was coming, but River is an unknown who we've let into our compound. Something we never do.

Whatever he decides, I trust it will be the right decision. Oliver and I went to West Point together. Both of us Army brats, but that is where the similarities end. Oliver's grandfather was a general and his father a colonel before he left the service to be a senator. Generations of service to our country and obscene family wealth is one hell of a legacy. Oliver wears the mantle of heir well.

My father was a grunt. Career military from the ground up. I lived on bases throughout the world. Army was drilled it into me from a young age. Tough and rough around the edges. I'm the guy you want by your side in combat.

Most of our classmates were surprised when Oliver and I

started hanging out, but we only saw the Army in our blood, not the status of our birth. Add in our inherent ambition, and our friendship was as easy as breathing.

While we both reached the rank of Major, Oliver is the one who leads Phoenix. His strengths lie in strategy and political maneuvering, which is only helped further by his mental power. My strengths lie in leading missions and tactical explorations, and my ability to manipulate fire comes in handy when dealing with the enemy.

The cameras show River and Greer with their heads together, talking low, but it's easy to see from their body language that there's a closeness between them. More than friendship?

"They look tight," I grit out, irritated by the sight. Stuck with following them for the last couple of days, I couldn't help but be a little pissed off. They never noticed us. What if we had been Raven?

Oliver throws me a speculative look. "Yes, it's obvious there's an attraction between them."

Brad frowns. "I don't like him. He had a quick answer for every question. Either he's telling the truth, or he's really fucking good at lying. My gut says it's the latter."

I agree with the old man, although I don't dare call him that out loud. Brad was an Army Ranger for a long time. He knows more ways to kill a man than I could even dream of learning.

Oliver pinches the bridge of his nose. "To make matters worse, Nash couldn't find anything on River after he dropped out of high school." Nash is our resident computer genius, and he always finds something, which tells us River's past is buried. "River said his mom took them off-grid, and it's possible he slipped through the cracks, but at some point, he popped up on Raven's radar. The question is—when? And why?"

"Do you believe his explanation of how he escaped at the

gas station?" Oliver turns and asks me. "He said the proximity of the forest boosted his power and gave him the strength to wake up sooner."

My gaze drifts back to the cameras. "I believe it. When he was knocked out in our SUV, I could feel his power reaching for the side of the road. Trees bent toward us. His command of nature is on another level."

Oliver absently nods. "I can feel his power through the cameras. It's close to matching the level of yours. Drawing on power reserves when someone is unconscious is incredibly rare, but not impossible." He lifts a shoulder. "I wonder if he developed his power naturally, or was he pushed past his limits like us?"

The military conducted a lot of experiments on us when they discovered we were more powerful than the first generation. Endless days of testing our physical and mental response to the most rigorous of trials. Dark times. The more boundaries we broke through, the more our powers grew until we were pushed to the brink of madness.

"Did you see his eyes?" I ask Oliver, handing him a picture of River from high school. "They changed—from blue to that startling green color."

Mine used to be boring brown. Nothing special. Until the experiments changed them into what I see in the mirror every day. Amber with a ring of fire, like my power can't be contained within my mind. It has to have a physical manifestation, too.

I stare at the dark-haired beauty by River's side. "How do you want to handle this?" Personally, I'd keep her here and dump the smirking shit out in the middle of nowhere, but again, it's not my call.

Oliver's blue eyes narrow. "Put her in the program. She has a lot to learn. Lionel sheltered her from this world, and Brad believes she needs basic survival skills. Maybe if she learns how to take care of herself, she'll stop relying on River."

Brad looks up and reluctantly informs us, "Lionel said she didn't have powers until last week."

"What is her power?" I ask, irritated that we didn't think to get that answer when we had her in the interrogation room.

Brad lifts a shoulder. "Lionel never said, but it has to be something special if Raven is hunting her, right?"

Oliver taps his chin with his finger. "I don't know. Something's off. There are no late bloomers." He looks at me. "Get her in to see Beckett. Tell him to dig deep. If she went all those years without using them, something powerful must have been blocking her."

"And River?" I sneer, unable to help myself. There's something about him that makes my gut clench. Maybe I should introduce him to Jax. He scares the shit out of everybody.

"Offer him his choice of classes," Oliver suggests with a pensive look on his face. "I'm curious to find out which ones he chooses. It could give us the answers we need."

River drops a brief kiss on her lips, and the two head toward the line to get some food. I grind my teeth together and leave the room to find Beckett. The sooner we separate them, the faster we can determine River's angle and re-establish the security here.

THE LIGHT FLICKS OFF, AND THE DOOR TO BECKETT's office opens, but the second his young patient sees me, he immediately backs away. Stifling my irritation, I attempt a smile and motion for him to leave, but he stares up at me without moving. Beckett walks up and places his hands on the kid's shoulders. With a soft exhale, the tension leaves the kid's body, and he walks out with a smile on his face.

"I'd tell you to stop scaring my patients, but I know that's not your intention," Beckett states firmly as he looks at his watch. "I've got five minutes before the next patient arrives. What do you need?"

Beckett was also at West Point with me and Oliver, but we didn't hang out together. His friends were cerebral in nature, geeks interested in military intelligence and technology. The field he would have entered if they had let him. When the Army found out Beckett's talent was psychometry, they used his ability to find the rest of us, turning him against his fellow soldiers.

Here, at Phoenix, his talents are used to help his fellow psychics instead of putting a target on their back. With a simple touch, he can glean information and emotions, but his ability to calm the overwhelming emotions that come with our powers is pure gold. It also doesn't hurt that he looks completely non-threatening.

"We have a new... woman... here. We don't know what her power is, but it apparently didn't show up until a little over a week ago," I tell him, stammering like a complete idiot. "Oliver thinks she needs to see you to figure out why she suppressed it."

Beckett's grey eyes light up with a spark of interest. "How old is she?"

"Twenty-three," I inform him.

"Hmm. Definitely a woman," he says with a straight face, as if I can't see the laughter he's holding back.

I'm thirty, not eighty. "Whatever. She likes this guy she came in with," I explain with a snort. "Maybe you should talk to him, too. My gut says he's bad news."

Beckett raises a single eyebrow. "I'm not sure your gut is

reliable. You didn't trust me either." He taps on his phone. "What are their names?"

"Greer Vickers and River Fulton," I tell him.

He types in the names. "Any relation to Colonel Vickers?"

"He was a surrogate father to her after her dad died," I inform him with a sigh. "Brad said she picked up his name when she went on the run. I don't know her real name." I pause at the thought and wonder what it is. "According to her, Lionel was killed by Raven."

Beckett looks up and waits for me to explain.

I summarize what she's gone through the last few days. "She's definitely telling the truth. Kind of self-contained but let loose when she saw Brad. I think he reminds her of Lionel. You can't fake that level of trauma, but Brad and his team didn't find Lionel's body. Raven could have taken it with them, but why? It's not something they usually do." Lionel was a good soldier. A man of integrity who led more top-secret missions than most of the special ops guys I know. He deserves a proper burial.

"I see," Beckett replies after a second. "Hopefully, she's open to diving into her psyche, because I agree with Oliver. It's odd for psychic powers to show up so late. Maybe she was subconsciously using them but never noticed, then they suddenly evolved or increased. Usually, I would speculate a low power level, but if they were, Raven wouldn't be after her."

His comment makes me sit up straighter. "Come to think of it, her power doesn't register at all. No wonder I forgot to ask her about it. I didn't feel it."

Beckett's eyes light up. "That *is* interesting." He makes a note on his phone. "And River?"

"You'll feel his power coming a mile away," I tell him. "Enhanced to the nth degree, similar to mine and Oliver's. We don't know what caused it, though."

He's practically vibrating with excitement. "Let's get them

in here tomorrow. You said they're in some sort of relationship?" I nod, and he dips his chin. "Good. I want to see her at 9 a.m., and him immediately after, at 9:30 a.m. If they know they're back-to-back, I could use that to ferret out more information."

Considerably more relaxed than when I entered, I shake my head at him. He obviously used his power to bring my emotional response down a notch. "Thanks. I was a bit wired."

He takes off his glasses to rub the bridge of his nose. "It's what I do."

Hand in hand, we head back to River's room after dinner. I keep expecting someone to stop us and make me return to my room, but no one does. River is right. They must be watching us. There's no way they would allow new people to roam around the place. I wouldn't, and they're a government group housing a bunch of people with what I'm sure is an alarming list of powers. Watching comes with the job.

River's room is identical to mine, and it makes me grimace. All the white is stressing me out. It's too sterile. I feel like a rat in a lab waiting for the door to the maze to open up so I can get the cheese.

River walks over to the bed and fingers the folded clothes sitting on top. "Someone's been here. I left these clothes lying on the floor earlier, and yet here they are, washed and folded for me. It's an invasion of privacy, and I hate it." He picks them up and tosses them into one of the dresser drawers.

"I wonder if Raven's headquarters is similar to this one," I say, speculating whether all government facilities lack personality. Probably. With no chairs in the room, I kick off my shoes and sit criss-cross applesauce on the bed.

River joins me on the bed, his back to the headboard, legs stretched out in front of him, then pats the spot next to him. I move to his side.

Since the moment we met, I've felt comfortable enough to fall asleep next to him multiple times—the semi-truck, in Jordan's apartment, and on that old leather couch in the warehouse. Biting my lip, I stare at him. Why does a bed suddenly make me nervous?

His thumb reaches out and pulls my lip from my teeth. "I don't want to be in this room or this place without you. When you're not here, all I want to do is find you. With you here beside me, all I want to do is run away and find someplace safe for the two of us to hide."

"That sounds so good," I admit with a sigh.

If only I hadn't killed Trent, but I did. I'm not sure there is anywhere safe for me to hide except here. Hightower and Raven will never stop looking for me. I want to tell River, but murder is a huge burden to put on someone else's shoulders.

His bright green eyes search mine, and whatever he sees makes him sad for a second, but his lips quickly lift in a smile. "All this free time. What should we do?"

Heat steals across my cheeks in a raging blush as my thoughts go back to the theater. Why do I feel like a teenager dreaming of her first kiss? I'm twenty-three, damn it. His eyebrow rises high, like he knows exactly what I'm thinking, and that makes it worse.

His chuckle is low and full of the same needy desire, but he shakes his head. "Stop, you're killing me. I promised sleep, and I'm going to stick to my word. Besides, my control only goes so far, and you in this bed is a temptation I'm not sure I can resist."

"Was it real?" I murmur, almost convinced the kiss was a dream. It had been that good.

"It was real," he said, leaning closer. "And when you're not exhausted and overwhelmed, I'm going to kiss you again to prove it." He picks up my hand and entwines his fingers with mine. "We need something to distract your dirty mind before you make me forget my good intentions."

My mouth drops open in surprise. Then, I decide a comment like that deserves a little punishment, and scoot in close, allowing my lips to hover an inch above his. "Twenty questions it is. I'll go first. Tell me about your… first kiss."

He groans. "You fight dirty, too." He lifts his other hand and sweeps the hair back from my neck before he glides his finger down the side of my neck. "So do I." While his finger continues its path, he proceeds to answer.

"My first kiss was in kindergarten," he says in a low voice. "She was five and a half, and I was five. Her name was Margaret O'Connell. She had red hair and green eyes, and I thought she was the prettiest girl in our class. At recess, I announced to everyone, including her, that she was my girl-friend. Then, I stretched up and planted a kiss on her cheek."

My lips twitch. "Older and taller. Was that your type?"

"And wiser. She proceeded to pop me in the eye," he reveals with a laugh. "Nobody warned me about redheads, but I learned quick. Never kissed another."

Laughing, I wink at him. "Good thing I don't have red hair."

His finger moves up and entwines a piece of my hair. "I'm not sure it would have mattered." The tension between us increases a notch. "Your turn. First kiss."

I twist my lips. "My story isn't as good as yours. I was in the fourth grade and rode the school bus. So did this guy, Clay, who was a sophomore in high school who I had the biggest crush on. One day, my best friend dared me to kiss him." I roll my eyes. "I never could resist a dare. As I was getting off the bus, I bent down and kissed his cheek, then ran off."

"A sophomore. Wow, you liked them really old," he says with a wink. "I might be way too young for you."

"Ha, ha," I mutter with a smile. "Obviously, I didn't think through the repercussions. Clay laughed it off, but the kids on the bus were ruthless about it. Thankfully, he got his driver's license shortly after and never rode the bus again." Funny thing, though. I never regretted it.

"That was a great story," he insists with a laugh. "Okay. Back to the questions. Favorite color."

"Blue. Well, turquoise," I tell him.

"Mine is purple. Any shade," he says in return, releasing my lock of hair. "You pick the next question."

Yawning, I scoot down on the bed and wait for him to join me. "Favorite or first pet," I say a minute later.

His eyes find me, and there's a wealth of sadness in them. "Frankie, my dog. He was the best. Definitely not a purebred. Short, with fur in a million different colors. We got him from the shelter when I was ten."

"Did he die?" I ask tentatively.

"Worse," he replies with a heavy sigh. "When we went on the run, I had to leave him behind. My mom took him to a friend of hers who had a farm. I loved him so much. They emailed her pictures of him every once in a while, but I couldn't bear to look at them. She said he looked happy, though." There's a raspiness to his voice that makes me wish I'd asked another question.

Without a word, I roll over and wrap my arms tightly around him. The sweet scent of him washes over me. "I'm sorry." The hurt in his voice is still there after all these years. He really loved Frankie.

He rests his chin on top of my head. "How about you?"

"Never had a pet," I tell him. "My mom was allergic. Honestly, I was a girly-girl. All I wanted was Barbies and pink sparkly things." It was true. My room looked like a pink glitter bomb had gone off in it.

His hand rubs down my arm. "Ever been in a serious relationship?"

"No," I answer slowly. "My parents died when I was sixteen. In a car crash." I pause, wanting to tell him the truth. "They were murdered. Lionel said my dad waited too long to get us to safety. Someone ran us off the road. I lived. They didn't."

"Raven?" he asks tentatively, squeezing me tighter.

I shrug but bury myself in the feel of his lean arms holding me and the scent of honeysuckle on his skin. "I guess. Lionel didn't say for sure, but my dad did have the ability to manipulate air."

"I'm sorry."

"Anyway, I had a hard time getting close to anyone for a long time," I finish with the answer to his question. *Until you*, I think, but don't say the words. His hand moves from my arm to my back, and as the soothing motion continues, my eyes droop. This has been the longest day ever.

"I understand. You're the first person I've gotten close to, too," he admits with a yawn, making me smile at his blunt honesty. "I'm tired. How about you?"

When I nod, he reaches down and pulls the covers over us, then pulls me back into his arms. "Sweet dreams." The ghost of his lips drift across the top of my head, and I smile at the warmth that the simple gesture leaves in its wake.

"What do you want to eat?" River asks, tapping the tray in front of me.

I eye the food in the metal containers in front of us, then reach for a spoon to scoop out some scrambled eggs. "Eggs and toast are plenty for me. When I was going to school, I usually only had a protein bar in the morning."

He piles his plate with a little bit of everything. "Breakfast is fuel for your brain and one of my favorite meals. Bacon, sausage, biscuits, eggs, pancakes... you name it. I love it."

"If I ate all that, I'd be bigger than a house," I tell him with a shake of my head. "And sleepy."

"That's the beauty of using your powers," he tells me. "It revs up your metabolism. In fact, if you use them to the point of depletion, you'll need to stuff yourself to recover."

I look down at my modest plate of food. "I'll take your word for it." The only time I used my powers, I passed out afterward, but when I woke, I didn't feel hungry. Just stressed.

Finding an empty table, I sit down and dig into my eggs. Not bad. "Needs a little salt, but they're good. How is yours?" I can't help but look at the pancakes, dripping with butter and syrup, on his plate. Exactly how I like them.

"Everything is good, but the pancakes are unreal," he teases me. I glare at him, and he laughs. "Here. Take one. You're drooling." He places a single pancake on my plate.

"Mmm, thank you." There's something universal about pancakes. Both my dad and Lionel used to make them for me. I take a bite and let out a little moan as the thick syrup and butter hits my tongue.

"Good to see you're eating," Quaid says, striding up to us, energy crackling around him.

Choking down the bite, I look up at the intense man and see he's carrying several items. At least he's not scowling.

"Here's a printout of your schedule and a map," he says, handing me two pieces of paper and a tablet. "Your first meeting is in fifteen minutes with Beckett. He's our resident psychiatrist. Everyone meets with him so he can help ease any concerns you might have and give you someone confidential to talk to."

River snorts. "Pass."

Quaid hands him a tablet. "The meeting with Beckett is non-negotiable. Your appointment is right after hers at nine-thirty. Once you're done, take a look at the list of classes and decide which ones you want to take. I'll meet you back here at noon to get the list."

With a frown, I glance down at the papers in my hand. One of them has a complete list of classes with days and times. "Why didn't I get to choose my classes?"

"Based on Brad's assessment, we created a list of classes for you. Most of them are focused on learning survival skills and how to use your powers," Quaid murmurs. "Don't tell anyone about that class."

Nervous, I look at River. "Why?"

River shares a look with Quaid. "Never give away all your secrets."

Quaid dips his chin in agreement and looks at his watch. "Exactly. You'll need to leave in the next ten minutes to make it to Beckett's office in time. It's on the map." He leaves as silently as he arrived, and I can't help the relieved sigh that escapes. That man rubs me the wrong way.

I'm finishing this pancake first, though. Hurrying, I quickly shove a couple more bites into my mouth and look over to see River laughing at me. "What? These pancakes are too good to waste."

He waves a hand. "Take them with you. We can bring the trays back at lunch."

I pause mid-bite and think about it. "I don't like the idea of walking around with a tray. My schedule is packed."

Ten minutes later, I've finished all my food, and after setting my tray down where I'm supposed to, I drag River out the door.

According to the map, Beckett's office is in the building next to this one. Bright sun blinds me the instant I step outside, but I soak it in. It feels good to be out of the white sterile environment.

Numerous tan buildings surround this one. Well, technically, they're a mustard-y brown color that sort of looks like a mix of tan and creamy yellow that looks like baby poo or something, but I can't stomach the thought. Tan it is. My nose wrinkles at the sight of them. Does the military not believe in color? With a shrug, I open the door to the one in front of me and walk down the hall until I reach room 103.

Entering, I find a small sitting area with a few chairs and a door with a light on top of it. Having seen enough psychiatrists' offices at the hospital where I did clinicals, I know the light is used to signal when another patient is in the room. Although it's not on, the black and white clock on the wall says eight fifty-nine, so I sit down.

River grabs the seat next to me and continues eating his breakfast.

"Oh good; you're here," a smooth voice says, and I jerk my gaze back to the door where I find a tall, lean man in jeans and a green button-down shirt.

I'm pretty sure my mouth drops open. Thick, wavy brown hair frames a perfectly symmetrical and utterly stunning face with a square jaw, a strong, straight nose, and smiling lips. Light-colored eyes framed with black glasses should make him look stern, but the intelligence gleaming from the depths of his eyes makes him lean toward sexy serious. Is that even a term? Probably not, but it should be. Sexy nerd. Sexy smart. Sexy...

River leans over. "Are you okay? Nervous?"

Reining in my thoughts, I nod and take a deep breath. "I'm good. Great. Yep."

I stand, then make my way toward Beckett, but the whole time, I'm wondering how I'm going to be able to talk about my feelings to someone who has a cleft chin.

"Hi, I'm W... Greer." Apparently, I'm also a mess.

He nods and stretches a gloved hand toward the interior of his office. "It's nice to meet you, Greer. I'm Beckett. Please come in."

I dart a glance at the gloves on his hands. Sometimes in rehab people wore gloves to protect skin that had been damaged badly in a fire, but those aren't the same. He's wearing thin black leather gloves. I stop in the middle of the room and wait for him to tell me where to sit.

The office is kind of boring. There's the obligatory couch. A few upholstered chairs. A large wooden desk with files and papers cluttering the top. The wall of windows makes the room feel light and airy, but there's little décor to give it much-needed warmth.

A glass of ice water sits on a coaster in the center of the coffee table.

"Sit anywhere you like." He motions to the options.

Uncomfortable choosing the couch, I contemplate the chair to the right of it, but I don't like the idea of sitting that close to the stranger who's trying to delve into my head. So, I sit on the edge of the couch and clasp my hands together.

He smiles and takes the seat across from me. "Once you get to know me, I hope you'll feel more comfortable in here." His words make me blush, and I scoot back a tiny bit. "We'll spend our time today getting acquainted. Sound good?"

Relieved, I nod. "Yes."

He leans back in his chair and studies me for a minute. "I'm sorry for your loss. Lionel was a good man."

His words melt a little bit of the stiffness in my spine. "Thank you. I didn't realize he knew so many people here." The image of Lionel lying on the ground at the gas station, sweat pouring down his face and his hand shaking while he tries to hold back the fire flashes in my mind, and I can't help but flinch.

"Want to talk about it?" he offers in a comforting tone.

"It's too fresh," I say with a shake of my head. "Can you tell me how you knew him? Was it here?"

He tilts his head to the side. "I met him ten years ago. At West Point. He came to speak to me and my fellow cadets about Army life and to offer guidance on the road ahead of us. Since then, I've met him a few times."

"Did you know he loved to cook?" I ask him with a sad smile. "He was really good at it, too. I'll miss having dinner with him, testing out his new recipes." I didn't even know that was on my mind until just now.

Beckett shakes his head. "I didn't know that about him." He taps his finger on his knee. "Did you live close to each other?"

"I lived in his garage," I tell him, my voice breaking at the mention of it. It's stupid, but I miss my apartment. My life. "He wanted me close but knew I would need some independence while I completed grad school, so he added an upstairs apartment to his garage."

"What were you studying in school?"

"Doctorate in physical therapy," I reply, almost choking on the answer. "Sorry. Losing Lionel, my life, finding out I have powers, it's all too much right now."

"What is your power?" he asks in a calm voice.

Surprised, I stare at him. "I thought you all knew. Water, I think."

"Think?"

I lift a finger. "I've only used it once."

He reaches up to adjust his glasses. "That's unlikely. We're born with our abilities, which usually manifest when we're teenagers. You would have used them long before now."

"I would have noticed if I had manipulated water," I insist, irritated by his assumption.

"My guess is you suppressed the memory for some reason," he continues, as if I hadn't interrupted him. "Using that as the basis of my theory, I pulled some information from your background. When you were sixteen, you were in an accident with your parents, correct?"

Great. Another raw memory to bring up. "For a casual conversation, you're bringing up a lot of triggers." He stares at me, waiting patiently for me to continue. "You're correct." The thought of talking about my parents and the accident so soon after losing Lionel is scraping raw nerves.

"The accident report says you woke up in a pond," he calmly states. "I looked up an old property survey and some other documentation. I also spoke to the family who owns the land. What would you say if I told you the pond wasn't there before the accident?" he reveals, to my astonishment.

Stunned, I sit there and stare at him. Does he honestly think I created the pond? For what reason? "Seriously? Why would I do that?"

"Maybe you used the water to cushion your fall. It would have been an instinctive move. Something your power would leap to do naturally," he informs me, unaware of the bomb he's just dropped on me.

"That's not possible," I tell him, pissed that he would even suggest it.

"Why does that upset you so much?" He asks calmly.

Shaking my head back and forth, I stand and look down at him, angry tears falling down my face. His theory is preposterous. "No. It's impossible. You're wrong. Do you hear me? Wrong. I didn't have any powers back then." Swallowing hard to dislodge the knot in my throat, I continue, "If I had, I would have used them to put out the fire that burned my parents alive." With a sob, I leave him sitting there and dash out of the room.

Beckett jumps up to run after me, but the second I hit the door, I look at River. "Stop him." River immediately stands and moves toward Beckett with raised hands. Shouts fill the air, but I don't stop.

At the end of the hall, I slam my hands against the door to the outside and keep going. Sobs slip from my throat at the thought of having the power to save my parents from burning alive. Their screams haunt me to this day. Could I have saved them?

Images and noises from that night bombard me. Bright lights. Something slamming into the car. Spinning on the road. My mom's screams. My dad shouting, but I can't hear what he's saying. The window opening, and my body flying through it. Darkness. Waking in the pond. Shivering in the cold water. Trees swaying in the night air. Crickets singing. A bright, steady light in front of me. It's our car. My parents. Burning. Darkness again.

Stumbling to a halt, my tears flow as I stare at the ground in front of me. There's something bugging me about that night. What is it? I begin walking again, hoping to clear my head. I've gone through that night so many times. What's different? Come on.

People start shouting, and I clap my hands around my ears to shut them out. *Shut up. Trying to think here.* Air stirs my hair. *Thud.* What in the world? I turn around and see the shadowy outline of a head nailed to a wooden post. It's a shooting range target. I move a few feet closer and see the hole in the center. *Shit.* Knees shaking, I drop to the ground. Was someone aiming at me or the target? Unsure, I stay low. Then I hear the sound of thundering feet.

"What the hell do you think you're doing?" a familiar voice shouts at me. I look up and see the guy who escorted me to the cafeteria yesterday. What was his name? Gabriel?. "You could have been killed. Did you not read the fucking sign?"

What sign? "Are they still shooting?" I ask shakily.

"What?" he spits back, then exhales loudly. "They're... taking a break. Did you not see the sign?"

"No. What sign?"

He practically throws his arm out of the socket, pointing to a red sign hanging on the fence about two hundred feet away. "The big fucking sign that says 'Stop. Gun range. Shooting in progress.'"

Right. Lesson learned. Watch out for signs. "Missed it." I'm sure he's wondering how someone could miss a sign that big, but I don't enlighten him. "Thanks, Gabriel."

He reaches down, grabs my arm, and pulls me to my feet. "It's Gabe. I know you're new, but you need to take this seriously." Folding his arms across his chest, his brows lower into a stern look. "You're damn lucky he missed."

"I never miss." A guy with white-blond hair sweeping across his forehead, a tattoo sleeve, scruff for days, and brilliant blue eyes strolls up. My height, but a little leaner, he stops in front of me. His hand, also tattooed, fingers my hair. "Although, surprisingly, I might have been off by an inch. Maybe the scope is off... or perhaps it's fate?"

"You're the one who shot at me?" I ask coolly, unimpressed with his casual admission.

I scan the length of him. Ragged jeans with holes in the knees. Combat boots. Black T-shirt. Probably doesn't care that he scared the crap out of me.

He laughs. "Not a chance. I shot at the target. You stepped into the bullet's path. Good thing you didn't die. I hate to do paperwork." His eyes sweep across my face. "You were crying. Must have been why you didn't see the sign."

Thanks, Captain Obvious, I mentally scream, but instead I lift my chin and quietly assure him, "I'll make sure to stay away from this area in the future."

Blondie shakes his head. "Unfortunately for you, you're in my afternoon class. Make sure you're on time. Two p.m." He turns and motions for Gabriel and the small crowd gathered around us to move back. "I'm Jax, by the way. I'll be teaching you how to use all sorts of weapons." His walk toward the cover at the far end of the field is pure swagger, but my eyes linger on every step he takes. He's almost there when he turns around and waves, catching me staring.

If there was a wall close by, I'd bang my head on it. Repeatedly.

WALKING SLOWLY DOWN THE HALLWAY, I PEEK AROUND the entrance to Beckett's office and see the interior door closed and the light on. River's gone, too. I look up at the clock. Fifty minutes have passed since I ran out of here. My tablet and the two pieces of paper are sitting on the coffee table. I pick them up and quietly walk out of the office.

Great. I missed one class, and my power class started ten minutes ago. There's no way I'm disrupting the class so everyone can stare at the new girl. I'll wait and go to the next one. With a sigh, I walk outside and find a bench in the sun.

Miserable and adrift without Lionel's comforting presence, I sit there contemplating the past. What if Beckett was right and my powers manifested that night? Everything happened so fast. I don't even remember all the details. Like how did I escape the car and my parents didn't? Water wouldn't have helped me. Did my dad use his power? I lean my head back, wishing I could remember.

"Already skipping my class?" a smooth voice asks, taking the seat next to me.

I lift my head and look to my right. Perfect posture in an immaculate suit, I muse. Sitting up straight, with his shoulders back, the man beside me exudes sophistication like it was bred in him. The elegant, charcoal grey suit gracing his tall body certainly conveys that perception, but his posture reinforces it.

He pinches the pleat on his pant and turns his head to look at me. Blue-grey eyes top a long aristocratic nose. Dark brown, wavy hair, longer on top with precisely trimmed sides, looks like the kind of expensive cut you see in the best of circles. Indentations under his cheekbones make them appear sharp and pronounced. Clean-shaven too. No nonsense lips pressed firmly together give me the tiniest hint of his ire.

"Sorry," I say, flipping up the page in my hand to see the name. "Oliver. This hasn't been the best day, and given that I was already ten minutes late, I didn't think my teacher would enjoy me disrupting the class." Come to think of it, where's the rest of the class?

"There is no class. Just you and me," he informs me. "Given

your age, I doubt you'd enjoy learning to use your power in a class with teenagers."

"Ouch," I remark with a shake of my head. No woman likes to hear those words, even if he didn't mean them the way they sounded. "No. Worse would have been the younger ones." When he lifts a sculpted brow, I continue. "Lionel's son burned the house down when he was five or six."

"Really? I didn't know," he replies with a thoughtful look. "On average, our powers manifest when we're teenagers, but it can happen earlier."

"But not later," I state with resignation.

"No," he confirms. "Your meeting with Beckett didn't go as planned."

Fidgeting for a few minutes at the idea of someone knowing what we discussed, I finally blurt, "Doesn't my discussion with Beckett fall under doctor patient confidentiality?"

"It does," he assures me. "He didn't give me any details, but I had to send Quaid in to diffuse the situation between him and River." There's a hint of anger in his eyes. "Beckett would never hurt another. Can you say the same about River?"

I frown at the thought of them actually fighting, but I don't answer.

"We vet each and every person for weeks before we let them come to Phoenix. Lionel vouched for you, so we relaxed the rules. But once you started traveling with River, we had to revisit things," he informs me. "Unfortunately, there is very little information on River past his freshmen year of high school. He's a very powerful unknown. Normally, we wouldn't have brought him here, but I promised Lionel I'd help you, and I didn't think separating you from him would be wise."

Is he going to force River to leave? If so, I'm going with him. I'm not tied to anything here. Surely there is somewhere safe out there. I shift uncomfortably in my seat while I wait for him to reveal what's going to happen next.

He shifts to look directly at me. "We take the safety of this compound very seriously. I've given him a warning. In the future, it would be best if you didn't invoke his... protection. If you feel Beckett is overstepping, come to me. I'll resolve the issue."

Feeling like a chastised child, I stiffly nod, but underneath, I'm secretly relieved that he isn't kicking us out. I need to know my powers and how to handle them, and River can't always protect me. He has a mother and a sister.

"I understand. I feel bad for leaving River and Beckett behind to deal with the situation," I grudgingly concede. The idea that I could have saved my parents was a punch in the gut.

"Good," he says, looking at the gold Rolex on his wrist. "Our time is up. Tomorrow, we'll focus on using your powers." He glances back at me. "What is your power?"

"Water," I reply.

He tilts his head to the side. "Interesting." While his face never changes, I can tell my answer isn't what he expected.

I wait for him to ask more questions, but he doesn't.

"I'll see you tomorrow," he murmurs, rising to his feet.

Totally looking forward to it. Not. "Do you know my room number?" All I want to do is hide for a few minutes. Maybe take a shower. Change clothes.

He taps on his phone, then replies, "113. There's a map of the rooms on the tablet. Anything else?"

"No, thank you," I tell him.

With one long look at me, he pivots and strides away, his walk as purposeful as his demeanor. A soldier, maybe? It suddenly clicks, and I want to smack myself on the forehead. Lionel said Oliver ran Phoenix. Guess that's Senator Jack Harrison's son. Major Oliver Harrison. I wince. Way to make a great impression. If Lionel was here, he'd be really disappointed.

I open the tablet and find my room. Through these doors, down one long hallway, then a right, and about halfway down the next one is room 113.

As I walk, I think about my conversation with Oliver. I need to learn my powers and some survival skills. If he thinks bringing River here is bad, he's going to be livid when he finds out the truth. I killed Trent. And at some point, I'm going to have to tell Oliver why Hightower and his men are really after me. They couldn't care less about my ability to manipulate water. Losing both his wife and son to someone with powers... Hightower will do anything to find me.

Part of me wants to close my eyes and shut out the world for the rest of the day, but I've already missed two classes. Showering makes me feel a bit better, but putting on a clean set of grey sweats brings my mood down. Where can I get some normal clothes? And my go bag. I don't like being without it. Needing some sense of normalcy, I decide to talk to Oliver tomorrow. Right now, I've got to get to class.

First one this afternoon is with Quaid. It takes me no time to get to the gym where he's holding class. Thankfully, it doesn't have the usual gym socks and sweat smell, but the cavernous tan interior matches the building's boring exterior all the way down to the light brown wooden floors. Although, this one lacks the obligatory basketball court. Odder still, the rear of the gym is in shadows. I stare at it for a second, wondering what the tall shadowy shapes could be before turning my attention to the rest of the class.

To my relief, there are roughly fifteen others here with me. If it was just the two of us, I'm sure something snarky would slip out of my mouth, and that would be bad. There's enough going on in my life without adding more conflict, and after he had to step in, I doubt he's happy with me. Also, he's a big guy and intimidating as hell, not that I'd let him know.

"Line up!" he shouts, eerily similar to a drill sergeant.

When we've all assembled in front of him, tall, muscular legs stalk up and down, eyeing each of us.

"I'm not going to teach you how to fight. Raven is full of trained soldiers. Some with powers and some without. In a fight, they will win."

Wearing his usual uniform of camo fatigues and a matching Army green t-shirt, he stops in front of me and studies me for a second, then continues, "I'm going to teach you defensive techniques to help you evade and escape. And finally, if all else fails, how to use your powers to *neutralize* them. Not fight. For example, I have the ability to manipulate fire. One way I could neutralize them is to light a ring around them, so I can escape."

A brave young man I've never seen before raises his hand and asks, "Why don't we use our powers to do more?" With his dark hair and eyes, as well as his complexion, he could be Hispanic. Maybe a year or two older than me and very good-looking. Well, except for the current of electricity coursing down one of his arms. That's a bit frightening.

"Good question," he tells him. "What happens if you hurt or kill one of their men? Purposely?"

"They'll use force against you," an older man states with confidence. With his receding hairline, I put him in his forties. Slim, with bent shoulders, he looks like life has taken a few hits at him. "Maybe it won't be just you they go after either. Maybe it's your wife who knew nothing about your powers. Or your children who inherited them."

Sadly, I look at him and nod, knowing he's right.

"Or they take video of you using your powers and threaten to release it to the public," a young girl with short black hair and kohl-rimmed eyes states in a clipped voice. "Or they force you to use your powers in front of regular humans, making them afraid of you and removing your support system. They're ruthless." Her voice rings with truth and anger.

A stubborn glint shines in the young man's brown eyes. "Or you take them out. Somewhere quiet. Where there are no working cameras."

Quaid folds his arms across his chest and stares at the guy. "If you do, they'll never stop hunting you. Their tactics include whatever is most useful to them: declaring you a dangerous person in the media, countering your powers with technology that neutralizes yours, or even taking you out from a distance. You are a thing to them. Not a person."

Chills run down my spine. Hightower will never quit. My goal was to leave here with a new identity and find the life I worked so hard to achieve, but I realize that's not going to be possible. At best, I'll have to live a small, quiet life, making few waves, my dreams lost to the past. Worst, he finds me. Is there a middle ground? Damn, I hope so.

Determination lifts my chin higher. Good thing I was wearing tennis shoes when I left my old life. Looks like I'm going to be doing a lot of running.

The young man looks away from Quaid's relentless gaze. It's clear he remains unconvinced, but I can see by the clench of his jaw, he's determined to learn whatever he has to in order to survive.

Quaid clears his throat and points to the darkened area of the gym. "Behind me is a replica of a city with buildings, streets, alleys, and Raven's men. You will have ten minutes to find a place to hide before I come looking. A horn will blow when the ten minutes is up. Make sure you're hidden by that time."

Everyone starts talking at once and he holds up a hand for silence. "Take this seriously. If I don't find you in fifteen minutes, you win a point. Points are rewarded. Failure results in laps."

He raises a small gun. "This is a paint gun. When I tag you, you're done. Return here and wait for the rest of the class. If I don't find you, stay hidden. When you hear the horn sound for the second time, it will be safe to come out."

Lights go up, and I see that what I mistook for a gym is actually a ginormous warehouse surrounding a small realistic city. I study the grey buildings and wonder if the Army used this for training purposes. When I return my gaze to Quaid, he's holding up five fingers.

"5, 4, 3, 2," he shouts, then pauses. "1. Go!"

I take off running into the streets. Stationed at the corner of the first building is a man in blue fatigues with an armband. Embroidered on the band is a black raven in mid-flight. River mentioned they had one on their uniforms, but the men at the gas station had been in suits, and I was too distracted to notice them at Jordan's. I stare at the beady red eyes of the bird. Sinister-looking, the image burns itself into my brain, leaving me with a lingering sense of foreboding.

Shaking it off, I head farther into the city. Most of the doors are locked. The few that aren't open to reveal restaurant kitchens, apartments, or offices with workers in them. I reach the end of the alley and spin in a circle. There's a dumpster, but that's too obvious. Some boxes. I look up and contemplate the railing on the building that leads to the roof, but what happens if I go up and there's no cover?

Aware of the clock ticking down, I try to remember the little bits River taught me, and I get an idea. Going back to one of the kitchens, I hurry to slip into position. A loud foghorn bellows in the air.

Shouts and screams come from outside, and my hands shake a little at the thought of being hunted. I can see why

Quaid does this. Everything about this feels real. Heart racing, I stand still, ears peeled for the slightest noise.

Minutes go by. The door behind me opens. From the corner of my eye, I see Quaid silently sweep through the kitchen, poking in cabinets and opening ovens. When he finds nothing, he stands completely still. I'm barely breathing, inhaling the shallowest of breaths. Sweat beads at my temples and the back of my neck while my muscles strain to hold my position.

Finally, he leaves. The door closes, but I don't move. Thirty seconds later, it opens again, and this time, it doesn't close. Is that so he can glance in here when he goes by? I continue to hold my pose, making sure I don't lock my knees and possibly faint. Gradually, I increase the depth of my breaths but not to the point that anyone can hear them.

Eons later, the foghorn sounds again. For a second, I slump against the stainless-steel counter, but there's little time for relief. Hurrying, I change out of the chef's clothes and back into my own. A minute later, I'm running back to class.

Five people are standing in front of Quaid without a speck of paint on them. I slip into line beside the girl with the short hair. The younger man made it. So did the older man. I nod at the remaining four ladies, who flash relieved grins back at me.

"Congratulations, you six evaded me," Quaid says with a grim smile. "But let's see how you really did." He lifts a remote and flips on the screens behind him. Images of the city appear. Quaid rewinds the cameras, then plays them forward. The second he spots one of the six, he fast forwards until he finds us in our hiding spot.

The older man hid behind a bookcase in the office. Thin, he barely fit in the impossibly small space, but a camera caught him entering and disappearing behind it.

"Hmph. Never occurred to me someone could fit back

there. Good choice, Edward. I'll be more alert to small spaces next time," Quaid assures him.

He followed me to the restaurant where I put on one of the mannequin's clothes, then put my hair up and added a chef hat from another. "Good tactic. Hiding in plain sight. Better to do it in public where you can't be trapped, but I applaud your decision."

Quaid continues to find everyone's hiding place except the young man's. "Good. You used your powers to short circuit the cameras around you. I would recommend you take out a few more so they can't use the void to follow you, but you did great."

He looks at the large watch on his wrist. "All six of you will get a point this time. Next time, watch for the cameras, and do what you can to avoid or confuse the person monitoring them. Okay."

He claps his hands together. "The rest of you, take a lap." He points to the track running along the wall, and they all groan, but no one argues as they get up and start jogging along the perimeter. "You six can leave."

Everyone starts filing out except me. Wringing my hands, I stand to the side until they're gone.

Quaid looks at me and raises an eyebrow. "Question?" His voice is curt, but I can't detect any anger in his tone.

Raising my chin, I look into his unusual amber eyes. "No, an apology. I'm sorry I asked River to intervene with Beckett this morning. Oliver told me you had to step in and... resolve the issue. I wasn't thinking at the time, only feeling, but it won't happen again."

Quaid grunts. "It will." He folds his muscular arms, and the tiniest hint of a tattoo peeks out from under the sleeve of his shirt, but I can't tell what it is. "A lot happened to you in a short amount of time, which kept you in fight-or-flight mode. You're safe now, but your emotions will continue to run high for a while. Even small things will trigger you."

He pauses. "My issue is with him. River will do whatever he thinks is best. Unfortunately, that may not be the best thing for you or Phoenix. I laid out our rules to him this morning. It's up to him to follow them. If he doesn't, he's out."

Irritated at his high-handedness, I scowl at him. "You have to give him time. He's not used to answering to someone else. He's been on the run for a long time."

He lifts a shoulder. "So he says. I'm not buying it. Things aren't adding up with his story, but I don't need to know his secrets. He can keep them as long as they don't jeopardize the security of this facility or the safety of its residents, including you. If he does, I'll remove him." He taps his watch. "Don't you have Jax's class next? He hates when students are late."

I open my mouth to defend River, but I know it won't do any good. From the minute Quaid met him, he hasn't liked him. I don't know why, but it doesn't matter. I won't be involving River in my disputes in the future. Tossing a glare at Quaid, I spin on my heel and head out the door. This isn't over, but Jax did warn me not to be late.

I'm actually running by the time I enter the shooting range for class. How in the world did I walk so far earlier today without even realizing it? I know I was lost in an emotional storm, but that had to at least be a mile. Entering the area, I see a long tan wooden structure portioned into sections at one end of a dirt field. Huffing and puffing, I join the group standing in another bare bones wooden stand, barely arriving a second before Jax blows the air horn he's holding in his hand. What is it with the horns? I'm tempted to plug my ears, but the sound cuts off.

Dressed in the same scruffy attire that seems to be his signature look, he ambles over to a nearby table and sets the horn down on it, then turns back to us. With one hand, he shoves the thick swath of white-blond hair on top of his head back. With his features and attire, he sort of reminds me of a surfer, but his attitude is intense and a little unnerving.

Like Quaid, Jax walks the line, but his entire focus is on our hands. Mine are resting beside my thighs. My neighbor on the right is restlessly tapping hers. I look at the person on my left and find large hands in a half curl.

Jax stops at the woman on my right. "It's okay to be

nervous. Guns are dangerous." He keeps walking until he gets to the man on my left. "Or excited." He moves back in front of me. "Have you ever shot a gun?"

One corner of my mouth lifts in a wry smile. "Tried, but it didn't fire." Several people laugh, but I'm not joking. Although I'm incredibly grateful I didn't shoot River at the gas station, I'd like to learn why.

Jax sweeps a cold look at the people who are laughing. "Laughing at another student in my class for any reason will not be tolerated. I don't care what experience you think you have. Here, everyone is a plebe until I say you're not. Do you understand?"

"Yes," I murmur along with several others, fighting a smile at his defense.

Jax freezes, then shouts. "I didn't hear you. Do you understand?!"

"Yes!" we answer in unison this time.

"Good," he replies with a sneer. "Next time, tack on a sir to that answer. I'm a fucking Sergeant in the United States Army and the best damn sniper you'll ever meet." The man next to me flashes a wide grin, and Jax comes up to him. "Don't get excited. I'm not going to teach you how to be a sniper. I doubt you have the capacity to learn all the shit I know."

His grin disappears. "What are you going to teach us?"

Jax narrows his eyes at him. "First, I'm going to teach you manners." Locking eyes on the guy, he waits until he turns his head to continue. "Then, I'm going to teach you how to pick up any weapon in reach and confidently..." he pauses for a second, "use it to defend yourself."

He waves a hand to the cover behind us. "Today, you will learn to shoot a handgun. Why? Because they're the most common weapon you'll come across." Walking over to one of the sectioned-off areas, he jerks a thumb behind him. "At every gun range, this is called the firing line. When I tell you to line up at the firing line, you will pick one of these booths and line up."

We tense in anticipation, but he shakes his head. "Stand down. Today, I'll teach you the basics: how to load the gun, grip the gun, position yourself into the proper shooting stance, how to distribute your weight, flip off the safety, sight your target, breathe properly, pull the trigger, and safely set the gun down when you're finished. Take this seriously. If anyone fucks around or doesn't listen, you'll be dropped from my class. Got it?"

"Yes, sir!" we state firmly.

He gives us a pleased nod. "Good to know you're capable of learning. Now, I'm going to demonstrate each of the basics, then I'll call you up one at a time and have you walk through each step. You will shoot one time. That's it."

For the next twenty minutes, we watch Jax demonstrate each of the basics. Using exaggerated movements, he shows the position we should take for each step several times. There's much more to shooting than I ever thought, and I doubt I'll remember it all. Biting my lip, I try to concentrate on memorizing the first couple of stances.

The guy next to me snorts, but thankfully, Jax doesn't hear it. "Overkill."

"I know you won't remember half the shit I just told you, but try your best," Jax says, finishing his demonstration. "First up, Overkill."

My lips twitch when I look to my right. Guess he heard him. Note to self—Sergeant Jax has Whisper 2000.

The guy stiffens but walks over to the booth. Jax motions for him to begin, and he immediately grips the gun and raises it to fire. He shoots, and the second his arm comes down, Jax pushes him off balance, grabs the gun from his hand, and mock shoots him.

"Bang. You're dead."

"I already know how to shoot!" the guy shouts from the ground. "I shouldn't have to follow all the steps."

Jax flashes a dark grin. "In my class, you'll do what I tell you, when I tell you, got it?"

The guy flashes him a sulky look. "That's not fair. Is there an advanced class I can take?"

"Do you think Raven will be 'fair'? What about a scared civilian who thinks you're a threat to his town? Think they will be fair?" He looks at the target and scoffs. "You didn't even hit your target, and you think you're ready for an advanced class. Get back in line."

"I'm an excellent shot," the guy insists, getting to his feet. He stomps over to the booth and holds down the button on the wall. The target flies toward him and stops. Grabbing it, he pulls it closer, then curses.

Jax claps him on the back. "Don't worry. I'll be sure to give you extra lessons. Get back in line."

The guy ambles back to his place beside me, muttering the entire way.

"You," Jax says, pointing directly to me. "Booth."

I walk up to the booth and stare at the gun in front of me instead of him. He'll only make me nervous, and I'll forget the positions. When I hear "Begin!" I pick up the gun and almost drop it. I didn't expect it to be so heavy. It looked like a toy in Jax's hand, but the weight tells me it's very real. I make the "v" he suggested for the grip with four fingers on one side of the gun and my thumb on the other and place my other hand under for support. Squaring my shoulders and torso toward the target, I get my feet into the staggered position he suggested and stop. I can't remember what to do next.

He leans in close, and the smell of sunshine and a slightly acrid, smoky scent, which I'm guessing is from shooting earlier, wraps around me. "Put your finger here." He places my finger on the trigger in the correct position.

I frown and turn my head to look at him. Piercing ocean-blue eyes, only inches away, meet mine, and for a second, I get lost in their clear depths.

Inhaling sharply, I spit my question out. "Shouldn't I wait until I'm ready to fire to put my finger on the trigger?"

"Mm, rain on a summer day," he murmurs, then steps away to ask the crowd. "Good question. She asked whether she should wait to put her finger on the trigger. Anyone have the answer?"

Blushing at both his words and getting called out in front of everyone, I wait for someone to answer. A young female voice pipes up. "Only pick up the gun if you're prepared to shoot. With your finger on the trigger, you eliminate the time between prep and shot."

"Very good!" he exclaims. "You've earned a reward point and jumped to the top of the class." Turning back to me, he sees my finger still on the trigger. "What's next?"

I release the safety, then lean slightly forward and align my sights. Stopping, I wait for him to put the ear protection over my ears. Since this is our first time, he didn't want us to put them on until we were actually ready to shoot.

He picks up the headphones, smooths my hair, places them on my head, then taps my right shoulder, the signal to shoot when ready.

Breathing in and out a few times to clear my head, I try to steady my trembling hands and pull the trigger. When I shoot, a small force pushes back on me, but the recoil isn't too bad. Carefully, I put the safety back on, set the gun down on the booth, and take off the headphones. My stomach is cramping from nerves.

He claps me on the shoulder. "Don't worry about bringing in the target. You missed."

My shoulders drop, and I return to the line while he calls the next person. A young woman strides up to the booth, and she's so confident, I have to wonder if she's the one who received the reward point. Her long, blond ponytail swings jauntily as she walks. In leggings and a grey sweatshirt, she stands out from the rest of us. I'm jealous. Not just because of her attire, although I'm very envious of those leggings. She seems utterly relaxed.

The second she picks up the gun, her experience is obvious. Her comfort with the weapon and each position is clear. She flows smoothly from one step to the next, then shoots.

Jax pulls in the target and flashes her a big smile. "Slightly to the left, but excellent shot. Make sure your grip is tight and completely squared up before you pull the trigger. A centimeter off can change the trajectory."

Maybe I should practice the positions a few times before the next class.

One by one, the rest of the class takes a turn. At the end, Jax calls out a couple of names for displaying excellent marksmanship. The young woman pumps her fist when he calls her name.

He dismisses us, and I watch her stride up to him.

"Where did you learn to shoot?" he asks her, as she reaches his side.

"My dad was a cop," she admits with a sad smile. "He taught me. I wasn't very good, but circumstances force you to get better in a hurry."

Hopefully that will be me in a couple of weeks... or months. I'm not sure. To be honest, the gun scares me, but I like Jax.

He's blunt but also really passionate about learning to shoot the right way. Although his personality is a bit intense, his handsome, relaxed surfer looks help balance it out.

As I leave the range, I see the big red sign Gabe pointed out earlier today, and I can't help but laugh. It's huge. No wonder he was so pissed off. After getting to know Jax a little better this afternoon, I'm surprised he wasn't, though. I glance back at him and see his bright blue eyes staring directly at me. Blushing, I duck my head and turn back around. There are way too many good-looking men here. It's almost annoying.

Dinner tonight consists of grilled chicken, mashed potatoes, and green beans. Having skipped lunch to stay in my room, I'm starving. Tray in hand, I stand in the middle of the cafeteria and scan the room until I find River, who's seated at a back table by himself. I walk over and stop beside him.

"Is this seat taken?" I tease with a smile.

He looks up at me and grins, but my smile immediately drops when I see the bruise around his eye.

"That's one hell of a shiner. Who did that to you?" I ask, dropping the tray on the table and reaching for him.

He grabs my hand and pulls me down beside him. "I'm fine. You should see the other guy." When the line doesn't get a laugh, he sighs. "Seriously. I threw the first punch. Quaid was only defending himself."

Quaid, I fume. This is about me.

"I'm so, so sorry, River. This is all my fault. I should never have asked you to stop Beckett this morning." Whatever happens, I need to face up to my reality and stop hiding from it. "Do you want me to get you some ice?"

He shakes his head. "Oliver gave me a bag when he

lectured me. It's all good." He squeezes my hand. "Are you okay? What happened in there? Nobody would tell me. Patient/doctor shit. And you don't have to get into the details. I just want to know if you're okay."

Not really. The whole thing is emotionally exhausting and frustrating. With a sigh, I lift a shoulder. "Sort of. Beckett told me my powers likely woke during the accident that killed my parents." I stop and take a breath for courage, then tell him what I remember from the accident and the realization Beckett pushed on me. "I've always carried this guilt around with me because I survived and they didn't, but it never occurred to me that I might have been able to save them. Everything about the accident and that night is murky because of the gaps in my memory. I don't know what to believe, but the possibilities are torturing me."

His arm comes around and squeezes me tight. "Or your powers might have already been depleted. We don't have much juice when our powers first activate. Barely anything, really. It's likely you used up your reserve creating the pond. Maybe it's best you don't know."

"Part of me wants to know," I murmur, wiping away the tear sliding down my cheek. "I've got so many questions about that night. Why were they after my dad?"

River snorts. "They were after you."

I shake my head. "My dad had Lionel change my birth certificate. They wouldn't even think I had powers."

"Plenty of people were doing the same thing at the time. It didn't help," River insists. "My mother stole our original birth certificates, and the copies, from the hospital and courthouse records, and yet Raven still knew about us. They're always searching, forcing us to run again and again." Bitterness coats every word.

Is that what I'm going to feel after years of running? "I'm

sorry you didn't have a normal childhood. All I could think about was my parents. I never realized I was lucky to have gotten away. But why didn't they come after me when I was with Lionel?"

"Lionel was in the Army, right? Maybe it has something to do with that," River speculates. "What was his rank?"

"Colonel," I murmur, taking a bite while I think about it. "Sorry, starving." Chicken is a little dry, but not bad. It's free food, and I'm realizing how valuable it is.

He takes a bite too. "That's a good rank, but not sure it would help. Maybe he knew someone higher up?"

Not wanting to reveal Lionel's missions with the special forces, I lift a shoulder. "I told you Lionel knew Jack Harrison. Former Army buddy. Senator. Head of Phoenix. Maybe that helped?"

"Probably," River concedes. His voice lowers an octave. "Will you stay with me tonight?"

My cheeks heat. "You still want me to? I understand if you don't." I dart a glance at his black eye. "Thanks to Oliver, I know how to find my room now."

He stares at me. "Of course I want you to stay with me. For however long I'm here, that will never change. Understand?" There's a note of something I can't place in his voice.

"I don't want you to leave," I blurt out, then wrinkle my nose. "Sorry. That's extremely selfish of me. I know your mom and sister are still out there hiding, and you'll have to go back to them." There's no way he'll stay here without his family. "I'm not sure I'll be ready to go with you, but if not, I'll be here when you get back."

His mouth compresses. "I don't know if I'll come back." When I only stare at him, he continues, "Look. I know you think this is the best place for you, but it's not for me. Not because of the rules, either. I don't want to live in a cage. Even one as padded as this place." His eyes silently plea for my understanding. "I'm hoping you'll go with me."

Torn between the safety here and him, I shrug. "We'll see. But promise me... no matter what... you won't leave without saying goodbye, okay?" I push back at him. "Goodbyes are important." Not having been able to say them to my parents had left this huge hole in my heart. "Promise me."

He hesitates for a long minute, but then solemnly promises. "I promise, I won't leave without saying goodbye."

Relieved, I nod and turn around to finish the rest of my dinner. "Did you choose any classes?"

"Spanish and martial arts," he informs me. "I only speak English, and I figured another language would be useful, especially with Mexico right next door. Maybe it would be easier to hide there instead of the States." His tone is nonchalant, but I can tell he's given the idea more than a passing thought.

"I've always wanted to go there," I tell him with a smile. "After dinner, would you teach me how to pick a lock? It could be an extremely useful skill, and I need all of those I can get. Although I did good hiding from Quaid today."

His face morphs into something comical. "You *hid* from Quaid?"

I snort and explain what he made our class do today. "I remembered what you said about the university and hiding in plain sight, and thought it was a great idea."

He frowns. "Yeah, but don't try it in closed spaces. You could be trapped."

I laugh. "Now you sound like Quaid. Maybe you two have more in common than you think."

River narrows his eyes. "Don't even go down that route. He's an asshole."

As irritated as he makes me, I don't think Quaid's an asshole. Protective. Intense. There's a lot riding on his shoulders, and despite the friction between us, I like knowing he's standing between me and the enemy.

Rolling my eyes, I tell him. "So are you. Not to me, but I can see that side of you." When he looks startled, I wink and change the subject. "Guess what? I shot a gun today!"

"So, you found the safety?" His grin tells me he's remembering me raising the gun at him and trying to pull the trigger. "I'll be sure to remember that in the future."

I shove his shoulder. "Whatever. Yes. I found the safety, Mr. Smartass. My aim, though, appears to be dismal."

He wipes an arm across his brow. "Phew, guess I'm good for a little while."

With a grin, I finish eating, then grab my tray. "Whatever. Let's go. I'm eager to learn another new skill."

Once we reach his room, he shows me his lock picking kit. "It includes tension wrenches, picks, and rakes. I'll teach you how to use this kit and a few other items like bobby pins, paper clips, and a knife. Once you understand how a lock works, you can try to find your own mechanisms."

Tilting my head, I study the pouch in his hand. "Why do you have a kit? Is this something I'll need to put in my survival bag?"

"Yes," he says fervently. "It's not how I got out of the handcuffs at the gas station, but I've used the kit a lot to get in and out of places. Definitely a must for your 'survival' bag."

After ushering us back to the hallway, he locks the door, then demonstrates the tools several times. "The bottom lever is for tension. Once you have that in place, you use the second tool to lift up on each of the five pins. You're looking for the pin that's the hardest to lift, which is called the seized pin. Keep wiggling the tool under it until it lifts. You might hear an audible click or not, but once it's up, you have to find the next seized pin. Once all five pins are up at the same time, it's unlocked."

He hands me the tools and places them properly into the lock. "There. Wiggle the top tool and try to lift the first pin."

Biting my lip, I focus on the tiny hole and finding the pin, but it's way more difficult than it looks. After thirty minutes, I'm sweating, hair is in my eyes, and my shoulders are aching.

"I need a break," I inform him, dropping my hands from the lock and slumping against the wall. "Who taught you to pick a lock?"

His eyes brighten with laughter. "My sister. Smart as a whip. When we went on the run, she looked up all kinds of things from lock picking to prepper survivalist stuff. She wanted to be prepared. She would learn something and make us learn it, too. Lily was insufferable."

I laugh. "How long did it take her to learn how to pick a lock?"

He winces. "Five minutes." I gape at him, and he shakes his head. "She's a genius."

Tilting my head, I consider the pink spreading across his cheeks. "And you?"

He mockingly frowns. "Twenty minutes. Lily never let me live it down."

Determined to get it right, I face the door again and insert the tools. Fifteen minutes later, I'm banging my head against the door. "I'm not getting it." Tossing him a mock glare for not telling me that this was hard.

He wraps his arms around me and places his hands on mine. "Being on the run creates its own urgency. Here. Let me help you." Resting his chin on my shoulder, he guides my fingers and the tools.

My concentration scatters, and it takes me a minute of mindless movement until I can rein in my focus. For the next twenty minutes, I ignore the press of his hard body against mine and the heat generating between us to pick the damn lock. Finally, success! The latch clicks, and I turn the handle. Shock renders me speechless as the door swings open, but River immediately picks me up and swings me around in a circle.

Wearing a matching grin, I wrap my arms around his neck. "I highly doubt it will be that easy on my own."

My eyes lock with his green ones, and I marvel at the gleam of happiness I see in them. Does he see the same in mine? Lionel's death broke my heart into a million pieces, and this new world isn't worth the toll I paid, but somehow, this exact second is full of life and hope.

Holding me to him, his mouth lowers. Strong and compelling, his lips coax mine into joining his in a joyous dance. Full of laughter and mingled desire, our tongues and lips play to a song only we can hear. Walking forward, he pushes the door open, then closed.

My back presses against the cool wood, giving me the leverage I need to wrap my legs around his waist and eliminate the gap between our bodies. His lean chest and hips align with mine perfectly, and we both groan at the feeling. Only skin against skin would be better.

The kiss goes on for eons. Chests heaving the few times we break to stare at each other before desperate need pulls us back for more. It's the best of tortures. Lost in the taste and feel of his lips against mine, I shove aside any rational thought and let the world drift away. Who knew kissing could be this good?

Eventually, he lifts his head. Green eyes drenched with desire stare down at me, but soon conflict creeps in, bringing reality with it. One path leads to something beautiful, but the other rips us apart. Are we willing to take the chance? Neither of us has any words of reassurance for the other. He can't tell me he's going to stay, and I don't know whether I'm willing to leave.

My hand smooths down the back of his head to his neck, and my legs fall to the ground, unsteady but willing to stand at his side no matter what.

Lids lower over bright green eyes, concealing his thoughts, as he pulls me into a tight hug. "From the first moment I saw you, something shifted inside me." He gives a low chuckle. "I didn't account for you. You make me want the impossible." He pauses, taking a deep breath. "But it's not just us. I have to think about them."

My lips turn down, but I understand his feelings. "If my mom and sister were out there and needed me, I wouldn't stay. It would kill me, but I'd leave. And I won't let you stay for the same reasons." Dropping my forehead on his chest, I let his warmth chase away the chill sliding over my body. "Who knows? Maybe fate will find a way for us to be together."

An alarm intrudes into my dreams, and I smile. I've missed waking up to one. Living without a phone has sucked. In my old life, it would wake me up, tell me about the world, show me my emails and calendar, and basically, rule my life.

River taps the phone in his hand to turn off the sound. "Good morning, Sunshine." After a stretch, he eases down and gathers me in his arms. "Looks like we've got a few minutes to relax."

My schedule has me meeting with Beckett every other day, but not today. Grateful for the small reprieve, I turn my attention back to the object of my desire. "Where did you get a phone? And why didn't you get me one?"

He grimaces. "Sorry. I don't like to be out of touch with my... family." Pausing for a second, he looks from me to the phone. "I can get you one, but why don't you ask Oliver first? They seem to be watching you pretty closely. Might be better if it comes from him."

I consider his words and nod. "A phone *and* my go bag. I don't like being without the means to leave." I dart a glance at him and see his smile brighten a bit. After the kiss last night, he tugged me into bed to snuggle. Both of us quietly agreeing to accept whatever happens. Let Fate have her way.

Pressing a kiss against his lips, I ease up from the bed and head toward the door. "I want to change and stuff before class."

I'm excited to see if my manipulation of water was a fluke or not. Until now, I've been scared of using my powers, but whether I like it or not, I'm a part of this world. Might as well start figuring out how to live in it.

He jokingly lunges for me but laughs when he misses. "Go. Learn new stuff. Tell me all about it later." His eyes are bright and happy again this morning.

Thirty minutes later, I'm walking toward Oliver's office, using the tablet as my guide, but as I near, I hear him talking. Not wanting to intrude, I look around for somewhere to wait, but unlike Beckett's office, Oliver doesn't have an outer sanctum with extra seating. I prop myself against the wall a little farther from the door, but I can still hear every word.

"More are arriving every day. You know what he does there. He can't be allowed to continue his operations. None of our actions have contained him. He's gained more power and become increasingly less concerned with following the established guidelines. It has to stop. If that means going rogue, we're ready," Oliver tells the person, his voice sharp and to the point.

Nobody replies, which means he must be on the phone. I wonder if he's talking about Hightower. Does that mean Raven's captured more individuals? What are they doing with them? I creep a little closer.

"I'll stand down for now, but we need to see movement. Fast," he states firmly.

For a second, there's silence, then I hear something slam. Listening intently, I wait, wondering if he's still on the phone. He strides out of his office but comes to a halt when he sees me lingering in the hall.

"Sorry, I didn't want to interrupt," I mutter awkwardly, tapping on the tablet. "Are we still having class?"

His perfectly pressed navy suit is molded to his broad shoulders as if it was custom made. There's something about a man in a suit. Or maybe it's *this* man in a suit, like he was born to wear it.

Oliver's blue-grey eyes seem more blue against the navy fabric. Too bad they don't give away his thoughts. Roving over my face and body, they relay nothing, which puts me on edge. I shift from side to side.

He slips off the jacket he's wearing, revealing a crisp white button-down shirt and surprisingly, well-defined muscles. "We are. Outside. I need to get out of this office for a while." One hand gestures for me to start walking.

"Okay," I agree, almost jumping when I feel his other hand come up and lightly rest against my back. A loaded tension fills the air between us. Frantically, I scramble for something to say. "Can I get a phone? And my go bag back?" Why do I sound like a two-year-old asking for milk and cookies?

Not once do his steps slow, but there's a heavy pause before he asks, "Are you planning on leaving?" He stares down at me, eyes watchful and cautious.

My hands wring together as I try to think about what I want to say, especially to him. "I'm very, very grateful for all of your help and Quaid's and Jax's, too." I nervously pluck at the grey sweatshirt, drawing it away from my body. "Obviously, I know I can't have my old life back, but this place feels like a prison. With everything so topsy-turvy, I need some sense of normalcy, like I'm still me." I wrinkle my nose. "Even the tan buildings make me feel like I'm either in the service, a criminal, or trapped in The Twilight Zone." Okay, maybe that was a *little* overboard.

His mouth twitches. "How do you know you're not?"

I jerk my head around and grin at him. "A joke? Damn. I'm definitely in an episode."

He laughs, and the dimple in his cheek deepens to something sexy.

I take a deep breath and continue, "Look, I know it's silly. It's just hard to leave everything behind, and without Lionel here to center me, I'm second-guessing every decision."

He's quiet for a few minutes. "I never thought about it like that, but that's not a surprise." With a grimace, he looks down at his suit. "I've been wearing some semblance of a uniform my whole life, carrying out orders given by others, and following their plans." His hand contracts against my back as if he wants to clench it into a fist, but instead, he sweeps it down my back.

After a deep breath, he continues, "Here's what I can do. I'll see if I can figure out a better clothing option for everyone, and I'll give you back your go bag, but no phone. I'm sorry. If we allow everyone to carry a phone, our security will be worthless. They're too easy to track. I can promise when you're ready to leave, we'll give you a phone to take with you, though."

Swallowing hard, I look away. I don't want to give away the fact that River has one or how desperate I am for my own. "Deal." Outside, the sun beats down on my forearms where I've pushed up the sleeves of my grey sweatshirt. "Where are we going?"

He points to the grouping of trees in front of us. "There's a stream in there. I thought it would be a good place for you to practice your power."

Butterflies dance in my stomach. "Okay, but remember, I've only used it twice, and both were in extreme circumstances," I say with trepidation. What if nothing happens? Will he be irritated?

"Tell me about the first time," he orders without any hesitation. When I don't say anything, he stops and places a hand on my arm. "This isn't going to be easy, but I need to know what triggered you to use your powers. It will help with unlocking them."

My brows come together. I'm not sure what he means, but since I don't even know how I used them, I don't ask. Quietly, I tell him what happened in the accident. "The next thing I know, I'm sitting in a pond, staring at my parents' car that's in flames with them in it. I don't remember what I thought or if I realized I used my power. The moment was brief and full of anguish. A blur, then I passed out."

"And the second time?" he asks softly as we reach the stream.

I stare at the slightly muddy water trickling through the sand and rocks. There's very little to indicate it's even flowing. No noise, only the tiniest movement against the backdrop of one of the rocks.

Nausea rises, forcing me to swallow hard. Procrastinating a few more minutes, I squat down and scoop up a handful of liquid, then let it slide through my fingers to the ground. "Someone was attacking me. I used water to defend myself." I stand and lift my chin, looking over at him. Bare bone facts, but it covers the basics.

He stiffens and turns to the side. "Thank you. That's helpful." He begins rolling up one sleeve of his pristine white shirt. "Has anyone told you about my ability?"

Anxiously, I stare at him and shake my head.

He finishes the second sleeve and drops his hands to his side, then turns back to me. "In its simplest terms, I have the ability to influence your mind." He holds up a hand when I step back in alarm. "Hold up. First, I want you to try to use your power without my influence. If that doesn't work, we'll decide together what to do next. Every choice is yours. I won't force you to do anything. I swear." His hand raises in a ninety-degree angle with three fingers showing, and I snort.

"Isn't that the Boy Scout oath?"

He dips his chin. "It is. I take it very seriously, too."

I stare at him, trying to decide whether I should trust him. Lionel did. Said he was a good man. His ability is making me uneasy, though. It's basically mind control.

With a sigh, I wave a hand. "Fine. Let's give it a go."

I look down at the stream. I don't recall using my powers during the accident with my parents, so I concentrate on the feelings I had when Trent was trying to kill me. Terror. Anger. Fear. Hatred. Letting the emotions swirl inside me, I close my eyes and picture Trent. The resolution on his face. His ice-cold determination. The smirk on his lips.

Fury at everything that's been taken from me rises, too. The maelstrom of moments that have brought me to this place. Here with Oliver. I raise my hands and open my eyes.

Water flows gently over the riverbed. Frustrated, I immediately close my eyes and try again, but the result is the same.

Oliver raises an eyebrow, but I clench my jaw and shake my head. I don't want his help. I try again. And again. And again. But no matter how many times I try, nothing happens. I want to scream my frustration to the world. Why isn't this easier for me? Blowing out a huge sigh, I finally drop my hands in defeat.

"You've suppressed your magic for years. Maybe as some kind of unconscious punishment for not saving your parents or perhaps because it scared you. Unfortunately, power that only deploys as a defense mechanism is unstable," Oliver speculates in a steady voice. "If you don't want my help, you're going to need to let Beckett in, which could mean remembering the night of the crash or the more recent attack and pushing through those painful memories."

Shuddering, I contemplate the thought of reliving everything and almost ask Oliver for his help, but the idea of someone influencing my brain is more terrifying than dredging up painful memories.

"Wielding power is much harder than I thought it would be," I admit with sigh. "Lionel made it look so easy. He manipulated the fire at the gas station for a long time. Only at the end did his hand actually shake, but I couldn't tell if that was due to his injury or the depletion of his power."

Oliver's head jerks toward me, his eyebrow raised. "What injury?"

"Raven shot him. In the back," I explain furiously. "It's why I left him behind. He couldn't walk and refused to let me stay. Hardest thing I've ever done. Last time I lost a parent, Lionel saved me—forced me out of bed, made me go to school, and basically, ensured I could live without them."

It's hard to remember those days. "Lionel was my rock. My anchor. Now, he's gone too." Those words cut through my bones like a scythe.

Oliver steps up beside me. "You know, I'm told I make a good rock. Older. Wiser. Solid. Dependable. Traces of humor." He drops his gaze down to his suit. "A bit stuffy, but that's not necessarily a bad thing."

I almost snort. This man isn't the least bit stuffy. He's a little older, certainly wiser, and his dry sense of humor is unexpectedly charming.

Is he being nice because of Lionel, or is about that sense of duty he wears like his suit? "Yes, but can I trust you?" His answer is key. Not because I'm looking for Oliver to be my rock, but because I need a little assurance about whether I should stay or not.

"I never lie," he informs me, his expression solemn. "However, I'm very aware trust is earned, not given. Instead of telling you, I'll do my best to show you."

The fact that he's taking this seriously smooths the ragged edges of the huge hole in my heart.

"Thank you."

I scan his serious features, trying to guess his age, but it's hard to tell. He's a major in the Army. If he graduated West Point at twenty-one and it took him around ten years to achieve his rank, he would be thirty-one or thirty-two. Eight or nine years older than me. I don't mind. I like the fact that he's older. He could be... I instantly reject the thought of him as an older brother... a friend. With a smile, I follow him back to campus, where he points out the direction of the gym.

Her hair is pinned up, exposing her delicate neck. I slide my gaze along the long lines to the curve at her shoulder. There's a slight flush to her cheeks. Is that because of the sun or that idiot River? I scowl at the thought of him. I don't care what Jax or Beckett say. I don't hate everybody on sight. Just him. Look at Greer. She's irritating and naïve as hell, but I like her. With everything thrown at her, she could have easily fallen apart, but instead, she's here, learning to navigate our world. River's hiding behind that arrogant mask of his.

Her eyes meet mine and narrow, and I toss her a challenging look of my own. She's feisty, and it fuels the fire in my blood. For some reason, I particularly annoy her. Good. That means I push her out of her comfort zone. Her lips press tightly together. Oops, guess I've been staring at her for a while. I tense, waiting for her to blast me, but instead, she turns away. Wait, what?!

Frowning, I tilt my head to look closer. There's a lot of thinking going on behind those forest green eyes of hers today. I'd ask if she was okay, but she refuses to let us help her, preferring to run to River.

"Everyone, line up!" I order, raising my voice over the chatter. "Today, we're going to learn some self-defense techniques. Before we begin, I want everyone to remember that we're only using these tactics to help us escape. Not fight. Got it?"

The young man with electrokinesis frowns but says nothing. He came in a week ago and hasn't settled down yet. I doubt he ever will. If he could control his anger, he'd make a damn fine soldier. Add in the power to manipulate the movement of energy, including the electricity he wields so easily, and he'd be an outstanding one. Maybe I should at least talk to him about joining us.

While it's top of mind, I sweep down the line, mentally tagging everyone I think would be ideal. Our time with the Army is coming to an end. We can't serve the needs of the government and protect the rights of those like us without conflict, but we need others who are willing to stand beside us.

The older gentleman is fast thinking and capable. The dark-haired girl, too. In fact, almost all of the six who evaded my capture yesterday would likely fit the mold. Except for Greer. I thought the loss of Lionel would fill her with the determination to fight against Raven, but instead, her main focus is a new life. A twinge of envy slides through me, but I shove it down. Normal life isn't for me.

"Greer," I call out, making her jump. "I need a volunteer." With a slight curl of my lips, I can practically hear her grind her teeth in response.

She flashes me an innocent smile, then turns toward the others. "Anyone else want to volunteer? I'm too nervous."

My lips flatten. Sneaky. I open my mouth to order her, but the girl with the dark hair strides forward, and I resign myself to working with her.

"Thank you for volunteering, Talia," I tell her, and everyone chuckles, including Greer. "Okay, let's get started. I'll put you in a variety of holds. You do everything you can to get out of them. If you escape, you get a point. If you don't, I'll teach you, and everyone else, several ways to get out of the hold."

Coming up behind Talia, I wrap my arms around her neck in a rear chokehold. "Go!"

Talia immediately drops her chin against her chest to create a bit of space between her neck and my forearm. Then, she goes on the attack. Reaching for my eyes, ears, or whatever she can grab. Once I'm distracted, she twists her head to the side, slides out of my hold and drops into a squat. Kicking back, she immediately connects with my knee, then jumps up and starts running.

I let out a piercing whistle to halt her sprint. "Good job! Now, let's go over some more options and a list of things that you shouldn't do. For example... the squat wasn't wrong, but you should avoid anything that takes you close to the ground. Losing your balance could cost you your life."

For the next thirty minutes, I put Talia in different holds. She does well. I'll definitely ask her to join us. Fast thinker and light on her feet. Plus, I believe she has the ability to control air and wind. Very useful.

"Okay, let's break up into pairs," I tell them, gesturing to the area around us. "One person will practice the holds, and the other will try to escape. In fifteen minutes, we'll trade off."

The young electro immediately walks up to Greer, and I see her smile in return. She points to an area in the gym, and they walk over to the spot. Interestingly, she takes on my role and puts him into a chokehold first. I watch him easily get out of it by following the techniques I taught them. Forcing my gaze to leave her, I walk around and slowly correct a hold or escape as needed. The whole time, my attention constantly drifts back to Greer and electricity boy.

David, that's his name, I mentally snap, irritated at my lack of detail.

Finally, I get around to where they're practicing and stop to watch them. All the laughing and joking ceases when they realize I'm watching. With a cough, David gestures for Greer to turn around so he can put her in a hold. She reluctantly presents her back to him.

He places her in a rear chokehold. She dips her chin and quickly escapes. Much faster than I anticipated. Maybe there is more to her defensive skills.

Intrigued, I decide to keep watching. They go through a few more, and she easily escapes each time. At first, I think he's letting her off the hook, but the longer I watch, the more I realize she has actual skills. Maybe Lionel taught her. That would make sense. Last hold.

David turns to face Greer, and I watch as her breathing increases. She's nervous about this one. He raises his hands and wraps them around her neck. Greer freezes, then shakes her head. Her expression changes to fear, and her movements become desperate. Her hands come up, and she beats against David's arms, but he remains firm.

Her eyes glaze over, and she raises her hands high, bringing them together in a circle. She looks up, and I follow, but there's nothing above her. I move to stop the exercise, but water suddenly shoots out of the bottles next to me, and I jump back.

"Greer! Snap out of it," I order her in a hard voice, but it doesn't pierce the barrier of the nightmare she's reliving. "David, let her go and back up." I'm hoping the removal of his hands helps her return to the present.

Eyes wide, David releases Greer and steps back several feet.

I move to her side and stroke a hand down her back. "It's okay, Greer. You're safe. I've got you." Water flies toward me, and I incinerate it with my fire. Hissing fills the air, and the faintest of smoke rises along with it. Greer pauses at the sound, then lifts her left hand and sends another stream of water at me. She's locked in the nightmare. The energy surrounding her increases exponentially.

With a grunt, I let the water hit, then spin her around, and clasp my arms around her in a chokehold, trapping her hands inside it. "Listen to my voice. You're safe. Release your powers." If she doesn't snap out of it, I'm going to have to put her to sleep.

"Please," she whimpers. "I've never done anything to you. Why do you want to kill me?" Her voice trails off as her hands continue to weave intricate patterns with the water. Fists clenching, she pulls the air taut as if a rope is in her hands.

After watching her movements for a minute, I realize what she's unconsciously doing. She's recreating a scene. I watch every motion and slowly realize what she's done. *Damn it.* I lean in close. "Greer. It's Quaid. You're safe. I won't let anyone hurt you. I promise."

"You promise?" Her voice is barely a whisper, but the fear in her tone is high.

"Nobody will hurt you," I assure her, tempering the anger in my voice. I want to know who attacked her. No wonder she's suppressing her power. She's terrified of it.

She shudders and sags in my arms, and I slowly release my hold. I turn her around to make sure she's back with us. Her green eyes stare steadily back at me, clear as crystal, then drop to the floor. I reluctantly step away.

With bright red cheeks, she turns to the class. "Sorry. I got a little carried away."

Her chuckle is forced, but few will judge her here. We're all in this together.

After seeing their acceptance, she walks over to David. "I'm so sorry. If I'd known that would happen, I'd have warned you."

He flashes her a wide grin. "We all have our demons, sweet pea. Don't worry about it." Walking over to her, he slings an arm across her shoulders. "Do you want to try again or give it a rest?"

It takes a minute, but her chin slowly rises. "Again." She looks at me in defiance as if expecting me to say no. But getting back on the horse is the best thing she can do, so I give her a nod of encouragement. Besides, I'm too busy reining in a storm of emotions.

My phone alerts me to the time. "Okay, one more hold, then get to your next class. That's all for today." I watch David gently put her in a wristlock. Good choice.

Deliberately leaving them, I stride out of the gym to text Oliver. I've learned a few things about our little bird today. She definitely has a trigger. More interestingly ... I didn't feel her power until she used it. Then it was like a tidal wave exploding into the room. We typically feel powers, active or not, but hers is completely dormant until it isn't. Like a switch.

When it's on, it's almost sentient, searching for water. But when it only found the small amounts in the water bottles, it wasn't appeased. She wasn't appeased. I felt her power increase. Unconsciously, she wanted more. Tried to pull it from the very air. It's why I put her in a hold.

Someone attacked her, choked her, and she used her powers to kill him. Although she didn't admit it, I'm absolutely sure. Lionel never mentioned it to us. Did he know? Was he afraid we wouldn't accept her if he told us? Or did he not know? Why the secrecy?

More unsettling was the tug I felt when she used her powers. Familiar and rare. It doesn't make sense. Why her?

Practically stumbling to my next class, I force one step in front of the other. If Quaid hadn't stepped in, I don't know what would have happened. I clasp my arms together, missing the feel of his strength wrapped around me. Yawning, I shake my head. Why am I so tired? An arm slips through mine and pulls me close. Startled, I turn to my right to see Talia, the dark-haired girl from class. She looks to be somewhere around my age. Maybe a year or two older. Hard to tell.

"You were channeling a lot of energy back there," Talia says with a speculative look. "Do you not use your power a lot?"

How can she tell? "No, why?"

"I manipulate air," she begins with an easy swirl of her finger. A cool breeze sweeps across my face. "At first, I had little control. Either it was barely working or blowing gale force winds. Unstable. Hungry. Today, your power felt similar."

"Good to know there's hope," I say with a sigh. "Most of the time, I don't feel the power inside me. Part of me is glad, though. It's destructive. I wish I didn't have any."

She slips her arm from mine and flashes a sympathetic smile. "I used to feel that way. My life was good, full of love and friends. Until they took it all away. Wishing for normal is useless." Her expression turns fierce, determination in every line. "You'd do better to embrace your powers. I'm glad I have the ability to protect myself. I wish I could do more... like fight." She pats my back and strides toward Jax.

Another Hightower and Raven victim. It's sad. More than ever, I wish I could go back in time. Save my parents. Save Lionel. Have a normal life surrounded by all of them. Instead, I'm here with River and Talia and David and all these others. Why? What are we trying to do? Find a fake life? It feels pointless.

Jax raises his voice. "Everyone, find a spot along the range and practice what you learned yesterday." His ocean-blue eyes find mine, and he raises an eyebrow. "If you need help, ask nicely."

Needing space from everyone, I head to one of the spots on the outer edge and pick up the headset. I eye the loaded gun with distaste. Another symbol of this war I don't like. I want to help people regain their mobility, not take it away. I thought it would help to learn new skills, but I'm second guessing this one.

A hand presses against my back, startling me. Jax plucks one side of the headset off. "Tough day, beautiful?"

I turn in the booth to face him. "I don't want to shoot. This isn't me."

His eyes rove over my face, and he lifts a shoulder. "You don't have to do this."

"Honestly, it's kind of terrifying," I admit in a low voice.

He picks up the gun and takes the stance to shoot. I hold out the headset, but he shakes his head. "My abilities give me everything a sniper needs, including the power to turn sound on and off. Put them on."

A shiver runs down my spine as I reach up and slide them

on. Tensing, I stare at the target in front of us and wait for him to pull the trigger. He shifts and fires. Again and again for at least a solid minute. Rapid firing. Then, he puts the gun down and lowers my headset.

"Let's see how we did," he says cheerfully. "Hit the button."

I bring the target in closer and stare at the paper in disbelief. Not only did he hit the target, but he created a smiley face around the bullseye. My eyes flick from the target to him.

With a grin, he reaches out and grabs the target. "See. Shooting can be fun. Not scary." He hands the paper to me. "A souvenir."

I shake my head, refusing to take it. "You keep it. I need... to go. I'll let Oliver know I want to drop this class." Pivoting, I hurry away from the booth and the man standing there with his artwork.

There's only one person I want to see right now. Entering the building, I hurry to his room and knock on the door.

He takes one look at my face and opens the door wider. "What happened?"

I step into River's arms and bury my face in his shoulder, the story rushing out of me in a plethora of incoherent sentences. "David choked me, and I somehow got trapped in the past. My powers burst out of me like they were alive. I couldn't control them. Quaid had to step in because I couldn't get back to the present." I sob. "I don't want this. Any of it."

River continues to rub my back and hold me until I can calm down. "It's okay." Then he leads me over to sit on the bed. "Start over. Who's David, and why was he choking you? Do I need to go find this asshole?"

I wave a hand. "Quaid's self-defense class. David is a student in my class. We were practicing holds. Everything was going fine until he put his hands around my neck, like he intended to choke me."

River's shoulders relax. "Good to know. So, this triggered a... nightmare?" His voice is hesitant, as if he's confused.

I freeze. I hadn't meant to admit that part, but I guess if I'm going to have to relive my worst day with Beckett, I'd rather do it with someone I trust first.

"My personal nightmare," I admit with a sigh. Scooting up the bed, I pull my legs up and wrap my arms around them. River joins me, calm steadiness flowing from his green eyes while he waits for me to tell him my story.

"In college, I had a stalker. Maybe two, but that's irrelevant. One of them saw the mark on my shoulder and researched my parents. He found out my father had powers, which meant I must have them, too. At the time, I didn't even know anything about powers or this world or Rh-negative blood. He did, though. Apparently, one of us killed his mother," I say bitterly. How the past shapes us all.

"Can I see the mark?" River asks softly.

I slip my sweatshirt off my shoulder until he can see the blob on my shoulder. I peer down at it and notice it's changed a bit since I last looked at it. That's weird. "It's a scar I got from the accident with my parents. From hitting a tree or something."

River mutters something under his breath.

"What is it?"

"Nothing. Sorry. So, what happened with the stalker?" He nudges me.

"He and his friends kidnapped me. Beat me. Threw me off a cliff," I blurt out quickly, wanting to get the worst part done. Some of the guilt I've been feeling dissipates with those words. They started it. Not me. At any time, they could have taken me home. Or even left me in the woods. Either of which would have been better than what they did.

"Fortunately for me, there was a waterfall with a pool below. It broke my fall," I continue. "Unfortunately, he saw I was still alive and came down to finish me off. So did his friend."

My fingers twist together as I try to find the courage to finish. River reaches over and entwines his fingers with mine, his thumb sliding across the back of my hand in a soothing manner. I flash him a grateful smile.

"All along, I thought he was crazy, but when his hands started squeezing my neck, he smirked at me. One little gesture, but the thought of his... glee at my death... something inside me stood up in fury. It consumed me until all I could think about was killing him. Water was lapping at my legs, and it's as if it spoke to me. Suddenly, I knew what I could do. So, I did."

I stare at him, hoping he'll understand, but his head is tilted like he's waiting for me to finish. "I killed them."

His thumb stills. "Who did you kill?"

I shake my head.

He gets up on his knees to face me. "Tell me who. I won't judge you. Please."

Staring at him, I bite my lip, thinking about it. Maybe it's time someone knew. Lionel's gone. If something happens to me, I want the world to know why.

"Trent. Hightower and his buddy."

"Fuck. Fuck. Fuck!" he says, punching the bed with each word. "He'll never stop hunting you." He drops his head into his hands. "There's nothing I can do. I can't keep you safe from him. He's too strong, and his reach is too far. Maybe Phoenix is your best hope. Lionel thought so."

Sadness drips from his tone, but I shake my head, refusing to admit defeat. "I can have a life outside of here. With you.

And your family. Oliver told me Phoenix will give me a new identity. We can find somewhere quiet or go to Mexico. I don't care. Don't... give up on me. Please. I want to live a normal life."

He pulls me into his arms. "I don't see how. You don't realize how ruthless he is. If you leave this compound, it's only a matter of time."

All the same thoughts I've been thinking but to hear them come out of River's mouth is even more devastating. I stare at the white walls around me. The lack of windows. It's suffocating. This will not be my life. I refuse to accept this existence. But those are my decisions to make, not his.

I'm glad he knows, though. Makes our decisions easier. River has a family. His mother and sister are his priority. I don't want to become another obligation, especially not one that comes with a bomb. I hug him tighter. He already saved me once. That's enough.

"How did it feel using your powers?" he asks, his voice hollow and distant.

I open my mouth to tell him how uncontrolled and unstable it felt, but there's been enough sharing today. I don't want to lie, though. "It felt kind of weird, but familiar, too. Talia, a girl in my class, said it would get easier the more I practice."

He nods but says nothing. What else is there to say?

River's silence pushed me to spend last night in my room. He protested, but I could tell he needed some time away from me.

When the alarm on the tablet goes off, I tap it off. Eyes gritty from lack of sleep, I stand in the hot shower and stare at the tan floor and the water flowing down the drain. My power might not be the coolest, but there's certainly an abundance of it in the world. Quickly finishing, I get out and dry off.

My lip curls when I reach for a clean set of grey sweats, but I force myself to thank the universe for something clean to wear. After all, I could be wearing the same clothes day in and day out. Jordan had very few clothes. Barely enough to fill a backpack. Ready to run, right?

Not wanting to see River, I rush through the breakfast hall, grabbing toast and juice, then head out the door to the bench I've claimed as my own. Set between two trees, the iron bench provides a peaceful place to sit in the sun.

Nibbling on my toast, I stare out into the field in front of me, waiting for the sun to show its bright face. I'm cold in places I didn't know were a part of me. Hollow alcoves inside my body where the darkness and sadness reside. I need the rays to reach those spots and shine their brightest light.

Two men come into my line of sight, running side-by-side near the fence, muscular legs in sync, chests out, as if they've done this a million times. Oliver and Quaid. Phoenix's fearless leaders. I stare at them, wondering what makes them take on such a role. Did the Army force them, or perhaps Oliver's father, Senator Jack Harrison? Or is it some sense of obligation to those of us with powers?

Their commitment to the people in this compound is undeniable. They work hard to prepare them for the outside world. A reality check on how to evade and survive. But is that enough? Based on what I overheard in Oliver's office, Raven's out of control, capturing more of us every day. The few soldiers I've seen here aren't enough to fight the enemy. At some point, Raven will turn its eyes toward Phoenix. Who will save them?

Their heads swivel at the same time to look at me, and the burn of their stares across the expanse of dirt and grass is enough to make me squirm. What will they do if they find out my secret? Kick me out? Maybe that would be for the best. At some point, Hightower will find me. Everyone around me is in danger.

My second alarm goes off. Ten minutes until class. The two turn in my direction. Tanned skin glistens in the morning sun, and I lick my lips, admiring the muscles flexing hard as they push their bodies to the max. Older but still hot. These are men in every sense of the word. Not wanting them to see me staring, I lift my face to the sun's warmth, but I don't need it anymore. All my hollow spaces are filled with heat.

"Is everything okay?" Oliver asks in a slightly breathless voice.

I open my eyes to find them both standing in front of me, their Army green shorts and tanks leaving little to the imagination, and I straighten under their scrutiny. I'm sure they're used to women drooling, but not me.

Oliver's unusual eyes are more blue than grey this morning. Intense, they drill into me, searching and assessing. Of course, Quaid's brows are pulled together in his usual scowl. His amber eyes are sweeping me from head to toe. He's either looking for a weapon or gauging my physical state. The two of them are quite a pair.

"Just enjoying the sun and my breakfast," I tell them, holding up my glass of juice. "Do you run every morning?" If so, I might have to find another bench to sit on. For my peace of mind.

Oliver's head tilts. "We do." He glances at his watch. "If I'm going to make your session with Beckett this morning, I need to grab a shower. You're good with me attending, right?"

Uneasy, I stare at him. "I didn't realize you were joining us." It makes sense, though. If he's going to help me with my powers, he'll need to know the best way to approach it. Me. "It's fine." Fine is such a fucked-up word. It's like these grey sweatpants, which are not fine.

Oliver must agree because a flash of concern sweeps across his face but instead of probing me further, his eyes dart to Quaid, who nods. "Right. I'll see you in ten." He takes off jogging toward the facility.

Quaid props his foot up on the bench beside me to stretch one of his long legs. Seriously? Is that really necessary?

"Are you doing okay this morning?" His tone is gruff, as if he's not sure how to proceed.

Don't look. Don't look. My eyes slide to the leg beside me and the muscles on display. Instead of hair, tattoos cover his thick, muscular thighs and one of his calves. I almost whimper. *You were almost a damn physical therapist!* I mentally yell at myself. You've seen skin. Muscles. Nothing new.

"All good," I reply, surging to my feet. "I'm fine." There's that damn word again. Now, I'm scowling. "See you later."

River's leaving. I'm trapped. I don't know how to get to point B or even where point B is. Will I ever be safe again? Can someone give me a manual for using my damn powers? And why the hell does Mr. Surly look so damn good? All that is the tip of the proverbial iceberg.

He grunts like he doesn't like my answer but doesn't stop me, which sort of pisses me off further. I dump the empty juice bottle on my way to Beckett's office.

Beckett's waiting for me when I arrive at his office, leaning against the doorframe, looking cool, calm, and collected, and it freaking irks me. His gaze narrows, and it's all I can do not to roll my eyes. He's probably evaluating my mental state, which, to be honest, is kind of shit this morning. Straightening, he motions for me to join him. I grab the same seat on the couch like last time, but this time, he sits next to me.

"I'm sorry. I pushed too hard on our first visit," he says, looking at me. His light grey eyes stare at me, waiting for an answer. They remind me of Oliver's when he's irritated, but Beckett's eyes don't have any blue in them. His are sort of silvery grey. "I mean it. I should have realized it was too much."

It was, but denial is my best friend. I open my mouth, but the only word that comes to mind is fine, so I close it. It's rude, but honestly, I'm not sure I care this morning.

Oliver arrives, dressed in a solid navy suit with a light blue shirt that brings out the blue in his eyes. Beckett moves to the chair across from me. The second he settles into it; a cloak of professionalism falls over him. That must be his usual spot. He motions to the seat beside me, but Oliver takes the chair on my right.

"Greer. Oliver wants to use his mental ability to help you discover the pathway to your powers. He's explained your reservations, though, which I completely understand. Having someone in your head is unnerving," Beckett begins. Oliver clears his throat, but Beckett ignores him.

"We also need to develop your control mechanism, correct?" he asks, tapping his pen on the notepad in front of him.

I nod. Quaid probably told them both what happened.

"This is your decision, not ours. What do you want?" he asks, flicking a glance at Oliver. "Do you want to use your powers?

Oliver immediately leans back in his chair, giving me space.

I look from him to Beckett. In the Army together for a long time, it's clear they all speak some second language. One the rest of us can't hear. Another aggravating point.

"I want to be normal, but since that doesn't seem to be on the table, I guess I need to find a way to use and control my abilities," I concede, knowing the choice was made that day by the waterfall. It just took me this long to realize it. "But I don't want to have to keep reliving that day in order to use my powers."

"Quaid said David's hands around your throat threw you into the past?" Beckett's question is light but probing.

"Someone tried to kill me," I admit, feeling a tightness around my throat. "The water came to my aid and shared its secrets with me. It told me I could use it as a weapon, so I did."

Both Oliver and Beckett sit up straighter. "What did you do?"

My lips tremble, but I spit out the truth. "I killed him. And his friend." Silence descends in the room, but I can't tell what they're thinking. Will they kick me out?

Oliver leans forward and takes my hand in his. Is he going to take control of my mind? Fear rises. Beckett reaches out, but with one look from Oliver, his hand drops to his lap.

Oliver gently squeezes my hand. "Does anyone else know? Do I need to send a clean-up crew to get rid of the evidence?"

I blink. Did he really offer to help me hide the bodies?

"We have a crew on stand-by," he assures me. "The last thing you need is to be looking over your shoulder."

If he sends a crew, they'll know I killed Trent Hightower. The son of our enemy. I shake my head several times. "No, it's f... good." Not fine. Definitely not fine. "Lionel helped me." Sort of true. He hid the truck, but not the bodies.

The corners of Oliver's eyes narrow, as if he knows I'm not telling the whole truth, but his gaze remains steady. "If you change your mind, let me know. The last thing we need is Hightower and his men using this against you. Or us."

I stare back at him, then force a smile. "Yep. Now that's settled, how do we begin?"

That was close. It's obvious I won't be able to stay here for long, though. If I do, this could end badly for them, which brings me back to the point of today. If I'm going to be on my own, I need to learn how to wield water.

Beckett stands. "I'd like to start with the same scenario that triggered you yesterday." He motions for me to follow him to the center of the room. "You, too, Oliver."

Oliver joins us and gives Beckett an uneasy look. "I can use my mind to do this."

Beckett looks at me. "Here's what we're going to do. Oliver is either going to wrap his hands around your neck, or he's going to use his mind to make it feel like he's choking you. The second you're triggered, and your powers rise, I'm going to calm you. Distance you from the pain and emotions. Then I want you to try to use your powers."

Although I hate the choking part, I get why he's starting with it. Normally, I'd protest Beckett's mental influence on my emotions, but after yesterday's more explosive reaction, I know I'll need it.

He raises an eyebrow, silently asking if I'm good with his plan. "I want to start disassociating your powers from the event. What do you think? Remember, you're calling the shots. If you don't want to do this, you don't have to."

I nod my agreement. "I want to."

Oliver shifts from one foot to the other. I wonder which one makes him more uneasy.

"His hands. Not his mind." The idea of mind control is terrifying. I like my mind the way it is. Without influence.

He stiffens, then dips his chin and moves in closer. "Ready?" Five inches taller than me, he's around the same height as Trent. He places his hands on my neck. Unlike Trent's cold fingers, Oliver's are warm, but the second they wrap around my throat, my pulse skyrockets.

I take a deep breath in and smell the soap he used in the shower. The clean scent isn't remotely close to the luxury cologne Trent wore, and it helps center me. "Yes."

"Close your eyes," Beckett tells me. "It will help you fall into the past faster."

I let my eyes drift closed.

"Squeeze," Beckett orders him. "She has to break through this barrier."

His fingers tighten, and my airway narrows. I try to take a deep breath but can't. My vision darkens, and I claw at the hands on my throat. Trent appears. His intent clear. My hands slacken as I almost give up, but then that smirk appears. My fury rises. The power inside me with it.

A hand slides across my shoulder, and the fury dies. But I still can't breathe. I inhale, but there's little air. Then wavering power finds its strength. To resist. To fight. Hands loosen around my neck. I inhale deeply, drawing in as much air as possible, then open my eyes.

Anger simmers in the blue-grey depths in front of me.

In reaction, I step back, automatically raising my hand against him. Water from the glass on the table arcs in his direction. He steps to the side at the last minute, and it falls harmlessly to the floor. I stare at my hand. A defensive reaction but nothing out of control like yesterday, and I was aware of it happening.

"I did it," I say, looking at my hand before I drop it back to my side. "I wasn't exactly calm, but I stayed in control."

"Good job," Beckett praises me. "I think this is going to work. We'll use this tactic until you can call it forth without a trigger. It shouldn't take long to map the neuropathways. Maybe a couple of sessions."

Oliver's fingers glide gently over my throat, and his mouth compresses. "I have to go." With one last look at my neck, he storms out of Beckett's office.

"Is he going to be okay?" I ask, hoping he's not angry with me.

Beckett looks at the door and tilts his head. "Eventually." His gaze slides to me. "We'll get you some cream for your neck. More importantly, how are you doing?"

"I'm good. Really good," I say, to my astonishment. My shitty emotions dissipating under a ray of hope. "Thank you."

Her dark green eyes full of fear, the almost imperceptible flinch when she saw my anger; it nearly brought me to my knees. I storm out of Beckett's office. Wrapping my hands around her throat felt wrong. *Bastard.* If he wasn't dead...

Fists clenched, I stop and force my anger to recede before it sweeps over the whole compound. It's been a long time since my control was tested. After a couple of minutes of concentration, a steady calm falls over me, and I continue to my office.

Lionel didn't mention she eliminated anyone, which is odd. The few missions we went on together showed him to be meticulous and well organized. Although Brad did say they were in a rush to leave. I make a mental note to ask him for more details.

Quaid's pacing my office when I arrive. "How did it go?" His amber eyes are almost burning with the fierceness of his emotions.

I tilt my head to study him. The only time he's ever calm is on a mission, but he's more on edge than usual. Amber eyes bright. Muscles tight and poised for action. Is it Greer or the conversation he knows is coming?

Crossing to the bar next to my desk, I pour myself a finger

of bourbon and down it in one gulp. Then, pour another and take it to my desk. "It went well."

His hands clench the top of the chair in front of my desk as he tries to rein in his impatience. He snorts, eyes falling to the glass in my hand. "Clearly. What happened? Is she okay?"

"She didn't want me to use my abilities," I inform him, knowing he's going to want every detail. He always does. Even at West Point, he gathered details like a squirrel hiding nuts for the winter. I spread my hands on top of my desk and stare at them. Today wasn't the first time I'd choked someone, but it's the first time without lethal intent. Never a beautiful young woman who needed my help.

He drops into the chair. "Damn." His hand rubs his head. "How did she do?"

"Beckett's plan worked," I tell him, swallowing the bourbon in my hand to get rid of the sour taste lingering on my tongue. "She maintained control and her awareness."

"You felt it, didn't you?" he asks, eyes narrowed on me.

Shifting my jaw from one side to the other, I return his stare. "I did. She's powerful. Or she will be when she learns to wield her abilities. Maybe it's because they've been repressed all these years. I don't know."

"You know what I mean," he states flatly.

With a deep sigh, I contemplate the empty glass but set it to the side. My calendar is jammed packed with meetings and decisions today. "The second she used her power; it tugged at mine, searching for a response."

Quaid leans back in satisfaction. "There's a connection. What it means, I don't know. We've felt it with others, but it's always been muted. With her, it's different. She sparks against me like a match."

Hearing noise outside my office, I put the empty glass into my desk drawer and stand. "We'll table this for later."

Jax, Beckett, and several other officers enter, and I slip into the leadership role I fought so hard to achieve. My brotherhood. I've spent years with these men. Serving our country, covering each other's six, carrying out the worst missions they could give us, and celebrating our rise in the ranks. It took sacrifice and dedication to achieve Major. Saluting my men one final time is bittersweet, but I do it because they deserve my respect.

"Thank you for coming," I begin, leaning forward, fists on my desk. "I received some disturbing news yesterday morning. Hightower and his Ravens have been busy, capturing prisoners... to the tune of almost a thousand captives."

Anger surges across the room, and they don't know the half of it. "According to my father's spies, he's killing the weak and unstable, experimenting on the most powerful, and using others as leverage to gain favors from their wealthy and politically powerful families. He's out of control. My father is working to stop him, but we all know politics takes time, and men are lost in the gaps." Each one nods. We've all been there.

I take a deep breath. "All my life I've had powers. They didn't define me. From an early age, my calling was to be a soldier and serve my country. Sure, I expected there to be conflict between the two. We all did." I look at Quaid, whose fiery nature battles with his cool intellect.

"In the Army, we follow the chain of command. At times, it chafes, but never has it felt wrong. For the last year, I've repeatedly asked for permission to strike at Raven's operations. Every day, I was told to stand down and wait for orders," I inform them, shaking my head.

Fists clench, but nobody says a word. Code and honor are bred into us from the beginning.

"But I can no longer stand by and enjoy the safety of my position while innocent people are sacrificed to appease a mad man's need for vengeance," I tell them. "I'm resigning from my position in the Army to stop Hightower's path of annihilation."

Quaid, of course, knew it was coming. We've had many discussions over the last year. It wasn't an easy decision to make for either of us. We knew at West Point we were career Army. It drew us together.

But after a year of trying to convince my father, my CO, and the rest of command that we need to act, I realized they're scared the world will find out about us but exposure is not an acceptable reason. Every day, the cost of our silence rises.

Varying expressions of shock or satisfaction, depending on the path they've taken to get here, appear on their faces. Several of them have been itching to fight for a while but have stood down because of me.

Jax steps forward. "The only thing I like about the Army is access to the latest weapons. Do you have a stockpile somewhere?" Hands on his hips, he waits for me to confirm what he already suspects.

"I do," I admit with a half-smile. "Can't wage war without them. I hoped it wouldn't come to this, but I've been preparing for the possibility for a while."

He nods in satisfaction and shrugs. "They were never going to promote me beyond Sergeant. Too unpredictable for their taste. I'm in."

Beckett's grey eyes have a sheen to them I didn't expect. "For years, I've lived under their thumb, forced to use my powers to influence my friends and fellow soldiers. This compound is the first time I've been able to use my abilities to help those like us. Thanks to you. I'm in."

Steven, a young officer, steps up. "My wife is pregnant. I can't leave the Army or the safety of this compound. She comes first. I'm out." He hesitates. "But I'll help behind the scenes. Now, if you'll excuse me. Plausible deniability and all that."

His arm snaps up in a salute. "It's been an honor serving you, Major Harrison." He strides out of the office.

Two others follow, leaving seven of us.

Jax looks around. "I assume you have a plan to grow this little group of ours?"

"Of course," I assure him. "I've been speaking to our field team leads. I'll send word tonight. Anyone who wants to join us needs to be here as soon as possible."

First Lieutenant James Brock, who has the incredible ability to conjure realistic illusions, raises a finger. "Why so quick?"

"It's taken some time, but we finally located one of Raven's facilities," I reveal in a quiet voice. "Our first objective is to slow or stop his current efforts. Give him a real target to focus on. If we strike a blow, a hard one, he'll turn his attention to us."

Sam whistles. "Guess we're jumping in with a bang. Surveillance?"

Quaid stands up. "We've got numbers, guard routines, and the usual. Right now, we need to finalize our team and get an understanding of the pool of powers at our disposal. Once we have that information, we can create an attack plan, which is where you come in. There are civilians here who want to fight. Powerful users. At least a dozen. I've met them all. David. Talia. Edward. Gabe. To name a few. All we need to do is ask. If they say yes, you and I'll assess whether they're ready to join this mission or in need of further training."

Adam, a young sergeant who joined us a year ago, steps forward. He's been in charge of the stealth missions to save those on the streets. The program has been highly successful. He's also the one who puts potentials to sleep so they can't reveal our location.

"I've got a team that's ready. They've been talking about

leaving and creating their own group. There's eight to ten of them. Powerful and trained."

Quaid nods. "Trained is key. If they're ready, let's get them up to speed quickly." Adam nods and sits down to jot a few notes. "Make sure you give Adam a list of their names and abilities."

Speaking of lists... I pick up the one on my desk. "Beckett, I need you to find us a new place." Because of the trials the Army put him through, his powers make it hard for him to engage in combat. "I've got a list, but I don't have time to vet them and get everything else done. Would you mind?"

A relieved smile appears. "Thanks," he replies, taking the sheet from my hand. "I assume we'll need it by Friday."

"Affirmative," I answer with a grimace, aware of the short timeline. "It can be basic. We'll figure out the rest."

Once everyone has their orders, they head out, leaving me to make the calls to the rest of our team. Most of my officers are aware of the other cells, but they don't have any details. That information has been closely guarded by my father and myself. Too often knowledge gets leaked because too many people are in the know.

But first, I have to make two calls. Technically, I should call my CO first, but the storm of my resignation will hit my father hard. I dial his cell.

"Oliver," he says in his deep, gravelly voice. "I don't have an answer for you. The joint committee is still debating."

I take a deep breath and slowly let it out. "I'm resigning. My next call is to my CO, but I thought you should know first."

I've been dreading this conversation all day. Disappointing my father isn't something I do. Exceeding his expectations is my usual M.O. Not once have I ever taken a stand against him, but I've spent a year handling this his way, lying low and saving the few I can. Essentially, keeping Phoenix a secret from the rest of the world.

"Don't be stupid," he says after a second. "We'll figure out a way to curtail Hightower, even if this committee doesn't give me the vote I want."

"They can't afford to vote in your favor," I reply with a sigh. "You and I both know it. If we don't stand, they'll crush us. We need to go on the offensive."

Everyone in congress knows I am one of *them*. The military documented every experiment they conducted and shared it with the powers that be. Those trials nearly shredded me and my team to the bone, but they got the answers and the lethal soldiers they needed.

"Give me forty-eight hours," he orders in a tone that leaves no room for disobedience. He's used to getting his way, but not this time.

"I'll call you tomorrow," I evasively reply. By then, he'll have heard from my CO, and it will be a done deal. "Good night... Sir." I tap the red button and hang up. So many times, I've wanted to call him Dad. The closest I ever came was Father, but even then, it didn't sit right. Sir has always been easier for us both.

Spitting out the toothpaste, I bend over to rinse my mouth and, eyes wide, watch the water flow up toward my mouth. I fill it with water, swish it around, then spit. The water turns and flows down into the sink again. That's new.

I didn't even notice my power rising. An unconscious thought to rinse my mouth and it flowed to do my bidding. Effortlessly. I wonder if this is why it looks so easy for everyone else... because it is.

A message pops up on my tablet. "New appointment." I tap on it and see a new meeting set up with Beckett for this morning. Curious, I swipe through the next few days and see one for every day this week. Are we suddenly in a rush?

Well, they can wait until after breakfast. I hurry to the cafeteria, hoping to see River. He said he had classes yesterday, but I'm pretty sure he's avoiding me. After what I told him, I don't blame him. Associating with me could put his family in danger.

He's sitting at a table dragging his fork through the eggs on his plate.

"If you want pancakes, I'll get you some," I offer with a tremulous smile.

He jumps at the sound of my voice, then chuckles. "Sorry, I didn't hear you walk up. Thanks for the offer, but I'm not hungry."

Biting my lip, I ask him, "If I grab breakfast, are you going to be here when I return?"

A tiny line appears between his brows. "Of course. Go, get food."

My stomach is cramping with nerves, but I force myself to grab a muffin and some juice, then join him at the table. Leaning in close, I whisper. "I used my powers yesterday." Barely, but it's a start. "And again, this morning." Although I'm not entirely sure how I did it.

He smiles. "That's great, Greer. I mean it. Sorry, I'm worried about my mom and sister. We've never been apart this long. I'm going to have to leave soon." He pauses. "I hate that you can't come with me."

My mouth turns down. "You never know what the future holds, right? We're here, together, right now. Let's meet up this afternoon. Okay?"

He drops his forehead to mine. "It's a date."

My tablet pings. "Sorry. I have to meet Beckett and Oliver this morning."

His brow furrows. "I thought you met with them yesterday?"

I explain the new appointments on my calendar and shrug. "Maybe they want to take advantage of yesterday's progress. Anyway, I'm glad. The faster I learn how to wield water, the better." Before I think about it, I drop a kiss on his lips. "See you later."

Frown still on his face, I leave him. Hopefully, things will be better between us this afternoon. When I enter Beckett's office a few minutes later, both he and Oliver are talking quietly. They stop when I step into the room.

"Greer, thank you for joining us on such short notice," Oliver says, a pleasant smile plastered on his face.

I ignore the smile and look at his eyes. They seem to be a better barometer of his emotions. Today, they're more stormy grey than blue. Interesting. He's upset. Is it me or something else?

Beckett is calm, of course. Does he ever allow himself to display other emotions?

"Yes, thank you, Greer. Given yesterday's success, I thought repetition would be best, so I've scheduled this session for every day this week. Hopefully, we can quickly establish a connection," Beckett explains with a smile.

Suspicious, I look from one smiling face to the other. "Why the rush?"

They glance at each other, then at me.

"Do you not want to do this? Was yesterday too much?" Beckett asks, the smile slipping from his lips.

Frowning, I shake my head. "No. I mean, yes, I want to do this, and no, it wasn't too much. I ... never mind. Anyway, it's working." I tell them about the water in the sink this morning. "Is that how effortless it is for everyone?"

Beckett and Oliver share a look.

"It was different for us. There isn't a physical manifestation of our powers," Beckett explains hesitantly. "People would often react the way I wished, but it didn't occur to me that I was the one swaying their emotions. It wasn't until I stepped into a fistfight and told them to calm down, and they instantly did, that I began to understand."

Horrified at the thought of having the power to instantly influence everyone's emotions, I shudder. "I know you used yours to calm me, and I'm grateful, truly, but I didn't realize the extent of your abilities. Does it feel wrong when you use them?"

He flinches. "Are you scared of everyone's abilities or only those with mental powers?"

Ouch. He's not wrong, though. Thinking about it, I realize I'm fine around others like River or even Quaid, although I refuse to admit that out loud. "I guess... only the mental ones."

Of course, he goes into analysis mode. "With all of the powers out there, I find it interesting that it's only our type that you find scary. I wonder if there's an underlying cause?"

Oliver huffs.

Beckett darts an irritated glance at him. "If you don't watch it, I'll make you smile all day." Oliver straightens but says nothing.

"Let's move on. Some of us will be leaving at the end of the week, but I would feel better if you had a grasp on your powers before we do." He smiles. "The incident this morning gives me hope that you will."

Nice try. "You're leaving?" I look at him, then Oliver. "You too? Who else?"

Oliver scowls at Beckett. "Damn it. That's top-secret information." He looks at me. "You can't tell anyone yet. Not even River. Promise me."

"I won't," I assure him.

Panic wraps around me. River's leaving. Now Oliver, Beckett, and likely several others. I'll be here by myself. "I don't want to stay if everyone is gone."

Oliver takes my arms in his hands. "I'm sorry. You can't go with us. It won't be safe. You'll have River, though." The worried expression on his face tells me he didn't expect my reaction.

I don't dare tell him River is leaving, too. Instead, I ease out of his arms. "You're right. It was a shock, but I'm fine now." That damn word. Oliver's brows crash together, but I ignore him and turn back to Beckett. "Can we get started?"

Beckett flicks a glance at Oliver. "Yes, we can. Oliver, get into position." His tone is firm and surprises us both, but I guess he's the boss in this office.

Oliver takes a half step closer and squares his shoulders as if he's bracing for the enemy. "I hate this." His voice is barely a murmur, but I hear him.

"I'm sorry," I whisper, closing my eyes so I don't see his expression.

A curse slips from his lips, and a moment later, his hands wrap around my throat. A shiver works its way down my spine, but not with the usual fear. There is something about having this commanding man put his hands on me. I take a deep breath and clear my mind. A minute later, I'm still standing there, barely breathing, but nothing is happening.

Beckett leans in closer. "You have to squeeze, Oliver."

"Give me a minute," he mutters. "You're welcome to take my fucking place."

"Calm," Beckett says, and a heavy sigh fills the air. "Greer, the second you feel your power, don't hold back. Let it flow through you. We've got you."

Seconds later, fingers squeeze my throat. Warmth twists into anger, and my power rushes to the surface.

Beckett's low voice penetrates the darkness. "Put aside the anger. Let your other emotions rise."

Unease fills me. I guess he doesn't have to be in my mind to pick up on my emotions, but I like the fact that he's letting me do it. My anger slips quietly away.

His voice moves behind me. "That's it."

Layers of guilt surface from the muddy depths of my mind. Copious amounts of guilt for so many things—my actions by the waterfall, Lionel's death, leaving him at the gas station, not using my powers to save my parents or him. It's all there. Layer after layer.

Hands slip from my throat, and I catch my breath as I feel them lightly rub across my skin before disappearing. Oliver hates doing this, and my continued resistance is making it worse. More guilt piles on.

Beckett breathes out. "Acknowledge it. Understand it. Now, let it go. Guilt is destructive and will tear you down from the inside out."

I shake my head, unable to let it go. Without the guilt, what do I have? The answer comes to me. Gut-wrenching sadness. Pain lances through me, and I hear Beckett suck in a deep breath.

"I can distance you from it," he offers. The timbre of his voice is like the warmest of blankets, wrapping around me. "You'll know it's there, but it will feel less sharp. Manageable."

Before I even think about it, I shake my head. I don't want him to influence my emotions. Besides, they deserve to be mourned. Family is everything. They were mine.

"You need to celebrate them, too," Beckett murmurs on my left. "They lived and loved. Don't let sadness dictate the memories."

He's right. Lionel used to say the same thing after my parents died. He helped me remember my father's laugh and the smell of my mother's perfume. All the birthdays we spent together, not just the last one. Now, it's up to me to remember Lionel the same way. His joy of cooking. The pride he showed when I graduated with my bachelor's degree. All the lovely moments we spent together. I miss him so much.

I open my eyes and stare at the man in the pressed suit, standing in front of me. "I've been sad for so long. It's hard to let go. Living without my parents felt like a punishment." The corner of my mouth lifts. "Lionel refused to let me 'wallow' as he liked to put it. He made me find a life. Yet, I couldn't move past it. I functioned. I succeeded. But I never let anyone but

Lionel close. I used to tell him I'd find someone after I graduated."

Lionel's dark green eyes, full of pain, surfaces, and I marvel at what a remarkable man he was and how much he meant to me. "Beckett's right. Lionel deserves to be mourned, but he deserves to be celebrated too. They all do."

Oliver reaches for me, but this time, he pulls me into his arms. Soap and a subtle musky cologne wrap around me along with his quiet strength. "Brad told me you were the daughter Lionel never had, and I believe it."

"I want to make him proud. I want his sacrifice to mean something."

Oliver raises a hand and sweeps the hair from my face. "I do, too. It's why I'm leaving. We're leaving." Beckett makes a sound, but the look Oliver gives him stops his words. "We can't sit on the sidelines anymore."

Chills race up my spine. Not only are they leaving, but they're going to fight. "Take me with you. I know I don't know anything yet, but I can learn."

He immediately places a finger on my lips. "No. It's time for you to heal and find your future, not confront the enemy."

Lifting my chin, I step away from him and shake my head several times. "You don't understand. I don't have a future." Alone, I'll have no chance. I have to make him understand. "Nowhere is safe. Hightower will hunt me to the ends of the earth."

Oliver's head tilts. "Why?"

Beckett lays a hand on my shoulder. "What makes you think that?"

Calm sweeps over me, and I jerk away from him. "Don't. I'm not hysterical." I bite my lip, knowing I'm going to have to reveal the rest of my secret. "Because I didn't kill a random college student. I killed his son, Trent."

Both men curse, and I flinch.

Wringing my hands together, I stand taller and look Oliver in the eye. "I'm sorry I didn't tell you. To be honest, this place doesn't inspire a lot of trust. You do, though." I wave a hand at the prison-like walls. "Regardless, I can't stay here, and I doubt I'll be able to protect myself if I'm alone."

Beckett moves to my side. "What about River? Won't he leave with you?"

"He has other obligations," I inform them.

Oliver scowls. "What obligations?"

I hesitate. It's not my secret, but I know he's too proud to ask them for help. Maybe Oliver can locate River's family and bring them here. "He has a mother and sister. Both of them have powers. He needs to get back to them."

The two men share a look.

"Where are they? We can bring them here," Oliver assures me.

"I don't know," I reply, realizing I never asked River for their location. I assume he didn't tell me because it wasn't safe. "I'll ask him. I guess that means you don't want me to come with you."

"We're going to war," Oliver patiently explains. "Everyone going is either a soldier or they've used their powers to fight the enemy. Unfortunately, we don't have the capacity to assign someone to protect you." He waves a hand. "To be frank, war is hell. With everything you've been through, it's better if I find you a safe place to go."

"Fine," I tell him, watching his eyes narrow at the word. He knows I don't mean it, but I'm betting he won't call me on it.

"Do you want to practice your powers?" he asks after a minute, proving me right.

"I need a break," I tell them, worn out from this session but also needing space to think, far away from them. "Is that okay?"

Beckett interjects before Oliver can answer. "It's your decision. Locate one of us if you decide you want to try again today. If not, we'll see you in the morning."

Crushed by the thought of everyone leaving, depressive thoughts swirl in my head. Maybe Oliver can help River, but will he want me near his mom and sister with this massive threat hanging over my head? Probably not, and even if he did, where would we go? Neither River nor I want to remain here, but staying on the run isn't an option, either.

Oliver's right, too. Do I really think I can go to war? The last thing I want to do is put others in danger because they're protecting me. Besides, I know absolutely nothing about fighting, only defending myself.

Beckett drops his head back on his shoulders and stares at the ceiling. "I sure as hell didn't see that one coming." His tone is full of disbelief at the bomb Greer dropped in our lap. "Hightower's son. No wonder he's on a rampage, rounding up record numbers for his prison camps. Damn." He drops his head to look at me. "She's right. She can't stay here. It wouldn't be safe for her or anyone else."

Sliding a finger around the inside of my collar, I loosen the tie I put on this morning. "No, she can't. Fuck!" I stalk over to the window to give myself a minute to think. My plate is full, but the thought of leaving her here without a plan isn't an option. I need to find a solution.

"I'll talk to River. See if I can get more information about his family's whereabouts. And I'll check with my father. Maybe he knows of another safe location," I say, running a hand through my hair. There are few protected places in this world. My father went to a lot of trouble to make this base disappear from the records, but nothing is truly ever gone. Still, there are a few small off the grid places.

"We could take her with us," Beckett tentatively suggests. "I'm not going to fight. She can stay back with me."

I scoff. "You've lived as a soldier. You know what to expect. She doesn't." I turn toward the door. "I need to talk to River before my next meeting. Let me know when you find our new headquarters."

"Maybe you need to examine why you're so adamant she stay safe but not with us," Beckett calls out as I stride out of his office.

I roll my eyes. He's always trying to analyze everyone, looking for a reason, but sometimes, there isn't one. Protecting people is my job. I call Quaid.

"Where's River right now?" I ask, knowing Quaid has his tablet on him at all times.

"Why? What happened?"

"Later. Location?" I prod, not willing to go into everything over the phone. He replies with the information, and I head to River's Spanish class.

When I get there, I slip into the room and lock eyes with him. Without saying a word, he gets up and follows me out.

Taking a gamble, I start with her secret. "Greer told me what happened with Hightower's son."

His eyes never twitch, telling me he's loyal to her. She obviously trusts him.

I don't want to reveal that the rest of us are leaving, but I need to find out if he's willing to take her with him. "She told me you can't stay because of your mother and sister?"

His jaw locks, but he says nothing.

"She can't stay here. You know that, right?" I ask, studying his reaction.

He exhales loudly. "Why not? It's not safe for her to leave." Worried bright green eyes drill into me. It's obvious he cares for her. Probably why he hasn't left yet.

"What if I help all four of you find a safe place? Somewhere off the grid. Would you take her with you and your family?" I ask.

He curls his lip. "No offense, but I don't trust you. You hide in this compound while Raven captures person after person. Very few even know Phoenix is real and on the streets *saving* people." He sneers as he says the word saving. "Not one mention in the discussion boards. No way for anyone to contact you. You choose who to save or not. Everyone thinks you're a myth. Personally, I think you're worse than Raven. Their agenda is very clear."

He's right. Every word. We started out with big goals of saving people, but the military is too afraid the world will end if it knows of our existence. While I've tried to broaden the scope of our operations, it has barely made a dent. Hence my resignation. River's anger is completely justified.

"You're right. I tried to change things, but the government is resistant. Hightower has their favor and approval," I admit with a frustrated sigh. "You know we can save your family. Look at you and Greer... and the others here. If you give me your mom and sister's location, I'll send a team right now."

"You mean the government is afraid of us." River scoffs. "Look. I appreciate the offer, but I don't trust you to save my family. I've got it covered." Despite his bravado, I can sense he's worried about the situation.

Might be best to back off for a day. Let him think about it. "My offer stands. I want to help you. Greer, too. If you decide to let me, text me." When I rattle off my number, his mouth drops open, and I almost snicker. I've been aware of his phone since the day he got it. Nash has this entire compound wired for devices.

I leave him standing in the hallway and stride off. Once I'm outside the building, I call Nash, my favorite geek. "I want you to use facial recognition to find where River's been the last two years. Every location." Hanging up, my brow furrows.

River made a mistake. He used the word "save" when he spoke about his family. Wherever they are, he needs to save them, which suggests they've been captured by Raven.

WHILE NASH LOOKS FOR THE INFORMATION I NEED, I head back to my office to greet the groups arriving this morning. Several field teams have been begging for a chance to take the fight to Raven instead of sitting on the sidelines. Once I resigned, I told each of them what we were planning and extended an invitation to join us.

Honestly, I wasn't sure how many would be willing to resign, but surprisingly, almost all of them said yes. They've seen a lot of action on the streets, and while they saved a few here and there, they've also had to stand by while Raven captured one after another. River was right. Few people said yes to the safety we offered because nobody knew if we could be trusted.

"Welcome," I tell them, striding into my office where I find Quaid and Beckett chatting with them. "Thank you all for coming at such short notice. We need to move quickly on the intel we received with the location of one of Raven's bases. Based on our surveillance, activity has died down at this site, which gives us a good window of opportunity."

Captain Walker crosses her arms. "That's suspicious. Activity has increased across the board. Are you sure the intel is accurate and up to date?" She raises an eyebrow.

Quaid jumps in. "I conducted it myself." He points to the table where we've been planning the attack. "It's a small place.

Maybe fifty rooms for captives. My guess is they've run out of space. Guards, both numbers and rotations, have decreased. Less supply trucks going in and out. They're in a maintain-only phase. It's been this way for the last three weeks."

She studies the map. "Looks like there's some ground cover with this nearby forest, but that's about it. How are we going to get in without them sounding the alarm?"

Quaid looks at the group and smiles. Everyone stiffens. "This will be a multi-prong attack. So far, we've worked out a few tactics, but nothing is finalized. We'll jam all outgoing communications. Once we're close, we'll have David use electrokinesis to overload the facility's electricity, shutting down all alarm systems. Oliver will use mind control to force them to open the gate and lay down their weapons."

The excitement in the room rises as they realize we're going to take the offensive. Crowding around the map, they begin offering suggestions for neutralizing any of the power threats we might encounter. We don't know who or what we're going to find in the facility, but since Hightower usually gets rid of the weak, the prisoners are likely powerful but unstable.

Over the past year, the few who have managed to escape told grim tales of experimentation designed to drive a person mad. Starvation and torture were an everyday occurrence, but tame compared to the experiments themselves.

Raven took it to a whole new level. They deliberately amped up powers, pushing beyond control limits, to expand abilities to their maximum potential, which sounds a lot like what the Army did to us. Unfortunately, Raven took it beyond the realm of safety into a potentially explosive situation, resulting in unhinged individuals with tremendous powers that constantly stretch their control.

Some had their powers neutralized, which didn't sound as bad, until they explained how Raven set them up as targets against the others. Without the ability to defend themselves, they were at the mercy of those with powers.

Not to mention the countless number of tests they had to undergo. Designed to help Raven figure out the most effective ways to capture, sedate, and kill us, they tested bullets, poisons, fire, ice, and so many other weapons without a care to the victims who died along the way.

While we have remained here at this compound, waiting for our orders. It's no wonder River is bitter. Others will be, too. Hell, I'm bitter. But hopefully, we can save the captives and shut down Raven. Stop the madness before it spreads to the next generation. The Army might prosecute us afterward, but I'll gladly face the consequences.

Quaid stands in front of a considerably smaller class today. David and Talia aren't here. Neither is the older gentleman whose name I can't recall. Of the six who evaded Quaid the first day, I'm the only one left. Apparently, a dud who can barely use her powers doesn't get invited to join the war.

Quaid's amber eyes settle on me, and for a second, I'm lost in their depths, but thankfully, anger comes to my rescue. Screw them. I'll figure out a way to take care of myself. First, I have to learn to use my powers. Clenching my jaw, I wait for Quaid to give us instructions.

"I'm a pryo," he begins telling the class. "I'm going to light my arm on fire. You're going to put it out. If possible, use your powers. Look around you. Be creative. This exercise is about thinking fast on your feet when presented with a challenge. Got it?"

Everyone looks nervously at each other, but not me. I'm ready. A grim smile stretches across my face. Water beats fire, right?

Whoosh! Fire flares around Quaid's outstretched arm. Heat blasts us, and I wince. For some reason, I didn't expect to actually feel the fire burning against my skin. Watching him use his powers. Something inside me wakes, reaching for him as if it wants something, and for a second, I'm distracted, but when I see him motion to someone, I shake it off.

Up first is Tessa, a quiet teenage girl. She nervously rubs her palms down her legs, then steps forward. Turning in a circle, she smiles when she notices a towel on the gym floor. Her hand does a lifting motion, and the towel drops on Quaid's arm, then winds around the corded muscles until it's tight, smothering the fire.

Quaid flashes her a wide smile, and I stare at him in disbelief. Where did that smile come from? I thought all he did was scowl.

"Very good!" he exclaims. "Next time, try to do it without moving your hand. Using only your mind gives you a bigger advantage. You don't want to give the enemy any clues regarding your ability or next move."

Next, a young man moves forward. His scowl rivals Quaid's usual demeanor, and it makes me want to laugh. I can't remember his power, but I like him already.

A hole opens up beneath Quaid, and he barely jumps out of the way. The fire goes out. "We'll pretend I didn't jump out of the way. Burying me. Good choice. See me after class." His gaze is speculative as he watches the young man walk back to the line.

"Greer!" Quaid calls out.

Swallowing the lump in my throat, I tell myself I've got this. This morning, the water flowed to me when I needed it. I'm hoping it does the same now. Moving closer to Quaid, I almost have to raise my arm to ward off the heat. My eyes lock on his. There's a glint in them I don't understand. Is that a dare?

I don't try to *use* my powers. Instead, I concentrate on how thirsty I am and how much I need water to quench that thirst. It's unbearable. I'm parched. Nothing happens. Pretending I'm in the bathroom, I bend closer to the fire. Sweat drips into my eyes and down my chin. My eyes lock on a nearby water bottle. It starts violently shaking. I stand up and let the need for water fill me. The bottle dances up and down. Suddenly, the floor opens, and water spews out in a huge wave, heading straight toward Quaid and me.

"Ease off," he orders.

My pride refuses to let me admit I can't control it, so I simply smile.

"Damn it, Greer!" His hand reaches for me, but I back away. Seconds later, the water slams into his body, sweeping him off his feet and putting out the fire.

Curious, I walk over and stare into the floor of the gym where a large silver pipe lies with a huge chunk out of the top and more water inside of it. I hope this isn't the water main for the entire compound. Dread fills me, but I force myself to turn and look at Quaid. I'm sure he's going to flip out on me.

The entire gym is silent, nervously watching him. Quaid stands up and shakes like a dog. Water flies everywhere. His mouth twitches, and just when I think he's going to start yelling, he roars with laughter. Hands on his knees, he bends over to try to catch his breath, but the laughter doesn't ease as his whole body shakes with it.

Minutes later, he wipes his dripping face, stands, and looks at the class. Fire erupts across his body, drying every little drop, even the clothes he's wearing. I'm so jealous.

"A little forceful, but you did awesome!"

Wait. He's *proud* of me. Why? I didn't have an ounce of control. You know what, who cares? My anger dissolves, and my lips curve in a large smile. Hell, I'm proud of myself. I did it. Without someone's hands around my neck. Without being in danger. Water came because I needed it.

With only a few sessions under my belt, I now know I can use my power. It's not perfect, and my control is iffy, but it responds to me. Maybe confidence is the key. In school, I had it in spades. Here, it felt impossible. I've floundered while everyone else has been using their powers. Not anymore.

Having achieved success, I start taking notes. I'm good at studying. A perfect student. There's a lot to learn, but I can do it. School is my comfort zone.

Ignoring Quaid's request to stay, I leave and head straight to the stream Oliver showed me. When I get there, water trickles over the rocks in a soothing manner, and I drop to the ground. My hands automatically reach for the liquid, and it responds, flowing up to meet them. I rub the water on my hands and cup it in my palms, making friends with the element that answers my call.

I still don't remember using it the night my parents died, nor why I suppressed it. Part of me wishes I'd known, but I'm happy to have had a normal-*ish* childhood. River had to go on the run at an early age and missed out on all the usual milestones.

River. I asked him if that was his real name, and he laughed and assured me it was. He was teased a lot in school, but it never bothered him. Apparently, his mother loves nature and thought the names fit him and his sister, Lily.

Sometimes I want to tell him my real name, but I can't. If he were captured by Raven, the only name he knows is Greer, not Willa. Honestly, I'm proud to carry Lionel's son's name, though I miss my girly name.

"There you are," River says behind me.

The water falls back to the stream, and I turn to look at him. He makes a noise and strips off his sweatshirt, then his shirt. Astonished, I stare at his surprisingly cut abs. All our nights together, and I've never seen him without his shirt. I've been missing out. My eyes trace every line and crevice.

To my dismay, he slips his sweatshirt back on. Crouching down in front of me with his t-shirt in hand, he reaches for my face. "Hold still."

I rear back. "What are you doing?"

"Your nose is bleeding," he replies tersely. "It happens when we overuse our powers. A couple of minutes of pressure should help."

Embarrassed, I take the shirt from him and press it against my nose. "Thank you."

He sits down. "How long have you been out here?"

I glance at my tablet and wince. "An hour. I've been playing with the water and thinking. About the past. The future. You."

"You told Oliver about my mom and sister," he says, picking up a rock and tossing it into the stream. "Why did you tell him? I told you that in confidence."

"Whether you like Phoenix or not, they have the resources to help people. They found us. We're here and safe. I thought they could do the same for your family," I tell him, fidgeting restlessly. I knew when I told Oliver I was breaking River's trust, but I was desperate to find an answer that would let us be together. "I'm sorry. I should have asked you first."

He tosses another rock into the stream, and I reach over and push it to the side. "It's blocking the flow." The water is barely trickling as it is.

"If I asked, would you leave this place and go somewhere safe with us?" His voice is quiet, but I can tell by the intense look in his remarkable green eyes that my answer is important.

I chuckle. "Leave this wonderful facility with its grey sweats and tan buildings? How will I ever cope?" He doesn't laugh, so I reach out and grab his hand. "Of course. There will be nothing left for me here."

"They can teach you how to use your powers. Plus, you seem to be getting close to Oliver," he suggests in a speculative way. "I wasn't sure if you'd want to leave."

Phantom hands circle my throat, stroking gently, and I almost choke at the thought of Oliver leaving to fight the enemy, but he's not mine. "He cares about all of us, not just me. It's why I told him about your family. Oliver needs to save people. It's ingrained in him. Duty, integrity, dedication. Lionel was like that, and my dad. Must be an Army thing."

River exhales heavily. "Okay. Let me figure out a plan. The tricky part will be getting back here. I've got a general idea of where we are but not the exact coordinates. Maybe Quaid or Oliver can help with that piece. I'll think about it."

"How do you know where we are?" I ask, looking around at the trees. Maybe if I knew what kind of trees those were I'd be able to guess, but nothing looks familiar.

River digs his hands into the dirt. "The land. It gives me a general idea. For example, this type of dirt." He raises his hand with a fistful of it. "We're not in Georgia. The dirt would have a ton of red clay in it if we were. This has clay in it, but it also has wetlands and Cecil soils." He looks at the area around us. "Add in the vegetation and trees. My guess is somewhere in North Carolina."

Impressed, I stare at him. "You're remarkable." I smile widely. I'm happy he asked me. The yearning to return to my old life has faded. It's time to find a new life with River and his family. That's enough, right?

His smile fades. "Here, let me take a look." He lifts the t-shirt from my face, then dips it into the small stream. "Bleeding has stopped. Let me wash your face so the others don't think I popped you in the nose, especially Quaid." He leans in close. "Personally, he scares the shit out of me."

Laughing, I tilt my face up and let him clean the evidence. "Me too, but I'd never tell him. He's already too damn arrogant. It infuriates me."

River stops washing to look at me, speculation in his eyes. "Hmm. I'm starving. How about you?"

"Famished," I reply in surprise. "Literally, it feels like my stomach is completely empty. I know I ate breakfast earlier."

River nods. "When you use your powers regularly, you burn a lot of calories." He pats his washboard stomach. "That's how I got the abs you were staring at earlier."

Sputtering, I shove him away and get to my feet.

He jumps up and grabs my hands. "I don't mind, you know. In fact, it feels good to have your eyes on me."

Pressing forward, I put my hands on his stomach and slide them up around his neck. "They're pretty awesome. If only you weren't leaving." We agreed to hold off until we figure out the future, but damn, it's so tempting.

River's the perfect height. I don't have to stretch to reach his lips. They're right there, waiting for me. Tilting my head, I capture them in a long, remorseful kiss. "Forgive me?"

He shakes his head. "You'll have to give me at least a dozen of those first."

"Deal," I capitulate, giving him the first of many.

"Listen up!" I order. "Our team on the ground has noticed some new activity at the facility, and it's not good. Last night, they loaded up a truck of prisoners and shipped them out. If we're going to rescue the rest, we need to hit them at dawn."

"Do we have a plan?" Captain Walker asks with a frown.

"Most of one," I assure her. "We'll figure out the rest now."

"Sergeant Sellers, Adam, will provide cover for Sawyer, who will create a massive sinkhole behind the facility," I begin, pointing to the young man who almost buried me alive earlier. "Something big enough to warrant Raven sending men out to investigate."

Sawyer's scowl never wavers. Earlier, when I asked him if he had the power to do what I needed, he raised a cool eyebrow and told me he could create a sinkhole large enough to drop the entire facility in it. Add in the amount of anger he's carrying, and I immediately brought him on board.

"Divide and conquer. While their attention is split Lieutenant Brock, James, will use an illusion to lead the next group to the entrance. Once there, David will take out the electricity, and Oliver will force the guards to put down their weapons and open the gates," I inform them.

"Jax will provide sniper cover. Pick out a good marksmen to lead the rear. I want you covering the front," I tell him, then resume. "Captain Walker, Leisa, you'll lead a team and take out the soldiers in the rear. Once you're finished, make your way into the building and sweep for any opposition." I'm confident they can eliminate the rest without our assistance.

"I'll lead the second group through the front. Once in the courtyard, my team will split up and enter the facility here and here to search for captives," I inform them, tapping the map to indicate the locations. "Oliver will lead a third team comprised of James, David, and Nash to the main office, where they'll gather intel on the operations of this facility and any others."

I straighten and look at each of the team leads. "Our time will be limited. My best guess is ten minutes max. Does everyone understand their orders?"

They nod, their faces reflecting the solemn nature of the meeting, but there's an underlying excitement I don't usually see in a war briefing. Even the youngest and most inexperienced members, David and Sawyer, are ready.

"Great. We roll at four a.m. That gives us six hours to load up and get in the air," I inform them. "Gear up. Weapons and vests are in the courtyard. Load up on ammo."

Everyone scrambles out of the room, senior leads pairing up with inexperienced soldiers to help them out.

I turn toward Oliver. "All good?"

Oliver slips off his jacket. "We need this win." He tells me as if I don't know what's on the line.

I clap him on the shoulder. "Trust me. If I have to take them all out myself, we're saving those prisoners."

He exhales a long slow breath, then nods. "Since we don't have a new place, we'll have to return here. Any captives will be offered the safety of this compound until they figure out what they want to do."

Stripping off the rest of his suit, he steps into his fatigues, shedding the sophisticated persona and donning the skin of the lethal soldier he's trained to be. He stands, snaps his shoulders back, and grabs his pack.

"We have a lot to do. Let's go," he says, striding out the door with me by his side.

RUMBLING FILLS THE CRISP MORNING AIR, AND THE ground shakes under our feet. A sinkhole seventy yards wide suddenly appears behind the facility. Minutes later, men rush out of the facility to investigate exactly as we anticipated.

"Cut the comms," I order Nash, looking over at him.

Tall and lanky, his dark hair falling in his brown eyes, wearing a pair of jeans and a sweatshirt instead of fatigues, he looks more like a grad student than a sergeant in the Army. The technopath dips his chin and flips the button on the grey, rectangular box in his hand. "Sweeping now." His eyes never look up from the laptop in front of him.

The biggest computer geek I know, I honestly wasn't sure how he'd do in the field, but like the rest of us, he's ready. "James, you're up. Leisa, get into place."

I glance at the screen on Nash's laptop and watch the footage from the drone feed. So far, everything has gone to plan. The element of surprise is on our side. Neither High-tower nor Raven expected us to attack them. We've never done it before. Next time, it won't be so easy.

Lights wink out at the facility, and a minute later, the gate opens to reveal soldiers, weapons on the ground, as they face Oliver, David, and the rest of James' team.

"Leisa, you're a go," I murmur into the comms at my throat. Turning to my men, I hold up my fist, then make the motion to move out.

Running out of the forest, we join the rest of our team at the entrance, then move in together. Nash breaks off to join Oliver's team. I tap five of my men and point to the other side of the facility. They'll provide initial cover, then break off to search for prisoners. I point to this side and raise my gun, leading my team into the facility. We'll take out any opposition along the way.

Angling myself in the lead, I drop a couple of soldiers, then hit the next hallway and do the same. My men search the closed doors behind me, clearing them one-by-one. Aware of the clock ticking down, I realize we need to move faster. Based on my best guess, we have about ten minutes until Raven figures out this facility is offline.

"Jackpot," I murmur, finding closed doors with glass windows set into them. I peer into one and see someone lying on a cot. I bang on the door. "Want out of here?"

The petite brunette jumps up and stares at the door. "Who are you?"

"Does it matter?" I ask her. When she merely folds her arms across her chest, I give her my best don't fuck with me look. "We're sure as hell not Raven."

Her eyes narrow for a second, then she shakes her head. "Get me out of this hellhole."

I break the glass and open the door. "Be careful, electricity is down. You're welcome to leave or go back to our compound, where it's safe. Up to you. How many are on this side?"

"A few," she replies tersely, unwilling to provide me with numbers. I don't blame her. "Get this collar off. I'll help."

Stepping back, finger on the trigger in case this goes sideways, I nod at the soldier to my right. He places the prod Nash designed on the collar and short circuits it.

She immediately rips it off and rubs her neck. Skinnier than I originally thought, she raises bony arms and extends her hands. Glass shatters and doors open all the way down the hall. Damn, she's powerful. I wonder if they're all at that level.

Men and women, boys and girls, of all ages tentatively shuffle into the hallway, powers held at bay by the collars around their necks. All of them bone-thin like the girl next to me. It's obvious Raven used starvation and those damn collars to control them.

"We don't have much time. Line up, and we'll get your collars off," I tell them, raising my voice so everyone can hear. "Once they're off, head outside. You can set out on your own or go with us." Power leaks from a few of them. "Every single one of the individuals in my unit has abilities. If you try anything, this will get ugly real fast."

A grey-haired older man steps forward. "Who are you?"

"Phoenix," I reply, motioning for him to move into line.

He snorts. "Phoenix is a myth."

That stings. "Well, damn." With only a thought, I hold my arm out and light it up. "Maybe you can't see me. There, that's better." Several people murmur to each other. "We're Phoenix. We have a compound that's safe. If you want out of here, get in line. If not, you're welcome to stay and greet Raven in five minutes, give or take."

The thought of Raven terrifies them into action. It takes little time to get the collars off. Several rush out of the facility.

A young man steps forward. Dark hair, tall, and practically a skeleton. He pulls the brunette closer and tucks her into his arm. "I'm Lance. This is Dani. We don't give a fuck who you are. Just get us somewhere safe."

Three minutes later, we lead our remaining group to the helicopter sitting in front of the facility. The other team is already outside loading up the ones they rescued, and I walk over to them.

"How many?" I ask tersely, keeping my weapon ready.

"Eleven rescued, seven are going with us," James gruffly informs me. His eyes are bright with unshed tears. "They look rough. Raven's put them through hell."

I clench my teeth but give him my numbers. "Nineteen on my side, fifteen returning." Thirty total prisoners. Not nearly enough, but it's a start. "Get Adam to put them to sleep and head back."

Lieutenant James Brock salutes me and steps into the bird where Adam is already administering his command to them. I raise a fist and step back twenty feet. Circling the air, I order the bird back to base. Once that one leaves, the second one arrives, and I motion for half of our men to load up.

Where the hell is Oliver?

"Major, get a move on. Enemy will be here any minute," I spit into the comms.

"On my way," he replies tersely. "Be there in two."

Damn it. "Stay alert." We took out roughly twenty of their men, but the rest are still standing in the courtyard where Oliver left them. No one has moved. I don't like the thought of leaving them alive to fight another day, but I won't kill an unarmed man.

At one minute and forty seconds, Oliver and his team round the corner in a full sprint.

"Failsafe triggered. Building's going to blow. Load everything up and get in!" Oliver yells as he hands a box to one of my soldiers. He jumps into the helicopter and begins grabbing boxes from Nash and David.

"Fuck me. Hurry!" I stand by the doors until the last soldier is on, then I jump inside. We lift off, and twenty seconds later, an explosion goes off in the rear of the building. It triggers one detonation after another until the entire building, including the courtyard full of unmoving soldiers, is gone. Vibrations shake the 'copter, but it remains in the air. Guess that takes care of the problem.

"What is all this stuff?" I shout, pointing at the boxes. I knew he was going for intel but thought Nash would copy it electronically.

"They documented their experiments," Oliver returns with a grimace. "We're going to make copies and get them to my father. He needs all the ammunition he can get to show the government what Raven's doing to us."

We're in the cafeteria grabbing breakfast when we hear the sound of helicopters. Rushing outside with River, I watch two Army helicopters land and unload passengers. From the nearest one, soldiers in camouflage, holding guns, emerge. My heart sinks when I see who steps out. Oliver, Beckett, Quaid, Jax, and several students I've gotten to know, like David, Talia, and Gabe. Now I know who's leaving. There won't be anyone left.

River's gasp has me turning to the other helicopter where emaciated people are rubbing sleepy eyes and slowly disembarking. These must be the captives. I swallow hard. They look rough. If it hadn't been for River, that would have been me. A pulsing power emanates from them.

Like the others, River feels powers. Maybe that's why he gasped. I haven't really felt them until now, but there's definitely an invisible wave coming off these people. They must be powerful if I'm picking up on it.

A tall, lanky young man with a petite brunette tucked under his arm is staring at us with a murderous expression on his face. Or rather, at River. The girl tugs on his arm, but he shakes her off and stalks toward us.

"Shit," River mutters.

"You bastard!" the young man roars before clocking River in the face. "You're a fucking traitor. Aidan, Jordan, Freddie, Mark, and Hector. Gone because of you. You sold us out! Why? Tell me!" he continues to whale on River.

River says nothing. Nor does he fight back.

It hits me. Lance. One of the guys from Atlanta who was captured. The group Jordan told me about who he felt guilty about not saving. River too. "Jordan is fine. He's living in Atlanta. Or at least he was when we saw him a couple of weeks ago."

His fist freezes in mid-air, and he turns to sneer at me. "You sure about that?" His voice is taunting. "What do you think, River? Or is she a liar like you?"

River shoves him. "Get away from her."

Quaid strides over and gets in between the two. Fire erupts across his body, physically forcing them to step back. "What the fuck is going on here?" His amber eyes flick over my body as if making sure I'm not hurt.

Lance suddenly splits into two. Literally. There's one of him standing by the girl and the other tackling River to the ground.

"Sergeant!" Quaid yells, and a stocky young man in fatigues comes running over.

He points at the two slugging it out, and the soldier quietly orders them to sleep. River and Lance, or rather both Lances, slump to the ground.

Hmph. That's the asshole who put us to sleep before we arrived here. I turn toward Quaid. "That's a shitty way to handle it. They're only going to be more pissed off when they wake up."

He lifts a shoulder. "I don't have time to coddle anyone. Tell them when they wake up that if they don't cool off, I'll throw them in the brig." He stalks off, muttering something about double trouble.

I look at the girl across from me. Anger simmers deep in her eyes. "Hi. I'm Greer."

"You with him?" she asks, jaw clenched so tightly she can barely get the words out.

"River?" I clarify. When she nods, I confirm. "Yes. Jordan told me Lance and the rest of them were captured, but there were too many for River and him to fight. They both felt incredibly guilty about it." I hope she's more reasonable than Lance.

She snorts. "I'm Dani. How long have you known River?"

"A couple of weeks," I reply. Wow, it seems longer.

"That explains it. He's lying to you."

A couple of soldiers come over and lift Lance's bodies. She positions herself next to them. "Lance is the best guy I've ever met. He'll do anything for his friends. Trust me. If he hit him, you can bet your ass River deserved it." She taps one of the soldiers on the arm. "I'm going with him." Her tone is firm and after glancing across the yard at Quaid, the soldier nods.

I wait, but no other soldiers come over to get River. Looking around, I see Quaid and Oliver watching him from across the yard. I learn why a moment later. Grass and dirt moves over River's body, covering him completely. Thirty seconds later, he sits up.

"What the hell?" he mutters angrily. "That bastard. I hate being put to sleep."

"Here, let me help you up," I say, reaching down with my hand. He takes it, but the second he stands, he pushes me away and stomps off. "You're welcome."

Frustrated and confused, I stare after him. Is he upset because he's hurt that his friend accused him, or is he angry because Lance is telling the truth?

Beckett walks up to me. "Would you mind helping me get these people settled? There are twenty-two of them. We need to provide each one with clothes and food, then give them time to decompress."

I paste a smile on my face. "Sure, but I don't think we should lock them in their rooms, though. They've been prisoners long enough."

A grim smile stretches across his face. "Completely agree. Follow me, and I'll show you where we keep the supplies." He scans my face. "I saw what happened with River. Don't judge him until you know the full story. Sometimes, this world forces us to do things we would never do, including hurting our friends."

Surprised, I turn to Beckett. "I won't. Believe me. I'm not qualified to judge anyone." After all, I killed two people. I acted in self-defense, but does that make it acceptable? I'm still not sure of the answer.

"I guess not," he muses. His silver eyes have darkened to grey storm clouds.

"Want to talk about it?" I ask, the irony not escaping me. "I might not have empathic abilities or whatever like you, but I'm a good listener."

"Some other time," he murmurs, shifting his feet. It's obvious he's uncomfortable being on the other side of the proverbial couch. He stops at a large building with no windows. "This is our supply warehouse."

"What is it with all the tan? Is that the only color the Army is allowed to use?"

He laughs, and the dimple in his chin deepens. Such a small thing, and yet, I'm practically drooling. "It is the official color. Want the real reason or the one they give us?"

Intrigued, I raise an eyebrow. "The real reason."

"Some important general visited the bases in the 70s and

decided everything needed to be uniformed and standardized," he says, then laughs. "And cheap, of course. The Army buys things in bulk, you know. We have warehouses full of this paint."

I laugh. "Clearly. This is an old base. Do the newer ones look like this, too?"

He tilts his head. "You never went to a base with Lionel?"

I shake my head. "Nope. He took a desk job when my parents died so he could be home with me. Most of the time, he worked from home reviewing contracts, or so he said. Now, I wonder what he really did."

"Hmm," he says, and I can tell he's curious, too. "Anyway, they call it Creech Brown after the general himself." He chuckles when I wrinkle my nose.

"And the official reason?"

"Technically, it camouflages the buildings. Enemies aren't able to distinguish important buildings like operations from less important ones like the mess hall. And, supposedly, it makes the buildings harder to see from a distance," he tacks on.

"Still fugly, if you ask me," I say with a laugh, and he agrees with a chuckle.

We pile the supplies into several rolling carts by the door of the warehouse. Once they're full, we start wheeling them toward the dorms.

I can't quite figure him out. "You know, I've been around individuals in the military my whole life. When I was younger, my dad's friends would come to visit. Plus, Lionel, of course." I pause, wondering how to put my question. "You don't seem like the military type."

His lips curve in a wry smile. "I grew up wanting to help others. At the time, I didn't know why. Now, I know it's because I didn't have any barriers. I used to soak up all the emotions from those around me. The weight of their feelings made me want to do something to ease their burdens. I thought about becoming a doctor, but I felt the emotions would be overwhelming."

I raise both eyebrows. "And war isn't?"

He shrugs. "When I joined, there was no war. I thought the brotherhood would be a great support for someone like me. And for a while it was." He glances at me, and I see an ocean of sadness in his eyes. "Like Raven, the Army conducted experiments on those of us with powers. They made me do despicable things to the men and woman I called friends and colleagues. When I resisted, they brought in someone with mind control to force me, which is why I understand your aversion to it."

"That's the real reason the government doesn't corral Raven," I say, with a dawning note of terror. "They want a way to use and control us like their own personal army." It makes sense. Why else would they condone Raven's horrible methods?

Wind catches my hair, whipping it into my face, and I stop the cart.

"Here, let me," he offers, smoothing it back from my face.

"Thank you," I tell him, staring up at this enigmatic man. "What happened after the experiments?"

"Except for Oliver and Quaid, everyone turned on me. When they were tapped to lead Phoenix operations at this compound, they submitted a list of soldiers to join them, and I was lucky enough to be on it. They knew I committed terrible acts, but they didn't hold the past against me. Instead, Oliver thought helping people would be a better use of my powers," he informs me. "His support saved me. And that's why I think you should hear River's side. All of it. Without judging."

"I will. Thank you for sharing your past," I say, wanting him to know how much it meant for him to tell me something personal about himself. Kind of evens the playing field between us. Not that he's going to be here for much longer.

"This is the last batch. Why don't I finish up and you go find River? He really needs a friend right now," he suggests with a gentle smile.

I reach up and place a kiss on his cheek. "Thank you again."

River's sitting by the stream with his hands buried in the mud when I find him. His relationship with the earth and nature is quite remarkable. It reaches for him when he's in pain and carves a path when he's running from the enemy. As I stand there, a flower curls itself over his shoulder.

"Mind if I join you?" I ask softly, not wanting to disturb him.

His shoulders droop at the sound of my voice. "I hoped to have more time before I had to confess my sins, but time is against us."

I sit down beside him and draw my knees up. "It always has been." I remind him. "Let's start with something easy."

He lifts an eyebrow. "Shoot."

"When that guy put you to sleep, how did you come out of it so quickly? I mean, I was standing there. I saw the ground cover you. Does it heal you?" I know it's an odd question, but I could have sworn the water did the same to me that night Trent and Tommy tried to kill me, because the next day, I woke with no bruises, broken bones, or soreness.

"It does," he replies with a grin, looking down at his hands. He pulls them out of the ground and shows me his dirty, bruise-free knuckles. With a sigh, he digs them back into the wet mud.

"There are so many things I have to tell you. I don't know where to start."

Part of me doesn't want to know, but I have serious decisions to make myself, and I can't do that until I know the truth. "Start at the beginning."

"The beginning is my favorite part because it led me to you," he says, looking at me. "No matter what you hear, please stay for the entire story. Okay?"

Shit, it's bad. I swallow but give him my word. I'm not sure I would have if I hadn't spoken to Beckett earlier, but he convinced me to hear him out. "I will. Promise."

"Our beginning wasn't at the gas station. It began on campus," he begins.

I raise my head to clarify. "My school? I would have remembered if we'd met."

He shakes his head. "One day, you ran into a football star. Unfortunately, he wasn't very smart. When he saw the mark on your shoulder, he decided to search his father's files. His father, on the other hand, is very, very smart. An alert immediately went to his phone informing him of his son's activities."

Chills erupt across my arms, and I pull my knees in close to my chest as if they can help protect me from whatever he's going to tell me. "Trent."

He nods. "Hightower thought his son was in trouble, and he sent me to save him." He pauses. "Remember when you told me about your stalkers? You thought you had two but weren't sure? You did. Trent was one, and I... was the other." He thrusts a hand through his hair, ruffling it up, then smiles.

"The first time I saw you, I thought the dunce had made a mistake. You didn't feel like you had an ounce of power," he says with a shake of his head. "You were also the prettiest girl I'd set eyes on in forever."

Shock renders me speechless. Of all the secrets I thought

he'd reveal, this wasn't one of them. Senator Hightower, leader of the Ravens, sent him to what... eliminate me? I look around the deserted forest. If so, he's had plenty of chances. I return my gaze to him.

He searches my eyes, then continues. "I stopped following Hightower's orders the moment I took that first photo. I was standing in the bushes, waiting for you. You came out of the library and stopped at the top of the stairs. Your hair was sticking out everywhere, and you looked so tired. I couldn't help myself. I thought you were beautiful."

He laughs at the look on my face. "For the first time ever, nature gave me away. A twig snapped and scared you off."

That jolts me out of my stupor. "The envelope with the pictures... that was you? You broke into my car? You followed me everywhere. Nowhere felt safe. You scared the fucking hell out of me." I shove him hard and stand, my body trembling with fury. "What is wrong with you?"

He jumps to his feet and grabs me. "I was trying to scare you! Make you run. Trent, the Hightowers, they wanted me to kill you. I couldn't do it. Most of us with powers are ready to run at a moment's notice. I didn't realize until later you didn't know anything about our world."

"So, this is my fault?" I ask in a dangerously quiet voice. Water splashes over my feet, and I look down and see the tiny stream has diverted itself. "You left me at the mercy of Trent and his buddy Tommy. Do you know what they did to me? They drugged me, kidnapped me, stuck me in a fucking shack in the middle of the woods, beat me, and threw me off a cliff!" My voice raises higher and higher with each word.

"And when that didn't work, they scaled down to finish the job. If I hadn't been by water or had these powers, they would have killed me. Where were you? If you wanted to save me, that would have been a great time to do it!" I yell at him.

I jerk my hands from his, but I have no intention of leaving. He has my full attention. I want answers. I deserve answers.

He clenches his fists. "I'm sorry. Hightower became suspicious and sent his goons to pick me up. I tried to get word to you that afternoon, but neither you nor Lionel were at the house. I swear, I didn't know what those neanderthals were planning. If I had, I'd have found a way to get you to safety," he says with a shake of his head. His green stare implores me to forgive him, but I can't.

"You could have come to me and Lionel. He would have taken you seriously. Instead, you let them ruin my life," I insist, trying to understand his point of view, but it's so damn hard. Not only did his stalker activities scare the shit out of me, but doing nothing to prevent them from kidnapping me made him their accomplice.

He sits down on a nearby rock and hangs his head. "Everything about you took me by surprise. I didn't know what to do. For the first time in my life, I put someone else ahead of my mother and sister. To be honest, I hated myself for it. I wanted to save you, but I knew Hightower would kill my family. I was stuck."

My jaw drops at his confession, but I'm still so furious. That's why he's so protective about his family. They're captives.

"You should have saved me. Period." If he had, I wouldn't have killed Trent, and I might have had a chance. Now, there's no going back. "You could have easily told Senator Hightower I didn't have any powers. He would have called off Trent. Instead, you selfishly stayed, which put me in Trent's sights, reinforcing his right to kill me. Or so he thought."

He winces. "Honestly, I didn't think he'd believe me. He's extremely paranoid. But you're right, I should have come up with another plan. You threw me for a fucking loop, and my whole head was spinning. I couldn't think."

His answer doesn't ease the anger, but it I force myself to exhale slowly and sit down next to him. "This story sucks, by the way."

He chokes on my words. "It totally does. You don't even know the worst part."

More? I angrily cross my arms over my chest and brace myself. "Tell me."

His voice is hoarse as he continues, "Lance is telling the truth. For three years, Hightower has held my mom and sister hostage while he sends me out to find a unique talent or a lot of power. I turned in Lance and the other guys. Not just them, either. Countless others. I convinced them to trust me and sold them out. I didn't know what else to do. When I first started, I thought I could do it a couple of times, then he'd let us go." A tear rolls down his face. "I was completely naïve. My success fueled his need for more. If I refused, he'd torture my mom or experiment on my sister. And me when I returned."

This is really, really bad. "Damn. You're the villain in this story. You're Raven."

After a bit of silence, he takes a deep breath and turns to me. "With Lance here, I have to leave. Tonight. I'm already on borrowed time. If Phoenix discovers what I've done, they'll hold me indefinitely. If I don't return, Hightower will kill my mom and do worse to my sister. You understand, don't you? I've been putting this off because I didn't want to leave you, but I'm out of options."

"Why didn't you save Lionel?" The question leaves my mouth before I can really think about it, but now that it's out, I have to know. My breath stalls as I wait for his answer.

"I tried to save you both at the gas station, but I was groggy from the drugs they gave me when they captured me, and my powers were muted," he says, looking at me. "I didn't have enough juice to do it all. I'm sorry. When I saw him go down, I didn't think. I knew I couldn't let you end up like him. I jumped out of the vehicle and ran to you. You know the rest."

I think back to the gas station. He hadn't been moving when they first arrived. Now I know why. "Knowing what I know now... it would have been so easy for you to fall back into old habits and let them take me like you did with countless others. But knowing it would cost you; you still saved me. I looked at those captives today, and I was so grateful I wasn't standing with them."

I'm not sure I would have survived. These last few weeks have been enlightening. Lionel sheltered me from the world and its dangers. So had my parents. If River hadn't been with me, I'm sure Raven would have quickly captured me.

With a shiver, I lay my forehead on his shoulder. "I'm still angry with you, but I can't say I'd have taken those same risks. I'd have been too scared. So, thank you."

He turns and pulls me into his arms. "Stay mad at me. I deserve it. Seriously. But I'm glad you know. I didn't want you to find this out from someone else, and with me leaving, Lance will happily tell you all my traitorous faults."

In the heat of the moment, I'd forgotten he was leaving. Tonight. I raise my head. "What can I do to help save your family? Tell me."

"Stay here where it's safe," he replies immediately. "Seriously. Everything is my fault. They were captured because I was bragging on the boards about my powers. Back then, I was a stupid kid. Didn't know anything. My mom tried to tell me, but I brushed her off. Raven sent a team to track us down. For three years, we've been under their boot. The last time I saw her, she begged me to take my sister and leave, but I refused to leave my mom behind. I promised her I'd find a solution. Instead, I fucked everything up. This is my only chance to save them and myself. To give us a better life."

"Let me talk to Quaid and Oliver," I beg him. "Please. They'll help you."

He adamantly shakes his head. "No, they won't understand. Nor will they let me go. I can't trust them." He sighs. "Besides, someone has to lead the fight against Raven, and I believe Oliver is our best shot. That's why I didn't give Hightower any information about this place or its location. Whatever Oliver's father did to hide this place, it worked. Raven doesn't have a clue about it."

There's a note of admiration in his voice I didn't expect to hear, but I'm not surprised. Oliver's willingness to help others is impressive, but his determination to take down Raven is pure steel.

"Don't worry. The compound is very small with few guards. Plus, they're used to me coming and going at odd hours. I'm going to slip in and out, and if I time it right, I'll hit shift change," he says, trying to convince me and himself that everything will work out.

"I'm going with you," I blurt. Once I say the words, I know it's the right thing to do. Doesn't mean I'm not scared out of my freaking mind, though. Or that things will ever be the same between us, but River needs someone in his corner.

He drops my hands and steps away from me. "Absolutely not. No fucking way. You don't get it, do you? You've been the best thing that has ever happened to me. You make me want to be a better person. To stop hiding behind my excuses. But the only way forward for us is to save them. I should have done it a long time ago, but I was in so deep, I couldn't see a way out. Now, I do."

He moves closer and tugs the neck of my sweatshirt until it exposes the mark on my shoulder. "Besides, you're special. This mark means something. I think you might have two powers. If you do, Hightower will kill anyone he has to in order to get his hands on you."

"This mark? It means nothing. I can barely use one power. How the hell could I have two and not know about it?" I ask him, freaking out about the possibility.

He lifts a shoulder. "I don't know much. I've heard him on the phone a couple of times, talking about those with marks.

When Trent searched the files, he specifically started with the one labeled marks."

My mind feels like it's going to explode with everything he's unloading on me. In the end, it doesn't matter though. I refuse to let him go alone. If I did, I'd feel like a coward for the rest of my life. I thrust a hand through my hair.

His hands, smelling of dirt and water—our elements, reach up and cup my face. "I don't want to live in this world without you. Stay here. Wait for me."

"Fine," I tell him, but unlike Oliver, he accepts the word without suspicion. His shoulders relax and he smiles. Thinking fast, I make a list of what I'll need. "I need to go by Oliver's office to grab my hair tie. Meet you in your room later? You won't leave without saying goodbye, right?"

He presses his lips to mine over and over. "I won't. I promise. Before I leave, I need to talk to Lance. I owe him."

"His girlfriend's name is Dani," I tell him. "She's nice but a little fierce. I wouldn't go to their room. Maybe the cafeteria?"

He laughs but agrees. "Whatever you think. Come on." Tugging on my hand, he heads to the compound.

I take one last look at the little stream and follow.

Parting at the bench, I head to Oliver's office. There's a team of soldiers in there when I arrive, but the minute they see me, all talking stops. Oliver steps outside and closes the door.

He frowns. "What happened? Did you fall?"

Puzzled, I stare at him. "What?"

"There's dirt on your face," he informs me, taking out a handkerchief from his pocket. "Here." Leaning close, he wipes my cheeks and under my jawline. The subtle mix of soap and cologne drifts toward me. I hold absolutely still as his head dips toward mine, then exhale when he moves away. "There. I got most of it, but you may want to wash up."

His eyes catch mine, and the blue in the center darkens. He

clears his throat. "Did you want to practice?" He looks at his watch. "I can carve out some time."

I shake my head. "You're busy. I came to get my go bag. You said I could have it?"

He raises an eyebrow. "Why now?"

Good thing I've already thought about this, or his stare would make me stumble. "The captives. I'd feel safer if I had my bag. With the burners. Just in case." He says nothing, just continues to stare at me. "Look. You're leaving. If I don't get it from you now, I might forget." I deliberately play into his guilt, which makes me kind of nauseous.

"Wait here," he tells me, heading inside and closing the door behind him. Minutes later, he steps out with my bag in hand. "Here you go." Instead of giving it to me, he holds it above my hand, and I bite my lip, hoping he won't ask any questions. "I'm still working on a plan for you. Somewhere you'll be safe. Please don't do anything rash." His hand clasps mine for several long seconds before he finally releases the bag.

Well, now I really feel like shit. "I'm not. Thank you." I'm not giving up on him. Honestly, I hope we'll make it back in time for him to get us somewhere safe.

He studies me for a second longer, as if reluctant to let me leave, then opens the door. "If you need anything else or want to practice, come find me."

Jax sticks his head out of the crowd in the room and winks at me. Oliver glares at him and shuts the door.

Another idea pops into my head. I run to my room and check the bag. The cash is still there. So are the burners, which I plug in to charge. I sling the go bag on my back, grab my tablet, and walk out of the building, staring down at the lit screen the entire way. If I don't have something to look at, I'll look nervous and anyone monitoring the cameras will notice my odd behavior. Outside, I keep walking until I get to the range.

All the handguns and ammo are stored in the locker next to the range. The big guns are stored elsewhere. I open the locker and pull out a gun and two boxes of ammo. I don't know if River can shoot, but I'll feel a hell of a lot better if we have some protection with us. Stuffing them in the go bag, I sling it back on my shoulders and return to my room.

Once I get there, I stash the phones in the bag along with my toothbrush and a few necessities, then complete one last task. Finally ready, I leave my room and go to the cafeteria to grab snacks. Bananas, muffins, waters, and some other small stuff. Then I head to River's room. When he opens the door, there's a defeated look on his face.

"Didn't go well, did it?" I ask softly. I didn't think it would, but I admire the fact that he faced him.

"Lance was the most powerful, so they kept him alive for their experiments, but Raven killed the others," he drawls in a heavy voice. "I don't deserve his forgiveness."

"None of us deserve any of this," I state with a frown. "Not even that douchebag Trent and his horrid friend, Tommy. But this world is brutal, and it's only going to get worse. Today, Phoenix took their first strike at Raven. Tomorrow, it will be an all-out war."

He lifts his head, and a spark returns to his green eyes. "Thank you. I sure as hell don't deserve you, but I'm never giving you up." His gaze drifts to the backpack on my back, and he starts shaking his head back and forth. "You're not going."

I step forward, pushing him inside. "Shh. If you refuse to take me with you, I'll sound the alarm. I mean it, River. I'm going. What will happen if you get to their facility and your mom and sister are in the same shape as those captives today? You can't carry them both out of there."

He continues to shake his head. "I'm resourceful. I'll figure something out. Besides, my sister is incredibly powerful. She'll help me."

Ignoring him, I open the bag. "Guns, ammo, cash, burners. Can you think of anything else we need? Grab your toothbrush and other necessities."

He tries to take the bag from me, but I jerk it away. "If you try to take this bag from me or leave me behind, I'll scream. They'll come running. You know they will. Do you think you're strong enough to take on Quaid and Oliver and the others?"

Tears fill his eyes, but he scrubs them away. "You're too damn stubborn. The sun set a few minutes ago. We need to leave while everyone is preoccupied with dinner. But I don't want to take the guns. You told me you can't shoot, and quite frankly, neither can I. Are you ready?"

"No, but I'm not letting you go alone," I admit with a sigh after dumping out the guns and ammo. "Let's go."

THE DINER APPEARS AT AN INTERSECTION A FEW MILES from the compound. It's obviously been here a long time. The worn sign on the corner has a couple of letters missing. Dirt is everywhere—the parking lot, on the windows, and even in the air. It coats my tongue, making me thirsty. There's only one car in the front parking lot. I'm guessing they don't get a lot of traffic these days.

"Blink, I need a couple of rides," River murmurs into the phone beside me. He listens for a second, then tilts his head toward the diner. "Can you ask them for an address?"

While the diner doesn't look like much on the outside, the interior smells like pancakes and grease. I inhale and smile, remembering the place River and I hit after walking out of the woods that first morning. Well, first for me. I still can't believe he was one of my stalkers. My smile slips.

"Excuse me, what is the address here?" I ask, pointing to River standing outside on the phone. "We're on our way to a friend's house and need it for directions."

She raises an eyebrow and flattens her mouth. "Sure, hon. It's 374 Sycamore, Candor, North Carolina." She holds up the coffeepot in her hand. "Coffee? Food?"

"No, but thank you," I say, heading back outside to give River the address.

He relays it into the phone. "Thanks, man. I owe you. See you in a minute."

I raise an eyebrow. "Who's Blink?" And how is he going to get here in a minute?

River grasps my elbow and ushers me around back. "He's a jumper. We need to get across the country to Texas. Public transportation has too many cameras with facial recognition."

"Does he need money?" I ask, dipping into the pack on my back. When River nods, I pull out a few hundred. "Is this enough?"

He takes it from me. "He'd do it for free, but he needs the cash. Thanks."

There's an odd noise behind me, and I turn to see a tall, auburn-haired guy with deep blue eyes, wearing a black leather motorcycle jacket, vans, and worn jeans. He scans me, then turns to River. "I can only take one of you at a time. Who wants to go first?"

Terrified, I glance at River and shake my head. "Is this safe?"

He laughs. "Teleportation is safe, but very disorienting. I'll go first. Make sure you have skin contact with Blink. Got it?" He grabs his hand and poof! They're gone.

I wrinkle my nose at the slight burning smell left behind. Am I really going to hitch a freaking ride with a guy named Blink? Shifting from one foot to the other, I look up at the night sky. There are so many stars out tonight. I pray my parents and Lionel are up there, looking down at me and keeping me safe.

Blink appears in front of me and holds out his hand. "I've never lost a person yet."

That's not quite reassuring, but I tentatively smile and place my hand in his. "I'm Greer, by the way."

"Mason," he admits in a cool tone.

Colors flash by, whirling around me, and nausea rises. Then it's gone, and I'm standing in a parking lot with puffs of prickly tumbleweed nearby.

Blink lets go of my hand and jerks his chin at River. "Later." He disappears.

For the next hour, I try to focus on our plans to hit the next facility, but forest green eyes continuously shatter any hope of concentration. Guilt about leaving her behind is eating at me. *Damn it.* I haven't found a solution that will guarantee her safety yet. She needs to be protected from that monster Hightower.

Quaid shifts restlessly beside me. "She's going to run. I'm telling you. Why would she ask for the go bag? I can't believe you gave it to her." His amber eyes stare at me accusingly.

"Where would she go? There's nothing for miles around," I remind him. "She's just on edge after seeing the captives today. It's a hard reality to accept." Even for hardened soldiers like us, the torture endured by those captives was tough to see. I look around the room and note the stoic determination on everyone's faces. We're more committed than ever to this path we've chosen.

I rub a hand across my chest. Why do I feel hollow inside? As if I'm missing something or making the wrong call? Quaid shifts next to me, bringing his hand to his chest too. I frown. Did we ingest something in the air at the Raven facility? I wouldn't put it past that bastard Hightower.

"You feel okay?" I ask Quaid.

"No, I'm irritated as hell at you," he replies shortly. "Why?"

"Something is off," I tell him, looking around at everyone else. Their attention is completely focused on Captain Walker as she outlines the plan she's devised for the next attack. None of them are rubbing their chests. "Don't you feel it?"

His hand stills. "It's her. She's gone." With a curse, he strides out the door.

Surely she wouldn't be so rash. Where could she go that's safe? Did River tell her about a place? I hurry to catch up with Quaid.

"The sun set over an hour ago. Her room," I tell him, watching him pivot away from the walkway leading to the bench and back to the dorms.

Instead of knocking, he pulls out the master key he keeps with him. Normally, I'd protest, but every inch of my gut is screaming. He thrusts open the door and stands there, taking in the room.

I step in and frown. Were we wrong? Feeling slightly stupid, I rifle through the clothes hanging in the closet. Two sets. Standard issue for every rescue is three, which means she's wearing one. Everything else seems in order. I move to the bathroom. Shampoo and conditioner in the shower. Soap is gone. So is her toothbrush.

Quaid curses, and I return to the bedroom. "She left a note. Addressed to you." His voice is gruff as he hands it to me and paces back and forth. "I'm calling Nash."

Oliver,

Please don't blame River. He begged me to stay here, but I wouldn't be able to forgive myself if I did. By saving me, he put his family at risk. As an orphan, I can't bear the thought of his family paying the ultimate price. Families deserve to be together. Seeing those captives today brought home the reality of what they're facing, and I can't bear the thought of safety while they remain in Raven's grasp. I hope we make it back here, to the safety you've promised, but if I don't, forgive me.

Thank you for everything,

Greer

"Damn it. Lionel put her in my care, and I fucked up," I curse, closing my eyes for a second to think. Failure is not an option. "Nash. What did he say?" I could hear Quaid talking on the phone while I was reading the note.

"Actually, he was just about to call you. I believe you asked him to track River's movements for the last two years. It took a while. River frequently changes his appearance, but once the software concentrated on the one feature he didn't change, he was able to connect the dots," Quaid states with satisfaction.

"His eyes," I pick up where he leaves off. "Where?"

"Nash said he moved around the country a lot, but always returned to one of three places," he replies in a hard tone. "Atlanta, Lubbock, and Asheville. Nash searched our internal data for bases in those areas but found nothing. But he thinks there's a secret list of government facilities that aren't listed in the larger database. Kind of like this place. Think your father can help?"

Without answering, I pick up my phone. When my father answers, he spends the first two minutes giving me hell for giving up my commission and leading an attack against one of our government facilities.

Having heard enough, I butt in. "Stop. Do what you do best —damage control. Right now, I need you to reach out to your contact in the Pentagon and find out if there are any government facilities near Atlanta, Lubbock, or Asheville. I need the information ASAP. I'll call back in thirty."

Quaid practically rips the phone out of my hand when he hears that last comment. "Thirty gives Greer and River one hell of a head start." He stalks to the door. "I'm going to get my gear, and you better pray we catch up to them. Who's our best tracker?"

"Jax, but Gabe would be easier," I answer, hurrying to follow him. "Did you ask Nash to start a new search for River and Greer in the cities surrounding us? We need a direction."

"Affirmative," he replies gruffly. His cool intellect already working out the possible routes. "He's on it. Meet you back here in ten."

I nod and round the corner, almost running into Jax. "Sorry. By the way, we're borrowing Gabe for a while."

Jax lifts a cool eyebrow. "Sniping or tracking?" His bright ocean blue eyes are watching me closely.

"Tracking," I reply with a wave. "Maybe both. Not sure."

He immediately moves in front of me, stopping me in my tracks. "What's happening?" Hands on hips, he looks relaxed, but I don't buy it. He's a master at disguising his real thoughts. Too many years spent in hidden places, preying on the enemy.

"Greer and River are gone," I tell him, trying to slip past. When he steps in my way again, I turn my stare on him. "Get the hell out of my way. Time is of the essence."

He raises his hands. "I'm better at tracking and sniping. Take me."

I consider it. He's the best, which is the reason I requested his reassignment to this compound, but he only follows the orders he chooses. "Fine. Inform Quaid. We leave in five." Pushing past him, I enter my office in a rush. "Captain, you're in charge. If we don't make it back in seventy-two hours, head to the location Beckett gives you. We'll meet you there."

She takes one look at my set face and automatically salutes me. "Roger that." Her nose wrinkles, then she chuckles. "Sorry, saluting is a hard habit to break. We'll continue working on the plan."

As my own hand automatically rose to salute her back, I flash a wry smile. "It is. Carry on." I grab my pack and head back out the door.

When I get to the courtyard, Quaid and Jax are waiting for me, along with Nash, who steps forward to hand me a satellite phone. "They hit a diner off of I-74. Cameras don't have a time-stamp. Straight west from here, a little under eight miles. Chopper is waiting. I'll continue to monitor from here. Good luck." His brown eyes sweep from Quaid to myself to Jax. "As soon as you hear from your father, relay the intel, and I'll work up an analysis."

I stuff the items in my pack and clap him on the back. "Thanks, Nash."

Quaid stalks toward the helipad. "Load up."

Less than a minute later, we circle over the compound and head toward the diner. The bird makes it in three minutes. Quaid must have told them it was urgent. They set down a click out, so we don't alert them, but when we see the diner, we know we're too late.

An old grey cinder block diner sits on the corner of nowhere, its asphalt parking lot full of cracks and weeds. Large dirty windows offer a murky glimpse into the inside. Beyond the garish orange neon sign, loudly proclaiming they're open, there's one soul in a booth eating, a cook, and a server.

The smell of greasy food hits me when I open the door, and my nose wrinkles. I make a quick call. "Nash, I need a picture of River and Greer." Damn it. Gnashing my teeth, I curse silently. I can't believe we left without one.

My phone pings two seconds later, and I walk over to the server. "Have you seen these two people?"

An older woman in her sixties, she quietly assesses the fatigues I'm wearing, then purses her lips. "They were here. Left maybe ten minutes ago. Why? They in trouble?" Her eyes widen when she sees Quaid stalk past the window. "He with you?"

"Yes," I say tersely. "Which way did they go?"

"Around back," she replies with a shrug. "Didn't see a car."

I nod at the cook and customer, who are watching the entire exchange. "Thank you." I place a twenty on the counter and head out the door.

Quaid stops pacing. "Well?"

"She said they left ten minutes ago. Around back," I tell him, watching him hurry around the building. "Jax."

Jax stops looking at the stars to follow me to the rear, where Quaid motions him over to a specific spot.

"I don't see tire tracks," Quaid informs him. "Think they took off on foot?"

Jax holds up a hand, then walks in a circle. He widens it once, twice, but stops on the third time. "They disappear." He frowns and returns to the center and retraces his steps again. "No car. Not on foot. They're just gone."

Surprised, I dart a glance at Quaid. "See any traces of ash?"

Jax squints, then pulls out a flashlight. Carefully stepping, he restarts the entire process. "Here." He looks at me. "How did you know?"

"Fuck!" I curse. "A jumper." Jax lifts a confused eyebrow. "A jumper has the ability to transport themselves anywhere. The best ones can bring someone with them. Although, I've never heard of one able to carry two passengers."

Jax mulls over my answer and continues to walk his circles. "He didn't. Looks like he made two jumps. Here and here." He points to the two piles of ash. "What's with the ash?"

I lift a shoulder. "Pieces of their clothing get caught in the jump. We think it's a chemical reaction, but we're not sure." I dial Nash. "Jumper picked them up. We're going to wait here another ten minutes, then call my father."

Jax looks at Quaid and me. "She has a mark, doesn't she?" His tone is mild, but we both hear the excitement in his voice. "Any idea why some of us have it and others don't? I mean, I used to think the most powerful got them, but that theory fizzled pretty quickly."

The marks used to bother me, but when nothing happened with them, I pushed the thoughts aside and concentrated on the day-to-day task of managing Phoenix. Now, I'm back to wondering. Instead of answering him, though, I call my father.

He answers on the first ring. "Nothing in Atlanta or Asheville. Cannon AFB in New Mexico is the nearest active base. Reese AFB was closed in the nineties, then turned into a wind research institute in 1997. The only other location listed near that area was a small weapons depot, but it was closed as well. Do you want to tell me what this is about?" His tone is cautious, as if he's not sure he wants to hear it.

"No, but be on the lookout for a truck full of intel heading your way. They kept documents of the experiments. It's worse than what they did to us in the Army," I tell him, trying to keep the bitterness out of my tone. Granted, we volunteered to assist the Army in their research, but we never realized they would take it that far. When my father found out what they were doing to us, he stopped it in its tracks.

"Hell," he returns softly. "I'll do my best with what you send me. Rumblings from the Capitol tell me Hightower's going for the jugular. I'm fighting him, tooth and nail. In the meantime, ditch your cell and call me on the other line going forward." He pauses for a second. "Good luck, son." The line goes dead.

It's bad if he called me son. I tap the off button and strip the SIM from my cell. Then, toss the phone in the dumpster. Quaid and Jax silently follow my lead without even asking. Good thing Nash sent a phone with us. This one is registered to the Army. We'll have to eventually ditch it, too, but for now, nobody but Nash knows we have it.

"Weapons depot outside of Reese AFB. Shut down in the 90s. We'll take the chopper to the airport. Have a private plane ready for us. Untraceable. The hunt for us is on," I relay to Nash. "Send the team to the location. Armed and ready. We'll meet them there."

I stop and think for a minute. "Kill the cells for the entire team. This phone is limited-use only. We'll pick up a couple of burners." Last order. "Tell Beckett to move us out asap. We can't wait for Friday."

"Where did you meet Mason?" I ask, looking at the strip mall next to us. When he lifts an eyebrow, I almost shake my head. Guys and their nicknames. "I mean Blink."

"Atlanta," he tells me. His head swivels around, and he motions to the car rental place. "We need a car. The place we're going is twenty miles west of here, but first, I need to pick up a hat and fake glasses."

Using my fingertips, I stretch the sweatshirt out. "New clothes. Normal ones. Non-negotiable." I didn't dare ask Oliver if he'd gotten me the clothes I requested.

"There's a Wal-Mart about a mile that way," he says, pointing down the dark street. Even with the streetlamps, it's tough to see much. "We need to hurry, though. I don't know how much longer the rental place will stay open."

Taking my hand in his, he takes off. A few minutes later, we turn a corner, and bright lights shine across a busy parking lot. Relieved to see people and normal life, I flash a smile at River.

Instead of his usual relaxed smile, his lips curve halfway, then flatten. "If someone calls my name, don't turn around. Keep walking. If they stop me, pretend you don't know me, okay? A lot of the guards come here." He stops at the entrance. "You remember their uniforms, right?"

An image of the bird's beady red eyes comes to mind. "Yep. Why don't we split up and meet back at the front in ten minutes?" I reach over and hand him the hundred I'd stashed in my jeans earlier. Then I walk through the doors directly to the clothes section.

I grimace at the sweatshirts, even the pretty ones, and settle for a couple of long sleeve t-shirts, a jacket, and pair of jeans. Plus, a few underthings. I head into the dressing room to make sure everything fits, which it does, but I also pull out several bills and stuff them in my jeans.

There's plenty of cash in here still, remembering the day Brad handed it to Lionel. I wonder where the money came from. Zipping it closed, I grab the clothes and head to the front.

I look around, but there's no sign of River. With a shrug, I move to the side of the aisle and wait. And wait. Surely he wouldn't leave me here in the middle of nowhere while he went and saved his family, would he? I bite my lip. He would. Just when I think he's ditched me, I see him striding down the aisle with a man in blue fatigues with a familiar armband.

I ease into the clothing rack behind me and watch the two of them laugh as they walk by. River catches my eye and subtly shakes his head. The two of them get in line to check out. Weaving through the clothes, I head to a cashier farther down. Slinging the clothes on the conveyor belt, I watch the two of them out of the corner of my eye, but not once do I turn my head.

Quickly paying, I head straight to the restroom to change clothes. I tear off the tags but keep them in my hands to show the person who checks the receipts by the door. Happily, I stuff the grey sweatsuit into the trash. When I get out, I look around, but neither of them is close by. I head out the front door. The minute I step outside, a hand grabs my elbow, and I jerk my head to the right and see beautiful green eyes staring at me.

"You scared the shit out of me," I whisper to him. "Where did he go?"

His eyes are bright with excitement. "He's off shift. Going home for the night." He holds up his hand to show me a plastic key card. "Our ticket into the facility. There's a side door with no guards."

I smile because I'm not sure what else to do. Sneaking into a government facility is absolutely terrifying. My eyes catch on the dark T-shirt and jeans he's wearing. They make his green eyes pop. "Much better than the grey sweats."

He leans forward and nibbles on my lips. "I can't imagine not having you by my side, but before we do this, I need you to promise me something."

I shake my head. "No, I won't leave."

He places a finger on my lips. "Promise me that if something happens, you'll think about me every once in a while. Good or bad. I don't care. Touch a plant, smell a flower. I'll feel it wherever I am."

"Promise," I murmur, barely able to get the words out. I know there's a good chance neither of us is going to make it out tonight. Stepping into his arms, I breathe in the spring smell that is such an intrinsic part of him. Honeysuckle and flowers and the earth.

"Do I smell like water?" I ask suddenly, wondering if my powers have changed the way I smell.

His lips twitch with laughter. "No? I mean, you smell nice. Very clean. But not like the ocean or anything."

I slug him in the arm. "Stop laughing at me. You smell like spring. I thought... never mind."

He laces his fingers in mine. "Let's go. We need to get to the rental place."

Aware of the clock ticking against us, we walk quickly back to the strip mall. River goes in and comes out a few minutes later with a set of keys. He walks over to a dark grey Altima and unlocks the door for me.

Nervous, I rub my hands on the rough denim, trying to ease the nerves attacking me. I have no clue what I'm walking into. If only I could have joined the raid... Instead, I have brutal images of what a place like this will do to its captives. I shiver. More reason not to get caught.

Fifteen minutes later, River pulls into a park. "It's a five-minute walk to the facility. Last chance to back out. You can wait here." His eyes drift from my eyes to my lips. "Please don't say no."

In answer, I get out of the car and slip my backpack on over the black jacket I just bought, then pull up the hood. A second later, he gets out and comes over to my side.

"You're so stubborn," he says with a sigh. "My mom's going to love you." He points to a dirt path. "We'll take this through the park to the side of the facility. Everyone thinks it's being used as a warehouse because there are so few windows. It's not very big, though. We can get in and out quickly."

Not willing to chance our voices carrying in the still night air, we're silent the entire way. Once we get to the side of the facility, I understand why they think it's a warehouse. It's a long rectangular building made of cinder blocks and painted Creech brown. Small windows top the structure, but that's it.

The standard military paint makes me smile as I think of Beckett's silver eyes twinkling with laughter as he told me that story.

River places his lips by my ear. "There are a few more guards than usual. Might be because of the raid yesterday. I'll go in first, make sure it's clear, then signal for you, okay?"

I nod.

He walks out of the trees and heads straight for the single grey door on this side of the building. A small light shines down on it. He slips inside just in time. A guard walks by a minute later and tests the knob. Locked. He moves on.

My eyes burn from staring at the door. To distract myself, I scan the building. Another guard goes by. Is he on a rotation? Should I be counting the minutes? I wish someone had given me a manual for this first.

The door eases open, and I hold my breath. River's head ducks out, and when he sees the coast is clear, he waves me forward. My legs are shaking like crazy, but I stumble out of the trees and jog across to him.

Once inside, he pulls me into his arms. "Put this on. There are a lot of guards here and your jacket will stand out." He thrusts a dark blue button down into my hands.

I look around the small room. There's a coffeepot on the counter and a table with four chairs. I pull off my jacket and put it in my backpack, then slip the button-down on over my t-shirt. He silently hands me an armband, and I slide the hateful insignia up my arm. He's going to owe me for this.

With my hand in his, he leads me out of the break room and down the hall to a janitor's closet. "Put your pack in here. We'll grab it on our way out."

Uneasy at the thought of leaving it, I swallow hard and stash the pack in the corner where someone won't see it. "Are they here?"

Tears fill his eyes. "They're here. In rough shape. Worse than Lance. We're going to have to help them out, but I have a plan."

Infirmary. He slips in and rolls out two wheelchairs. "We'll get my sister first. She's more mobile, and her powers can help us, if needed."

He wheels the chair down the stark white hallway filled with fluorescent lights quickly and with purpose. A guard walks by but doesn't stop. He's wearing the same dark shirt and armband as us.

River stops and swivels the wheelchair around to face a door. He presses the key card against the electronic lock, and when it clicks, enters first.

"Hey, Brat, I've missed you," he says in a low voice full of emotion.

A beautiful, but skeletal, face topped with long white-blond hair turns toward River and smiles, bright blue eyes sparking with disbelief and happiness. Using the table, she pushes herself up and slowly walks over to her brother. "You shouldn't have come, but I'm happy I get to see you one last time." Her frail arms wrap around River.

Tears roll down his face. His eyes, heavy with guilt, turn toward me, and he shakes his head. "I'll always come for you, Lily."

I swipe the wetness from my cheeks. This is wrong. In what world do they have the right to destroy someone so beautiful? I look around the small room. A cot, a small table with two chairs, and a nightstand with a lamp. I peek in an open door and see a closet with one shirt and two pairs of matching cotton pants. That's it. No bathroom.

"We actually have it better than a lot of the others," she says softly. "Hi, I'm Lily." She holds out a fragile hand, pale as snow. I realize it's been a long time since she's been outside.

I reach out and enfold her in a gentle hug. "I'm Greer, River's friend. I'm so, so sorry. You're too beautiful and sweet for this horrendous place. Once we get you out of here, we'll find you a comfy couch in the sun where you can lie like a cat all day."

"I haven't seen the sun in years. I'd like that," she says wistfully, then looks at the clock. "Shift change is in forty minutes. They've quadrupled the number of guards this week, so we need to be gone before sunrise. Mom's at the end of the hallway." Shuffling over to the wheelchair, she eases into it.

I look at River. How are we going to get them across the park? There's no way I can pull a wheelchair across the dirt and grass.

He looks at me. "Stop worrying." His fingers slide along Lily's neck. "No collar?"

Her laugh is full of bitterness. "No need for a collar when you have very little strength or when they can threaten your family. Mom doesn't have one either."

"Fuck. I'm sorry." He clucks her under the chin. "Hang on." Spinning the wheelchair around, he zooms to the door, making her laugh. It's hoarse and thready, but full of affection. He ducks his head out, then motions for me to follow.

This time, we don't pass anyone, but the hall is full of doors with windows on them. Like Lily's. I move closer to the wall and peek in when we pass by, seeing a person in each one. A captive. My feet slow.

River looks back and hisses, "Hurry up."

I point to the doors. "What about them? We can't leave them."

"We'll tell Oliver when we get back. See if he can send men to get the rest," he promises me. "Please, please hurry. This is my only chance to get them out."

"River," Lily says with a shake of her head. "She's right. Every one of these people has been here with us since the beginning. We can't leave them."

River glares at us both but doesn't reply. He simply speeds up. A minute later, he stops at a door. I look back. It's a long way to the exit.

He wheels his sister into the room, and I follow. "Mom."

The body on the bed slowly turns over and stares at him for a solid minute before recognition slips into the depths of her light blue eyes. "River. I knew you'd come. Come give me a hug. I've missed you."

He bends down and wraps his arms around her small body. "I'm here to save you," he says, tears muffling the words. "I should have done it a long time ago, but I was too scared to go against him. I'm sorry. So sorry." He breaks down, clutching her to him.

"Hush," she tells him, wiping the hair back from his face. "My beautiful boy. You're here now. That's all that counts." Like Lily, she has a head of white-blond hair. Supposedly River does, too, although I've only seen him with the brown.

"We need to go," Lily interjects in a worried tone. She turns toward me. "Please."

Taking a deep breath, I push the wheelchair over to the two on the bed and touch River. "We have to get them out of here."

He flinches, but I gently tap his mom on the shoulder. "Let me help you into the chair."

His mom looks up at me and tentatively smiles. "Introduce me to your friend, River." It's clear she isn't sure whether to trust me or not.

Lily leans forward and whispers, "This is his girlfriend, Greer."

Not technically, but with a shrug of acceptance, I look at his mom. "Nice to meet you. Unfortunately, we need to leave right now." I lean over and help lift her fragile body into the chair. "There. Let's go."

"I'm Susan," she replies, then catches River's hand in hers. "You'll never make it with me tagging along. Save Lily. Please. Do it for me. Knowing my children are safe is all I've ever wanted."

I pull his hand out of her tiny one. "We're all leaving together." I know I'm being abrupt, but honestly, I'm not sure I can leave her behind either. With a twirl, I turn the chair around and head straight to the door.

"I like her," Lily says with a snicker. "River. Now." She knows it's urgent we leave immediately.

We walk quickly down the hall but not too fast. A couple of guards pass by, but none stop. Each time I hold my breath, and I hear his mom do the same. I squeeze her shoulder. Skin and bones are all I feel beneath her thin gown.

Anger builds every time I look at Lily and Susan. Innocent. Tortured almost to death. Why? For revenge? Or something more sinister? Hightower's an evil, evil man. So was Trent. Warped by the same mindset as his father.

River slows at the janitor's closet, and I reach in and grab my bag. I tuck it in the chair with his mom, then follow him to the break room. When we get near, several soldiers walk out.

One looks at us, and his eyes narrow. In response, River continues walking down the hall to throw him off.

"There's another exit up ahead, but it will put us too far from the park," River murmurs to the three of us once we're past the soldiers. "We need to go back." He slows, looking behind him, then turns the chair around when he doesn't see anyone.

I do the same. Please, please let us get out of here. But when I turn, the guard is coming back around the corner, several armed guards with him.

Lily curses and raises her hands. Locks click up and down the hallway, releasing the prisoners held inside. Weak and wearing collars, they shuffle outside, but the second they see the soldiers, they launch themselves at them like rabid dogs, tearing into them with their hands and teeth. The collars restrict their powers, but do little to restrain them, giving us precious minutes to escape.

We roll through the break room and out the door. Thankfully, there's nobody waiting for us, but the tree line looks so far away. Even if we make it, how are we supposed to run with the guards right behind us?

I look at River. This is hopeless. "How?"

His eyes grow brighter. "With nature's help." Vines slither out of the park and hoist the two wheelchairs in the air. "I'll get..." A shot rings out, and River's body jerks. He drops to one knee, and the wheelchairs crash to the ground.

I run to help Susan into a chair, then Lily.

Soldiers hurry out of the building and push both wheelchairs away from us. One grabs my arm, while two others grab River. With little effort, they haul us toward the front of the building. I search the grim faces around me. Nobody looks at me, but they're watching River very closely.

Once in the front, they shove us to the ground. Clapping

echoes in the dawn air. Confused, I look up and see Senator Hightower himself, standing there with a broad smile on his face. Dark wavy hair, perfectly combed, tall, with an athletic physique; he's an older version of Trent. Fury rises in me.

Next to him is a dark-haired man with the darkest of brown eyes, almost black in color, around five feet nine inches tall. Dressed entirely in black, he gives off a menacing air, but when his gaze moves to me, there's a look of... anticipation in his eyes. They almost sparkle with excitement. My head pounds every time he looks in my direction. Why does he look so familiar? What does he want? His face smooths of all expression when Hightower turns toward him.

"Right again, Hernandez," he says, then turns away, clearly dismissing him. The man steps back but doesn't leave. "River, I have a conundrum. On one hand, I'm very disappointed in you, and you know how much I loathe disappointment. It's clear you were trying to defect, and I told you a long time ago that wasn't going to happen."

He walks over and helps me stand. "On the other hand, you've also made me very happy. Bringing me the young woman I've been hoping to meet for so long." Once I'm standing, he grips my chin and pulls my head up until my eyes meet his. Unlike Trent's chocolate brown eyes, Senator Hightower's eyes are lighter in color. Cold and calculating, he stares down at me. "Willa, is it?"

The sound of my real name coming from his lips pisses me off, and I jerk my chin from his fingers. "Actually, it's Greer." He doesn't deserve to say my name.

"Take them back," he orders the soldiers, motioning to the two wheelchairs.

Lily and Susan look at each other.

Susan forces herself to stand. "I'm not going back." Her chin lifts in defiance.

River drags himself up and lunges for her. "Don't, Mom." He tears his gaze from her and looks at Hightower. "Please. I'll do anything you want. Don't hurt her."

Hightower laughs. "For years, you and your sister have been defying me, and I've graciously overlooked these small, hardly noticeable rebellions, but not anymore. Maybe you both need a valuable lesson."

He looks from River to Lily. "Lily. Lily. Lily. I leave your collar off, and this is how you repay me?" A split second later, he dips his chin, and the soldier behind Susan steps up and places a gun to her head.

Lily's hands begun to glow blue, but she quickly stifles them. "Please. I'll wear the collar." Tears fall rapidly as she begs Hightower. "She won't last much longer. Let us spend her last days together. Please."

River strains against the two guards holding him, blood dripping into the dirt. "I'll do anything. Anything at all. I know a jumper." He spits out, desperate to save his mother. "He's remarkable. The perfect addition to your collection."

My attention shifts to River in horror, and I realize this is what he's always done. With very little leverage, he plays the cards in his hands. Except for me. For some reason, I was the line he wouldn't cross.

Susan calmly looks at both of her children. "From the moment you were born, I've loved you more than anything in this world. We had the best of times together. On the road. In the parks. Quiet spaces meant for us. I can't hang on any longer. It's my time." She looks down at herself. "My strength is gone, but my love for you will never end. I love you."

Hightower nods and the gun goes off. Susan slumps down in the chair, a surprisingly neat hole in her head, the ground to her right splattered with blood and gore.

Lily screams and screams. Her hands begin to glow with a blue light, and with a single flick, she sends the soldiers behind her to the other end of the long field. Pushing to her feet, she raises her arms and whirls them around. Men and dirt go flying, caught up in the tornado of her power.

Weeds erupt from the ground, latching onto ankles and dragging soldiers down, smothering them with the dirt.

Hightower laughs and signals to a man on his right. Wrists in chains, but no collar, he stares at Lily. Her power cuts off. Then he does the same to River.

"River, I don't think you've met Henry," Hightower says with a smirk. When River doesn't answer, he shrugs. "Henry has absolutely no offense abilities, which is why he doesn't have to wear a collar. He's fantastic as a defensive weapon, though. Nulls everyone's powers very effectively."

Lily howls with anger, but River goes silent.

Hightower turns to me. "Tell me, Greer. What are your abilities?"

For some reason, I laugh. "Water. That's it. Nothing special."

"Ah, but that's not true, is it?" He says with a pensive look. "You're marked, which means you have a second power, correct?"

"Not that I'm aware of," I reply with a chuckle. This man is going to kill me for my ability to make a stream of water rise or burst out of a pipe. Big whoop. "I'm kind of a dud. Didn't River tell you?"

River turns sad eyes in my direction. "She hasn't found a second power. However, she's beautiful and kind with a big heart. A great kisser, too. I fell for her the moment I looked between the leaves of that bush at the university and haven't been the same since. That's her greatest power."

He looks at his sister. "Lily. I'm sorry I didn't save you and Mom. All these years. I should have been a better brother. Gotten you two out of here."

Lily's bright blue eyes spark with anger. "You're the best brother. Nobody would have sacrificed so much to save us. I love you, River. Are you ready?"

He smiles at Hightower. "I'm ready, are you?"

Henry's head explodes, and he drops to the ground. Puzzled, I look from him to the hills beyond the facility and see men and women with guns heading toward us. Quaid's storming across the field, bullets blazing, while fire flicks out like a whip, burning everything before him. Beside him strides Oliver with his perfect posture, wearing fatigues instead of his usual suit, also firing a gun, but his real power lies with his mind. One look and soldier after soldier surrenders to his will.

I exhale in relief.

Henry's death releases Lily and River's power. Both of them erupt into a whirlwind, taking out soldiers right and left.

Hightower taps something on his phone, and an alarm goes off in the building behind us. Blaring loudly, soldiers begin running out of the building to join the fight.

Hightower strides forward and grabs my arm. I look around, but there's no water anywhere. Panic tries to take hold, but I squash it by pretending I'm in Quaid's class. His arm is on fire, and I need to put it out. I close my eyes and open my senses to the world around me.

There is a small amount of water under my feet, possibly the facilities pipeline, but it's not enough to save me. I keep searching. Bingo. A large body of water lies to the east. Concentrating hard, I try to move it closer, but the thread connecting us keeps slipping from my grasp. Damn it. It's too far away. Why the hell did they have to build this facility in the freaking desert?

The soldier next to Hightower drops and another one yells, "Sniper!"

I smile, knowing it's Jax. His power is faint, but I can feel it.

Hightower ducks down and shoves me forward.

Taking advantage of the distraction, I drop to the ground and roll into the legs of the soldier next to me, knocking him down, then try to stand and run. He grabs my leg. I kick back.

"Greer!" River shouts, turning in a circle. He spots me on the ground and dirt flies up and into the face of the man behind me, blinding him.

I jump up and run toward River.

Helicopters arrive. For a second, I hope it's reinforcements, but soldiers in Raven blue file out. My heart sinks. I look around the field. We're clearly outnumbered.

Hightower runs to the nearest helicopter, points to me, then gets on board. It takes off. Men rush over and start dragging me toward the other aircraft.

Lily screams and goes down. River races to help her.

A blazing line of fire appears, splitting the soldiers into two groups. Quaid emerges from the dust, firing shot after shot into one group, while his mind wields fire against the second.

Oliver protects Quaid's back, shooting any who get close, but when soldiers raise their guns to shoot him, they find themselves shooting each other. Scared, they try to resist, but their minds aren't strong enough. I shiver when I see the fight in their eyes turn to resignation. Oliver's power is terrifying.

Electricity arcs high in the sky, then lands on the shoulders of a soldier. Like hopscotch, it jumps to the next and next, electrocuting every single one of them. David emerges from the crowd, arms energized with power.

Shots continue to ring out. Everywhere. Pain hits me, and I look down, expecting to see a bullet wound, but instead, I see a taser. The damn soldiers hit me again, and my body violently convulses. I scream for help.

Soldiers rush Oliver and take him to the ground. Quaid stalks over to help him, fire preceding every step, gun easily eliminating those who manage to avoid the flames.

Someone picks me up and begins carrying me to the helicopter. Panicking, I focus on the water in the distance. The ground shakes, but nothing appears.

An anguished shout from River has me whipping around to find him. Lily's on the ground. Not moving. He shakes her, but her head lolls from one side to the other. He bends down and picks her up. Tears falling, he carries her over to his mother and lays her down. He arranges their bodies carefully. Hands clasped together. Flower crowns in their hair. Petals of all different colors covering their bodies.

He staggers to his feet, power bursting out of him in green waves. It quickly begins eating up the ground around him, creating a forest full of spiky flowers, carnivorous plants, and sinister trees. Soldiers in the path of destruction are quickly assimilated into the forest he's creating, some turning to dust, others absorbed into the very fabric of nature.

"No, River, don't!" I yell, but he doesn't hear me.

His eyes search the crowd around him. Shots hit his body, but the bullets are quickly spit out again. Wounds healing in an instant. Nothing can stop him. His power continues to grow, spreading across the ground like a wave of locusts, covering the bodies of his enemies.

"River!" I scream, biting the hand holding me. When the soldier curses and lets go, I shove him away and run toward River. "Stop. Please stop."

His green eyes find mine, and he falters for a brief second, but when another bullet slams into his shoulder, his hatred and grief returns.

I reach for him, taking his hand in mine. Time slows, then ceases to exist. The two of us in a bubble of our own making. "Don't leave me." I plead with him.

"I love you, Willa. Greer. Whatever name you want to call yourself. The moment I saw you, my life changed forever. The last few weeks with you have been heaven. Because of you, I lived. Now, I'm free." A vine crawls up from the ground and caresses my cheek. "I've done so many bad things. Unforgiveable acts. This is my chance to redeem myself and save at least one of the people I love. You." His eyes slide to Susan and Lily. "Don't cry for me. The three musketeers will be together again."

"I won't ever forget you, River," I tell him, reminding him of my promise. "Because of you, I live." The ground trembles, and I release his hand, then step back.

His power erupts like Old Faithful, spewing across the soldiers, wiping half of them out. Vines and flowers and plants rise from the ground, covering his body, and for a minute, I think they're healing him, but instead, his power consumes his body, and he becomes one with the very nature he loved so much. Lilies, in a rich pink color, cover the ground where his sister used to be, and black-eyed Susans, with their bright yellow petals, blanket the spot next to her.

Guards scramble around me. Grabbing my arms, they try to drag me toward the helicopter, but my eyes are glued to the beauty unleashed by River. My heart breaks into a million pieces for their loss. Sorrow like nothing I've ever felt before wells up and overflows my heart. Not for one person, but for everyone whose lost loved ones to the fear and vengeance hatefully wielded by Hightower and his flock of Ravens. To all the fallen. And for what? For the power that resides in our veins. Our blood. Our heritage.

The ground shifts, and the water answers, but I release my grip on it. I don't want the water to come and wash away this tribute to River and his family. In a daze, I stare sightlessly at the chaos around me, and that's when I feel it. Water. In their bodies.

Power rises and joins with mine, more than I've ever wielded. It's almost nuclear, but unlike River's unleashed fury, I have complete control of it, and I know what to do.

I touch the nearest soldier, and he falls to the ground, his shriveled body a husk. I touch another, then another. I hear someone order me to stop, but I can't. I won't. I want our loved ones back. I want the people they stole from us. My head swims, and the faces around me blur. The world dims. My knees give out.

Strong arms catch me. "I've got you." Oliver cradles me to his chest. "Quaid. We need to get out of here before reinforcements arrive. Rescue the captives in the building. Eliminate the evidence. We don't need this getting out."

I shove against Oliver. "Not River and his family. Don't burn them."

A warm finger trails across my cheek. "I won't." Quaid's rough voice promises me.

Heat burns the very air around us, and a bright light sears my eyes. I turn my head into Oliver's chest. "You came."

"I had to... you left," Oliver replies in a low tone.

Like every day the last week, she lies in the bed without moving. I stare, waiting, and when her chest rises and falls, I can finally sit. Her silky dark hair fans out around her pale face. What I wouldn't give to see her forest green eyes shooting sparks at me. With a sigh, I pick up my book.

Beckett comes in and raises an eyebrow, but I shake my head. His mouth turns down, and he quietly leaves the room. Jax swings by and drops into the chair on the other side, then turns the TV on.

I scowl at the little shit. He knows this is my time slot. "Get out."

He flicks an unimpressed glance in my direction, then continues to flip through the channels. "She's probably bored to death with you in here. What are you reading? Some dry ass book on war strategy?"

I tuck the book into the chair to obscure the title, but the smirk on his face tells me he knows. "Have you carved out a place for the range?"

Beckett found us a place in the wilds of Wyoming. With the Grand Tetons on one side, and flat range on the other, it's the perfect place to hole up while the shit dies down. The old ranch has a ton of habitable outbuildings that we're slowly turning into quarters, a mess hall, and an equipment and weapons depot. Operations and the war room are located here in the main house. Along with Greer.

He waves a hand. "Of course." His chin drops to her. "Why hasn't she woken?"

There's a note of worry I don't think I've ever heard in his voice. I shrug. "Pulling on our powers overloaded her system. We're used to wielding a lot; she's not. When her body has rested, she'll wake," I explain confidently, although I'm purely guessing at this point.

With the volume lowered, he stares at the screen, but I can see the wheels turning in his head. The same as the rest of us. Although she only drew power from Oliver and me, all the marked felt a bond snap into place on that field. One born of power and blood. But why was Greer the catalyst?

He abruptly sits up and increases the volume.

Irritated, I glare at him. "Turn it down."

"Look," he fires back, pointing to the TV. "Hightower's holding a press conference."

Oliver comes racing into the room, along with Beckett, but they stop when they see the TV on. "Turn it up."

Jax looks at me. "I was just about to." He punches a button on the remote, and the newscaster's voice fills the air.

"If you're just joining us, armed men burst into Simon's, a well-known dining establishment for members of Congress, and kidnapped Senator Jack Harrison at gunpoint. We have few details right now, but we're hoping Senator Thomas Hightower can shed some light on the situation," she announces, turning toward the cameras. "We're going live at Capitol Hill."

The scene changes to the Capitol building, where Hightower is standing at a podium. "At this time, we know very little. Senator Jack Harrison was dining alone at Simon's. He was the only target. We have received no ransom demands. That's all we have to share right now."

"Bastard," a weak voice spits out, jerking our heads in her direction. "Help me sit up." Her hand reaches toward me, but I ignore it and wrap my arms around her back and gently pull her up into a sitting position.

"Welcome back," I say gruffly, relief filling every cell in my body. "That's it. Give him hell."

Her eyes, full of hatred, turn back to the TV.

I sit down and look over at Oliver. This is hitting him hard. Not just him. Hell, we're all feeling ambushed and pissed off.

After a barrage of questions that give us few answers, High-tower steps away from the podium to join a group of men. With a wave, they turn and head back inside the Capitol.

Oliver drops into a chair and rubs his hand down his face.

We've been waiting for them to make a move, but we never expected this to be it. Not once. Hightower has balls. Kidnapping a fellow senator of the United States. There isn't any line he won't cross to win this war. He must think taking out Jack will cripple us, but now that we've left the Army, we have a lot more options.

"Wait... rewind!" Greer suddenly yells. Her eyes are glued to the screen. Fingers white with tension grip the sheet. Jax rewinds it back to the podium, then hits play. "Stop. Right there."

We all look from the screen to her and back again. "What is it?"

"It's Trent," she says, her voice barely audible. When none of us says anything, she narrows her eyes. "I'm not crazy. It's him. Can you zoom in or something?"

"Nash!" Jax shouts, and we hear feet running from across the house.

Breathless, Nash walks into the room. "What? Where's the fire?"

"Can you zoom in on that group of men?" Jax asks, pointing to the screen.

Nash curses and flips off Jax. "Let me get my laptop."

He returns and grabs a seat at the small desk in the room. Fingers fly over the keyboard as he finds the broadcast, splices it up, then loads it to another program. He clicks on the images on the screen to zoom in closer. "Done. Let me put it on the TV."

We all watch as Senator Hightower leaves the podium and crosses over to the group of men. He places his hand on the back of the one next to him. A familiar gesture, but it tells us nothing.

Nash clicks through to the next frame and zooms in. The man next to Hightower turns and looks back at the camera, perfectly capturing the features of the good looks he got from his Italian mother.

"Son of a bitch," I say, staring in disbelief at the face on the TV. "I completely missed it."

She grimaces. "I wish I had. It's hard to forget the face of someone you've killed." She swallows hard. "You know what this means?" When we all look at her with confused expressions on our faces, she huffs. "He's one of us. Which means one of his parents is, too. The mother, maybe? Or Hightower?" Her voice drops as she considers the ramifications.

We all share a look. "Are you sure you killed him?"

"I snapped his neck. When I woke up the next morning, he was still lying on the ground next to me, eyes open, staring sightlessly at the sky," she recalls. "But there was a moment when I reached the top of the cliff where I thought I saw him smile." She blows out a frustrated breath. "I don't know. Damn it."

"We'll look into it, but first, we need to rescue Jack," I say with a frown, turning toward Oliver.

Oliver's head rises, his eyes flashing a dark stormy grey. "I should have seen this coming. For some reason, I thought my father's position kept him safe. Fuck Hightower. The gloves are coming off." He stands and starts pacing. "We're not going to win this battle in a direct fight. With the government behind him, he has access to endless troops."

"We're not stopping the rescues, right?" Greer butts in, her lip between her teeth.

I reach over and pull it out. "Hell no. We'll find a way to infiltrate the facilities from the inside. Right now, we need to let things die down. Throw him off the scent. We need new plans." My mind buzzes with the possibilities. "We need to take down the foundation under Hightower's feet."

Oliver's determined face nods in agreement. "My father has a few trusted men who I can tap into for intel. Up until now, he's made all the calls. It's time for us to make a few moves."

"With me included. I'm done sitting on the sidelines," she says, her eyes shifting from me to Oliver, knowing we lead the team. "I have a few ideas on how to expand this group of ours. Create a larger network. All they need in return is hope." She raises her hand, and the water arcs out of the glass by the nightstand, freezes mid-air, then returns, proving her ability to wield and control the element. "After we find Oliver's father."

Oliver comes over and picks up her hand. "And kill the bastards who took him." He leans down and stares into her eyes, then his gaze darts to mine with a command. I subtly turn my head to look deeper into their green depths, and that's when I see it. Two slivers of color—blue-grey and amber.

Stunned, I look at him, wondering what the hell it could mean.

THANK YOU!

Thank you for reading! I've always wanted powers, magical or psychic, I didn't care lol. I thoroughly enjoyed writing this book and look forward to the next. I'd love to hear your thoughts. Whether it's "give me more," or "I want to see a book with…" reviews help me write the next story. Please consider leaving one for this book.

*If you find an error, email me at Stellabrie@stellabrie.com.

*Playlists for all my books can be found on YouTube @authorstellabrie and on Spotify @Stella Brie Author.

*Pirating can have severe consequences, preventing authors from creating new stories. Please don't read pirated copies.

AWESOME PEOPLE

Special thanks to all these lovely people!

To my readers, friends, and fans! Thanks for all the wonderful words of encouragement, friendship, and love for my books! And for participating in my shenanigans and all the other weird things I post. You guys rock! I couldn't do it without you!!!

My awesome beta readers. They catch so many big and little things, help me with names, show me such amazing friendship, encouragement, and excitement, and they can't even share it with anyone! My books are a thousand times better because of their feedback. Thank you, Nia, Bianca, Iliana, Melissa, Rachel, Sandi, and Debbie for everything!

My ARC team who gives me so much support and enthusiasm even though I drop things on them at the last minute. Ooh, look, cover reveal! Book's launching in a week! Seriously, I appreciate all of you!!

My biggest supporters—my husband and mom. I'm so lucky to have you both! Love you!

And always… a special thanks to all the wonderful authors in the writing community who support each other day in and out. Writing would be a lonely and weird world without you. It would be me and my characters sitting around chatting (drinking) while we plot the next book. Your friendship and support mean a lot to me!

ABOUT THE AUTHOR

Stella Brie lives outside of Nashville, TN, with her husband. After mentioning her desire to write a book a million times to her husband, he challenged her to sit down one day and write a paragraph. Instead, she wrote her first book, *My Salvation*.

She traded in her career in digital marketing, working on big brands, for this wildly creative one. Armed with a notebook crammed full of ideas, she's constantly thinking about bold heroines, sexy men, and HEAs. Whether it's a paranormal book full of creatures and magic or a contemporary romance full of heat and drama, she's dreaming about bringing her books to life.

Latest News and Updates:

Facebook Group: Stella's Stalkers

TikTok: @stellabrie_author

YouTube! Playlists (all books): @authorstellabrie

Spotify Playlists (all books): @Stella Brie Author

Instagram: @stellabrie_author

Website: Stellabrie.com - Exclusive sneak peeks, cover reveals, giveaways, and more!

BOOKS BY STELLA BRIE

URBAN FANTASY WHY CHOOSE

KILLIAN BLADE SERIES

The Rowan (1)

The Rowan's Stone (2)

The Rowan's Destiny (3)

Wicked Savior - Lucifer's story (MF Romance) - (3.5)

The Light Falls (4) - Meri's story

The Dark Rises (5) - Meri's story

GENESIS SERIES

Bound by Water (1)

CONTEMPORARY WHY CHOOSE

THE SAVAGES SERIES (Duet)

Savage Traitor (1)

Savage Ruin (2)

Lethal Vengeance (Standalone + Spin-off)

My Salvation (Standalone)